ORPHANS
OF WAR

A gripping and emotional wartime saga

SYLVIA BROADY

Joffe Books, London
www.joffebooks.com

First published in Great Britain in 2022

Cover art by Jarmila Takač

ISBN: 978-1-80405-474-1

This book is dedicated to Julia Bricht, the inspiration for Juliette. Sadly, Julia lost her life at Auschwitz Death Camp in 1944 at the age of three.

CHAPTER ONE

Kingston upon Hull, May 1941

The screeching whirling sound of the siren filled the night air, as Charlotte Kirby hurried with her mother Martha and their neighbours from Newbridge Road to the air-raid shelter as the Luftwaffe relentlessly targeted the city's docks, railways, factories. Inside the shelter, the smell of frightened bodies permeated the dank air and the fabric of the building. Settling on a bunk, Charlotte turned, expecting to see her mother next to her, but she wasn't there. Peering through the gloom, she expected to see her mother talking to a neighbour. But no. She stood on tip-toes for a better view, surveying the bunks, but there was still no sign of her mother.

'She went back for her handbag,' a neighbour said.

The handbag, which held all her mother's precious documents. Suddenly, an almighty explosion sounded, and the shelter rocked from side to side.

Charlotte felt the blast deafening her ears, and she wobbled and banged her arm against the support of the bunk. 'Mam,' she cried, craning her neck to see if her mother was near the door. Why hadn't she come into the safety of the shelter?

The noise of the explosion ringing in her ears, her heartbeat racing, her body and mind in overdrive, she pushed past people to reach the door.

'Charlotte, you can't go out there,' a neighbour cried out.

'I must, Mam's out there.'

A man's bulky body barred her way. 'You can't open the bloody door. You'll get us all killed.'

A whooshing sound, followed by a deathly silence, and then the foundations of the shelter shook again and bodies catapulted from bunks. Children cried, women shrieked.

The big man toppled sidewards and Charlotte dashed forward, wrenching open the door.

Out in the street, she gasped in horror to see leaping flames running riot through toppling buildings. Coughing, her mouth full of acrid smoke, she feebly called out for her mother. She stumbled and fell with her arms stretched out before her, hot masonry raining down on her. Searing pain shot through her as it cut into the burning flesh of her knees and hands. Desperate to find her mother, she scrambled up, and with no thought for her own safety, hobbled to her mother's haberdashery shop and their living quarters.

She stood still in confusion. She must have gone in the wrong direction, because there was nothing there, only a pile of smouldering hot rubble. Wildly, she looked around, not sure of her bearings.

'Come on, you can't stop here, Missy,' said the Air Raid Warden.

'I'm looking for Mam and our shop, Mrs Kirby's Haberdashery.' Her voice wobbled and smoke filled her eyes, mingling with her tears.

'I'm sorry, luv, but it's a gonner,' he indicated the pile of smoking rubble. 'Come with me, I'll tek yer to the clinic and see if your mam's there.' Gently, he took hold of her arm, manoeuvring her away from the devastation that was once her home.

Charlotte could not think, she wanted to, but her brain was numb, her head still rumbling with the sound of the exploding bomb.

Inside the safety of the clinic, someone thrust a mug of hot, sweet liquid in her hand. As she drank, her head began to clear. She put the empty mug on a tray and looked round, searching for her mother. The room was filled with injured people, one young lad clutching hold of his mother, who had blood running down her face from a wound on her head. Charlotte walked frantically among the injured, searching for her mother, desperate to find her.

'Who are you looking for, my dear?' asked one of the Women's Voluntary Service ladies, known as the WVS.

'My mother,' Charlotte's voice broke into a sob. 'I can't find her.'

'Come with me to the information desk. They will help you.'

The woman at the desk checked her list for the injured taken to hospital. 'No Mrs Martha Kirby.' She looked up into Charlotte's grey-streaked face, the smell of the burning rubble ingrained in her skin and her clothes, and added, kindly, 'She could be at one of the first aid posts. Best stay here until we've checked all the relevant information.' She called a volunteer over. 'You go with this lady and she will show you where you can rest.'

Lying on a lumpy mattress, Charlotte listened to the snores, coughs, and cries of other people around her. She couldn't sleep, not until she knew where her mother was. From the window high up above her, she could see the burnt umber sky and flames still flickering. She watched the night sky gradually slip away to reveal a dark grey, murky dawn. Quietly she rose and tentatively made her way in between sleeping and restless bodies, to the small washroom in the far corner. Above a stone sink hung a mirror, and catching sight of her reflection, she gasped. Her light brown hair was interwoven with bits of debris and her eyes were two black holes, her face streaked with grey and mucky white. She looked like a monster in a horror film. She started to laugh hysterically, and she couldn't stop. It went on and on until she felt someone holding her, the thrust of a sharp needle in her arm, and then oblivion.

* * *

Hours later, she opened her eyes. A light above dazzled her, and she turned to her side.

'You're awake.' A harassed-looking nurse stood by her side and checked her pulse. 'The doctor will be on his rounds soon. How old are you, Charlotte?'

'Sixteen, I work with Mam in the shop. Where is Mam?' she sobbed.

'Come along, dry those tears,' soothed the weary nurse.

An orderly brought her a cup of tea and a meat paste sandwich. Charlotte drank the tea, but her stomach was churning too much to eat the food. All the time her mind raced, wondering where was her mother?

After her wounds were attended to, the doctor discharged her, and she was then taken to a washroom where she could freshen up. A WVS lady came to give her a set of old but clean clothes to wear: undergarments, a skirt, blouse and cardigan, shoes and socks. Feeling more human, but still concerned as to where her mother could be, she kept looking round, expecting to see her smiling face and her assurance that everything was all right.

Later Charlotte was shown into an office where an efficient looking woman sat at a desk, studying a document.

Before she could stop herself, Charlotte blurted out, 'I want my mother!' Her self-control slipped, and she burst into tears.

The woman came over and placed a comforting arm about Charlotte's shoulders. When her sobbing subsided, she dabbed her eyes with a handkerchief the woman had given her. 'I'm sorry.'

'You've had a shock and now I must tell you, my dear, that sadly, your mother died in the bombing raid. She was outside the shop when it took a direct hit. We found her body on the road, still clutching her handbag.'

Charlotte's body sagged and her emotions drained. She felt as though her mind and body were being ripped apart. An array of images flashed through her mind, none of them making any sense. She could hear her mother singing, her sweet voice rising high and then fading away, out of reach. Her beloved mother gone? Charlotte bit on her lip and whispered, 'I need to see her.' They could have made a mistake. In the confusion after the bombing, her mother could have been taken to another centre.

'Yes, I'll arrange it,' said the woman. Thankfully Martha Kirby's body was still intact. Not like some poor souls who were blown to smithereens, nothing left of them but dust of the earth.

Then she glanced at the document. 'We have contacted your aunt.'

'Aunt! I haven't got an aunt,' Charlotte hiccupped.

The woman checked again. 'Yes, you have, your mother's sister, Mrs Hilda Bilton.'

One of the WVS ladies accompanied Charlotte to an anteroom where coffins on trestles were placed in neat rows. Charlotte hesitated, having never seen a dead body before. Her throat tightened and her heartbeat quickened. She wanted to run away from this room full of the dead. Biting her lip slowly, taking tiny steps, she moved forward.

The WVS woman spoke softly, 'She never hurt you when she was living, my dear, and she will not hurt you in death.'

She gazed down at her mother, looking so peaceful. And gasped, 'She's not dead, she's just sleeping. She should be in a bed, not here!' Reaching out to clasp her mother's hand, she screamed as she felt its hard iciness. She kept on screaming and the WVS woman held her close until Charlotte's body stopped convulsing and became calm.

Gently, the woman released Charlotte, smoothed back her hair and gave her a handkerchief to dry her eyes, saying. 'Now, my dear, it's time to say your goodbye to your mother.'

Once more, Charlotte gazed upon the figure lying so still in the coffin. Gulping back a sob, she whispered, 'Love you, Mam, forever.'

That night, in the makeshift dormitory, she tossed and turned on the lumpy mattress. She didn't sleep. Grief wrapped round her as the image of her mother, cold and alone in her coffin, stayed with her.

* * *

The next day one of the ARP wardens brought a canvas bag to Charlotte, still intact. 'Is this your mother's? We found it not far from her.' Inside was an assortment of wools, needles, silks and odd scraps of material.

'What about Mam's handbag? It's got all her documents in it.'

'The authorities have it.'

While waiting for the aunt she never knew existed, Charlotte sorted and smoothed out the pieces of material and silks.

'What're you gonna do with them, love?' asked a woman sitting opposite her.

Charlotte looked up. 'I'm going to make a picture of my Mam.'

The aunt didn't arrive that day, but sent word she was coming the day of the funeral. So Charlotte spent another restless night on the lumpy mattress, but the WVS ladies were kind and she never went hungry.

On the day of her mother's funeral, Charlotte was up early and used the washing facilities before anyone else was awake. This gave her a chance to wash her hair. She gave it a good lather with a tiny sliver of soap and rinsed thoroughly until all the dust and bits of debris disappeared. Rubbing it dry on a rough towel, she felt her scalp tingle with freshness.

'You've golden glints in your lovely brown hair,' remarked the voice of a woman who had just entered the washroom. 'You can borrow my comb.' She rummaged in her bag and handed Charlotte a tortoiseshell comb.

'Thank you,' Charlotte said shyly and began to drag it through her tangled hair.

'Let me comb the back for you, love.'

Charlotte closed her eyes, feeling the tenderness of each stroke and imagining it was her mother. A task Martha had loved to do. Charlotte was transported back in time, absorbing the feeling, savouring every loving moment, wanting it to last for ever and ever. Then the spell was broken, when the woman spoke.

'There, it looks beautiful.'

'Thank you for being so kind,' Charlotte murmured, close to tears.

Later, sitting at a long table with other people made homeless by the bombing raid, Charlotte ate a breakfast of bread and jam and a mug of tea. Listening to an old woman bemoaning the senselessness of war, Charlotte agreed with her, for she couldn't comprehend why human beings would want to kill one another. At school and Sunday school, she'd been taught to be kind and helpful to everyone.

A WVS lady escorted Charlotte to another room, where she was given a dark green coat with a black diamond sewn onto the sleeve. 'What's it for?' she asked, pointing to the black diamond.

The kind lady explained. 'It's a mark of respect for the dead,' she said, fitting a black beret on Charlotte's head.

Then she waited for this unknown aunt to arrive.

'There you are,' came a cold voice.

Charlotte turned to see a tall, thin woman, dressed in black, staring at her with grey, unsmiling eyes. The very opposite of her mother, who had warm, loving, smiling, blue eyes.

Before she could stop herself, Charlotte blurted out. 'Are you sure you're my mother's sister?'

Hilda Bilton glared at Charlotte, snapping, 'For her sins, yes. Now come along, time's money.'

She turned and started to walk from the building and Charlotte, feeling lost and confused, followed her.

The funeral service, along with those of many others who had perished as a result of the bombing raid, was held in the small chapel nearby. The bodies were to be laid to rest at the Eastern Cemetery, and the clergyman would travel with the cortege to represent the families and loved ones who were unable to be present.

Her body numb, Charlotte let the tears flow. She didn't want to leave her mother, and longed for the warmth of her hugs. Instead, she had this unbending, emotionless woman called Aunt Hilda. Going to touch the coffin to say a final goodbye, she thought she heard her mother's voice saying, 'Charlotte, be strong and brave and be happy.'

Determined to honour her mother's words, Charlotte walked from the chapel with her head held high, though her heart felt laden with sadness.

CHAPTER TWO

May 1941

Charlotte and her aunt boarded the train at Paragon Station, squeezing into their seats in the crowded compartment. The short train ride to the village of Mornington was uneventful. As they alighted from the train, Charlotte thought how quiet it was compared with the hustle and bustle of her home city of Hull. Her aunt marched down the platform and Charlotte followed, having no idea where she would be staying. Her aunt seemed a woman of few words, and her stiff manner offered no chance to ask questions. Trudging along a narrow lane, Hilda turned towards a building looming up, with a sign swinging at an odd angle. Charlotte could just make out the words, Travellers Rest Inn. Her aunt held the open door for her to follow.

To Charlotte's surprise, it was filled with men drinking from tankards. They turned to stare at her and, not used to such attention, she felt her cheeks redden.

One man shouted out, 'What a pretty, young lass. She'll liven the place up.'

Charlotte lowered her eyes to look down at the sawdust on the wooden floor.

'Now then, Jed, show a bit of respect,' called the man behind the bar counter. 'This young lass is Hilda's niece, and she has just lost her mam in the bombing raid in Hull.' Charlotte kept her eyes downcast. The men turned to resume their drinking and chatter.

Hilda, stony-faced, beckoned Charlotte to follow her behind the bar, through a door and up two flights of stairs, to an attic room. Hilda pushed open the door. 'You sleep in here, it's the only spare room we've got.'

Charlotte looked in, surprised. The room was under the eaves and quite large with the walls painted a pretty primrose yellow, a bright rag rug filled the centre, and the edging of wooden floor-boards were stained a light oak. Blackout curtains framed the window and over them were pretty curtains with a design of colourful butterflies.

Putting the oil-lamp she'd been carrying on a chest of drawers, Hilda said. 'Come down in half-an-hour and you can have supper.' Then, abruptly, she left the room.

Charlotte sat down on the single brass bedstead, her trembling fingers tracing the patchwork quilt. Fear overwhelmed her and her heartbeat raced. She wanted to run far away. But where to? Deep breaths, she told herself, like the nurse at the hospital instructed. Gradually, her anxiety dissipated. She made herself look round the well-furnished room, sensing a strange, sad eeriness about it. She saw a bedside table, a wardrobe, with a long mirror, a stand with an ewer and bowl. She thought of the room back home in Hull, which she'd shared with her mother. A sob caught at her throat and she put her hand over her mouth to mute the sound, burying her face in the pillow.

Coming up for air, she rinsed her face in the cold water from the jug, patting it dry on a fresh, white towel. An image of her dear mother's face swam before her and tears misted her eyes again. She stood in the centre of the room, uncertain what to do. She didn't want to be here. Why couldn't she have stayed in Hull where she knew people? The first chance she got, she would go back home. Home. What home?

Remembering the pile of smouldering bricks and debris and the big empty hole, she shuddered.

Frantically, she looked round and saw the battered attaché case standing near the door where she'd dropped it. She picked it up, placed it on the rattan chair and opened it. Inside were items of clothing, a change of underwear and nightwear, a blouse and a cardigan, a spare pair of stockings, a toothbrush and paste, a comb, and an embroidered handkerchief. Gifts from the ladies of the WVS, which she felt grateful for. She'd lost all her personal possessions in the bombing raid, along with the contents of the shop. She had her mother's bag, but not even a photograph of her. She clamped her hands over her mouth to ward off her cries, but no sound came. Her insides felt all dried up.

She heard her aunt calling her down to supper. Her mother had instilled good manners in her, and she knew she should be thankful to Aunt Hilda for taking her in, but the feeling in her heart told her differently.

She picked up the lamp and wondered whose room it had been?

* * *

Charlotte woke with a start, hearing an unfamiliar sound, and wondered where she was.

Rubbing sleep from her eyes, she tumbled from the bed and crept to the attic window to peer out. Perched on the swaying branch of the nearby tree, a blackbird sang. A bird she'd only seen in a picture book, never for real. There were only sparrows where she'd lived. She gazed entranced, tears welling her eyes, for this was the first sign of welcome she'd received on entering this place. Last night she'd eaten a lonely supper of bread, cheese and a cup of cocoa, and had then been banished to bed by her aunt.

Today, she wasn't sure what to expect. She and Mam always rose early, had breakfast together, and then they both worked in harmony in their haberdashery shop. Saturday afternoon was their half-day off and she and Mam would go, with her friend Joyce, up town and then to the pictures or sometimes a show. On Sundays, after the morning chores and a roast dinner, Mam would rest while Charlotte went to the pier or the park to meet up with friends. And now . . . ?

'Charlotte, are you up?' called her aunt from the bottom of the stairs.

Hastily, she washed and dressed and went downstairs to be met by Hilda, who thrust a broom into her hands.

'You can earn your keep by sweeping the bar floor.'

On entering the bar, Charlotte gasped at the stench of stale beer and rancid smoke clinging to the very fabric of the walls and the heavy blackout curtains. She knew she would have to earn her living, but had foreseen nothing so repugnant. She wrinkled her nose and began the task, to sweep up the sawdust, which contained men's spit and other obnoxious things.

When she had finished, she emptied the contents into the huge dustbin outside in the yard.

'Breakfast up,' Hilda called. Her husband, George, came up from the cellar, and Charlotte washed her hands under the outside tap and dried them on her skirt.

As she approached the kitchen, the tantalising aroma of bacon twitched her nostrils and her stomach rumbled. George was already sitting at the table with a plate piled high with bacon, eggs and fried bread. Charlotte stared, having never seen so much food. She perched on a wooden stool and Hilda placed a smaller portion of breakfast in front of her and then poured out three mugs of tea from the huge brown teapot. Charlotte watched her aunt moving about the kitchen until she came and sat opposite George. Neither her aunt nor uncle uttered a word. She thought back to meals with her mother. They always chattered about the day's happenings or what new stock to buy.

The food tasted delicious, much tastier than what she and Mam had bought from the corner shop. When George had cleared his plate and drank three mugs of tea, he spoke.

'Now then, nipper, this breakfast will set you up for the day because we ain't got time to eat when the bar is busy. You're here to work. Bar cleaning was yer first job. After breakfast you'll clean and polish tables and chairs, and when the bar opens, yer clear tables and wash up. Right, jump to it.'

Charlotte noticed that Hilda never spoke a word. A woman of few words. Charlotte would have loved to ask her why Martha had never spoken about her. When young, they must have lived together, both having the same mam and dad. At least, she assumed so. She began her task of cleaning and polishing the chairs and tables and could see they had been neglected because of the brown gunge which rubbed off them on to her cloth. She had never envisaged working in a public house, but she must pay her way, and she had been taught to take pride in her work.

Later on, the bar was full of men drinking and mulling over the events of the day and the latest news of the war.

Charlotte didn't like moving close to the men. Some were polite, but some liked to rub against her body, which she didn't like. She discovered a little snug where three elderly women sat drinking. The three witches, as the men called them. Edna, May and Dot.

Charlotte found them a welcome relief and she would serve them their glass of stout and chat with them.

'Elbow 'em, love,' Edna remarked.

'Pardon?' Charlotte replied, not sure what she meant.

'Like this.' Edna levered herself from her stool and put her arm across her breasts, and jutted her elbow outwards.

The other two women, May and Dot, laughed.

Charlotte took Edna's advice. It worked, and over time, she began to feel less intimated by the crowds of men. She loved to serve the three friendly women and chat with them.

One night, from her attic bedroom window, which faced towards Hull, she witnessed the sky engulfed in flames, destroying her beloved city. Charlotte felt as though her heart had been torn from her body. 'Oh, Mam,' she cried. 'Why were you taken from me? I need you here with me.' Tears streamed down her face as she watched the enemy ravage her childhood home and her past life disintegrated before her eyes. Her last link with her childhood torn from her. She closed her eyes to conjure up her mother's lovely smiling face, and wrapped her arms around her body, imagining it was the warmth and love of her mother holding her close. She missed the hustle and bustle, the friendship of neighbours and the customers who came into the shop. They would often stay and chat, happy to pass the time of day and sometimes tell their troubles to her mother who always had a word of sympathy. She opened her eyes, her city was still on fire, but the planes had gone. She shuddered, knowing the enemy would be back and felt guilty that she was here in relative safety.

She heard her aunt moving about, and Charlotte found it hard to imagine her mother and Hilda being sisters because they were so very different. Hilda's only redeeming feature was that she was a good cook, so Charlotte never went hungry. And George was a man's man. Charlotte wondered why they had no children, but daren't ask. In fact, she asked Hilda nothing.

Months passed, and she was allowed the odd hour from work duties. During her precious time off, she would escape to her room. She loved to sit and sort the scraps of materials and silks salvaged from Mam's bag. Today she was sewing the pieces of material together. Delicately, with her finest stitches and love, she fashioned the oddments of material together Finally, with a sign of satisfaction, she appraised her handiwork, feeling pleased it was a wonderful likeness to her mother. As she held it up, the light caught the twinkle in her mother's blue eyes. A lump stuck in Charlotte's throat and tears threatened.

Later that evening, she asked the ladies if they knew of anyone in the village who could frame her work.

'There's old Jack on the edge of the village, he's handy with wood,' offered Dot.

* * *

On a beautiful bright autumn day, Charlotte walked along a leafy lane towards the far end of the village. Despite the war raging, she felt at peace. A happy feeling, though how long it would last, she didn't know.

Perhaps it was because she was away from her aunt. Hilda was a strange woman in many respects, as if she carried a great weight on her shoulders. Something must have happened in her past. Why had she and Martha had no contact? Had something terrible happened? As Charlotte walked along, breathing in the fresh, unpolluted air, she thought about her family. Her memories of her father were few, only the smell of his pipe tobacco, and the visit with him to the Hull Fair lingered. He had died in an accident when a runaway horse and cart ploughed into him. Then there was her Granny Kirby, a stiff, straight-backed woman who had been a staunch member of the Methodist Church and often took Charlotte with her to the services. Charlotte hadn't known her mother's parents and she couldn't recall her mother speaking about them. Tears welled as a picture of her mother's sweet, smiling face popped into her head.

She turned a corner and dashed away her tears, delighted to see a small cottage. Its front garden was full of late-cropping fruit and vegetables, and welcoming smoke curled upwards from its chimney pot.

She knocked on the sturdy oak door and heard the barking of a dog within. 'Quiet, Jip,' she heard a man's voice say. The door opened and a slightly bent elderly man, with a weather-beaten face, a thatch of silver hair, and twinkling dark blue eyes, stood there. This must be Jack, the carpenter the elderly ladies had told her about.

'Sorry to disturb you,' she said shyly.

The old man opened the door wider. 'Come in, dearie. You'll be Martha's girl.'

'Yes,' she said, wondering how he knew.

'You're the spitting image of her when she was a girl.' He ushered Charlotte in and closed the door. Jip came to sniff at her legs and, satisfied, went to curl up on the rug in front of the log fire blazing in the grate.

Jack poured her a strong cup of tea from the pretty pink teapot warming on top of the fire oven. She gripped the mug tightly, glad of something to do with her hands, and lowered her eyes to gaze into the fire. He must have sensed her mood, because he said, 'I am sorry about your mother, she was such a sweet girl.'

Tears filled her eyes as she kept her head low and asked. 'How did you know my mother?'

'Why, when Martha was a girl she lived here in the village.'

Charlotte's head shot up in surprise. 'I didn't know that. Mother never mentioned it. Why did she leave?'

She watched Jack reach for his pipe and baccy from the fire-stool top and begin filling it. His brow furrowed as he concentrated, and she wondered if it was because he was try-ing to remember or whether he was deciding what he should tell her. She glanced around the kitchen cum sitting room, which was clean and tidy. An oak table dominated the centre of the room, with four beautifully carved oak chairs. On the far wall stood a dresser filled with Royal Worcester china and a photograph of a lady with a round, smiling face.

'That's my Doris. She was a good 'un.' His eyes clouded, and he puffed on his pipe, lost in his memories.

Charlotte broke the spell by putting her mug on the hearth 'Should I come back another time?'

'No, it's fine. You were asking about Martha. She left the village when she married James Kirby.'

'My dad died when I was five, so I only have a vague memory of him. I wonder why they went to live in Hull.'

Jack puffed on his pipe. 'He worked in Hull,' he replied eventually. Then, changing the subject, he asked 'What brought you to my door?'

She related what the three ladies had told her. Opening the canvas bag, she carefully took out the tapestry picture of her mother, slowly unwrapping the tissue-paper. She held it up for him to see.

He laid his pipe on the hearth and studied it for a few moments. Your mam was a bonny woman. Good craftsmanship.' He peered closer and then straightened up. 'It will need a fine frame, not too heavy. Leave it on the table for now and come with me to my workshop.' He heaved himself up from his chair, and Charlotte gently replaced the tapestry in its tissue-paper and placed it on the big table. She followed Jack, with Jip in tow, out of the door and along a path to his workshop.

Stepping inside, one of the first things Charlotte noticed was the natural light coming from the two enormous windows. The second was the soothing yet powerful smell of wood seasoned with years of growth. The third was Jack; he came alive in here, as though he was a young man again. She watched him sorting through his stack of wood, a man in his element, touching various pieces of wood as though they were his children and for a while seemed to forget she was there. Jip, used to his master, curled up on some sacking and went to sleep. Charlotte moved to look at some carved pieces of wood and Jack looked up.

'Sorry, lass, I get caught up in my world in here. Come back to the house, I've something to show you.'

Inside, she followed Jack to his front room. When he opened the door, she gasped with surprise. In the room was the most beautiful carved furniture, table, chairs, sideboard, bookcase and a set of occasional tables. But it was the walls which attracted her attention, for they were full of the most exquisite tapestries, quilting and embroidery, all in the most delicately carved frames. 'So beautiful,' she whispered as she stood in awe, gazing at them.

'Your wife's?'

He nodded, and she could see the tears glinting in his eyes. She would have liked to ask him more about his talented, late wife, but she didn't want to upset him.

In the kitchen, Jip had gone straight back to his basket, knowing he wasn't allowed in the front room.

'Your work will be safe with me. Come back in a couple of days and I'll have it done for you,' Jack promised, as Charlotte was taking her leave.

'Thank you, Jack.' On impulse, she stood on tiptoe and kissed him on his cheek.

Back at the pub, a stony-faced Hilda met her. 'You're late. Get yer apron on and get into the bar,' she commanded.

'Sorry,' Charlotte muttered. But she would not let Hilda's lack of warmth spoil the lovely afternoon she'd spent with Jack.

CHAPTER THREE

October to December 1941

Charlotte gazed at the framed needlework portrait of her beloved mother, running her fingers along the silky wood of the frame. 'Oh, Jack,' she whispered, gulping back tears of emotion. 'It's beautiful.'

Jack's face beamed with happiness. 'It was a pleasure.' And Jip barked his assent.

Suddenly embarrassed, she felt the redness spread across her cheeks. 'I've no money to pay you with. I just work for my board and keep,' she whispered. The lack of money in her purse hadn't bothered her until this moment.

'Don't worry about that, lass. I like to have my hands occupied. It helps to pass the time. I don't get out much, except for a short morning walk with Jip and pottering in the garden. Shopkeeper sends lad up with my few groceries. The best thing is your company, that's when you can spare it.'

Feeling much happier, Charlotte replied, 'That's no hardship, I love coming to see you.'

'That's settled, then. Now we'll have a mug of tea.'

Later, arriving back at the pub in good time and so excited about the framing of her needlework portrait of her mother, she dashed into the kitchen to ask Hilda if she could use a hammer and hook so she could hang it on her bedroom wall.

'No,' was Hilda's curt response to her request.

Undeterred, she countered, 'Why not?'

'Because I said so,' Hilda shouted. 'I'm not having that woman on my walls.'

'Now then, what's all the commotion about? We can hear yer in the bar,' George strutted into the kitchen.

Not speaking, Hilda turned away, busying herself at the stove. Charlotte stared at her aunt's stiff-backed figure, wondering what was behind Hilda's outburst of rage against her sister, Martha.

Not looking at George, she fled from the kitchen.

Upstairs in her room, she placed the picture on the chair and then flung herself on the bed, sobbing for her beloved mother. Wanting to feel her comforting arms about her, helping her make sense of Hilda's behaviour. She couldn't understand her aunt's bitterness towards her, and her manner of coldness. Something dreadful must have happened between the sisters. But what it might have been, she couldn't think. Would George know? She doubted it. He only ever spoke half a dozen words to her each day, and they were about bar work.

She slid from the bed and went to the dresser and splashed cold water from the basin onto her face. Patting it dry, she glanced at her reflection in the mirror. Her red-rimmed eyes looked back at her. She tidied her hair, fastening her brown curls back with a tortoise-shell slide. Then she tied on her dark blue apron, trimmed with white edging, and went down to begin her work in the bar.

She avoided eye contact with the men, going to the snug to see the ladies. They were as pleased to see her as she them.

'Hello, love, what have you got to tell us then?' asked May.

So she told them about the lovely frame Jack had made, and how her mother's picture looked a treat.

'Have you hung it up?' asked Dot.

Not sure how to answer, Charlotte settled on, 'Not yet,' then changed the subject.

Later that night, lying awake in her bed, Charlotte wondered if any of the ladies had known her mother when she lived in the village.

A few nights later, she plucked up courage to ask the ladies. 'My mam, Martha, lived in the village until she married Dad and went to live in Hull. Did you know her?'

Three pairs of eyes looked at her, but remained silent. It was Dot who broke the spell.

'Martha, yer say. What was her surname?'

'Sheldon, Martha Sheldon. Aunt Hilda is her sister, though my mother never spoke about her. And I didn't know of her existence until Mam died.' As she thought of her mother, a lump came into her throat and tears threatened.

'Charlotte,' shouted George from the bar.

'I'd best go.' She hurried away.

The bar had filled up with soldiers' home on leave. 'By heck, things are looking up, George,' said a ginger-haired one. 'What's yer name, darling?'

Blushing under the scrutiny of the soldiers, 'Charlotte,' she whispered, her eyes downcast.

'She's the wife's sister's girl, so you lot behave, or Hilda will have something to say. Refill, lads?'

As the evening wore on, when she served the ladies again, Charlotte was too busy to stay and chat and her question about her mother remained unanswered.

The soldiers were a jolly lot, and they livened up the bar. One of them played the piano and the others gathered round and sang the popular songs of the day, their happy voices were now belting out, 'We're going to hang out the washing on the Siegfried Line . . .' They came again the next night and continued the jollity. But on the third night, the bar was quiet and Charlotte asked one of the regulars, 'Where are they?'

'Overseas posting,' he replied. She felt sad and missed their company.

On her time off, she escaped to Jack's cottage whenever she could. She told him about Hilda refusing to let her hang Martha's picture on her bedroom wall.

He looked thoughtful before replying. 'Hilda was always a strange girl. I could never fathom her out. She and George are an odd couple, but I suppose they suit each other.'

Charlotte thought about her aunt and uncle. Somehow, they didn't seem to connect with each other, not how she imagined married couples to be. But then, what did she know about marriage?

She and Jack sat in companionable silence, both lost in their thoughts, drinking their tea. She loved the tranquillity of Jack's cottage and the relaxed atmosphere after being at the inn, though she enjoyed talking to the customers, especially the three ladies. With Hilda and George, she felt she had to be on her guard though for what she wasn't sure, and she kept telling herself how grateful she was to them for taking her in when she was homeless and had no other family.

'I almost forgot,' Jack said. Jip's dozing eyes pricked up. 'I've been having a rummage around and I've found some of my Doris's bits of material and threads, so you are quite welcome to them. Come with me.' He levered himself up from his chair and walked stiffly to the front room. Charlotte followed him.

On the polished table top stood a wicker basket with a handle. 'Have a look,' Jack said.

Peeping inside the basket she was amazed to see an array of different scraps of material in rich jewelled colours: reds, blues, greens, purples and pure white. She touched the soft fabrics of velvet, silk and satin, and marvelled at the bobbins of coloured threads. 'They are beautiful.' She picked up a piece of fabric, holding it close, breathing in its scent.

'They are yours, lass. To do with as you wish. You can have the pleasure. I can make lighter frames, if you decide to make more pictures.'

She looked at him, seeing his eyes alight with happiness. 'You can do that?'

'Aye, it will be a challenge, but I'll do it.'

Feeling reluctant to leave the homely cottage and Jack's company, she sighed, saying, 'I must be going.'

He glanced at the clock. 'That time already?'

Outside, the December wind blew down from the north across the fields, whipping round her body, its icy bite stinging her cheeks. She hugged her scarf closer, holding on tightly to the bag of material pieces and threads as she hastened down the lane.

Inside the pub, a log fire crackled in the big grate, and a delicious aroma of rabbit stew wafted from the kitchen. Today was Friday and Hilda cooked a meal for the customers, if there was meat available, which today was rabbit. The ladies, who lived on their own, side by side in tiny one-bedroomed cottages, loved to come. It was Charlotte's first job to set the tables, at Hilda's insistence, white damask tablecloth and best cutlery for the ladies and blue checked cloth and ordinary cutlery for the men.

She hurried to her room and stored her precious bag in the wardrobe out of sight, for she knew that Hilda often came into her room. Charlotte had caught her once, just standing in the middle of the floor with a sad look on her face. On seeing Charlotte, she had left the room without a word.

She tidied her appearance, put on her clean apron and went straight into the bar.

Once, she'd popped into the kitchen to say hello to Hilda and exchange a few pleasantries. But Hilda rebuffed her by saying, 'I haven't time for idle words.'

On Friday nights, May, Dot and Edna wore their best dresses of colourful crepe de chine. The first time she saw them in their finery, she remarked, 'You all look lovely.'

'We like to dress up on a Friday night, it's a bit special,' Dot told her.

And May chimed in, 'I know Hilda's a strange one, but she's an excellent cook.'

Charlotte could attest to that. She had to keep telling herself how fortunate she was to have a bed and not go hungry. And now she received money each week. A few shillings, so she could buy essentials and save in the post office. It was a step forward, and she was luckier than most.

Edna, not wanting to be left out of the conversation, said, 'Wait until Christmas. Hilda serves a banquet, though with food on rations, it could be dicey this year.'

Charlotte laughed, served the ladies with their stout and then left them to their good-humoured banter.

The run-up to Christmas in the pub was hectic, and so it was often late before Charlotte flopped into bed. One evening they were extra busy so Charlotte decided that when finished in the bar, she would go into the kitchen and help Hilda with the clearing up. She never said a word to Hilda, nor Hilda to her, but she dived in. After all, she had helped her mother run a business and do the household chores.

Finished, and feeling exhausted, she was ready to crawl into bed when George lumbered into the kitchen with a bottle of malt whisky and three glasses on a tray. Placing them on the table, he said to Hilda and Charlotte. 'Sit down.'

Without another word, he poured three liberal tots and then said to Charlotte, 'Sip it slowly.'

She was glad of his advice, because although it tasted smooth as it trickled down her throat, it was hot. She watched him down his in one and pour himself another. To her surprise, she enjoyed the drink, loving its warmth and the relaxed, comforting feeling in her belly. And she was even more surprised when Hilda laughed, a girlish laugh, at a story George related from the bar.

Charlotte looked at Hilda as if seeing her for the first time. Her face was aglow. Was it the result of the whisky or something else? Whatever it was, this was the better side of Hilda, and she liked it!

CHAPTER FOUR

December 1941

Charlotte sat on the train as she headed towards Hull, excited. Her aunt and uncle had given her the Saturday off, though with strict instructions to return for evening duty. Two days ago, she had posted a card to her old schoolfriend, Joyce Goodwin, asking if she could visit and received a card by return of post with a big 'Yes'. As she glanced out of the window at the fields rolling by, excitement filled her as she thought of her beloved hometown. Although she was grateful to her aunt and uncle for taking her in when she was homeless, she never thought of the inn as home. And Mornington was just somewhere to live and work.

Steam billowed from the train as it came into Paragon Station, and Charlotte helped a young mother and her child to alight. She hurried down the platform through the barrier and on towards the bus station to catch the bus for Holderness Road. Sitting on the top deck, she looked out of the window at the familiar landmarks: the swimming baths where she learnt to swim, and the library, when as a child she had spent many happy hours choosing her books.

She'd always been an avid reader and bought books with the money she earned from working in her mother's shop. The Bronte sisters' books were her favourite and those of George Eliot she enjoyed as well. Sadly, the books had been lost in the explosion which had destroyed the shop and her home. There were no books in her aunt's home so now she was earning, she would save up to buy one.

She alighted two stops before her stop, because she wanted to soak in the homely atmosphere she so much missed. The noise hit her. She had forgotten the buzz of people talking, the constant hum of the road traffic. Without realising it, she had become attuned to the countryside noises. It upset her to see the destruction of her city. The terrible gaping holes where once stood homes and shops. She noticed the fatigue etched on the faces of people passing by. She nodded to a few women who used to come into the shop to buy wool to knit socks for the troops, or sometimes just for a chat.

Joyce lived down Rosemead Street, across Newbridge Road from Sherburn Street. Charlotte didn't quite know why she was walking down Sherburn Street. Their shop had been on the corner of the street and Newbridge Road. Stopping, she stared at the gaping hole where her home had been and found it difficult to comprehend. She should have taken a different route to Joyce's house and avoided the site, but an inner compulsion seemed to drive her forward, and all she could do was to follow until . . . she heard the screeching of the siren and felt her heartbeat racing too fast. Then her head began whirling and a strange sensation filled her body, and she was no longer in control of her movements. Reaching out, she clasped hold of the window sill of a nearby house for support. The noise in her head grew louder and the pavement beneath her feet shook, jerking her back in time. Reliving that dreadful night. She was in the air-raid shelter, hearing the bomb exploding. Rushing outside, she'd witnessed the devastation, the shop and her home nothing but a pile of rubble. That same bomb had taken the life of her beloved mother. The screaming came from a distance, becoming louder, reverberating in her head.

Suddenly warm arms held her close and a calming voice said, 'You're all right, love. I got yer.' It took some time for her head to stop spinning and clear. The arms holding her relaxed. Her saviour, a woman, spoke, 'You be Martha's girl.'

Charlotte stared into a pair of warm grey eyes She recognised the woman. She had been a regular customer in the shop. 'Mrs Osborne,' she whispered.

'What are you doing here, raking up those dreadful memories?'

Between hiccupping, Charlotte said. 'I'm going to see Joyce.'

'Ah, she's a nice girl. Come indoors with me and splash some cold water on your face to bring back your colour.'

Sitting in Mrs Osborne's kitchen, Charlotte sipped on a cup of strong, sweet tea, her strength returning. She felt calm. 'I don't know what came over me,' she whispered.

'You've had a shock and it's best out than bottling it up,' said the compassionate woman.

Charlotte contemplated this theory and thought that Mrs Osborne was right. Her Aunt Hilda had not once asked her about how she felt about losing her mother and losing her home and livelihood. It was as if the entire episode had not happened. Crushingly erased from her memory. But Charlotte knew, buried deep in her soul, she would never forget.

'Now it's in the open. You can move on. And another word of advice. Before you leave and go back to Mornington, visit Martha's grave and have a word with her. Let her know you are all right.'

'Thank you, Mrs Osborne, I will.' She rose from her chair and hugged the good woman.

Her heart felt much lighter as she crossed over Newbridge Road towards Rosemead Street, and before she could knock on the door of her friend's house, it flew open. And Joyce stepped forward to envelop Charlotte with a big hug.

'Oh, I've missed you so much.' Charlotte's tears were welling in her eyes, which she dashed away with the back of her hand. She followed Joyce through the hallway to the hub of the house, a lovely enormous kitchen. Warmth and the delicious smell of something tasty cooking in the oven, greeted her, and she felt her stomach rumble, reminding her that she hadn't eaten that day, skipping breakfast because she was so excited at coming here.

She sat at the big kitchen table, with Joyce's mother, father and two brothers, the men home for dinner from the shipbuilding factory where they worked. After telling her news of where she worked and lived, she listened to their news. The two brothers, aged eighteen and nineteen, were enlisting in the forces and over the meal were having a dispute as to which service. She listened to the good-natured family banter; it brought back memories of happy times spent with her mother, of their discussions over shop matters and the loving bond they shared. She missed her mother so much. She gave a deep sigh.

'That was a big sigh, love,' said Joyce's mother.

Charlotte blushed, not realising she'd sighed out loud. 'I was thinking of Mam.'

'Aye, a lovely lady, God bless her.'

Five minutes later, the men jumped up and returned to work. Charlotte helped Joyce with washing and drying the dishes.

'Fancy the pictures?' Joyce asked. 'There's a good one on at the Savoy.'

'Oh, the pictures, I haven't been for ages.' She was just about to say since her mam was killed and stopped herself. 'That would be lovely and it will give me just enough time to visit Mam's grave before I catch the train.'

'I'll come with you, if you like.'

As much as she loved Joyce's company, she wanted this first visit to be just her and Mam. 'It's kind of you, but . . .' She couldn't think of the words not to offend her friend.

'It's all right, you're a dafty, I understand,' Joyce piped up, giving Charlotte a hug.

So the two young women linked arms and went to the Savoy Cinema to see *Gone With The Wind* starring Vivien Leigh and Clark Gable. Afterwards, they both came out of the cinema, dancing on air in the street. 'I want to wear one of Scarlett's dresses and go to a ball,' Charlotte held out her skirt as if it was a gown.

'I just want a man like Rhett Butler,' Joyce said.

A man in front of them turned round and round, a twinkle in his eyes. 'Will I do, love?'

The two girls giggled, and linked arms, strolling along, when suddenly, Joyce blurted out.

'I'm going to join the Women's Land Army and do my bit for the war.'

'Why?' asked Charlotte. At this moment, she wanted nothing to do with war and its destruction.

Joyce shrugged, 'I fancy a change, and adventure. Why don't you come?'

While not thinking of Mornington as her home, she didn't have the urge to move again to another strange place. Thoughtfully, she replied, 'I'm not sure what I want to do for the war effort.'

Hugging her friend, she waved goodbye, and they promised to write to each other.

Charlotte set off walking down Newbridge Road and on to Craven Street, reaching Hedon Road, shivering as she hurried past the jail, trying not to think of the prisoners locked up in their cells.

At Eastern Cemetery, the steward gave her the plot number and the directions to her mother's grave. Carefully she walked along the narrow path, which separated each grave until she came to the far side, near to a wooden railing fence. She stopped in front of the plot number, where no headstone marked Martha Kirby's resting place. Charlotte stared down at the mound of brown, dry earth and bit on her lip, unable to believe that her mother was here all alone in this nameless grave. Dropping to her knees, she sobbed for her beloved mother, stretching out her arms across the grave in a hugging embrace.

Time passed, and she didn't move. Her tears of sorrow mingled with the earth.

'You all right, miss?' a male voice asked.

Slowly, Charlotte lifted her head to see the steward standing a short distance from her with a concerned look on his face. She made to rise to her feet, but pins and needles numbed her feet and legs from being in a cramped position and she stumbled. He darted forward and caught her arm and steadied her. 'Thank you,' she whispered.

'I'm about to lock up. I've got to dash home for my tea and then I'm on warden duties.'

As she walked by the steward's side to the main entrance, she asked him, 'What must I do to get a headstone for my mother's grave?'

'I can give you a leaflet with details. And check to see if your mother had an insurance policy.'

She caught the bus back to Paragon Station and, with minutes to spare, she boarded the train back to Mornington. Settled in her seat, she studied the leaflet about headstones and the stonemason who made them, but it gave no indication of a price. She pondered the steward's mention of an insurance policy and decided to ask Aunt Hilda for advice.

Charlotte returned late to the inn. It was a hectic Saturday night, full of local men talking about the war or farmers bemoaning the fact that their sons had joined up in one of the armed forces to fight the German enemy. 'Aye, it's a rum business,' one farmer scratched at his sparse grey hair.

'Charlotte, clear them glasses off yon table,' George bellowed over the din.

It wasn't until later in the week that she found the time to ask Hilda if Martha had had an insurance policy so that they could erect a headstone to commemorate her mother's passing.

They were in the kitchen and George was in the cellar when Charlotte put the question to Hilda.

Her aunt frowned. 'I know nothing about any insurance policy. Didn't you lose everything when the bomb hit? So I don't know where you would get any money from.' With a dismissive air, she turned to the stove and continued stirring the pan of porridge. George came up from the cellar and Charlotte laid the table for breakfast, her face set with determination. She would not give up on marking her mother's place of rest.

Next afternoon, before her evening shift, she had two hours to spare and pulling on her outdoor clothes, she walked down to see Jack and his dog Jip. On offer at the bakery were fresh scones, still warm from the oven. She counted out her pennies and bought four.

'Hello Jack and you too Jip.' The dog jumped up to be patted and to sniff at the scones.

'They smell good,' Jack's knees cracking as he pulled himself up on his feet. He moved the kettle across to the fire, saying, 'You'll be wanting a cuppa.'

'That would be lovely,' she replied, her voice full of forced jollity. He gave her a quizzical look, but didn't speak.

They settled before the fire to eat and drink. Jack smacked his lips. 'By, they were good.'

He had devoured two of the scones, and fed titbits to Jip, who was now sleeping contentedly at his master's feet. Jack eyed the last scone and Charlotte pushed the plate towards him.

Every crumb eaten, Jack filled his pipe and lit it, then looked straight into Charlotte's eyes. 'Now then, lass, what's bothering you?'

Charlotte felt a lump in her throat and then the words came spilling out about her mother's grave with no headstone to mark it.

'That's not a problem,' Jack said.

She looked at him with surprise, wondering what he meant. 'I'm not taking your money,' she stressed.

'I am not offering it, but I can make you a marker for your mother's resting place.'

She looked at him, and asked, 'Do you mean from stone?'

'No. I'll carve it from a piece of good solid oak. Just tell me the words you want on it.'

She jumped to her feet to hug him, her voice a whisper. 'Oh, thank you, Jack.' Jip, woken up from his slumbers, nudged against Charlotte's legs, not wanting to be left out. She bent down to stroke him.

With a lighter heart and a spring in her step, Charlotte returned to the inn.

CHAPTER FIVE

December 1941 to January 1942

Christmas and New Year passed in a haze of work and cheerfulness The giving of presents at Christmas didn't seem to be part of Hilda and George's ethos. They preferred the ringing of the till as the money flowed into it. Dropping into bed late one night, exhausted, Charlotte conjured up memories of the Christmastime festivities she had celebrated with her mother and friends. The pictures in her mind were clear. In their small community nobody was ever alone at Christmas.

After church, they'd usually had neighbours in to share their Yuletide meal and other friends would drop by and take part in the musical evening that followed. And if it snowed, she would entice her schoolfriends out to have a snowball fight and build a snowman and they'd stay out until they were frozen before dashing indoors to have hot fruit punch. She gave an enormous sigh, and hugged her arms around her body, keeping in the spirit of friendship and happiness, clinging on to these precious memories that she held so dear. With these lovely thoughts in her mind, she drifted off into a deep slumber.

Charlotte felt her life was plodding along, as if she was waiting for a bus, which never came.

Weekday nights at the inn were relatively quiet. A few local men would meet to talk about the day's happenings and made a pint of beer last nearly all night. Trade picked up on Friday nights, which were especially popular when Hilda cooked a meal. Charlotte enjoyed it when the pilots and crew from an airfield, a few miles inland, would descend on the inn as a change from their local watering hole. They were a lively crowd and someone always played the piano and a sing-song would follow. The young men from the village and surrounding area, home on leave from the forces, had returned to their duties. As she polished the tables, Charlotte recalled hearing not one of them speak about where they were stationed or posted to. And no one asked them either. She supposed they wanted to forget the war for the time being and enjoy themselves.

'You'll polish that bloody table away,' George called from behind the bar where he was working. 'Not a lot to stock up with. Brewery ain't much left, though I reckon supplies will be harder to get from now on,' he grumbled, more to himself than to Charlotte.

Finishing her cleaning, Charlotte went through to the kitchen, where Hilda was preparing a meal. 'Peel them potatoes,' she said, without looking up.

Charlotte was now used to Hilda's abrupt mannerisms, without quite understanding why she behaved as she did. Glad to be occupied, she set to work. In the background, music played on the old battery wireless and she hummed under her breath quietly to herself because Hilda didn't like any frivolity. She seemed to deem it a sin. Charlotte couldn't understand how two sisters, Martha and Hilda, could be so different in every way. Hilda came across as a sour and unsociable woman, the very opposite to her sister. Her mother had been a happy, friendly woman, always willing to help those in need. Charlotte wondered if anything terrible had happened in Hilda's life. She thought of her mother's loving, sunny nature and wished God had spared her and taken Hilda instead.

'Oh!' she uttered, clamping a hand across her mouth. That was a wicked thought, when her aunt had taken her in.

Hilda turned round, saying sharply. 'Have you done them yet?'

That evening Charlotte welcomed the warm presence of Dot, May and Edna as they sat in the snug. All three of them had been born and bred in the village and had gone to school together, later going dancing together, meeting up with their prospective husbands. Married, they drifted apart. Dot lived in Hull where she raised her family of four children. May went to live in Beverley. Sadly, she didn't have children, and her marriage floundered. 'I kicked the womanising bugger out,' she chortled. Edna raised her family in the village, and she had told Dot and May about the alms-houses to rent for retired ladies.

That night, Charlotte couldn't sleep because the sound of an air raid on Hull boomed across the countryside and searchlight beams criss-crossed the sky. She stood at the window, watching and praying that no one would be killed or injured. A sense of guilt filled her. She was here, away from Hull and in relative safety. She should be there, helping with war work, not stuck in this village inn. When her next free day was due, she would see what she could do. Maybe join the forces. Anything not to be dependent on her aunt and uncle.

Over the next few weeks, trade picked up. At the first opportunity, when she had three spare hours, she dashed to Hull. Jack had finished the wooden cross to mark her mother's grave. She cried when she held in it her hands and traced her fingers lovingly over the intricate carving of her mother's name and details, so beautiful and yet so poignant. The cross felt warm to her touch and not cold like a headstone. With tender hands, she wrapped it in brown paper and tied it with string.

Holding it close to her heart as she travelled by train and then bus to the Eastern Cemetery, she drew strength from it, remembering Martha's loving kindness.

Arriving at the cemetery, she sought the help of the kind steward. He came along with her to her mother's grave and helped her to anchor the cross in place, according to regulations, which she did not understand. 'I'll leave you to it, Miss,' he said and turned away back to his duties.

The spring day felt fresh, and a breeze blew, rustling new leaves on the trees and bushes. Charlotte glowed within, feeling the warmth of her mother reaching out to touch her soul, as if to give her blessing for her future life. She dropped to her knees, the touch of the soft earth comforting, and bowed her head. She tried to think of a prayer, but words jumbled in her head and so she simply muttered the Lord's Prayer.

After some time, she rose to her feet and whispered, 'I'll come again, Mam. Love you.'

Tears ran unheeded down her cheeks as she stepped backward, not wanting to turn away. A blackbird flew over and startled her and she glanced upwards, noticing the sky had turned to a murky grey. She shivered as the wind whipped round her body, pulling at her beret. She drew the scarf around her neck closer and thrust her hands deep into her coat pockets as she stepped onto the gravel path, her feet echoing a hollow crunching sound as she made her way out of the cemetery to catch a bus back to the station.

Arriving at the station, she dashed onto the platform to see her train pulling out. Now she would be late for her evening shift. She went into the station buffet and bought a cup of weak tea and a stale bun, because she would miss her evening meal.

Hopefully Aunt Hilda would put it in the warming oven, and she'd eat it when she'd finished working. At this moment, she didn't care.

* * *

One day in early spring, Charlotte was on her way back to the inn after visiting Jack when a woman driving a pony and trap pulled up beside her. She had seen the woman about the village, though never spoken to her. 'Good afternoon, my dear. I am Mrs Carlton-Jones and I am looking for volunteers to help me.'

Charlotte glanced at her, wondering what help she needed.

The lady, having gained her interest, continued. 'Mornington House on the far side of the village needs a good clean-up. The authorities have negotiated with the owners to use the house for child refugees. I need to check over the house and I could use another pair of eyes. Would you be free tomorrow afternoon?'

Without hesitation, Charlotte replied, 'Yes, I am.'

'Excellent, my dear. Your name?'

'Charlotte Kirby.'

Back at the inn, she bubbled with enthusiasm. 'Where've you been?' Hilda grumbled. 'Sneaking off without saying.'

Charlotte decided not to mention anything yet about Mornington House.

The next afternoon, at two o'clock, Charlotte waited outside the inn as Mrs Carlton-Jones drew up in her pony and trap. There was just enough space for her to squeeze in next to her. Brought up in the city, she had only ever ridden on buses, trams and trains, never in a pony and trap before. She loved the gentle pace as the pony trotted along and noticed the admiring glances from the village folk as they passed by, the old men doffing their caps. Though it was for Mrs Carlton-Jones, Charlotte gave them a wave.

The house was on the road leading out of Mornington towards the east coast. It was built sideways on from the road with a low brick wall around it that once had an iron gated entrance, long gone to aid the war effort. They both climbed down from the trap, and Mrs Carlton-Jones tethered the pony to a nearby tree with a grass verge for it to munch on. They walked up the drive, which was overgrown with a tangle of bushes spilling out onto it and weeds running amok. Mrs Carlton-Jones inserted an iron key in the front door, which was warped with age and weather, and took a lot of budging to open it. Inside, Charlotte sniffed the damp, musty air and glanced about. Catching her hair and face on a hanging cobweb, she brushed it aside, trying not to be squeamish.

Mrs Carlton-Jones produced a pencil and notebook, writing her observations as they moved from the hall through to the spacious sitting room, dining room, and several smaller rooms and then through into the kitchen. Charlotte had never seen such a large kitchen, with a double-sided cooking range, lots of cupboard space and a walk-in pantry. Off the kitchen was a laundry room with a deep sink and an overhead pulley. Going into the large hall, they climbed the curved staircase to the eight bedrooms and one bathroom with a toilet.

Everywhere they walked, the floors were thick with dust and mouse droppings. Opening the door leading to the attic staircase, Mrs Carlton-Jones sighed and said to Charlotte. 'My legs won't make it up those steep stairs. Would you mind, my dear?'

'Of course not.' Without effort, she climbed to the top of the house. Counting four rooms, two in front of the house and two at the back, she inspected them closely before coming down to report her findings. 'Three of the rooms' sloping ceilings are damaged where rain has poured in, they'll need repairing. The fourth room is full of old trunks and boxes.'

They went outside through the kitchen door and found a sheltered alcove with a wooden bench and sat down. While Mrs Carlton-Jones consulted her notes, Charlotte looked out at the trees and the waist-high grass and the tumble of rambling roses clinging to the side of the house and the garden wall beyond. She wondered who had lived here. A family? She listened to the drone of bees and closed her eyes when she heard the voices of children playing quite close by. Opening her eyes, she looked around, but saw no one.

Mrs Carlton-Jones closed her notebook and Charlotte asked, 'Who used to live here?'

'No one. Not for a few years. There was an accident.' She jumped to her feet, saying, 'Time we were going. I have all the information I need.'

When they arrived at the inn, Mrs Carlton-Jones said, 'Thank you, my dear, for accompanying me. I would, at some stage, like to involve you further. If you are willing?'

As she jumped down from the trap, Charlotte replied eagerly. 'Yes, I am.'

On her next afternoon visit to Jack, she mentioned to him the plans for Mornington House.

He scratched his silver thatch of hair. 'Well, I wish the kiddies good luck who stay there.'

CHAPTER SIX

Summer 1942

Up bright and early, chores done, Charlotte was on her way to see Mrs Carlton-Jones at Mornington House. Today she would have the list of the refugee children who were coming. It was sad, she thought, how all those city children must leave their homes and families to be with strangers for their safety. She thought of the kindness of the three ladies when she first arrived in Mornington, leaving her home city to live with strangers and working in the inn when her grief for her mother was raw. The ladies had given her so much comfort, as did the kindness of Jack. Her aunt and uncle, strangers, had taken her in out of duty. Nothing more. No kindness, no warmth, no asking how she felt. They were immune to her. She was a commodity, like a barrel of beer. She shrugged off her morbid thoughts and called hello to two young mothers pushing prams towards the shops.

When Charlotte reached Mornington House, an agitated Mrs Carlton-Jones greeted her with the words. 'This is an emergency; it's not what I thought.' Charlotte, unsure, waited for her to continue, noticing a pile of documents on the wooden bench, which served as a desk. Mrs Carlton-Jones motioned Charlotte to look at the topmost document which lay open, saying. 'It is a list of their names.'

'Oh, so we know who is coming,' she answered, wondering why this was an emergency.

Mrs Carlton-Jones, known for her unflappability in the face of any problem arising, usually dealt with difficulties in her stride.

Charlotte glanced at the French names; she would need practise to pronounce some of them. And then she looked at the date of their arrival. She looked at Mrs Carlton-Jones, saying 'They're coming in three days' time.' Now she knew what the problem was. There was a lot to do in less time.

'I have told the authorities that I will do my best.' Then she rounded on Charlotte, her tone sharp. 'I hope you can still help?'

'Yes, of course,' she replied, moving to one side, away from the older woman's spray of spittle.

The imminent arrival of the foreign children became the talk of the village. And that evening, Charlotte faced George, her voice firm. 'I am doing volunteer work for the war effort by helping with the child refugees. That leaves me enough time to still do six evening shifts and clean the tables.'

He glared at her and boomed, 'What about the floor?'

She shrugged. 'You'll have to get someone in.' Then added cheekily, 'The inn's making a good profit.' She turned, leaving him speechless.

The next day, Charlotte hurried down to Mornington House, which they had scrubbed clean yesterday, from top to bottom, leaving the windows washed and sparkling.

Tomorrow, the first group of ten children would arrive. 'Another group next week,' exclaimed Mrs Carlton-Jones, now completely back in charge of the situation.

Charlotte carried a pile of bedding up the magnificent mahogany staircase to the bedrooms. There were five iron bedsteads to a room, and as she made up the beds for the children, she sang the catchy tune 'Run Rabbit Run', which the locals were fond of singing to annoy Farmer Huggate.

The sheets and pillow cases were white and the blankets army grey. Covering each bed were colourful counterpanes, made by the women of the village. During evenings in the snug, Dot, May and Edna had been busy, using a crochet hook to interlock loops of wool and material: silk, cotton, anything to hand they could use. She'd watched, mesmerised, marvelling at how nimble their fingers were and how they never made a mistake.

Charlotte met the pleasant, middle-aged couple, Mr and Mrs Grahame, the live-in staff, 'We are so looking forward to caring for the children,' they enthused.

The daily cook, Mrs Jolly, a village woman with ten grown-up children, was in the kitchen making a list of provisions she needed. 'Hello,' said Charlotte. 'I'm one of the volunteers.'

Mrs Jolly beamed a welcoming smile, replying, 'Bit different from working at the inn, I expect?'

Mid-morning, when all the bedrooms were ready, Mrs Jolly made a big pot of tea, and Charlotte joined the other volunteers in the kitchen for a well-earned cuppa. She studied the names of the children on the list, and turning to Mrs Carlton-Jones, asked. 'I only know a smattering of French, so I'm wondering how best to communicate with the children. In a strange country and separated from their families they will feel homesick and frightened.'

Mrs Carlton-Jones replied in a matter-of-fact voice. 'I am sure that won't be a problem. I understand when they have settled in, an English teacher will come. Children are very adaptable and no doubt they will soon learn English.'

Charlotte wasn't too sure. In a strange country, far from their homeland and loved ones, and bearing in mind what horrors they must have witnessed, it would take time for them to settle. To offer them love, care, food and a warm bed would be a good start.

Rising from the table, Mrs Carlton-Jones said briskly to the helpers, 'Come along. We have more work to do.'

The rest of the morning and into the afternoon, Charlotte sorted clothes donated by various charities. When it was the afternoon break, instead of heading to the kitchen for a refreshing drink, she went for a walk round the grounds. She meandered through the overgrown garden, noticing the wild bramble bushes and weeds, which had taken over the vegetable plot. Further on, she stopped to shield her eyes from the summer sun to gaze across the expanse of a neglected pond full of green algae with bulrushes and reeds at its edges. Surrounding the pond, a wooden stake fence had recently been erected. Its stillness held an air of sadness, and she felt a strange sense of, what? A time warp? She wasn't certain. Suddenly the water rippled, and ducks swam among the reeds and bees buzzed as they went about their work. Birds landed on an overhead branch of a willow tree and sang. Glancing up, she saw an aircraft flying towards Driffield Aerodrome. It glinted in the sunlight, and she wondered if one of the women in the ATA piloted it. Amy Johnson, the famous aviator from Hull, had flown with them until she sadly lost her life the year before. Charlotte reluctantly made her way back to the house.

They finished early. 'Everything is ready for the children, so you may go home,' said Mrs Carlton-Jones. 'And thank you, for your good work.'

Arriving back at the inn and knowing she would be busy working that evening, and then tomorrow at Mornington House, Charlotte went to her room for a rest. The inn was silent, with no sign of her aunt and uncle, and she relished the quietness. She was surprised to see her bedroom door standing open, for she felt certain she'd closed it that morning. Stepping nearer, she heard a strange sound, like an animal in pain, coming from her room. Cautiously she stood in the open doorway, and shock rippled through her to see Hilda sitting on the bed.

Uncertain what to do, she watched as Hilda rocked back and forth, sobbing for someone called Milly.

Charlotte took a step forward. 'Aunt Hilda,' she whispered. But the woman didn't seem to hear her. Charlotte stood in front of her and asked, 'Aunt Hilda, can I help you?'

Hilda looked up, her eyes glazed and her expression vacant, as if she didn't know where she was. And then she mumbled, 'It's the anniversary.'

Charlotte waited for Hilda to enlighten her, but she began rambling incoherently and sobbing again.

Making a quick decision, she hurried downstairs and was relieved to hear George whistling outside in the yard as he attended to some task. Stealthily, she slipped into his tiny office and found the bottle of brandy. Picking up a glass off the shelf, she poured a generous measure.

Back upstairs in her room, Hilda was now quiet and staring into space. Gently, Charlotte placed a glass in her hands and whispered, 'Drink this.' She watched her aunt for a few moments and then she went over to the window to stare across the fields towards her home city, wishing her mother was here. She missed her so much, feeling her loss like a physical pain in her heart. Not for the first time, she wondered why a good person like her mother should have been taken so soon. She closed her eyes and wrapped her arms around her body, lost in her thoughts of bygone days.

'She would be ten now.' Hilda's voice broke into her reverie.

Charlotte turned round, surprised to see a serene look on her aunt's face. 'Who?' she asked.

'Milly, my daughter.' She looked into Charlotte's face. 'You didn't know I had a daughter?' Charlotte shook her head. 'Doris Mansfield took my Milly to play with the children up at Mornington House, which she often did. I remember it was a warm, sunny day, and we were busy. They had a pond and a dog. Doris was in the kitchen having a cup of tea and the children were playing in the garden.' She became quiet and Charlotte sat on the chair, sensing there was more to come. Hilda's voice trembled a little as she continued. 'We were never sure what happened, but we thought the dog had gone into the pond and got tangled up on some netting. The children went into the pond to rescue it. The dog broke free and the children . . .' Hilda gave a deep wrenching sound, her words coming from deep down within her. 'They all drowned.'

Charlotte held her breath, staring in disbelief at Hilda. Tears filled her eyes, and she went to her aunt and sat by her side, wrapping her arms around her, holding her close, feeling the trembling of her body.

After some time, Charlotte murmured, 'Was this Milly's room?'

Hilda disentangled herself and sat up, her face blotchy with tearstains. She nodded.

Just then, George boomed from below, 'Hilda, where are you?'

A startled look came into her eyes and she made to jump up, but Charlotte put a restraining hand on her arm. 'You go and freshen up. I'll make the pot of tea.'

When Hilda came downstairs, George looked at her, but didn't say a word. He drank his tea and immersed himself in the newspaper.

For the first time, Charlotte felt sorry for her aunt and uncle. To lose a child must have been devastating for them. How do you come to terms with that? Never. Now she could understand their off-hand ways. She was in her bedroom, once their daughter, Milly's room. She couldn't rest, she just lay on the bed, staring up at the ceiling.

That evening, as she served the three ladies, May remarked, 'What's up with you, love? You look a bit down.'

Charlotte glanced towards the bar to see George talking to a customer and sat down on a stool at the table. 'I feel so sad. Aunt Hilda told me about her daughter Milly and the terrible accident.'

'I wondered if she'd tell you. It wasn't our place to.'

'No, of course not. It must also have been devastating for the parents of the other children.'

'Aye, it was. Broke their marriage up. She went to live in London. He stayed in the house on his own, living like a

45

hermit. When war came, he joined up and went away.' May finished, and they all lapsed into silence.

Then Dot chirped up. 'It'll be good to have kiddies again at the big house. Have they fenced the pond off?'

'Yes, it's safe, but I guess it could always be a temptation to children.'

* * *

Next day, Charlotte was early at Mornington House, looking forward to the arrival of the children. Mrs Carlton-Jones called staff and volunteers into the dining room. She waved a telegram in her hand. 'This has just arrived. The children were staying in temporary accommodation on a military base. Not an ideal situation, but it sufficed. Now the military want them all to be moved at once. So today all twenty children will arrive.' There was a murmuring of voices. 'Quiet,' she ordered, and turned to speak to the two men present. 'Are you able to set up the extra beds?'

'Yes, Missus,' they replied in unison, and off they went.

Mrs Carlton-Jones continued, 'Bed linen to be sorted and beds made up. Mr Mackay is baking extra loaves to help us, but I will need someone to collect them.'

'We will,' said two women at the back of the room. 'We can load them on to our old pram.'

'I've got the rabbit stew on and I'm about to make the rice pudding,' said Mrs Jolly, wanting to get back to her kitchen. 'I've got more to do than listen to her clap-trap,' she muttered to Charlotte.

'Right.' Mrs Carlton-Jones waved her hands in dismissal.

Charlotte went to sort out the bedding and to make up the beds. 'The children sound as though they've been pushed around a bit,' she said to her co-worker, Laura, a young girl of fourteen who had recently left school and volunteered because she wanted to escape from her domineering mother.

Charlotte pulled back the blackout curtains to bring more light into the room. The original curtains had been tatty and so they had taken them down, though they saved some of the material to make draw-string bags for the children to keep their belongings in. She smiled at Laura, liking her. They worked well together and soon had all the beds made.

Carrying a pile of towels into the huge bathroom, Charlotte hung one on each wooden peg. 'We need more combs and brushes, and we have just one bar of precious soap.' The time passed, and it was two p.m. before they finished. Cook had made a pile of cheese sandwiches and a big pot of tea for them.

Charlotte and Laura sat outside on a bench, smelling the newly mown lawn, and taking in the freshness of the air after being indoors for such a long time. They let the summer sun warm their faces.

'What time are they due?' asked Laura.

'On the three thirty train.'

'They'll have a long walk from the station.'

'Let's see Cook about some refreshment for when they arrive.'

Surprise filled Charlotte's face to see George in the kitchen having a cup of tea. 'He's brought the kiddies a case of lemonade and I've made jam tarts,' said Mrs Jolly.

Rising to his feet, he told Charlotte, 'We can manage tonight so you best stay here and help.'

Before she could utter a word of thanks, he'd gone.

CHAPTER SEVEN

September 1942

Charlotte watched as the two hay wagons halted on the driveway of Mornington House. The taut bodies of the travel-weary children stared out with blank faces and expressionless eyes. A bewildering stillness surrounded them. Her heart wrenched with pain for these frightened and unhappy children so far from their homeland and their missing loved ones. Anger welled up inside her for the senseless act of war that had torn innocent children away from everything they held dear in their lives. In that split moment, she vowed to do everything in her power to support the children in making their lives secure and happy and free from fear.

Swiftly, she stepped forward, her arms open wide to lift the children down, saying gently, 'Come, we have refreshment for you after your long journey.'

Soon the children were inside the dining hall, staring vacantly at the refreshments on the table, not sure if they were for them. Charlotte noticed they didn't talk though some glanced about but most kept their eyes downcast. 'Eat.' She offered round the plate of jam tarts, and poured lemonade from a big enamel jug into glass beakers. One little boy's nose was running, dripping onto his jam tart. She bent down to wipe his nose with her handkerchief, and felt him flinch from her. 'It's all right, little chap,' she said gently. She looked at the label pinned to his coat. 'Raymonde, that's a good name.' His blue eyes wide, he looked at her and then, unsure, he lowered them and stuffed the tart into his mouth.

Afterwards, the children went outside into the garden to take advantage of the daylight and fresh air. They stood, unsure of what to do. One of the helpers brought out a football and some of the older boys, nervous at first, kicked the ball, while the other children just stood motionless, eyes cast downwards. Charlotte, her heart going out to them, realised it would take time and care for these children to trust and feel safe, and to adjust to their new way of life.

Later, after their hot, nourishing meal, some of the younger children yawned. 'They have had a long, tiring day,' remarked Mrs Carlton-Jones. 'So bedtime is in order.'

Used to boisterous children back in her home city of Hull, Charlotte felt her heart contract with concern for these children who were so quiet as they covertly watched each other. Going upstairs to the bedrooms, the children moved like ghosts, keeping to the sides of the walls, their eyes watchful, their bodies alert, ready to run from danger. She understood from a member of the organisation, who had rescued the children, that they had been living rough in buildings bombed by the enemy, and scavenging for food to survive. They had endured a perilous journey from their homeland of France, and on arriving in England, they had stayed at a camp down south where, after a thorough medical examination, they went through a delousing process.

There were twelve boys, six to each bedroom, and eight girls, four to each bedroom. Mr Grahame supervised the older boys, aged eight to ten, and Mrs Grahame the younger boys, aged five to seven. Charlotte was caring for the four youngest girls, aged three to five, and Laura the older girls aged six to ten. Helping Lucie, the youngest child, to undress and slip on her nightgown, Charlotte felt shocked at the state of the girl's body. So tiny and fragile that a puff of wind would blow the child away, like a floating balloon. How on earth had she survived? The leader of the rescue organisation, a woman referred to as Auntie, reported they'd found her just in time. She was on the brink of starvation, and so were some of the other children.

The drawstring bag made for each child was filled with a few essentials, including more items which had been donated by a kindly women's group in the village: a flannel, toothbrush and paste, and combs and hairbrushes, which was something they had been short of. Charlotte gave a drawstring bag to Lucie who hid it under her blankets, and no amount of coaxing from Charlotte would persuade her to hang it on her bed post. Fear filled the child's eyes so Charlotte tucked her into bed and was about to kiss Lucie's forehead when the child shrank back, slipping down in the bed.

'Night, night,' she said softly to Lucie, and to the other three girls, all tucked up in bed.

Charlotte lit the night light, which she set high on a shelf so that no child could reach it. She remained there until she felt sure every child was sleeping. Exhausted, but feeling happy, she went downstairs into the kitchen where all were to report and hopefully have a cup of refreshing tea.

Mrs Carlton-Jones was talking about drawing up a time-table for each of the volunteers. 'So that you can use your time wisely.'

'She thinks we're a bunch of school kids,' one volunteer mumbled.

* * *

Some of the children settled in, but others were cautious. 'It's a whole new way of life for them,' said Charlotte to Laura. 'And the language barrier is a bit of a problem.'

'Not at mealtimes,' Laura laughed.

Charlotte thought they were coping amazingly well after such upheavals in their young lives, though deep down, scars remained of their nightmare lives, which gave rise to occasional emotional outbursts. One day, Raymonde threw a tantrum and refused to wash his hands for dinner and ran off into the garden. Charlotte watched him run in the opposite direction, away from the pond. Her heart went out to him, the poor mite. Wrenched from his family and his homeland and being moved constantly about had unsettled him, so he retaliated in the only way he could to express his feelings and fears of the unknown.

'He will not have any dinner until he learns good manners,' rebuked a stern Mrs Carlton-Jones.

Charlotte looked at Mrs Jolly, who nodded, putting a plated meal in the warming oven.

After the dinner and the dishes had been cleared away, Charlotte went to look for Raymonde. She walked along the gravel path, looking to either side where bushes grew and he could be hiding. Stopping to listen, at first she could hear only the wood pigeons in the distance. As she neared the vegetable garden, she saw old Tom, a retired gardener, who had taken up voluntary work. He was busy raking soil in readiness for a crop to plant in spring. He appeared to be talking to himself. But as she drew closer, she saw Raymonde squatting with a trowel in his hand and turning soil over. She stood for a few moments, watching. She walked round so Raymonde could see her approaching. She didn't want to frighten him by coming up behind him unexpectedly.

'Hello, Tom. I see you have a willing helper.'

He glanced at her. 'Aye, Miss, he's a good 'un.'

She held out her hand to Raymonde, and his bottom lip quivered. Gently she said, 'Come and eat.' She made a display of using her fingers to shovel food into her mouth. 'Then you can come back and help Tom.' She pointed to the gardener, who grinned, showing a fine set of false teeth.

Later, before her shift finished and before the other volunteers came for bedtime duties, Charlotte went to find Mrs Carlton-Jones. She wanted to seek her approval of the plan she'd been mulling over. Carrying her notepad of ideas and a pencil to jot down any new ones, she found her seated at a table in the corner of the dining room.

Seeing Charlotte approaching, Mrs Carlton-Jones said, 'Ah, the very person I need to talk to.'

Charlotte drew in a deep breath and wondered if she'd found out about her saving Raymonde's dinner and waited for the reprimand.

Without preamble, Mrs Carlton-Jones launched in. 'I have other duties to attend to and some matters are pressing, so I need your cooperation. As you know, Mrs Grahame has overall responsibility for the running of the house and the children's welfare, and Mr Grahame is in charge of maintenance of the house and grounds, and helping with the older boys. And arriving tomorrow is Miss Elder, the children's English teacher. She will teach them in the mornings until they are fluent enough to attend the village school. I require you to organise the afternoon sessions, with help from other volunteers. I don't want the children to roam aimlessly around the house and grounds, getting into mischief. Have you any ideas, Miss Kirby?'

Charlotte smiled. 'If I may sit down, then I will tell you what I have in mind.'

She produced her notepad, cleared her throat and began. 'After dinner, when the children have cleared away their pots, will be outside recreation time.'

'Outside,' cut in Mrs Carlton-Jones. 'They should have quiet time.'

'With respect, after their morning English lesson which requires serious concentration, they need to exercise outdoors to use their energy and take in fresh air. A game of rounders for the older children, skipping for the girls and a game of hopscotch.' She saw the good lady frown and so she didn't enlighten her about drawing a hopscotch grid on the flagstones of the courtyard.

'After tea, they can take part in board games, or the girls can learn handicrafts like knitting, crochet and needlework.' She saw the good lady glance at her wrist watch, so added hastily, 'Later, when the children are more settled, they could take part in village activities.'

She waited for Mrs Carlton-Jones to disagree with her plan for the children. But she stood up, pulling on her gloves. 'Your ideas are sound and interesting, but we do not wish to overwhelm the children, given the disruptions in their lives. I suggest you introduce the ideas gradually to give the children a chance to adapt to living here.' Then, as an afterthought, she added, 'Well done, my dear. Must dash.'

Charlotte remained on her seat, concentrating on the list. After some thought, she decided that as a first step, with supervision, the children might enjoy exploring the grounds and getting to know their surroundings.

The next day, Mrs Carlton-Jones informed the volunteers, 'I have other commitments to attend to. From Friday, I will be here once a week. Charlotte, Miss Kirby, will be in charge the rest of the days in my absence.'

There was murmuring among them and glances in Charlotte's direction and someone remarked, 'She's nowt but a lass.' Then Mrs Carlton-Jones called on Charlotte to speak.

Charlotte stood before them, feeling her inside tremble. She cleared her throat. 'Our paramount aim is to help the children to settle in so they can enjoy their young lives after the terrible turmoil they have suffered. Do you all agree?' Five pairs of eyes stared at her. She held her breath, waiting.

'Of course we do, Charlotte. That's why we are here. To help the kiddies,' one of them said. The others nodded. 'Just let us know what you want us to do.'

Everyone began speaking and Charlotte released her breath, feeling the elation sweep through her body.

Her elation was short lived as unforeseen problems stepped in. While the children were now being well fed and had a bed to sleep in, pilfering was part of their lives, and their old habits were hard for them to break. While making the beds in the boys' room one morning, Charlotte found chunks of bread in Gilbert's bed, under the pillow. And in the drawstring bags of other boys, she found food, and also hidden in corners of the bathroom. It was a similar situation with the older girls. 'Food is too precious to throw away, so what can we do?' Charlotte asked the other helpers as they sat in the dining room, having a cup of tea on their morning break.

'What about a midnight feast?' suggested Laura.

'Don't be daft,' said one of the volunteers.

'Yes,' Charlotte mused, 'it is daft, but it might work.' And after discussing it with Mrs Grahame, they agreed that the feast would take place the following night, Saturday, but only for the older children.

They had gathered all the pilfered food up, except the mouldy bits. Cook supplied a jar of her best strawberry jam and a jug of milk.

On the stroke of midnight, Charlotte, Laura and two other volunteers entered the bedrooms and switched on the overhead lights. Soon the children stirred awake, sitting up and staring at the food, which they'd hidden away and which was now in full view. It was set out on trays in the centre of the floor, with a few fresh slices of bread. As an extra treat, Cook had baked fairy buns. Laura supervised the girls' bedroom, the other helpers in the boys' rooms, while Charlotte helped between the three rooms.

'Midnight feast,' she said clearly, and got the children to repeat the words which, with hand gestures, they seemed to understand, though she didn't think it would be in Miss Elder's vocabulary when teaching the children English. The children enjoyed their midnight feast, tucking into the food and drinking the milk. After a trip to the lavatory and handwashing, they were tucked up in bed. Charlotte told the children, 'This will only happen on special occasions so, children, do not hide food, because we have our rations and you will not go hungry. Do you understand?' They nodded and grunted in agreement.

Later, Charlotte and Laura discussed whether it had been a success. Charlotte said, 'I think most of them understood, but some children will still pilfer until they forget to do it. We don't know what really happened to them when they became orphans of war and had to scavenge for food. More often they would have gone hungry, so food to them represents survival.'

Tears welled in her eyes and a lump came in her throat. She glanced at Laura to see her dash away her tears.

'I love caring for the children,' Laura whispered. 'But I don't understand why they couldn't be looked after in their own country.'

Charlotte gave a heavy sigh, and replied, 'The Germans occupy their country and, from what I have read in newspapers and seen on the Pathé News, they are only interested in power.'

The next morning the children were up and dressed and down for breakfast, full of talk about their midnight feast. Charlotte smiled at Mrs Grahame as she listened to the chattering and then yawned. She'd only snatched a few hours of sleep and soon had to be on duty at the inn.

As she walked towards the inn, breathing in the chilly morning air, she wanted nothing more than to care full time for the children. She would have to wait until the authorities secured more funding, but for now, she loved being a volunteer.

CHAPTER EIGHT

Christmas 1942

The children's topic of conversation for the next week was the midnight feast. Somehow, it opened them up and helped them to relax and to be just children. And gradually, the pilfering stopped.

Although like any children, they often pinched a jam tart from the cooling tray, it was to eat, not to hide. The worst time for the children was when they had to wear a gas mask and go down to the cellar for safety when the siren sounded, warning of a bombing raid. Charlotte felt her heart ache as she witnessed the terror in their eyes, the fear of what might happen to them etched on their faces. As the war progressed, the targets were airfields around Mornington and the searchlight station up on the Wolds. The worst bombing raids were concentrated on her home city of Hull, targeting the docks and factories and much more.

Step by step, the children settled in, their fear not so apparent now. She and Laura and the other staff would read stories or they would all sing, play guessing games, anything to distract them from the war raging outside.

Their fears lessened as Christmastime fast approached, sparking off a fragment of recognition for some of the older children who called it Noel.

Today the children were having their last English lessons with Miss Elder and she joined them for dinner. Charlotte and Laura were in the dining room busy setting the table when Laura asked, 'Do the children celebrate Christmastime similar to us?'

Charlotte paused before laying the last knife and fork, and recalled her own childhood Christmases, which were always full of fun. 'I'm not sure,' she replied. 'But whatever we do for them, it will be better than what they've experienced over the last few years.'

Laura sat down for a moment, her voice full of enthusiasm. 'Yes, let's make it the best Christmas for the children. I'll start with showing them how to make papier mâché figures and baubles, so I'd best start scrounging old newspapers.'

Wishing she didn't have to work evenings at the inn, because she wanted to stay permanently with the children, Charlotte enthused, 'Yes, we'll make it the best ever.'

She made it her mission to encourage the villagers to make the children feel welcome by providing any toys and books no longer in use. Edna, May and Dot, eager to help, made little crochet dolls and knitted scarves and gloves, and enlisted the help of other ladies. Jack made wooden toy trains and cars, and the ARP wardens made a couple of boogies from wheels of old prams and wooden crates. The village school closed for the festive period and the children and teachers had donated paper-chains to hang up a bright star and angels to decorate the branches of evergreen cut from trees in the wood.

On Christmas Day, Charlotte burst with happiness. 'I don't have to work at the inn tonight, because it's closed, so I can spend more time with the children.'

Laura, helping with Charlotte, beamed, her laugh infectious. 'Isn't it lovely to see the children so happy!' They watched the children, loving the surprise and wonderment on their faces.

'Yes,' Charlotte replied. 'It fills my heart with joy and gladness.' Tears pricked her eyes and dampened her lashes to see the excitement in the children's eyes as they opened their presents received from Father Christmas. They bunched together when they had first seen him, frightened of this man in a red outfit, not sure of him. Friend or foe?

Old Tom, the gardener, who had donned a Father Christmas outfit and grown his silvery beard long and sported a moustache, gave a jovial laugh, his faded blue eyes twinkling as the children warmed to him.

The younger children were not aware of who he was, but she noticed two older boys giggling at each other and pointing to Tom's working boots. She caught their attention and put her finger to her lips and shook her head. And they understood.

After a delicious Christmas dinner of roast goose and trimmings, no Christmas pudding, but jelly for the children and mince pies for the adults, the children played quietly for some time and then a fight broke out between two boys. Charlotte, who was helping to do a jigsaw puzzle, rose to her feet and clapped her hands. 'Now children, we will go outside for a brisk walk, so put on your outdoor clothes.'

A mad scramble to the cloakroom ensued. Mrs Carlton-Jones, who had popped in to see the children, breathed a sigh of relief, settled back in her armchair and closed her eyes.

Mrs Jolly, finished in the kitchen, came into the sitting room. 'Peace at last. I think I'll have a nap.'

Charlotte found Mr and Mrs Grahame in the dining room, preparing a light tea for the children. 'Laura and I are taking the children walking in the grounds for half an hour.' They nodded with a look of relief.

Out in the garden, an overnight sprinkling of snow rested on bushes and trees. They took the path through the woods, letting the older boys, so full of energy and strong limbs, scamper in front. 'They look healthier now than when they first came,' Charlotte remarked to Laura as they strolled along, holding the hands of the smaller children.

'Yes, they're like proper children now.'

And they were, thought Charlotte, though they never talked of any family members. She couldn't imagine the terror they must have suffered at being parted from their loved ones.

Though she knew the pain of losing her mother to enemy bombing, she hadn't been a child sent to a foreign country.

'Miss Charlotte, look.'

A shout from one of the boys walking ahead jolted her from her reverie. Still holding the children's hands, she hurried forward. It was the pond. The children shrieked with delight, but she caught the anxious look in Laura's eyes, for she knew the story. The canopy of trees formed a frame over the water and from their position on the path, it gave the pond a beckoning, alluring quality. She caught the word 'swim'. 'No, too cold.' She gave a shiver to emphasise her meaning. Then she clapped her hands, saying, 'Time to go back for tea.' They understood the word meant food and eagerly they turned to hurry back towards the house. She walked by Laura's side and said, 'I will have to talk to Mrs Carlton-Jones about the children's reaction to seeing the pond.'

'It's fenced off.'

'Yes, I know, but I sense these boys want adventure.'

Once inside the house, Charlotte and Laura supervised the children in the cloakroom and, having changed into their soft shoes and washed their hands, they entered the dining room. Charlotte loved to see their faces when they saw food, and soon they had demolished the assortment of sandwiches, jam tarts, jelly and milk. Charlotte was hoping to speak to Mrs Carlton-Jones, but she had gone home.

Later, both Charlotte and Laura were staying on because the evening volunteers had family commitments. They played I Spy and board games with the children and admired their Christmas gifts once again. Soon it was bedtime and story-time for the younger ones, the older ones preferring to read themselves.

* * *

After Christmas, the children would be attending the village school for the first time. They seemed to welcome the prospect. Charlotte accompanied Mrs Grahame and the children on their first day at school. Mrs Carlton-Jones had provided a list of the children's names and their known details. 'Hopefully, Miss Elder's teaching of English came up to standard,' Mrs Grahame said to the teacher.

Miss Holderness replied, 'These are troublesome times and children are resilient. Come along, children.'

They watched the children go, and Charlotte whispered to Mrs Grahame, 'I think we are dismissed.'

Charlotte returned to meet them at dinner time and afterwards accompanied them back to school. However, when they arrived, Lucie refused to let go of her hand, and she couldn't persuade her to do so. Charlotte looked to Miss Holderness, who surprised her by saying. 'Miss Kirby, I suggest you join the class.'

Feeling like a child herself, Charlotte went with Lucie, still clinging on to her hand, to the infants' classroom. She stayed until playtime, when another little girl, an evacuee staying in the village, asked Lucie to share her skipping rope. For a while, she observed the girls at play and Lucie appeared quite happy, no longer wanting to cling on to Charlotte's hand. She informed Miss Holderness she was going and that Laura would collect the children later.

* * *

Spring 1943

'Hello ladies, lovely to see you,' Charlotte said to Dot, May and Edna as they sat in the snug one evening. 'Your usual?'

They nodded in unison, and she went to the bar with their order. Except for two men drinking at the bar, the ladies were the only customers.

As she waited for George to fill the glasses, he grumbled, 'Not sure how long I can keep open if business doesn't pick up.'

One man gave a hearty laugh and said in a loud voice. 'Haven't yer heard? There's a load of them foreigners gonna be billeted in village, so postwoman said.'

'I aint heard nowt,' said the other man.

'Nor me,' George said. And as soon as he'd served Charlotte he went to the telephone in his cubbyhole office off the kitchen.

Placing their drinks in front of the ladies and seeing as George wasn't in view; she sat down at the table and repeated what she'd heard.

They shook their heads. 'Foreigners, I wonder where they'll go,' said Dot.

'There are them huts up Driffield Road,' Edna suggested.

'They'll need a good clean out. I'm sure someone kept chickens in 'em,' May remarked.

'Do yer reckon we should clean them out?'

'Shovel 'em out, more likely.' Edna laughed and picked up her glass of stout.

Charlotte left them to their discussion, feeling pleased at the prospect of seeing more customers drift in.

Everyone in the village seemed to be talking about the foreign soldiers who, according to gossip, would take over the village. It didn't bother Charlotte who they were. Her only interest was the children. They filled her every thought. Caring for them was her vocation. She felt their pain and sorrow and shared in their innocent laughter. They enjoyed their life at Mornington House, except for having to go down into the cellar. At school, some of them had made friends, and Charlotte knew for certain, because of their alert sense of survival from when they'd lived in their war-torn homeland, that other children would never bully them. And little Lucie appeared happy with her playmate, though sometimes she still cried out in her sleep for her mère.

George began stocking up with supplies, though Charlotte never enquired where from.

Hilda didn't seem to care about what was about to happen and Charlotte could now understand, though not fully, her aunt's mood swings.

With her head full of the children, Charlotte, who was serving the ladies with their next order, didn't hear May's question. 'Sorry, I wasn't listening.'

'Got a young man, then?' May asked.

'No.'

'Then what was you thinking of?'

'The children.'

'Children! A young lass like you should be out enjoying herself. We were at her age,' she said, addressing her companions.

Then Dot chimed in, 'You might get one of them Frenchies that are coming.'

'Frenchies?' Charlotte repeated, not sure what Dot meant.

'Aye, it's the Free French soldiers that are coming next week. You never know your luck.'

The three of them chuckled, then began reminiscing about their young, carefree days.

CHAPTER NINE

Spring 1943

The day the Free French soldiers were due, excitement grew as the villagers of Mornington lined the main street to see them. They marched from the station at the side of the village to their billets, the Nissen huts. Charlotte stood on the edge of the crowd, who had gathered to watch the incomers. She'd never seen foreign soldiers before and expected them to look different but, apart from their uniforms, they were the same as any British soldier. Some of them looked mere lads with washed-out faces and thin bodies and others looked tired with dark, haunted eyes. 'They are a scruffy lot,' a woman standing next to Charlotte remarked.

'They look like they've been travelling for days and need a good nourishing meal,' Charlotte replied.

'Well, I hope they don't think they can have our rations,' the woman spoke indignantly.

'What about our troops in a foreign country, we wouldn't want them to go hungry?'

'You're right, my dear,' said Mrs Carlton-Jones. 'We must make them welcome and the least we can do is provide hot soup and bread for them.' With that, she strode off.

'She's a do-gooder who pokes her nose into everything,' said the other woman.

Charlotte watched Mrs Carlton-Jones disappear into the crowd and had to admire the good lady for her fortitude and her willingness to help those in need. She loved her volunteer work with the children, and if time allowed, she would help the Free French soldiers too.

Later she talked to the ladies in the inn 'I'd like to help to provide a nourishing meal for the soldiers.'

'Though Mrs Carlton-Jones can be a bit bossy, she gets things done.' Dot said.

'Always organising something,' May chimed in.

'Aye, as long as they do the same for our lads in foreign parts, I'll willingly help out,' said Edna. The other two nodded in agreement.

'How will we find out how to volunteer?' Charlotte asked, picking up the tray and starting to move away as she saw George glancing her way.

'Village Hall notice board.'

Early next morning, before going to Mornington House, Charlotte went to the village hall. And sure enough, written in bold lettering, was a notice tacked to the board asking all villagers to contribute to making the Free French soldiers welcome by providing a buffet meal to include soup and bread and whatever other wholesome food they could provide.

Reading the notice, Charlotte murmured to the man standing next to her, one of the ARP wardens, 'I'm puzzled. Why are the Free French here and not in Europe fighting the enemy?'

The man lifted up his cap and scratched his thinning grey hair, 'I don't rightly know, lass, maybe they're on special training.'

As it happened, Hilda needed Charlotte to help make the soup, and then to serve it to the soldiers. She dashed over to see Mrs Grahame at Mornington House, to explain why she couldn't volunteer that day.

'Not to worry, Charlotte, we'll manage.'

* * *

Later at the village hall, the Free French soldiers were sitting on wooden benches at long trestle tables and Charlotte was helping to serve them, while Hilda dished up the soup. Other helpers were slicing freshly baked bread and piling it onto plates which they placed on the tables so the soldiers could help themselves. The men nodded and murmured words of thanks, '*Merci.*' No one in the village spoke French, though someone thought the vicar might.

The huts, where the men were billeted, had been scrubbed and cleaned thoroughly by a willing band of women, including May, Edna and Dot. 'They're cold and draughty, but their bodies will soon warm the place up,' Edna said, in a knowing way.

Dot was quick with a reply. 'So, you've had experience of lots of men's bodies?'

'You've kept that quiet,' quipped May.

Edna's face flushed red and then, eyeing her two friends, she replied. 'Watch it! I could say a thing or two about you two, so don't you forget it.'

Charlotte loved the banter between the three ladies who had known each other since school days.

Turning towards the kitchen, a pile of empty soup dishes in her hands, Charlotte came face to face with a soldier. '*Merci, mademoiselle,*' he said.

Charlotte found herself staring into his weary face with crinkled lines around his brown eyes. He looked slightly older than some of the other soldiers. She blushed and whispered, 'You are welcome.'

'Time we were getting back,' hissed Hilda's voice in her ear.

Charlotte hurried into the kitchen.

In bed later that night, her thoughts drifted to the French soldier who had thanked her. There was something about him, but she couldn't pinpoint quite what it was on that first shy encounter. She liked him. She'd never had a proper boyfriend though sometimes she and Joyce teamed up with two lads and went dancing or to the pictures, but nothing serious, no one special. So why was she thinking of this French soldier? Was it because she had been starved of love and affection since the death of her beloved mother, or was she just letting her imagination run away with her? If only she could talk to Joyce about her thoughts. She loved the banter with the ladies and chatting to others in the inn who often told her about their troubles, and Jack's company was comforting. However, she had no one to whom she could confide her innermost feelings. She sighed and turned over, trying to get comfortable, and eventually she drifted into an unsettling sleep.

* * *

Just over a week later, four of the French soldiers opened the inn door and peered in. They stood uncertainly on the threshold, in their dark mustard-coloured uniforms, a bit darker than what the British soldiers wore. George, making his presence known, strode over to welcome them and ushered them to the bar. Playing the amenable host, George asked, 'What's it to be, gents?'

They stared at the half empty array of bottles on the bar shelf, and the hand pumps. One of them pointed to the bitter beer pump, and the other three nodded their heads. George drew four pints and placed them on the counter, waiting for the soldiers to count out their English money. This scenario was quietly watched by a handful of local men, with Dot, May, Edna and Charlotte, standing to get a better view. The first soldier took a long, thirsty draught of the beer and spluttered, spraying the counter, which George hastily wiped.

'Tek it slow, mate,' hiccupped one of the locals, who had already drunk too much. It was Farmer Huggate, whose two sons had gone off to war and whose daughter, who was supposed to work on the farm, had run off to London and joined the ATS.

After a few attempts, the soldiers began to master the art of drinking the local beer. It was that or nothing, because no one in the community drank wine. 'Them posh lot in Driffield might,' someone called out.

The next weekend, more French soldiers drifted down to the inn. A soldier lifted the lid of the piano, and tinkled the keys. 'Nowt that we know,' grumbled the locals. One evening one of the locals brought his mouth organ and played a tune, 'You Are My Sunshine', and the locals began to sing, including the three ladies. Charlotte watched the French soldiers pull sceptical faces and turn away from the crowd now gathered around the mouth organ player. Then one of them glanced over his shoulder and nudged the soldier next to him and they sauntered over to the piano and entered into the spirit. He soon picked up the melody, and the other soldiers crowded round the piano, mixing with the locals, and everyone was having a joyful sing-song, 'like a party atmosphere,' as someone remarked.

George encouraged this entertainment as everyone drank more, and his profits flowed.

One evening, a couple of nights later, after serving the ladies, Charlotte turned round to see the soldier with the brown eyes, who she'd noticed when serving soup in the village hall, looking in her direction. She smiled at him and as he smiled back she felt a wonderful fluttering sensation she'd never experienced before, and quickly placed her hand over her heart before someone noticed. Used to mixing with customers, she worked her way round to the table where brown eyes sat at the end of the bench, slightly apart from the other soldiers.

'Hello, another drink?' she asked, pointing to his empty glass.

'*Oui, merci*,' he replied, looking deep into her eyes.

She blushed with pleasure and picked up his glass for a refill and threaded her way to the bar. Hilda came bustling from the kitchen with a huge pile of sandwiches of freshly cooked shank of ham, and a big jar of pickled onions. The French soldiers certainly did have ravenous appetites, Charlotte observed as she stood back from the bar as one of them rushed forward to take the plate to offer the sandwiches to his comrades and the locals.

Pushing her way through to brown eyes, she waited as he took his last bite of the sandwich and set his drink on the table. 'You enjoyed it?' she asked.

'*Tres bon,*' he replied, smacking his lips.

She laughed and noticed how sensuous his lips were and the same wonderful feeling gripped her again and instinctively her hand went to her heart.

He smiled and copied her gesture, putting his hand on his own heart.

Oh my God. He thinks I'm a loose woman. She turned to flee when he caught her hand.

'Friend?' he asked, a pleading look on his face.

Feeling ashamed, she drew a deep breath to slow down her unpredictable heartbeat, and asked, 'What's your name?'

'Emile.' He then pointed to her.

'Charl . . .'

There was a sudden crash of glass as someone knocked over their beer. Charlotte hastened to collect a brush and shovel and clear up the debris and wipe down the table. When she finished her task, she looked round for Emile. But he had gone.

* * *

Next morning at Mornington House, with the children away at school, Charlotte and Laura had finished changing the sheets in readiness for the two laundry women who came twice weekly.

In the kitchen, Mrs Jolly poured out tea from the big pot, and the conversation centred on the village topic.

'What do you think of these Frenchies, Charlotte?' asked one of the women, a look of mischief in her eyes.

'Me, why me?'

'You see them most nights. You're not saying you don't look at them?'

'They seem very nice.'

'Very nice! Who are you kidding!' They all laughed.

'I fancy working at the inn, but my old man won't let me. Too much temptation, he said.'

More laughter, and Charlotte joined in. 'You could organise a Barn Dance, then you'd get a chance to dance with them,' she added, her eyes twinkling.

'What a splendid idea!'

They all jumped to their feet and made to leave as Mrs Carlton-Jones entered the kitchen.

The good lady held up her hand. 'A splendid idea. I shall put it to the committee. If they agree, I shall need helpers, so I will bear you kind ladies in mind.'

Eyes wide, speechless, they left the kitchen, all with a smile on their faces. And Charlotte thought of Emile, hoping to see him again.

CHAPTER TEN

May 1943

Mrs Carlton-Jones brought the pony and trap to a halt alongside Charlotte, who stopped walking, and waited. Without preamble, Mrs Carlton-Jones announced, 'I am organising a social event for the French soldiers. The Church ladies' group are providing food and George Bilton will run a bar, so you, my dear, along with the other village girls, will be required as dance partners. I am on my way to see Farmer Huggate, who now has land-army girls working for him. Gee up.'

Hastily Charlotte stepped back as the pony and trap sent a spray of dust and dirt up. Charlotte admired Mrs Carlton-Jones' vitality, her ability to get things done, especially for getting George to give her Saturday night off.

When she arrived back at the inn, the air oozed with anticipation and excitement. Something which had been previously missing she realised. George was busy stock-taking, a cigarette dangling from his mouth, and Hilda hummed as she polished glasses. Charlotte observed the scene, waiting for George to speak with her, but he seemed unaware of her presence.

But Hilda glanced her way instead. 'Put kettle on.'

That evening, the bar buzzed with the talk about the forthcoming social at the village hall.

Only Farmer Huggate seemed aggrieved. 'Just got bloody lasses working on farm and lady do-gooder has gone and hijacked them.'

'A load of nonsense, it's only for one night. You could have stood up to her,' one man said.

'Um,' he retorted, gulping down his beer and banging his empty glass on the counter.

As Charlotte served the three ladies their drinks in the snug, she noticed the gleam in their eyes and caught the last few words of their conversation. 'We'll have a little practice.'

'Practice, what?' she enquired.

'We were flappers in our day,' May answered.

Puzzled and not having a clue what she meant, Charlotte waited for an explanation because all she could think of were seals honking and flapping like she'd seen at the cinema.

'She means dancing, you know, the Charleston. They called us flappers,' explained Dot.

'I've got a picture somewhere; I'll show it to you.'

'We're going to the social,' said Edna. 'I've always fancied a Frenchman.' The other two cackled and Charlotte returned to her duties, amused by the ladies' good humour.

The question of what to wear for the dance haunted her for the next few days. The only clothes she had were those given to her when her home was bombed and all her possessions destroyed. 'What shall I do?' she spoke to the framed portrait of her mother that she kept on her bedside table. Gazing lovingly at her mother's gentle, caring eyes, a lump came into her throat and tears threatened. Oh, how she missed her beloved mother. It was so sad that she couldn't talk to Hilda about her, and so hard to believe they were sisters. Hilda was still cold and distant, as if she'd erected a steel barrier around herself.

The following day, Charlotte was pleased to find Jack in his shed, whistling a jaunty tune. Jip came running down the garden path to greet her, nuzzling the basket she carried, smelling the scent of the warm rabbit pie from the bakery.

'Hello,' she called, fascinated as she watched Jack finish painting, in bright red, a little wooden cart with a pulling handle.

'All done,' he was rubbing his hands on a piece of rag.

'Who's the lucky child?' she asked.

'Why, it's for the refugee children.'

She smiled with pleasure at his kindness and relayed to him the excitement of the village social dance for the French soldiers.

'Seen anything of Emile?' he asked, with a mischievous twinkle in his eyes.

She'd mentioned Emile to him in a previous conversation, and she blushed as she replied. 'Not lately. I heard they are training with tanks.'

They sat in silence for a few minutes, drinking tea, when Jack asked, 'Got a pretty dress to wear? As I recall, lasses like to dress up and catch a lad's eye.'

'I lost all my clothes when we were bombed out. I'll go shopping to Driffield or Beverley for a dress or material to make one. I have enough coupons.'

'No need, Charlotte, I've plenty of my Doris's clothes still in the wardrobe. You're welcome to anything you fancy.'

Jack led the way into his bedroom and Charlotte noticed how clean and tidy it was, with everything in its right place. She smelt the refreshing fragrance of beeswax. He sat down on a cane chair and pointed to the biggest wardrobe; an Edwardian mahogany wardrobe with a central long mirror, which reminded her of her mother's. Hesitantly, feeling as if she was intruding, she opened it and the lovely scent of lavender wafted from the little bags hung between the amazing collection of dresses in all colours and materials.

'We loved dancing, me and my Doris,' said Jack softly.

Charlotte went to him and hugged him, kissing his forehead. 'Doris was a lucky lady to have you for a husband.'

'Aye, we both were lucky,' as he looked fondly at the framed photograph of Doris on his bedside table.

They spent about thirty minutes looking at the dresses, she holding each one up for Jack to see and loving the joy on his face as he recounted his fond memories of his wife wearing each dress. She chose a blue silk dress, the colour of a summer's day sky and embroidered round the sweetheart neckline and the edge of the sleeves with tiny daisies. 'It's beautiful,' Charlotte enthused as she held it to her slender figure and looked in the mirror.

She swirled the dress around her body, loving the feel of the silk material. But it was too big for her and needed altering to fit. She wondered how to mention this to Jack, when he spoke. 'You keep the dress as a gift from me, Charlotte. It matches the colour of your eyes.'

She turned to him 'It is lovely, and thank you,' her eyes filling with tears of joy.

'I'm pleased to see another bonny lass wearing the dress.' She hugged him tenderly.

Back at the inn, Charlotte spent most of her free time up in her bedroom, altering the dress to fit. And with the spare material cut from the dress, inspired by the glimpse of Doris's photograph, she created a silhouette. Sewn with a delicate thread, she fashioned the material together to create a likeness of Doris. A keepsake for Jack to remember his wife wearing the dress and dancing in his arms. She wanted to take it to Jack as soon as possible.

Downstairs in the kitchen, she rummaged for paper to wrap it in. 'This will do,' she said aloud. She turned around to see Hilda staring strangely at what she was holding. Feeling slightly unnerved by her aunt's odd behaviour, though she should have been used to it by now, Charlotte said the first thing which jumped into her head. 'Do you like it?'

'It's Doris Mansfield,' Hilda whispered. 'She used to . . .' she stopped in mid-sentence and fled from the kitchen.

Charlotte, mystified, went back to her room. But by the time she'd arrived at Jack's cottage, she had forgotten about Hilda's behaviour.

Jack beamed with pleasure. 'It is beautiful. I've got a good piece of wood to make a nice frame.' Charlotte left him happy and contented in his workshop making a frame.

* * *

On the last Saturday in May, Charlotte looked at her reflection in the mirror. The blue of the dress made her eyes sparkle. She lightly dabbed powder on her shiny nose and teased a stray curl into place. Slipping her feet into a pair of strappy silver sandals, a gift from Edna, she gave a twirl and tapped her feet. She gave a sigh, saying aloud, 'I'm ready for the dance.'

Hilda and George were already at the village hall setting up the bar. Walking down the street to the hall, Charlotte heard her name being called. She squinted in the summer evening sunshine to see three young women strolling towards her, and then one broke away and ran towards her. 'Joyce,' she called with glee. They collided and hugged. 'What are you doing here?'

'I told you, I've joined the land-army and I'm stationed at Huggate Farm.'

'How wonderful,' she said adding, 'I've missed having a friend to confide in.'

'Tell me more,' Joyce said, and they both laughed and linked arms and entered the village hall.

The band, made up of a piano, accordion, banjo and saxophone, were tuning up. Not your usual dance band, but unique in their own way. The hall glowed with coloured lanterns and paper chains. A long trestle table stood against the wall nearest to the kitchen, and ladies wearing pinafores were setting out tiny savoury nibbles, which looked deliciously inviting.

'Where's these Frenchies then?' said Joyce. 'I hope they can dance. I fancy a good spin around the floor,' she enthused as she tested the spring of the floor.

There were quite a few young girls with their mothers as chaperones. The band began to play, and four young girls braved the dance-floor, eager to escape their mothers. They watched the door, waiting for the French soldiers to arrive and dance with them.

Charlotte and Joyce sat at a table drinking lemonade, chatting about their dancing days back in Hull. Suddenly the outside door burst open and in walked about a dozen French soldiers, all eager for excitement after their gruelling training. And straight away, some of them split the girls from their partners to dance with them. Some went to the bar, ready to sample the beer. Two soldiers carried a crate between them loaded with French wine.

'Compliments of the officer in charge,' one of the soldiers said, nodding in the direction of Emile.

Mrs Carlton-Jones hurried to Emile to thank him and to introduce him to the chairman of the village hall committee and other members. As he followed the good lady, he saw Charlotte watching and winked at her.

'He fancies you!' Joyce nudged Charlotte's arm.

'He sometimes comes to the inn,' Charlotte replied, and quickly added, 'with the others.'

'I'll make an appearance in this inn of yours. I'd definitely want to get to know them,' Joyce said, pulling Charlotte to her feet. 'Come on, we'll dance and get split up.' And they did.

It was much later before Emile, after his duty dances, came to ask Charlotte to dance. He held out his hand, and she slipped into his hold, feeling the quickening of her heartbeat at the nearness of his body close to hers. His cologne smelt of the freshness of a sea breeze and a lock of his dark brown hair fell across his forehead. She wanted to brush it away, but daren't because it would be too much of an intimate gesture with so many eyes watching them, including Hilda's.

She introduced Emile to Dot, May and Edna who looked splendid in their flapper styled dresses. Emile danced with each one of them while Charlotte sat and watched. She waved to Joyce who was clearly enjoying herself, and so were the other land-army girls.

The food was delicious; the ladies who prepared the buffet had done wonders in spite of war rations. She paid her compliments to Mrs Mackay, who'd baked batches of sausage rolls, and whose face was bright red after she'd danced a polka with a soldier.

Finally, Emile came to ask Charlotte for the last waltz, and she snuggled into his arms, loving the feel of him holding her close. She rested her head against his chest, feeling the rhythm of his heart, contented. She wanted the dance to go on forever. They didn't talk, but he softly hummed the tune, and she wondered if it was a French one. Around the dance floor they glided, both unaware of the three ladies watching them with faraway looks in their eyes.

As the music came to an end, Emile whispered in her ear, 'Can I walk you home?'

She lifted up her head to look into his rich brown eyes. What she saw made her heart beat even faster. 'Yes,' she whispered, and couldn't resist the desire for a cuddle to feel his body close to hers. Feeling his lips brush the top of her head sent a thrill of desire running up and down her spine. A feeling she wanted to last.

CHAPTER ELEVEN

May to June 1943

Charlotte and Emile walked together down a dark lane, and she felt their fingers touch, sending a shiver of pleasure running down her spine. She wanted to speak, break the silence, but no words would come. The moon suddenly appeared from behind a cloud and she glanced up at Emile's face as he stared straight ahead, seemingly deep in thought. She wondered what he was thinking. She knew nothing about him, she only knew that she felt a deep attraction to him. She wondered about his home life in France. Did he have a wife and children? He never spoke of this, and she didn't like to ask him. Perhaps the emotions she felt for him were just a romanticised fantasy on her part. And him, he was far from home and lonely, so he welcomed her attention. Maybe it was best to keep their relationship on friendly terms only.

By now they had reached the inn and she could see a faint chink of light peeping from the bar blackout curtains, which meant Hilda and George were back. Turning to Emile, she said politely, 'Thank you for walking me home. I must go in to help Aunt and Uncle tidy up.' She wanted to reach up and kiss him on his beautiful, sensual lips. Instead, she turned and fled indoors.

She leaned against the door, her eyes closed, waiting for her rapid heartbeat to slow down.

'There you are,' George grumbled. 'Time you were back.'

For once, Charlotte was glad to hear George's sardonic voice. Tying an apron around her dress, she set to work off her mood of indecisiveness.

Later, she tumbled into bed, tired and longing for the oblivion of sleep, but it eluded her. The picture imprinted on her mind was Emile's startled look as she fled. She felt sorry for the way she'd treated him. Did he want more from her? More than she was willing or able to give. Through the night until the early hours of the morning, she alternated her thoughts until sleep pulled her down.

After only a few hours, she awoke from her restless slumber. She dressed and slipped silently from the inn. The cool early morning air slapped her face as she walked at a brisk pace, wanting to clear her ragged thoughts. Passing the village hall, she noticed the door wide open. Had it been open all night? Cautiously, she peeped inside and was surprised to see Mrs Carlton-Jones. She was wearing a floral overall, and a turban scarf tied round her head, and she had a bucket of hot water and was wiping down the tables.

On seeing Charlotte, she said. 'You are a godsend, my dear. Mop and bucket are in the kitchen.'

Collecting the gear, Charlotte wondered if Mrs Carlton-Jones couldn't sleep either. The steady rhythm of mopping the wooden floor soothed her tangled mind. Once the floor was cleaned, a sense of fulfilment filled her for completing a simple task. She also realised what a fool she was being. What harm would a mild flirtation, a kiss or two, with Emile do? So far from home and lonely, missing his family, not knowing if tomorrow he might die. She shuddered at the thought of her dear mother, whose life had been cut short by an enemy bomb.

'Tea up,' called Mrs Carlton-Jones.

Charlotte's stomach rumbled at the delicious aroma of warm sausage pastry which greeted her as she entered the kitchen. 'This is a treat,' she said as she tucked in to the savoury delight.

Later, she walked the children to school, which some of the older children seemed to resent and always ran ahead. Arriving back at Mornington House, Charlotte mentioned this to Mrs Grahame, and it was decided, as a trial run, next week for the older children to go to and from school unaccompanied.

Having a free afternoon, Charlotte called in at the bakery, on her way to see Jack 'I've an apple pie,' Mrs Mackay sounded somewhat aggrieved. 'I hear that Frenchie he's got billeted with him brings him food and wine. So will my apple pie be good enough for him?'

'Oh, I'm sure it will, Mrs Mackay. Jack always enjoys your pies,' she said soothingly, not liking to see her upset.

Jip came running down the garden path and sniffed at the pie she was carrying. Jack was in his shed, whistling a merry tune. As she stood in the doorway unnoticed, watching him absorbed in sanding down a piece of wood, his face shone with pleasure, and her heart burst with happiness for him.

Then he sensed her there and looked up. 'Hello, lass. Nice ter see yer. I hear you've been busy up at big house with the kiddies. I'm making a couple of rounders bats for them. Yon officer who's billeted with me is a genius at woodwork and keen to help me. It's right good to have a man's company.' Adding hastily, 'and I love your company too, lass.'

On Saturday night, the French soldiers came into the inn and soon one of them started playing the piano and a couple began singing a sentimental song. 'Bloody hell,' said Farmer Huggate, 'you'll have us crying into our beer. Give us something cheerful.'

One of the old men pulled his harmonica from his pocket and began playing and soon the pianist picked up the lively tune and the locals sang, and the soldiers made an effort, adding a few antics, making everyone laugh.

Charlotte served the ladies and chatted to them, but watched the door, wondering if Emile would appear.

'He's late,' May was looking at Charlotte's solemn face.

'Isn't that him just coming in?' said Dot. 'He's a bit of all right.' And all three women giggled like young girls.

As in a trance, Charlotte moved forward, her gaze fixed on Emile as he searched the room.

And then their eyes met. Her heart beat faster. She hadn't seen him since the dance. He wound his way through the crush of bodies to her side and their fingers touched. She edged nearer to him and . . .

'Charlotte, here,' boomed George's voice.

She looked towards the bar counter where Hilda stood with a tray piled high with sandwiches. She pushed the tray towards Charlotte and hissed, 'Don't you get tangled with one of them Frenchies. No good will come of it.'

Charlotte stared at her, dumbfounded by her aunt's outburst. She stood for a few moments, watching her aunt turn away.

Charlotte picked up the tray and circled the tables. Emile lounged against the far wall and she proffered him the remaining sandwiches and stood by his side. She glanced in George's direction and saw he was deep in conversation with the regulars. Putting the tray on a nearby table, she looked into Emile's face, her heartbeat racing.

He smiled at her and leaned forward, whispering in her ear, 'Charl, I have missed you. Can we meet?'

'Yes,' she whispered back gazing into his eyes.

'Tomorrow morning at the crossroads?'

'I'll be there.' She felt his hand slip round her waist and he pulled her closer, his body heat mingling with hers.

Everyone had departed, and Charlotte cleared the debris and wiped down the tables. As she worked, she sang to herself one of the catchy French songs that the soldiers had sang.

She finished her tasks and was going to her room when George called out. 'Charlotte.' Her heart sank, wondering what he wanted.

'We've had a very profitable night.' He carried a tray with three glasses of brandy into the kitchen.

He was in a jovial mood, unlike Hilda. It wasn't until she'd downed the glassful that her face lightened up. She pushed her glass towards George. 'I'll have a top-up.'

Surprisingly, he did her bidding. He motioned to Charlotte as well, but she shook her head.

She quickly drained her glass and rose from the table, saying, 'I'm tired, I'm off to bed.'

She wanted to be up early.

Next morning, excitement soared within her as she hurried from the inn, down the lane to the crossroads. Her black lace-up shoes shone to perfection, and she wore her best pair of stockings. Although she'd given her coat a good brushing, it was still shabby, but her soft wool blue scarf was practically new, bought from a village jumble sale. Her freshly washed brown hair tumbled down around her face, curling to touch her shoulders.

She saw Emile before he saw her. He sat on a low wall, smoking. She walked on the grass verge so he couldn't hear her footsteps approaching, but just as she neared him, he glanced up. His serious face lit up, and his eyes shone as he looked at her. Her heart did a double somersault. He jumped to his feet and ground out his cigarette. The next moment she was in his arms, and he kissed her tenderly on the lips. He smelled fresh and manly, as she snuggled in his arms but, aware of people making their way to church for the morning service, she pulled away, wanting to avoid any gossip reaching the inn. Not that she was ashamed of Emile, but she knew Hilda and George would not approve and while she lived under their roof, she didn't want any nasty scenes or insults directed at Emile.

Contentedly, they walked side by side, holding hands when they were alone. Passing Mornington House, she said shyly, 'I've volunteered to help with the children in my free time.'

He slipped his arm around her waist and drew her close. 'You want children?' he asked.

She drew away from him, staring unsmilingly. His words made her feel uncomfortable.

'Sorry, I get my English words mixed up. You like children?' He explained, smiling at her.

'Yes, I love caring for the children.' And then she surprised herself by saying. 'But I'm too young to have children of my own.' He didn't reply, but nodded his head solemnly.

The June sun warmed her face and her heart sang, happy in Emile's company. It felt so natural to be with him. She chattered away, telling him about her mother and how she died in an air-raid and the destruction of the home and shop.

'Your father?' he asked.

Her father, she thought, and surprisingly, tears came into her eyes. Emile stopped walking and gently, with his forefinger, wiped away the tears.

'Sorry,' she whispered. 'It's a long time since I thought about my father. He died when I was quite young and my memories of him are few. I recall sitting on his knee and watching him blow smoke rings with a cigarette.'

She was about to ask about Emile's family, when she felt a slight stiffening of his body beside her, so she didn't. Another time, he might mention them, or perhaps he didn't have a family. She shivered, and he gripped her hand tightly.

Keeping to the quiet, narrow country lanes, hearing the birds chirping in the hedgerows, for a brief moment in time, she imagined there was no war. Then the illusion of peace was shattered by the roar of planes overhead, returning to the nearby airbase. They strolled slowly back to the village, not wanting their time together to end.

'My Cherie, duty calls,' he said softly.

Suddenly, it occurred to her, remembering that officers were now billeted in village homes. 'Where are you billeted now?' she asked.

His eyes twinkled mischievously as he answered, 'With this lovely young woman, whose eyes follow me every time I am in her company and I always want to kiss her inviting lips.'

And before she could utter a word, he pulled her into his arms and kissed her. She melted into his embrace, tasting the hotness of his lips crushing hers, a kiss of such depth and passion. When they came up for air, her body churned with pent-up emotions, emotions she'd never experienced before. Gently he brushed the tangle of hair off her face and looked deep into her eyes. 'You are a special person, my Cherie.'

She caught her breath and felt moved to tears. No one had ever told her that. They walked on in silence, holding hands until they reached the crossroad where, reluctantly, they parted.

Remembering he hadn't told her, she called to him. 'Emile, who are you billeted with?'

He stopped walking, turned round, and with a mischievous look in his eyes he replied, 'With Jack, Mr Mansfield.'

CHAPTER TWELVE

June 1943

Later that evening, Charlotte and Emile only had a quick chance to talk, as the inn was busy.

'So, you are Jack's mystery officer, helping him make toys for the refugee children?'

And he replied, 'You are the mysterious lady who Jack talks about. Should I be jealous?'

They both laughed, and then someone called her. Their fingers entwined as she moved away.

Later, as she served the three ladies, Dot remarked, 'Still friendly with him, then?' She pointed to Emile, who raised his glass to them.

Charlotte put down her tray and began to tell them how Emile was helping Jack to make toys for the children.

'So, you won't need us any more then?' Edna said huffily.

Not wanting to upset the ladies, she soothingly replied, 'They're for the boys and your lovely toys are for the girls.' She gave them all a hug.

'You are a dafty,' they chorused, smiling with pleasure.

Charlotte loved having the ladies in her life. They helped to compensate for the loss of her mother.

Later that week, Charlotte had a couple of spare hours and decided to go and see Jack. Like the ladies, she counted him as part of her surrogate family. As she neared the bakery, she smelled the mouth-watering aroma of newly baked bread. It evoked memories of when she lived in Hull, when Joyce's mother, who made hot cakes oozing with golden syrup, would bring a plateful to the shop for Charlotte and Mam. A childhood treat.

Thankfully, bread wasn't on rations and had become a huge part of a staple diet, especially for big families with many mouths to feed. Her own mother had often made a bread and butter pudding from stale bread.

'I bet that French soldier won't take Jack any bread as good as ours,' said Mrs Mackay as she wrapped a loaf in a piece of muslin.

Jack, as usual these days, was in his shed and Jip came running to meet her, sniffing at her parcel. Fondling his coat, she said to him, 'Next time, old fellow, I'll bring you a bone.'

And as if he understood her, Jip wagged his tail.

Jack came out from the shed, wiping his hands on a rag cloth, saying, 'It's good to see you, lass. I'll put kettle on and I've got a nice bit of French cheese to go with the bread.'

After they had drunk the pot of tea dry and eaten their fill of bread and cheese, Jack lit a pipe. 'I feel quite contented.' She eyed him, thinking he meant the food. Then he continued. 'War is strange and destructive, though sometimes good comes from it. As well as your company, I now have Emile's company. Who would have believed it, a Frenchman living in my cottage?'

The talk came round to the children, and she happily told him stories of how, despite their troubled backgrounds and the fact they were all now living in a foreign country, they seemed happy. 'I would love to work full time caring for the children,' Charlotte added wistfully, 'Maybe when the authorities have more finances they might employ me.'

'I'm sure they will, lass. They won't want to lose a good worker like you.'

She glanced at the clock on the mantelpiece. 'Time to go.'

Stiffly, Jack levered himself up from his chair. 'Before I go back to shed, I'd better put the clean sheets on Emile's bed.'

'Can't he do it himself?' she asked

'He does usually, but he's away somewhere. It's the least I can do for him because he helps me no end.'

She glanced back at the clock. 'I've time. I'll do it. You rest.' She watched him sink back down into his chair and close his eyes.

She collected the sheets from the airing pulley and went into the bedroom. She stood for a few moments, feeling an intruder into Emile's private space. And then she shook herself and began to make up the bed, hoping he didn't expect hospital-type folded corners.

Lastly, she smoothed out the patchwork quilt, thinking this must have been crafted by Jack's late wife, Doris. Straightening up, she glanced around the comfortable, light, airy room with the sunlight streaming through the casement window. Her gaze rested on a small bedside table, the sun catching the silver framed miniature picture. For a moment, she froze, and then something moved her forward. Her heart beating at a rapid rate, she reached the table. But then she hesitated, not wanting to see a photograph of Emile's wife. For who else could it be? Intrigued, she looked.

She was surprised to see a photograph of a young girl aged about two or three, wearing a flowered dress with a peter-pan collar and a pinafore over it. Perched on the top of her head was a big bow of ribbon fastening back her long dark hair. Her big eyes held an uncertain look, and she clutched a doll in her arms. Charlotte felt mesmerised by the photograph, wondering who she was.

There was a sound of movement behind her and Jack's voice broke the spell. 'Pretty, isn't she?'

She spun round, nearly bumping into him. 'Yes,' she whispered.

In the kitchen she collected her coat. 'Must dash, or I'll be late.' She gave him a quick hug.

In her head a voice kept spinning the words, like a gramophone needle stuck: *he's married, he's married.* She arrived back at the inn with no recollection of walking the distance.

'You're late,' George shouted at her as she hurried past him to her room, ignoring his words.

She dreaded the coming weekend and seeing Emile. She argued with herself, spending restless nights debating the best way to ask him about the photograph.

Joyce came by and they went to sit on the stone seat in the quiet church- yard. She told her friend about the photograph of the little girl. 'What should I say to Emile?'

'Ask him straight out.'

'Ask him what?'

'Simple — are you married?'

'And the photograph of the little girl?'

'If he's married, she's his daughter. If not, his niece.'

Charlotte felt her mind whizzing like the waltzes at the Hull Fair when they stop, and your body carries on the sensation. She clutched hold of the cold, firm stone seat until she felt steadier. 'What do I do if he's married?' she whispered.

Joyce laughed. 'Have fun. I would. I've got my eye on a gorgeous pilot. I shall pounce on him soon.'

They sat in silence for a few moments, listening to the gentle breeze rustling the branches of the yew tree. Charlotte's thoughts wandered. Was she reading too much into her friendship with Emile, because that was what it was? But, when she was with him, her heart beat faster and she felt the sensation of electricity charging her body, bringing it alive. He made her feel wonderful, special. Maybe it was because he was far from home and . . .

She jumped up, startling Joyce by saying aloud, 'Yes, just friendship. Anything else depends on who the girl in the photograph is.'

The week dragged, and on Saturday night the French soldiers descended on the inn. They seemed full of good cheer and soon the pianist was belting out English tunes as they sang a mixture of French and English words and phrases, the locals joining in. The jovial mood filled the inn, and Charlotte guessed it was a way of releasing pressure, like a great train engine billowing out steam. Her mood by contrast was subdued, smiling automatically as she served the good-humoured soldiers. And she couldn't stop glancing in the direction of the inn door.

She had just finished serving a crowded table of men, glancing again towards the closed door, when she felt a soft touch on her arm. Charlotte half turned to look into his familiar face.

'Charl,' he whispered, his eyes searching her face. 'You have missed me?'

She stared back into his beautiful large eyes, so full of tenderness and his lips so inviting.

'Yes,' she whispered back, unable to control the rapid beating of her heart.

'Meet me at the crossroads tomorrow.' His hand slipped round her waist in a caressing movement.

It took all her willpower not to crush her body to his. 'Yes,' she said. And then someone called her name, wanting a refill.

Later that evening, Charlotte cleaned down all the tables so she could get off early the next day to meet Emile before going to Mornington House. Satisfied with her efforts, she went into the kitchen.

Hilda sat at the table drinking a glass of brandy, something she'd recently taken to. Charlotte glanced at her, about to say goodnight, when Hilda motioned her to sit down. Charlotte looked round for George.

Picking up on her thoughts, Hilda said, 'He's down in the cellar,' her words slurred slightly. She poured another glass of brandy and pushed it across the table to Charlotte.

She didn't fancy it, but not wanting to offend her aunt, she sipped the golden liquid, feeling its warmth run down her throat. Hilda poured herself another glassful and gulped most of it down in one go. She hiccupped and then laughed.

The drink loosening her tongue, she babbled. 'I could have been your mother. Do you know that?' She wagged a finger at Charlotte.

Not sure of the meaning of her aunt's words, she kept quiet.

'Yessss,' Hilda slurred, obviously a bit drunk. 'I walked out with Edward first.'

Charlotte wasn't sure who Edward was, having never heard her aunt mention him before.

'Edward loved me and she, the bitch, took him from me.' She then broke down and began sobbing.

Charlotte stared at her aunt, astounded by her weird behaviour. She jumped to her feet and was about to try to soothe her when George lumbered into the kitchen.

'Is she bloody well at it again? You get off to bed. I'll see to her.'

Glad to escape this bizarre scene, she glanced over her shoulder as she left the kitchen and gasped in disbelief. George was hauling Hilda to her feet.

The next morning, nothing was mentioned about last night's happenings. Charlotte finished her duties and then went up to her room to change into her outdoor clothes. She wished she had some prettier clothes to wear instead of these tired ones. She sighed. But there was a war on, and clothes were on coupons, and what money she earned, after buying a few basics, she saved. She loved her hair this length, and glancing in the mirror, she picked up her comb and swept up the sides of her hair, rolling it into a semi-wave, letting the rest of her hair hang loosely.

Outside, Charlotte looked up at the scudding clouds and the darkening sky. She turned up her coat collar and walked briskly on to meet Emile.

When she reached the crossroads, there was no sign of him. So she sat on the low wall of the church to wait. Last night she hadn't slept much, wondering how to approach the subject of the girl in the picture. It was fine for Joyce to say ask him outright, but she couldn't be so blunt though she wished she could. He would wonder why she had been in his room, though she hadn't been prying. Just helping Jack with a task. Words kept reverberating in her head and she bit on her lip. Best to tell him the truth, that she was helping Jack by putting clean sheets on his bed when she noticed a picture of a pretty little girl. And let him explain who she was.

A voice broke into her reverie. 'Has he stood you up?'

She looked up into May's concerned face. And then glanced down at her wristwatch. She'd been waiting over half an hour. 'He might be on duty,' she said, feeling disappointed.

'Come home with me and have a cup of tea. From my sitting-room window, you can see the church wall so you will see him, when he comes.'

Charlotte looked down the road, seeing only children playing double ball on the gable end of a house. Slowly she turned to go with May.

May's cottage was tiny, but comfortable and scented with the fragrance of lavender. The room had a bay window, and peering through it, Charlotte could see the church wall. Still no sign of Emile.

'Take off yer coat and sit down,' chided May, indicating one of the chairs at the table in front of the window. And then she bustled into the kitchen.

Charlotte sat down and looked through the window, but saw only a woman carrying a shopping basket. Both her head and her heart told her that Emile wasn't coming. Finding out the identity of the child in the photograph, and whether he was married or not, would have to wait. Turning from the window, she took in the cosy room with its brass plaques on the walls, each depicting one of the four seasons. By the fireside was a chintz-covered armchair and an occasional table and on it lay a ball of red wool and knitting needles.

May carried in a tea tray and noticing what Charlotte was looking at, explained. 'I'm knitting dolls clothes for the kiddies. Dot's making the dollies and me and Edna are making dresses from any odd bits of material.'

Charlotte remembered the bits of material that Jack had given her, which she hadn't got round to using, and made a mental note to bring them round. Meanwhile, she'd enjoy the cup of tea and a delicious scone.

'Fresh from the oven,' May said.

After they had finished, Charlotte said to May, 'I am hopeful that soon I can be caring for the children full-time.'

'Will your aunt let you go?'

'I love caring for the children, so I won't let her stop me.'

'By heck, you're a different lass from when you first came. You wouldn't say boo to a goose back then,' May chuckled.

After another half hour had passed, Charlotte glanced towards the church wall. Still no sign of Emile.

CHAPTER THIRTEEN

June 1943

That evening, she learned that the Free French soldiers were away on a training exercise, somewhere in the East Riding, so Emile hadn't stood her up intentionally.

As the evening progressed, the locals were talking about the foreign refugee children and how well behaved they were. It warmed Charlotte's heart to hear this.

'Bloody village is overrun with foreigners,' grumpy Farmer Huggate growled.

'Shut up, you're a mean bugger. Just be thankful that our kiddies are safe,' admonished an airman, home on leave.

'Hear, hear,' chorused the other locals.

'Bill Huggate has always been a moaner ever since he was a young lad.' Edna remarked, as Charlotte set down their drinks on the table.

In her room, she talked to her mother's portrait, which she often did. It comforted her.

'Emile didn't stand me up,' she confided. Sometimes, in her head, she could hear her mother's voice responding to her. She never mentioned this to anyone, for they would think her weird. 'He makes me feel special.' Then tears filled her eyes. 'Just like you made me feel.' Was that it? The loss of her mother had left her with an overwhelming need to have someone who made her feel special?

A week later, Charlotte broke into smiles as Emile came through the inn door. She wanted to run to him and fling her arms around his neck and hold him close and feel the warmth of his nearness. Instead, she waited for him to sit down at a table with the other soldiers, and made her way slowly to him, conscious of Hilda watching her from behind the bar. But she didn't care, nothing was going to dampen her spirits.

Reaching his side, their eyes met, and a quiver of excitement raced through her body.

'Sorry, I couldn't let you know,' he said.

'You're here now,' she whispered.

Towards the end of the evening, when everyone had been served with their last order, Emile nodded towards the door and rose from his seat to go outside. Charlotte cast a quick glance around and, seeing George and Hilda engrossed in talking, she slipped out of the door.

A rush of cool night air fanned across her cheeks and she breathed in its freshness.

Letting her eyes become accustomed to the darkness, she saw him. Without thinking, she was in his arms, the nearness of him giving her a satisfied pleasure.

Gently, he released her, just enough to look into her eyes. 'I've missed you, my Cherie,' and then he kissed her, long and tender.

'I have to go,' she whispered. Not wanting to leave because there was so much she needed to ask him.

'Tomorrow, can you come to Jack's about eleven o'clock? I have an hour spare before I leave for headquarters,' he said.

'Yes.' The door opened and drinkers tumbled out and she hurried in, reluctant to leave him.

The next morning, she rose early to get her work done. She worked in a trance, her mind going over what she would say to Emile until her head ached. She had escorted the younger children to school and then returned to tidy the bedrooms, first asking Mrs Grahame if she could have a couple of hours off.

On her way to see Emile, the fresh air cleared her head, and she knew what she wanted to say.

Jip came running down the garden path to greet her, his tail wagging, and she bent to fondle him. When she straightened up, it was to see Emile watching her. 'Hello,' she smiled.

She followed him inside the cottage, surprised not to see Jack. 'He's in his shed,' Emile said.

It felt strange, being indoors, on their own, sitting in the fireside chairs opposite each other.

Emile opened the conversation by saying, 'I have something to explain to you, yes?'

She nodded.

'Jack told me you have seen the photograph of my daughter.'

Her heart thumped and her hand went to her mouth. *So, he is married? And I am just someone to fill his arms and body while he is away from home. Is that what I want? To be a comforter?* She didn't know the right answer. Whatever, it wouldn't last, because soon he and his battalion would leave to fight in the war and she would be forgotten. She thought of her friend Joyce's idea, just to have fun. Momentarily, she closed her eyes.

When she opened them, he was looking at her, waiting for an answer. 'Yes,' she answered. And then, as if taking on another persona, her voice deliberately icy cool, she remarked, 'She's a pretty girl. Does she take after her mother?' Then she stared at him, watching his face blanch white and the muscles in his neck contract. And in that instant, she hated herself for being so direct with him. But she had to know.

He stood up and concentrated on lighting a cigarette with trembling hands. How could he tell her? He drew hard on the cigarette, willing his nerves not to shatter as they had done when it happened. He blamed himself. He'd insisted on taking them to safety. If only he hadn't. Her death was on his hands forever. Constantly, over the past two years, he'd relived that terrible moment. Meeting Charl, this beautiful young woman, with the warm caring eyes, had helped his pain to heal, though the scars would always be there. Like now, so visible and raw.

He must explain to her. Would she understand his terrible crime? Or would she cast him aside?

Broken in spirit, joining de Gaulle's Free French to fight for the freedom of France, was his saving grace. His way to atone for . . .

Sweat drenched his back, and he lit another cigarette from the stub of the first and drew on it too hard, catching the back of his throat and making him cough. He strode over to the sink for a glass of cold water, swallowing it slowly. No longer able to hide the words. He turned, seeing Charl's puzzled face. He put out his hand and fumbled for the chair and sank into it. He glanced at her again, seeing her uncertainty. He gave a deep sigh and looked away from her. He couldn't bear to see the revulsion on her face. He coughed, cleared his throat, his voice low.

'In 1941, came the fall of France. We lived in Paris, which became a Nazi stronghold. I joined the army to fight the enemy, but I was reluctant to leave my wife and child in an unsafe city. I decided they would be safer in the quiet countryside, near to the village of Oradour-sur-Glane on my parents' farm where I grew up. So, we joined the exodus, leaving Paris, carrying only a few personal possessions. We travelled by train until we were hauled off by the German military. We trekked with the other passengers through the night, stopping only for short rests. I was anxious to get my family to safety as quickly as possible.' Emile paused. He wasn't sure if he could carry on. He pulled another cigarette from its packet and lit it. He drew in a deep drag. Not looking at Charl, but aware of her presence, he continued.

'The sky was a cloudless blue and glancing up, I saw it coming. My daughter, fast asleep in my arms, my wife a few paces behind, was talking to another woman. Get down! Get down! I yelled.' Everyone made a mad scramble for the roadside ditch. He closed his eyes and fished in his packet for a cigarette, but it was empty. He felt the shuddering inside his body, the bile in his throat rising. And then the touch of a cigarette between his lips. He opened his eyes to see Charl bending over him. He reached out to hold her hand, feel her warmth. Then she returned to her chair. For a few moments he smoked silently, drawing a molecule of strength to carry on.

'The bastards fired on us. An easy target. For some time, no one moved, just in case they returned. Gradually we began to shift. My daughter cried with fright and I soothed her and turned to look for my wife. She still lay in the ditch. I called for her to get up, but she didn't stir. A woman she'd talked to earlier went to see if she needed help. And then she screamed, a high wailing sound. I shoved Juliette into another woman's arms and ran to my wife. She was dead. Shot through the heart.' His body convulsed in shock as he relived those terrible moments, he couldn't stop the sobbing. His outpouring of grief.

Charlotte gasped in disbelief. How could she have been so cruel to let him relive the tragedy of the death of his wife? She went to him and held him in her arms as he sobbed out his grief. Holding him close, she stroked his thick brown hair, noticing its interwoven threads of grey. After some time, his sobs stopped and his body relaxed. But still she held him close, wanting to take away his pain. Then, gently, she eased away and had a poke around in Jack's cupboard, hoping he would forgive her. There was half a bottle of red wine which she guessed Emile must have brought.

She poured out a liberal measure into a tumbler and placed it in Emile's hands. She knelt by his side, pushing back a lock of his hair from his face, and whispered, 'I'm sorry I made you relive such a terrible tragedy.' He didn't reply, but sipped on the wine. Her heart sank. She wanted to gather him up in her arms, hold him close again, but suddenly felt scared to do so.

What right did she have, anyway? Instead, she stayed by his side, ignoring the cramp in her legs and thinking of that terrible night when she lost her mother.

Trying to free her mind of the atrocities of war, she listened to the silence of the room.

Suddenly, Emile put down his tumbler on the small table, gathered her up into his arms and held her close, hiding his face in her hair, as if he wanted to bury the past there.

Then, holding her at arm's length, he broke the silence. 'Thank you, Charl, for being here. As you Yorkshire people say, I needed to get it off my chest, though I am sorry to inflict my pain on you.'

She looked into his eyes and saw the sad rawness, and whispered, 'I'm glad I was here for you.' Rising to her feet, she reached for his hands. 'Emile, can I ask you a question?'

A wariness flashed in his eyes, but he nodded.

'Your daughter, is she safe?'

His face lit up as he replied, 'Juliette is safe with my parents on their farm.'

She felt the relief flood through her body. She pulled him to his feet and slipped her arms around his waist, feeling the strength and the heat of his body mingle with hers. Then she stood on tip-toe and kissed him passionately.

As she walked to Mornington House, Charlotte knew without doubt that while Emile was stationed in the village, she would be his girl. If that meant giving herself to him body and soul, then yes. The game of war was precarious, for who knew what tomorrow would bring. The game of love was more satisfying. For how long, she wasn't sure. But it was a chance she was willing to take.

Entering the house, the first person she saw was Laura, who commented. 'You've a lovely glow about you.'

CHAPTER FOURTEEN

December 1943

The last of the daylight filled the sky. Overnight there had been a sprinkling of snow, only resting on bushes and trees.

After a cup of tea together, Charlotte and Laura left Mornington House after a full day's shift, walking as far as the crossroads and parted. Laura lived in the opposite direction. She had a torch to guide her and Charlotte wished she had thought to bring one, for there was no moonlight. She shivered in the still, eerie darkness. The sound of someone whistling rang clear in the night air and she listened. A catchy tune, one she'd heard before, for it was a tune sung by the soldiers in the inn. Then came the sound of hurrying footsteps drawing nearer. She glanced over her shoulder, a tinge of fear gripping her. She started to run, caught her foot on the rough edge of the road, and tripped. She cried out in pain as she wrenched her ankle.

'Charl,' a voice rang out. 'Is that you?'

'Oh Emile, I'm here,' she sobbed with relief. Then she felt his strong arms helping her to her feet and holding her in a loving embrace. She clung to him, not wanting to let go.

'My Cherie, you shouldn't be out on your own in the dark.'

His fingers touched her face, and then she felt the tenderness of his lips on hers. She felt safe with his arms locked around her, she didn't want to move. Over the past five months, their relationship had grown from strength to strength, and she couldn't now imagine life without him. 'Where were you going?' she asked.

'To see you at the inn.'

'I worked extra time at the house.'

'Charl,' he whispered, 'I will see you home.'

Home, the inn, would never be her home. Reluctantly, she released her grip and slipped her arm through his for support. Her ankle was only sprained, but it made walking very painful.

No sound came from the inn, but a faint light was visible through a chink in the blackout curtains and she knew her aunt and uncle were waiting up for her. They didn't trust her to have a key.

Emile gave her a quick kiss and whispered, 'I will see you tomorrow night,' and he was gone.

Inside the inn, two glum faces glanced at her. 'You're late, and we wanted an early night,' George grumbled.

'Sorry, but we stayed to tidy up. Mr and Mrs Grahame were tired.'

'Don't know why you didn't stay the bloody night.'

Charlotte wished she'd thought of that.

Upstairs, in her bedroom, she sat on the bed and picked up the portrait of her mother. 'I miss you so much, Mam,' she whispered. In her heart she knew her mother would have approved of Emile and welcomed him into their home. Here, her aunt and uncle never asked her if she'd made friends with anyone of her own age. To them, she was just a worker, though Hilda had briefly let her guard down when she spoke of her daughter who died so tragically.

Perhaps that was it. They lost their only child and whatever compassion they had, simply dried up. And this is how they chose to cope with their lives by not getting close to anyone, including her. 'Sorry, Mam, I didn't mean to burden you with my thoughts.' Gently she kissed the image of her mother and placed it back on her bedside table.

She prepared for bed and bound a cold-water bandage round her ankle to alleviate the swelling. With luck, it should be fine in the morning. Turning off the light, she drew back the curtains revealing the distant searchlights criss-crossing the skies on the lookout for enemy aircraft. Then she hobbled to her bed.

But sleep eluded her, and thoughts spun round in her head. At first, she thought of Emile, wondering if they would ever share a bed together. She dreamed of it, though she remained doubtful that such a thing would ever become a reality.

She woke early and lay in bed thinking about her future, caring for the children. Tossing it over in her mind, she made a decision. She would ask Mrs Carlton-Jones if she could live in at Mornington House. She loved her work with the children and found it so rewarding that she wanted to help them blossom as individuals. Somewhere, deep down, hidden away were their true identities, before the atrocities of war caught them up in its machine, separating them from their homes and families. She wanted to make their lives happier and give them hope for their future.

* * *

Charlotte was extremely busy from Christmas to New Year's Eve, at the inn and with the children. And so was Mrs Carlton-Jones, who was organising a dance in the village hall to welcome in 1944. 'I want to show the battalion of the Free French soldiers how we celebrate the New Year,' she enthused to the staff and volunteers at Mornington House.

'Let's hope the Germans celebrate it,' piped up a voice. 'Send Herr Hitler an invite,' someone else put in, and everyone laughed.

Hilda and George were busy checking stock for the bar they were running at the dance.

Charlotte hoped they wouldn't need her, though, just in case, she told them, 'I am going to the dance with Emile.'

Hilda gave her a long, hard look, but didn't speak. But George was vocal. 'Our lads not good enough for you? I should watch them Frenchies, they'll leave you in the lurch, and then where will you be,' he sneered.

Ignoring him, Charlotte escaped up to her room. Glancing at her watch, she saw she had a couple of spare hours so she could go and see Jack. Now, with her work with the children taking up so much of her time, her visits to her dear friend were infrequent. She had something she wanted to mull over with him.

The late December day was cold and grey, and she doubted if Jack would be in his shed.

She called into the bakery on her way. Mrs Mackay was clearing away.

'You're out of luck,' she said as she looked up and saw Charlotte.

'Oh, I was hoping to take something for Jack.'

'Hmm, that foreign soldier tek him treats, so I hear.' Then her voice softened. 'Though nowt as good as what we bake. Just a tick.' She disappeared and came back with two bread cakes still warm from the oven. 'Them Frenchies don't know how to bake bread.' She wrapped them in a piece of muslin cloth. 'See you bring back the cloth,' she said, handing over the delicious smelling bread.

So pleased was Charlotte that she said, 'I could give you a big hug.'

'Be on your way, lass,' laughed Mrs Mackay.

As she left the shop, Charlotte wished her aunt could be more like Mrs Mackay.

She said as much to Jack as they sat by his roaring fire, drinking tea and eating bread with butter and cheese, and giving Jip a few titbits.

Jack looked thoughtful. 'Perhaps it's best if you know what happened between Hilda and your mother, then you'd understand more.'

Charlotte watched as he lit his pipe and wondered what he was going to tell her.

'Hilda was the eldest and Martha was five years younger. Hilda, in those days was a fine figure of a woman, and Martha a pretty girl with big blue eyes and golden curls. Hilda worked in a ladies clothing shop in Driffield and Martha in a haberdashery shop. Hilda met Edward, and they courted, and there was talk of an engagement. Anyhow, Edward was invited for tea to meet the parents and to ask them formally for their daughter's hand in marriage. And then he met Martha.'

Charlotte gasped, putting a hand over her mouth. Jack looked at her, and she nodded for him to continue.

'He couldn't take his eyes off her. He was so besotted by her he forgot to ask the parents for Hilda's hand in marriage. This caused a big row between them and Hilda hit him, giving him a black eye in front of a crowd of villagers. This caused a lot of bad gossip and Martha was sent to live with an aunt in Hull as Hilda threatened to hit her too.'

'Edward never came back to the village. Two years later, we heard that he and Martha had married and were living in Hull. Hilda became a very bitter woman. She worked part-time at the inn and married George Bilton. They had a daughter, Milly, who drowned in the pond. So, you see, Charlotte, Hilda hasn't had a charmed life. After their daughter's loss, Hilda had a breakdown. She never really recovered. George carried on, playing the tough man with a bad temper, but underneath that bravado, he was suffering.'

The room was silent. Even the fire stopped crackling. Charlotte shuddered and sadness filled her. Now she could understand her aunt's strange behaviour and her uncle's brusqueness. And then she had been thrust upon them, adding to their sadness and rubbing salt into old wounds. How Hilda must have hated her mother and now her. Charlotte felt sorry for her aunt and didn't want to add to her burden any longer. Charlotte had her mother's petite build and hair colouring and her father's eyes, so she must be a constant reminder of that terrible time in Hilda's life.

'Jack.' He looked up, and Jip stirred. 'Thank you for telling me everything.' She gave a big sigh. 'I now understand both Hilda and George, their attitude towards me.'

They sat in silence, and she watched him refill his pipe. Then she said, 'I am going to ask Mrs Carlton-Jones if I can live in at Mornington House to work there full time because I love being with the children, and I want to know them better. What do you think?'

'By gum, lass, that's a good idea. Those kiddies need someone like you. Mr and Mrs Grahame are nice and run the house well, but young blood is what the children need.' Then he gave a mischievous wink and continued. 'And you can tell Madge Carlton I said so.'

Puzzled, she asked, 'Madge Carlton, who is she?'

'Mrs Carlton-Jones, she's married to Jimmy Jones, Colonel Jones. Carlton was her surname before she married him. She's a bit bossy, but good 'em at heart is Madge, but don't tell her that.'

Walking to the inn, Charlotte considered the best step forward. She would broach the subject with Mrs Carlton-Jones after New Year, when it was quieter. Hopefully, she would agree to the plan. She walked on, her steps lighter.

CHAPTER FIFTEEN

December 1943

Excitement filled Charlotte, for she was looking forward to her trip to Driffield with Joyce.

She loved it when they met up because they always had fun. Not that she didn't enjoy her time with the children and Emile, but Joyce, a friend since they could first walk, always radiated infectious joy. Glancing out of her bedroom window at the late December morning, and seeing a bright, but ice-cold blue sky, she dressed warmly, glad of the soft knitted scarf, which she wound round her neck, and the matching beret and gloves, gifts from May, Dot and Edna. Running down the stairs, she called goodbye to her aunt and uncle.

Joyce was waiting for her, with their mode of transport, an old battered bicycle each. Laughing, they set off, wobbling at first as they negotiated the potholes. Down the country lane they rode singing, 'One Man Went to Mow...' An army truck came honking behind them and they nearly ended up in a ditch. Luckily, they arrived safely in Driffield.

Off the main street down an alley, they found a shab-by-looking shop with peeling yellow paint, and in the small bow window arranged to its best advantage sat a big Teddy

Bear. They gazed at it like two children, for hanging from the teddy's outstretched arms were necklaces and bangles intertwined with a rainbow of coloured ribbons glowing like precious jewels.

Pushing open the door, they could hear a bell jangle and a deep voice called from somewhere inside, 'Come in, my lushy darlings.'

Charlotte glanced around to see the owner of the voice, but there was no one there. She nudged Joyce, who giggled. A door opened in the far corner and a woman, with long silvery hair, wearing a flowing dress embroidered with butterflies, entered carrying a tea tray.

'Hello,' she said. 'I thought I heard the doorbell ring.' She laughed when she noticed their bemused faces. 'That was Casanova you heard.'

'Casanova!' they chorused, looking at each other, thinking they'd entered a madhouse.

And then Charlotte noticed the parrot and pointed to it, feeling stupid. 'It's not stuffed.'

As if taking umbrage, Casanova called, 'Sod you too.' This set Charlotte and Joyce off into fits of laughter.

Finally regaining their composure, they apologised to Greta, the owner of the shop, who smiled and sat down to enjoy her refreshments while they browsed through the shop.

It was like an Aladdin's Cave, offering up haberdashery, second-hand clothes, shoes, hats, broken jewellery, half-empty bottles of lavender oil, and boxes to rummage through. They spent a delightful couple of hours searching around on the dress rails and finding faded treasures belonging to a bygone age, like a long string of pearls and a tiny manicure set with mother-of-pearl handles. In one box, Charlotte found a slim copy of *Guide to the Bronte Country*, which included a map and pictures of the area, plus interesting information about the sisters. She loved the Bronte sisters and enjoyed reading their books, but had never visited the Parsonage at Haworth where they'd lived.

* * *

At last, New Year's Eve arrived and everyone seemed in high spirits. George whistled a cheerful tune, knowing the bar takings at the dance would be high and he'd make a decent profit. As Charlotte polished the glasses in readiness for the evening, she wondered what he did with his money, because he and Hilda never went anywhere to spend it. Maybe they were saving it for their retirement, but whatever they were saving it for, they never discussed it with her. Correction, they never discussed anything with her. She finished polishing the glasses and went to her room to get ready for the dance. Her dress was the colour of cherry blossom, with darker shades of fuchsia pink flowers in a lovely silk rayon. Brought from Greta's shop, it had needed altering, so she had spent long hours after work, unpicking the full skirted panels and sewing on new sleeves, replacing the torn ones. Now, looking in the mirror, she smiled. The dress fitted to perfection and the long string of pearls added a touch of glamour. Her long hair, which hadn't been cut since she arrived in the village, she brushed up the sides in waves secured by tortoiseshell combs. She looked at her reflection in the mirror. So different, quite grown up. Then a sadness swept across her face. In the time she'd lived with her aunt and uncle, she'd had two birthdays, both gone unnoticed, and now she was eighteen. Her mother had always made her a cake to celebrate and brought her a book or a trinket. Mentally, she shook herself and turned away from the mirror. It was pointless dwelling on the past, though she would always hold the treasured memories of her mother close to her heart.

Her aunt and uncle had already gone to the village hall, and she waited outside for Emile to call for her. The night air was crisp and the sky a midnight blue with a trillion stars twinkling. Searchlights criss-crossed the sky, looking for signs of enemy aircraft. She pulled her coat closer and made sure the scarf covering her hair was secure and held tight the string bag with her dancing sandals inside. Another good buy from the treasure trove shop.

Suddenly Emile appeared and hugged her, kissing her on the cheek, saying. 'You smell nice, just like my . . .'

He stopped in mid-sentence and she wondered if he was going to say, just like my wife.

Someone called their names. It was Joyce with her RAF pilot, Robert.

After the greetings, they strolled down to the village hall together.

Once inside, the two friends went to the ladies' cloak-room and Joyce produced her stub of deep pink lipstick for Charlotte to apply, 'Adds a bit of glamour.'

The band was in full swing and already couples were dancing and the hall buzzed with laughter and the clinking of glasses. Charlotte saw Emile at the bar with Robert, so she and Joyce circled the dance floor to join them.

'Shandies, ladies,' Robert offered, as he handed them the drinks. The table was full, so they stood on the fringe of the dancers.

Charlotte inched closer to Emile, and he turned to smile at her, slipping his free arm round her waist. He drew her to him so their bodies touched. There was a bit of commotion and a man came in trundling a barrow piled high with wooden folding chairs. Robert and Emile helped to unload them and set them up. Soon, the four were seated at a table. Joyce and Robert were up first to dance a lively Military Two Step.

Emile slipped his arm protectively around Charlotte's shoulder and whispered in her ear.

'I've missed you.'

A thrill ran through her body and she turned her face to his, saying, 'I've missed you too.'

Their lips touched, gently at first. Then she felt an over-whelming passion of wanting more.

Emile drew away from her, and she was suddenly aware that the music had stopped and Joyce and Robert were sitting down opposite them. For a few moments she'd forgotten they were surrounded by people. She felt her cheeks flush and, feeling a little embarrassed, she picked up her drink. Sipping her shandy, she studied the band, noticing they were an eclectic mix of RAF and Free French instrumentalists along with a couple of the local men, one with an accordion and the other with a banjo.

The band began to play a waltz and Emile stood up and held out his hand to Charlotte. In his arms, she looked up into his warm brown eyes, seeing the crinkles at the sides of his skin.

Laughter lines, or stress lines, she didn't know. And she thought of his daughter. Was she safe? Was she maybe fretting for her dead mother? Charlotte knew that she missed her own mother, Martha, but as an adult, she was better able to cope than a child. She wondered if Juliette was too young to understand why her mother was no longer with her. A picture flashed before her, a little girl with big sad eyes peering out of a window, waiting for her mother, who would never come.

She gave a gasp of sorrow.

'Charl, are you not well?' Emile's concerned voice brought her back to reality.

'Sorry. I'm fine.' She smiled up at him and rested her head on his shoulder, feeling secure in his arms.

Soon all four entered into the spirit of the evening and joined in the popular dances, Palais Glide, Gay Gordons, Hand-knees-and-bumps-a-daisy, Hokey Cokey. Charlotte laughed at the look of surprise on Emile's face when they finished the Veleta and went straight into the Barn Dance, where you changed partners after each sequence of the dance. She danced with other Free French soldiers, RAF pilots from the nearby base and some of the local forces home on leave.

Finally, Mrs Carlton-Jones announced the buffet was open and after the energetic dancing, they were ready for refreshments and a breather. They tucked into plates full of cheese and spam sandwiches, savoury sausage rolls, pickled onions, baked jacket potatoes and mince pies. Charlotte waved to the three ladies who sat at a table with friends and were drinking tea with their food.

Considering wartime rationing was on, there was quite a good spread. Something villages could do better than city folk, Charlotte mused.

When they finished eating, Emile, Robert and Joyce were enjoying a cigarette, so Charlotte collected their empty plates and gathered more on her way to the kitchen. 'Here,' someone shouted and threw a teacloth at her, so she obliged and chatted with the other volunteers while she helped dry the dishes.

When the music began again, she went to find Emile. But she couldn't see him anywhere.

Joyce and Robert were dancing, and she wondered if Emile was dancing too. She stood on the fringe of the dance floor, scanning the couples waltzing by, but saw no sign of him. She waited until the dance finished and the happy couple, all smiles and looking flushed, came back to their seats. 'Have you seen where Emile went?' she asked them.

'No, he was here just now, so he can't be far,' said Joyce.

Joyce and Robert got up to dance again, and Charlotte glanced around, hoping Emile would appear, but he didn't. She decided to see if he was outside. She went to collect her coat and scarf, and behind the cloakroom counter, a lady she recognised from the village sat knitting.

When she saw Charlotte, she smiled. 'I have a note for you from your soldier,' and handed over a scrap of paper.

Charlotte turned away to read the hastily scribbled note.

Sorry Charl, I had to rush off, problem at camp. Emile.

She stared at the words, feeling flat inside. The evening, like a wonderful big balloon so full of life, suddenly deflated. She went outside into the darkness to walk back to the inn alone, feeling sad that they hadn't wished each other a happy New Year.

Saturday, New Year's Day, and the inn was open as usual. Charlotte wondered if Emile would come. Servicemen home on leave and making the most of their freedom kept her busy. Every few minutes, she glanced towards the door. But Emile didn't appear and neither did any of the other French soldiers. She must remember that Emile was a soldier who must act under orders. And then a dreadful thought occurred to her. He and his battalion wouldn't stay here forever. They were training for war, and that meant they could leave at any time. She shivered. In her naivety, she'd assumed that Emile would always be around.

Why? Because she imagined him in her life forever, she told herself.

'Give us a smile, love,' a grinning red-haired airman said, catching hold of her arm.

Startled, she looked into the rawness of his eyes, where his smile didn't reach. He would be returning to war and not knowing if he would be coming home again. On impulse, she leaned towards him and kissed him full on the lips.

'Wow!' was all he could say.

'You're a lucky bugger,' one of his mates called, and they all laughed.

Charlotte, her face flushed, escaped to the snug.

'That was a nice thing to do,' Dot said to her. 'Yon Ginger's mam told me his girlfriend has packed him in and got herself one of them Yanks.'

'Your friend not in tonight?' asked May.

Charlotte just shrugged her shoulders and, hearing her name called, went to the bar to see what Hilda wanted. She pushed a plate of sandwiches towards her, saying, 'For them lads over there.' She indicated towards Ginger and his pals.

Balancing the plate aloft, Charlotte handed the sandwiches around and they soon wolfed them down. A soldier began to play the piano, and the others gathered round, and soon a rousing sing-song ensued. Next day, they would be reporting back to duty. And then who knew what?

CHAPTER SIXTEEN

January 1944

Charlotte had made her decision. However, it was a few days later before she got the chance to speak to Mrs Carlton-Jones. She found her alone in the dining room making notes on a writing pad. As Charlotte entered the room, she put down her pen and rubbed her hand across her brow. Her eyes looked dull and there were lines etched deep round them. 'Sorry, Mrs Carlton-Jones, am I interrupting your work?' said Charlotte, not venturing further into the room.

'No, my dear, I need a break. What can I do for you? Sit down.'

Charlotte eased down onto the chair opposite. 'I am considering doing more war work.'

Mrs Carlton-Jones looked horrified. 'You're not thinking of leaving us?'

Surprised by her reaction, Charlotte reassured her, 'No, just the opposite. If you agree. I want to work with the children permanently and sleep in if possible.' She waited, holding her breath and casting her eyes above to the far wall, staring at the portrait of a family group which hung there.

She'd never noticed it before and wondered if it was the tragic family who'd lived here before the war. She'd heard the man was serving in the armed forces, and the woman was involved in war business in London.

'You, my dear Charlotte, are the answer to my prayers,' Mrs Carlton-Jones beamed at her.

Charlotte lowered her eyes from the portrait to stare at her, wondering what she meant.

'Mr and Mrs Grahame are finding the care and the overall responsibility of the children more than they anticipated,' Mrs Carlton-Jones told her, glancing at the pad of notepaper before her. She continued, 'They have asked me to employ an assistant to live-in.' She looked up at Charlotte. 'Is that what you had in mind?'

Charlotte felt her insides bubble over with joy and couldn't believe her luck. 'Yes,' she answered clearly.

'What about your work at the inn with Mr and Mrs Bilton?'

Charlotte drew in a deep breath and sat up straighter. 'My aunt and uncle will understand my need for independence, and to move on with my life.' She crossed her fingers behind her back. 'And for my wish to devote myself to the care of the children.'

'Excellent, then that's settled. I shall inform Mr and Mrs Grahame and discuss with them where your quarters will be. I shall also inform the authorities regarding your remuneration. I do not foresee any problems.' She stood up and extended her hand to Charlotte, who hoped she didn't feel her own hand tremble.

After finishing her duties, Charlotte slowly walked to the inn, a place she would never call home. Her decision made to leave the inn, she felt jittery about how to tell her aunt and uncle without sounding ungrateful to them for giving her a place to live.

That evening as she served customers, her mind kept coming back to the problem of how to tell them.

'Now, what's up with you, Charlotte?' A female voice broke into her thoughts.

For a split second, she forgot where she was. She blinked her eyes to look into the curious faces of May, Dot and Edna. 'Sorry, I was miles away.' Quickly glancing to the bar, she was relieved to see George engaged in conversation, and Hilda nowhere to be seen. She slipped into the vacant seat in the corner of the snug and told the ladies of her offer of caring full-time for the children at Mornington House. She paused and three pairs of eyes stared at her, waiting for her to continue. She cleared her throat. 'How do I tell Aunt and Uncle without sounding ungrateful?'

'Ah, well,' said Dot. And then they all lapsed into silence. Then someone called Charlotte's name, and she got up to go. 'We'll think of something,' Dot with twinkling eyes.

And later, as the ladies were leaving, Dot said, 'When you finish with the kiddies tomorrow, call in to my cottage.' With a flourish of cold night air, they were gone, leaving Charlotte mystified.

She piled her tray with used glasses and went to wash them. Hilda gave her an odd look, as if to say, what are you up to?

The next day Charlotte was in demand with the children, especially the younger ones.

After a brisk walk in the grounds and through the woods, they were served their main meal of the day, cottage pie with mashed turnip, and bread and butter pudding for afters. She watched them eating, some of the older children gobbling down their food, as if it was going to disappear from their plate. One boy, Joseph, aged seven, always curled his left arm around his plate, protecting his food from anyone who might steal it. Not that they would, but it was a habit he couldn't break. Mr Grahame went to him and tried to stop him doing this, but Joseph resisted any attempt and made growling noises, like an animal. Mr Grahame tutted and walked away.

There was a scraping of chairs as the children took their used plates and dishes into the kitchen, and then raced into their play room with Laura.

When she'd finished tidying the dining room, Charlotte went to help with the washing up in the kitchen. She described to Mrs Jolly the incident with Joseph and continued, 'It's difficult to understand how anyone could make children suffer so much. To be snatched away from your mother and loved ones and then starved and caged like animals is beyond belief. It's inhumane.' Tears welled in her eyes.

Mrs Jolly, a practical woman, replied. 'Yon kiddies are now thriving with loving care, that's the best thing for them.'

Charlotte knew that the main reason she wanted to work with the children was to make their everyday lives happy, and to give them hope for their future.

She returned to the play room to read to some of the children, while others did jigsaws with Laura. Jimmy, aged twelve, from the village had come with his miniature railway track and engines and wagons, which some of the older boys had laid out on the floor away from the others. Charlotte glanced in their direction to see the boys sprawled out, absorbed in the slow process of trundling the engines along the track, repeatedly, never getting bored.

The young ones loved the story of the hen crossing the road with her brood of chicks following behind and then one gets lost. A page in the book showed a cluttered farmyard scene where the lost chick was. The children would lie flat on their tummies with the page of the book open in front of them, searching to find the lost chick. It amazed her, no matter how many times she read this story to the children, that they always wanted to look for the lost chick, although they knew exactly where it was hidden. When Charlotte was with the children, time passed quickly, stopping her ruminating on not seeing Emile.

Later, she called at Dot's cottage, as instructed, to see Edna and May also there. They lived in a row of almshouses, founded by a landowner benefactor in the eighteenth century. Inside the tiny cottages were a sitting room, kitchen cum diner, bedroom and a new addition of a bathroom. All three were dressed in skirt, blouse, cardigan, lisle stockings and neat button shoes. The only difference was their necklaces; Dot wore a string of pearls, Edna, a silver locket and May a gold cross and chain.

Charlotte slipped off her dusty shoes, left them on the doormat and was ushered into a warm, cosy sitting room with a table set with a tea tray and a plate of scones. 'This looks inviting.' She shed her coat and scarf which she hung on the door hook.

'Sit down, love,' said Dot.

As she sat down, she glanced at their faces, wondering what they had in store for her, but they gave nothing away.

She drank the welcome cup of tea and ate one of the warm scones topped with homemade plum jam, which tasted delicious. She recalled when she lived in Hull that jam had been difficult to come by and when they'd managed to get hold of a jar, it was dubious what fruit it contained. Ration restrictions in the countryside as opposed to the city were not so tight.

'What about a big party with balloons?' Dot tried to pull Charlotte from her reverie.

She stared at the three ladies in disbelief until they started to laugh. 'Your face is a picture,' they chorused in unison.

Now May took command of the situation. 'Usually, when you leave work, you have to give a week's notice, though with you living in, it's best to do a bit of soft-soaping.'

Baffled, Charlotte stared at May, repeating, 'Soft-soaping?'

Edna interjected, 'What she means is perhaps give your aunt and uncle a gift or a token of your appreciation for them taking you in. We could pool our rations and make a cake for them with a bit of fancy wording on it. And you could make them a nice thank-you card. What do you think?'

Charlotte felt tears filling her eyes, and her voice choked as she answered. 'You're all so wonderful. I shall miss seeing you in the snug each night.' She jumped up from her chair and hugged each lady in turn.

On her free afternoon, rain lashed the countryside. She managed to get a lift on a cart going into Driffield. 'Thanks, see you in one hour,' she called to the carter, as he dropped her off in the main street. Hurrying down the side street to the treasure-trove shop, she pushed open the shop door. Its bell tinkled sedately and then went on a wobble. Charlotte hastily shut the door, expecting to hear the parrot, but it didn't appear to be there.

Today there was another shopkeeper, a woman of indeterminate age, with a mob cap perched on her head of frizzy grey hair. She sat behind the counter, unravelling an old jersey to reuse the wool again. 'All right, dearie?' she asked.

Charlotte nodded and began rummaging in boxes, looking for some kind of memento for her aunt and uncle. Apart from the inn, she didn't know what else they liked or if they had any special interests and hobbies. In a glass case littered with old-fashioned brooches, she spied one designed as a colourful basket of flowers, but not too gaudy, just right to add a dash of colour to her aunt's drab dresses. Her uncle was a problem and time was getting on. And then she spied a pewter tankard with an inscription on it. Peering closer, she could just make out the words: Samuel Bilton Brewery.

'This is a lucky find,' she told the shopkeeper, as she paid for her purchases.

'Why's that, dearie?'

'It's for my uncle. He owns the Travellers Rest Inn at Mornington and he's a Bilton.'

Before meeting the carter, she just had time to pop into the grocery cum off licence to buy a small bottle of whisky for Jack, who she hadn't seen lately.

Settled on old sacking in the cart as it rumbled along the road, she felt pleased with the gifts for Hilda and George. And happy that she was going to see her old friend Jack, whose company she so enjoyed. A thought surfaced in her mind. Might Jack know where Emile was stationed?

CHAPTER SEVENTEEN

January 1944

On her journey from Driffield to Mornington, Charlotte slumbered in the cart, and woke with a jolt when the cart halted. She felt cold and stiff as the carter helped her down at the crossroad. 'Thank you,' she murmured. Pulling up her coat collar and tightening her headscarf, she set off with a brisk step in the direction of Jack's cottage.

'Come in,' he called to her light tap on the door. He was ensconced in his chair by the fire and made to rise to his feet. Jip came to her wagging his tail, and she fondled his ears.

'No, don't get up, Jack. You look so nice and cosy.' Though she thought he looked a bit peaky. She pulled off her coat and scarf and hung them on the door hook. 'Sorry I haven't visited you of late, but I've been busy up at the house with the children.' From her bag, she withdrew the small bottle of whisky.

'Just what I need,' he croaked.

'Hot water or tea?' she asked.

'Hot water, but not too much.'

She poured half the bottle into a tumbler and lifted the kettle, resting on the side oven hotplate, and added the water.

She placed it in his unsteady hands and sat back to watch him sip it slowly.

When he'd drunk half, he licked his lips. 'Just what the doctor ordered.'

He certainly looked a little better. 'Do you need me to bring you any shopping?'

'Nay, lass. Neighbours are good and often bring me my dinner, if he's caught a rabbit or two.'

'That's good,' she smiled, thinking that when she lived in Hull, a rabbit was a rarity, but the countryside was different. Perhaps the methods of obtaining said rabbit weren't strictly legal, but the village policeman turned a blind eye as long as it wasn't for monetary gain.

'Make yerself a cuppa, Charlotte, then tell me how the kiddies are.'

Charlotte stood at the kitchen table pouring the tea into a cup, when a movement from behind startled her. And a masculine voice whispered in her ear, 'I could quite get used to the English custom of afternoon tea.'

The teapot clunked on the table, and slowly she turned, almost falling into the arms of Emile. He held her steady as she looked into his amazing brown eyes and at his moist full lips slightly apart. She held his gaze, sensing his anticipation. The beat of her heart quickening, her body, weightless, seemed to float above and around her. He pulled her closer, anchoring her to him and she felt the soft touch of his lips on hers. She closed her eyes, feeling the sensation of unbelievable pleasure ripple through her body. Just to be near to him was all she desired.

'Ah, you're awake, Emile,' said Jack, half-turning in his chair.

For a brief moment, Charlotte had forgotten they were not alone. Her voice a little shaky, she asked, 'Would you like a cup of tea, Emile?' She felt his hand slip down the curve of her spine as he moved away from her.

'Yes, please,' he replied as he pulled up a chair to sit next to Jack. From a safe distance, she handed him his tea, not looking at him. She sat down opposite them, cradling her cup in her hands, and stared into the dancing flames of the fire. Although she avoided looking across at Emile, the love she felt for him radiated from her in waves. She wasn't sure if Jack knew of her feelings for Emile. It wasn't something she'd mentioned. She sipped her tea and half listened to the two men talking. Glancing at the mantelpiece clock, she stirred, rising to her feet. 'Time I was going,' she murmured.

Emile's eyes were fixed on her face and then he looked at Jack. And Jack grinned, saying, 'Emile, why don't you walk Charlotte back ter inn. It's dark out there for her to walk alone.'

Emile jumped to his feet, his gaze on Charlotte's face and she felt heat flush her cheeks.

'Delighted.' He helped her on with her coat, his fingers caressing the nape of her neck, sending tingles down her spine. She remembered part of a conversation she'd once overheard when she helped her mother in the haberdashery shop. Two customers were discussing a film they had seen.

'They say Frenchmen are the best lovers,' one of them had confided. They'd both laughed and the other one said, 'Don't let your Bill hear you say that.' She wondered if Emile was a good lover. Though she'd never been intimate with a man, so she had no experience to compare.

'Bye, Jack, and take care,' she called. Jip stirred at his master's feet, lifted up his head in farewell and promptly went back to dreamland.

Emile shrugged on his overcoat, and opened the door. Outside, the darkness engulfed them.

His arms encircled her, and she felt the warm closeness of his body. Their lips touched, tender at first and then a passionate urgency erupted and they clung together, not wanting to be apart. 'I missed you,' he whispered into the softness of her hair, her scarf falling on to her shoulders.

'I missed you, too,' she whispered back, her body shaping to his, not wanting to let go.

Someone coming their way was whistling and they drew apart. She slipped her arm through his and they walked on.

She told him of her decision to leave the inn and to work with the children.

'You love children, don't you?' he said.

'Yes, I do. I want to help them to be happy and have fun in their lives. For who knows if they will ever be reunited with their families. Whatever the outcome, I want to give them hope for their future.' He didn't comment, and they walked on in silence. She wondered about his daughter. 'Emile,' she began, not quite sure whether to mention her, but she took a deep breath and ploughed on. 'Your daughter, Juliette, do you ever hear from your parents how she is?' She felt him stiffen beside her.

Then he spoke, his words measured. 'My mother writes an occasional letter with news of Juliette's progress. Letters are censored, and she only mentions the mundane, because anything else is forbidden. Their village is a quiet one and, so far, they are safe from German interference, but the Nazis are unpredictable. And that worries me.'

He became silent and she didn't offer any comment. She wanted to say, don't worry, Juliette will be safe, but what did she know about a country whose citizens lived under enemy occupation? She only knew about her own homeland which suffered constant bombing and air raids. Instead, she gently squeezed his arm and moved closer to him.

When they reached the inn, his words surprised her. 'Charl, will you accompany me to a formal dance at the Floral Hall in Hornsea?'

She looked up into his handsome face and answered, 'I would love to. I've never been there before. And to be with you is special,' she added shyly.

He kissed her lightly, saying, 'Au revoir for now.'

She watched his tall, upright figure walk away and felt an overwhelming love for Emile. He was a bright light in her life, making her so happy, and she wanted to spend as much time as possible with him. And she wondered if, and hoped that, he felt the same way about her.

Inside the inn, all was quiet. In her room, she slipped off her coat and shoes and lay down on the bed. Closing her eyes, she stretched out an arm, wishing she could feel Emile lying by her side. She lay daydreaming until she heard Hilda calling her name. Hastily, she splashed cold water from the jug on her face, tidied her hair and went down for the meal before the evening shift.

They ate their meal in silence, as usual. Charlotte's thoughts raced, wondering what would be the best time to tell her aunt and uncle she was leaving the inn to work permanently at Mornington House with the children. She could put it off until tomorrow. She let out a deep sigh.

Hilda snapped, 'What have you to sigh about?'

Charlotte felt the flush of heat on her cheeks and carefully placed her knife and fork on her plate. She coughed and cleared her throat. 'I've something to tell you both.' Hilda stared at her, while George drank noisily from his glass of beer, eyeing her over the rim. Her words rushed out in a gush. Somewhere the slow drip of a water tap filled the silence surrounding the three of them sitting at the table, their expressions frozen.

After what seemed an eternity, Charlotte spoke again, her body trembling. 'It means I shall be leaving the inn.'

George took another loud sup of his beer, but it was Hilda who spoke. 'You can't go,' she blurted, her voice high pitched. 'Yer too young.'

'I'm eighteen, old enough.'

'But you are fifteen.'

She looked at her aunt in amazement. 'I was fifteen when I first came here and I have had three birthdays since.' They had never acknowledged or celebrated her birthdays, and she never mentioned it to them. On her special day, she would think of her mother and relive happier days. She looked at Hilda, and it was impossible for her to believe she was Martha's sister.

'You can't go. You're needed here to work,' Hilda whined.

George jumped to his feet, his chair scraping the floor. 'Let her bloody well go. She's a bloody drain on my profits.' He charged into the bar, muttering as he went.

Charlotte looked at Hilda, saying, 'I'm sorry, but if I don't care for the children, I was going to join one of the women's forces anyway.' She rose from the table and began to clear the dishes. She washed them up while Hilda sat staring into space. Job done, she made a pot of tea, set the tray on the table and poured out two cups, putting one in front of Hilda and sat opposite her.

After some time, Hilda spoke, 'Will you come and visit?' Surprised by this request, Charlotte answered, 'Yes, of course I will.'

'I've got used to having you around.'

After a decent interval, Charlotte escaped to her room, needing to steady her nerves before the start of the evening shift.

Later, Charlotte served the three ladies in the snug and told them what she had bought Hilda and George as a 'thank you for having me' gift. They nodded in approval.

'We'll make a few savouries for George and the men, and a sponge cake for Hilda and the ladies.'

Three pairs of eyes looked at Charlotte for approval.

'Oh, that's lovely,' she enthused, and hugged them in turn. 'I'm going to miss you ladies,' and she hastily brushed away the tears wetting her lashes.

'I hope you will come and see us,' Edna said.

'Yes, and you can come and see me, and perhaps teach the girls needlework or knitting skills.'

'Look! He's here, that young man of yours,' May beamed at her.

Charlotte saw Emile entering the room. She made her way to him, and their fingers entwined.

She was kept busy and there wasn't time for talking, not until she'd finished her shift and slipped outside to find him waiting for her. He held out his arms and she snuggled up to him, feeling the roughness of his coat and smelling his maleness. He kissed her tenderly, and she could taste the beer on his lips and inhale the tobacco from his breath. She loved everything familiar about him.

They talked about the dance next Saturday. 'I will be at Mornington House then, ready to start work on Sunday.'

'When is your last night at the inn?

'Friday. Hope you can come.' She told him what she'd bought for Hilda and George and the ladies' contributions.

'A party night.' He grinned mischievously. Playfully, she dug him in the ribs.

The last customers left the inn and it was time for a last kiss. As she watched him walk off into the darkness, she shivered, thinking she'd love to have him to cuddle up to on a cold winter's night instead of sleeping in her lonely bed. She looked up at the night sky, seeing a lone twinkling star. 'I can dream,' she murmured.

CHAPTER EIGHTEEN

February 1944

Charlotte didn't have time for any more daydreams, for her life became far too hectic. She was busy working nights at the inn, and spending daytime with the children. And today, she was trying to sort out her living arrangements at Mornington House. She trudged up the two flights of stairs with a panting Mrs Grahame slowly following behind her. Charlotte surveyed the rooms in dismay. They were full of boxes and trunks and junk from days gone by, though the leaking roof had been repaired. Brushing aside cobwebs, she ventured into the darkening room, feeling for a light switch, but there was no electricity installed. 'It doesn't look promising.' Charlotte sneezed as the dust filled her nostrils and her feet slipped on mouse droppings.

Mrs Grahame sat down heavily on a trunk and puffed until she'd got her breathing under control. Then she spoke. 'The alternative is the old butler's rooms.'

Downstairs, they followed the passage leading away from the main part of the house. Mrs Grahame produced a bunch of old keys and cursed under her breath when the key refused to turn. 'Let me.' Charlotte took hold of the key.

She gripped it tightly and turned. It made an awful noise as it groaned and shuddered, and so did her insides with the effort. And then the door creaked, inching open. 'It needs a can of oil!'

Inside the room, a swirl of dust and the smell of decay rose up to fill Charlotte's nostrils and mouth, making her cough. She managed to push open a sash window, gladly inhaling the cold winter air and did the same in the smaller room, used as a bedroom. At first glance, she felt dismayed with the sitting room-cum-kitchenette, seeing a small fireplace and hob and oven, and sink. Until she spied a door tucked in a corner. She still had the bunch of keys in her pocket and, selecting the largest one, fitted it into the lock. It needed oiling as well, but with a certain amount of wrangling, the door opened to reveal a small paved courtyard with a gate and a path, which probably led to the front drive. Perfect, she thought. Her very own domain with a private entrance. Elation filled her, as she whispered to the cloudy sky above, 'A place of my very own,' and drew in a deep sigh of contentment.

Laura helped her to clean out the rooms and soon every cobweb and dust mote had vanished. They sat on the floor drinking tea, which Mrs Grahame had brought them. She had gone off to confer with Mr Grahame, to source furniture, to furnish the rooms with.

'Aren't you lucky,' said Laura, 'I have to share a bedroom with my two younger sisters so I have no privacy, and they keep pinching my things.'

Charlotte shook her hair free of her headscarf tied in turban style and laughed. 'You're the lucky one. As an only child, I missed having a sister to play with.'

'You can have mine anytime,' Laura grumbled.

Mr Grahame and old Tom half-dragged, half-carried a mismatch of furniture, which they'd found stored in an outhouse, to her little haven. A huge bed, made of solid wood and shaped like a swan, filled the bedroom. Plenty of room for two, Charlotte thought as she gazed at it. In the kitchen, she laid a fire and struck a match, watching the flames curl up the chimney. The fire smelled of pine and apple logs. Tom had stacked a pile for her in the hastily constructed shed in the courtyard, to protect them from the elements.

'Best let the rooms air for a few days before you make up the bed,' Mrs Grahame advised.

Back at the inn, Charlotte spent a few nights lying awake, her mind full of moving on to her new venture. Tonight was her last night at the inn and Emile was coming. She pictured his face, the creases around his wide brown eyes, his sensual lips. He was twenty-five and she eighteen, yet when she was with him, she felt his equal. When she'd mentioned this to Joyce, her friend had asked her to explain, but Charlotte couldn't put it into words. She felt it here; she placed her hand on her heart.

'Charlotte,' her aunt shouted up the stairs.

With a quick glance round, she checked her belongings, which were all packed. Not that she owned much. Her clothes, a few books and the wooden framed needlework picture of her dear mother. A quick glance in the mirror and she saw her cheeks were a healthy glowing pink, matching the touch of the precious stub of lipstick she'd applied to her lips. Her dress matched her blue eyes, which lit up with eagerness. She picked up the two wrapped gifts in brown paper for Hilda and George.

Downstairs, customers were arriving, for they'd heard of a bit of a party happening and wanted a good seat. The local men liked their favourite positions at the bar and the routine of chatting about the day's happenings. Their wives preferred sitting at a table, enjoying the party atmosphere, hoping for a sing-song.

Flushed with happiness, Charlotte appeared in the bar and went to the snug to see the three ladies.

'Look,' May pointed to a table laden with trays of food, sweet and savoury, covered by a white tablecloth. 'Most of the villagers have donated.'

Charlotte gazed in wonderment as she peeped under the cloth and felt a lump in her throat and tears spring to wet her lashes. 'Thank you,' she whispered, overwhelmed by the kindness of everyone.

Soon the inn became packed, with everyone in good humour, including George and Hilda, who were both busy behind the bar serving drinks and the till rang constantly. Suddenly the door was flung open, heralding a host of French soldiers. Immediately Charlotte saw Emile, and she moved expertly through the happy crowd to reach his side. She wanted to fling her arms around him and hug him close, but instead she reached for his hand, feeling his strong, sure grip, and smiled up into his beloved face. And then Joyce came in with her airman, all smiles, and they chatted and Charlotte became swept along away from Emile. He smiled at her from a distance.

Round about 8 p.m. someone banged a gong, and the room went quiet. Everyone looked round expectantly, and all eyes seem to rest on Charlotte. For one frightening moment, she froze. And then she saw Emile's face, his reassuring smile, and Dot, May, Edna and Joyce came to stand by her side to give her their support. 'Speech!' someone called.

Something she hadn't thought of.

Joyce nudged her, saying, 'Drink this.' She put a small glass into her hand.

With trembling fingers, she put the glass to her lips and swallowed the fiery liquid in one go. It raced down her throat, warming her up and loosening her tongue. She coughed and cleared her throat. 'Thank you for coming.' She flashed her eyes around the room, all faces watching her. 'This is to say a big thank you to Aunt Hilda and Uncle George for taking me in when my home in Hull was bombed, killing my beloved mother. Please raise your glasses.'

Everyone dutifully did, murmuring their appreciation to Hilda and George. 'I now declare the buffet open,' cried Charlotte.

There were cheers.

Charlotte picked up the two small packages and the card she had made and went over to her aunt and uncle. 'Just small gifts to show my appreciation of your kindness for taking me in.' They both looked at her in surprise and it registered to her that they were not expecting anything from her.

George was first to open his. He tore at the brown wrapping paper and squinted at the inscription on the tankard. 'By, heck! Well I never!' Proudly he read out the inscription.

'Samuel Bilton Brewery. My grandad's brewery.' With much pride, he showed the tankard to the men standing at the bar.

Hilda looked on at her husband and slowly began to undo her gift, her fingers work-worn and clumsy. And then her eyes shone, lighting up her face. She looked at Charlotte and whispered, 'No one has ever bought me anything so grand before.' Touching the brooch lovingly with her finger tip, she sighed with pleasure.

She was about to close the box lid when Charlotte said, 'Let me fasten it on your dress.'

She slipped behind the bar counter and, to the delight of the amazed Hilda, fastened the clasp securely to her grey dress. Instantly, the stones in the brooch sparkled, reflecting in Hilda's eyes, which shone with tears and happiness. Charlotte pressed the card into her aunt's hand, saying, 'Thank you.'

The three ladies brought the refreshments to the bar, a plate of savoury food and a plate of assorted tiny buns, placing them on the counter. Then they turned to admire Hilda's brooch.

While they were engaged, Charlotte sidestepped away to find Emile. He was with the crowd around the piano, and she edged close to him. He sensed her presence and put his arm around her shoulders, and she felt the warmth of his body.

The song they were singing was one she knew from her schooldays, 'Frere Jacques'. Then they belted out 'One Man Went to Mow a Meadow', and the French soldiers couldn't keep up with the counting and everyone fell about laughing.

Next was a medley of songs sung by Vera Lynn when she entertained the troops.

Emile went to the bar to replenish their glasses and Charlotte leaned on the wall, the voices all around her drifting away. It was surreal, and she felt a little sad at leaving the inn.

She'd miss the companionship of seeing the regulars, especially the three ladies, who she now regarded as friends. But she had an open invitation to visit them anytime. And she knew they welcomed the opportunity to visit Mornington House and teach the girls knitting and needlework, after school and weekends. They loved being busy and worked tirelessly, knitting socks and gloves for the troops and the French soldiers as well.

'Daydreaming?' Joyce whispered in her ear.

Charlotte laughed. 'Yes, I shall miss the jolly, friendly atmosphere here. But I am moving on to a new phase in my life. A challenge. I love caring for the children.'

Joyce hugged Charlotte, saying. 'For me, war is topsy-turvy. I love working on the farm and I'm having a fabulous time, with the airmen. But we must beat old Hitler at his game and not let him win. Just think, if he ruled Britain, we would be his slaves. So, I do my bit to provide food so we don't go hungry.

And of course, I keep the morale of our lads up.' She gave Charlotte a wicked grin, leaving her in no doubt what she meant.

Emile appeared at Charlotte's side and Joyce went off to her airman. Above all the hustle and bustle, they found a quiet seat in the snug. The ladies were circulating and enjoying the attention. He set down the drinks on the table and took Charlotte into his arms and kissed her tenderly, holding her close so that their heartbeats became as one.

'My Cherie, I've yearned to kiss you all night.' He leaned back in his seat and looked at her.

'Was it worth waiting for?' she said impishly.

He smiled with satisfaction. 'You move across to Mornington House tomorrow?'

'Yes,' she sighed.

'I have the whole weekend off so I can help you to settle in, if you wish.'

'Yes, please.' Suddenly into her mind flashed the image of the big double bed. She was about to tell him about it when the ladies arrived in the snug, looking rather flushed, but happy.

CHAPTER NINETEEN

February 1944

A tinge of sadness swept over Charlotte as she left the inn, with a promise to visit her aunt and uncle. She was surprised when George gave her an extra week's wages, 'A bit of a bonus,' he said. And Hilda gave her a clumsy hug.

Now, as she walked by Emile's side, excitement and happiness occupied her on her journey to the next phase of her life. The walk to Mornington House took longer than usual because the villagers kept stopping to wish her well, 'Looking after the kiddies,' and 'My, you'll have your work cut out if those kiddies up at house are like my two evacuees.' Mrs Mackay presented her with a tray of shortbread biscuits. 'Something to keep your pecker up.'

'The villagers are so kind,' she said to Emile. Tears sprinkled her lashes.

'You are lucky to live where people care and are not frightened by a knock on the door.'

'A knock on the door,' she repeated, not sure of his meaning.

'Sorry. I do not want to dampen your spirits.' He glanced sideward at her and she held his gaze, as if to say, explain. He stared ahead and said, finally, 'My home country is occupied by the Germans, and in certain areas a knock on the door could mean a labour camp or prison.'

He didn't tell her of the brutality and the killings, and people who disappeared without trace. And so much more. He glanced at her face and saw she was about to speak, when a group of women entering the village hall stopped to talk to her. He put down her case which he had been carrying and lit a cigarette to steady the tautness of his nerves. He hadn't heard from his parents, and nor had his message to the family on the next farm been acknowledged.

He desperately wanted to know they were safe. He cherished the love and companionship Charlotte gave him so readily, which helped to stop him from dwelling on dark matters and kept his mind strong. Perhaps they consoled each other. She, of course, had lost her home and her mother to the enemy bombing. He watched her face light up at what one of the ladies was saying to her. He would be sorry to leave this relatively peaceful village and the area. He felt drawn to it and the hospitable people he came into contact with. Especially Jack, who reminded him of his grandfather who had died many years ago, when Emile was a young boy.

He had told him tales of how the Great War had been fought and won, a war to end all wars, until this madman came along with his intention of conquering the world and hacking anyone down who stood in his way.

Charlotte said goodbye to the kind people, and gently touched Emile's arm. 'You were far away.'

Not wanting to upset her happiness, he replied. 'I am thinking of the dance tonight and how much I'm looking forward to holding you in my arms.'

She smiled at him and asked, 'Is it going to be a posh do?' She was wondering what to wear for a grand occasion. Though her choice was limited.

'Posh do?' he queried.

She laughed, 'Will there be dignitaries and high-ranking officers?'

'Yes, but you will outshine them all with your beauty.'

She felt the blush creep up from her neck to her face at his words. Did he really think she was beautiful? She'd never considered herself so. Though she recalled her mother saying, beauty was in the eye of the beholder.

When they reached Mornington House, two of the younger girls were off school recovering from a cold and cough and were having their morning break of milk and a biscuit.

They jumped off their seats and rushed to Charlotte while Emile stood slightly back. And then Charlotte drew him to her and Emile said, '*Bonjour les enfants.*' At the sound of this man speaking their mother tongue, they became silent and shuffled their feet, hiding behind Charlotte, fear in their little faces.

Charlotte realised that the uniform and his language must have triggered terrible memories for the children. For who knew what they had suffered before coming to Britain and safety.

Mrs Grahame came bustling up. 'Now children, time to rest,' she said, shepherding them away from the dining room.

Neither Charlotte nor Emile spoke as she led the way down the passage to her quarters.

She flung open the door. 'Welcome, to my humble abode,' she chanted, wanting to lighten the atmosphere.

Stepping inside, he couldn't erase the look of fear on the children's faces. His thoughts were with his daughter, Juliette, and he was desperate to find out if she was safe. He couldn't bear it for her to suffer like those poor children. He must write to his parents again and to the neighbouring farm. Soon the battalion would be mobile and letters might be delayed. And then how would he know of Juliette's safety? His heart and head spun in turmoil. At a touch on his arm, he flinched. He stared down into Charlotte's concerned face.

'Emile, are you all right? Come sit down.' Gently, she guided him to one of the mismatched kitchen chairs. He didn't offer her any explanation, but she had an inkling what caused his distress. There was no fire lit so she couldn't make him a hot drink, so she filled a tumbler with fresh cool water and handed it to him. She watched him drink his fill, and slowly his face relaxed and the dullness from his eyes cleared. 'You are worried about Juliette?' she offered.

Surprised, he gazed at her. 'How did you know?'

'The children.' He nodded in reply. 'Have you heard from your parents yet?'

'No, and I am concerned.' He paused, debating whether he should tell her without betraying any confidences. 'Charl.' She looked into his deep brown, troubled eyes and his heart beat with longing to . . . He mustn't think like that. 'If I write to them and their reply is delayed and I am not here . . .' He paused again, unsure. And then, as if she had read his mind, she spoke.

'Emile, give your family or any of your contacts my name and address. For if they are experiencing difficulties trying to contact you while you are . . .' The words stuck in her throat.

She sighed deeply, for she knew he and his battalion would soon be leaving. 'They can write to me, if they wish, and I will forward them on to you or keep them safe here.'

'Charl, how can I thank you?' he asked, relief flooding through his body.

'For a start, you can help me unpack.' She leaned towards him and gave him a fleeting kiss on the lips. Laughing, she said, 'If you are good, I might kiss you again.' He laughed then.

Later, he went back to Jack's to change for the evening dance. Charlotte laid out her clothes, her best underwear and the deep red dress, one of Jack's wife's, that she'd altered, adding black lace around the neckline, giving it an elegant look. Then she had a good strip wash and washed her hair, rinsing it with rainwater she'd scooped from the butt in the courtyard.

Emile had lit the fire earlier, and the kitchen glowed with warmth. She sat on a low wooden stool in front of the burning wood flames dancing in the grate, towelling her hair dry. Then shaking it free, she let it fall onto her shoulders. It swayed with the movement of her body as she turned. Brushing it, she let it fall into natural waves, teasing little curls at the side of her face, like she'd seen actresses in American films do. She brought her hand-mirror from the cold bedroom and sat at the small polished oak table to apply her powder and to coax out the last remains of the stub of red lipstick. Joyce had given her a precious pair of nylon stockings, courtesy of a GI that she'd met.

Emile was coming to pick her up for the dance at seven. She had told him to use her courtyard entrance so that the children and staff wouldn't be disturbed. She had spoken to Mrs Grahame earlier to say she would be late back from the dance, and was surprised by her reaction.

'Why don't you begin your duties at dinner time tomorrow and then you can tell us all about the dance.' Mrs Grahame had a faraway look in her eyes.

Charlotte thought of those words as she waited for Emile, and the idea appealed to her. A lazy morning in bed was something she hadn't done for some time. Then a wicked thought dropped into her head. Just then, she heard the sound of a vehicle coming to a halt in the courtyard. And not wanting to keep Emile waiting, she slipped on her coat, and tied a scarf over her head to protect her carefully coiffured hair from the winter elements. Picking up her evening bag which she had made from a piece of black velvet trimmed with sequins salvaged from an old-fashioned bonnet, she gave a quick look round, turned off the light and locked the door behind her. The key was too big and heavy to put in her bag, so she placed it safely under a brick. She reached the gate as Emile appeared. He kissed her on the cheek and led her to their transport for the night, a jeep.

'I have it until tomorrow.' He helped her to climb in.

Soon, they left the village behind and were travelling along the narrow country lanes, only occasionally lit by the moon coming from behind a cloud. Emile concentrated on driving and she didn't speak, content simply to be by his side.

She couldn't see the sea, but she heard the crashing waves on the beach and smelled its tanginess. Time had flown so fast since she'd last visited Hornsea, long before the war. A lifetime ago. It had been one of her mother's favourite places to take the train to in those halcyon days of summers long gone. A touch of melancholy swept through her. She didn't belong to anyone now that her mother had died. No matter how much she tried, she couldn't ever think of Hilda and George as family. Jack and the three ladies were her dearest friends but, truly, the person she felt closest to was Emile.

The jeep came to a halt and Emile leapt out and helped her alight. He slipped an arm around her waist, drawing her close as they walked to the entrance of the Floral Hall.

The door opened, and they were greeted by a smart, uniformed man. She was shown to the ladies' cloakroom by a pretty young woman, also in uniform. After being relieved of her coat and scarf, Charlotte tidied her hair and went to find Emile. She could hear the sound of a band playing in full swing, and the atmosphere was more formal than the village dances. Women were mostly wearing long dresses, and she self-consciously smoothed down the skirt of her modest dress. Feeling a little shy at first, as she wasn't used to such grandeur, she was cheered by the sight of a couple of land army girls she'd met in the inn, who waved to her as they danced by.

'May I have this dance, mademoiselle,' came the soft timbre of Emile's voice in her ear.

She spun round and into his arms, feeling a surge of love running through her body.

He led her onto the dance floor and they glided round the floor. The glitter ball suspended from the ceiling and twirling around added to the magic of being in each other's arms, their bodies touching close and intimate, the music divine.

All too soon, the music stopped and she and Emile were seated at a round table with other soldiers of the French Battalion and their partners. Emile introduced her to them and she smiled and acknowledged them politely. Out of courtesy, she danced with a couple of the soldiers and found them entertaining. At one time, only Charlotte and a high-ranking officer, judging by his uniform, were at the table. At first he appeared stiff and formal and she felt nervous in his company until he asked her about her work. Full of enthusiasm, she told him about the refugee children, adding. 'It is a joy to work with the children. I feel sad when the younger ones cannot remember their families though some of the older children choose not to remember.' He held his head slightly on one side and gave her a quizzical look. She blushed under his gaze, but spoke clearly despite her racing heartbeat. 'From what I observe of the children, they want to block out their painful past and just enjoy being children.'

He reflected for a few moments. 'Very commendable. Excellent work, mademoiselle. And what of your own family?'

A fleeting sadness crossed her face and quietly she replied. 'My father died when I was quite young. My mother was killed in an enemy bombing raid in Hull.' Suddenly tears pricked her eyes and she hastily dashed them away.

'Forgive me, mademoiselle, I did not mean to distress you.' He laid a gentle hand on her arm.

She looked deep into his eyes and saw they were full of sadness. She was about to ask him about his family when the dance finished and the others returned to the table. The soldiers all remained standing until the officer rose and took his leave of them. Emile, seated next to her, took hold of her hand and the jollity returned.

Later, as he drove her home, she asked the officer's name. 'He is my commanding officer, General Jacques-Philippe Leclerc. He is a man I regard very highly.'

CHAPTER TWENTY

February 1944

On the journey back, snow was falling steadily. They didn't talk as Emile was concentrating on driving and negotiating the treacherous sharp bends. Charlotte rested her head on the seat, enjoying the wonderful harmony existing between them, feeling safe and content to be in Emile's company.

They reached Mornington House just after midnight and the grounds and gardens looked like fairyland, covered in a layer of pure white cotton-wool. Reaching the courtyard, Emile helped her down from the jeep and swung her up into his arms. Laughing, she wrapped her arms about his neck, her cold face touching his cold face, and yet at the same time feeling a delicious warmth of being in his arms and never wanting to let go. The key under the brick was hidden by snow. He set her down and, laughing, they hunted in the snow until he located the brick, retrieved the key and opened the door.

Once inside the kitchen, so dark after the brilliance of the outside whiteness, the blackout blind already in place, Charlotte lit the oil lamp on the table. She turned to Emile, feeling the coldness of his hands in hers.

He kissed her gently and whispered, 'I should go now.'

With a fierceness she didn't realise she possessed, she said firmly, 'No.'

In the light of the flickering lamp, he stared deep into her eyes, seeing the longing he felt in his heart reflected back at him. He drew her into his embrace, both heedless of their wet outdoor clothing.

She whispered, 'I don't want the night to end.'

'Are you sure?'

'Yes.'

Quickly they shrugged off their outdoor clothes, and she opened the bedroom door, drawing him in. Wildly undressing, their discarded clothes were scattered around the room. For a few seconds, they stood naked before each other. And then, laughing, she slid into bed and opened her arms to him and they snuggled down, hugging each other for warmth. The touch of his strong, muscular body wrapped round hers sent signals of undiluted pleasure racing to every part of her. She sighed, drinking in this enchanting feeling of love and letting it enfold her in its embrace.

'My Cheri,' Emile whispered, 'I have dreamed of this moment for a long time.'

'So have I. I want to belong to you,' she whispered back. She wanted, needed him in her life to make her feel a whole person to be loved and cherished. Though she knew their precious time together was short. She'd heard rumours, though she didn't mention it to Emile.

The Free French were going down south. It was uncertain if she and Emile would ever meet again. Whatever the outcome, knowing they had given themselves lovingly to each other, gave her hope. Her lips found his, her hands stroking his neck and down to his chest, arousing him.

His hands caressed her body as she yielded to his desire.

Through the night they explored each other's bodies, taking pleasure in their thirst and passion for each other. Each time their love reached dizzy heights, she luxuriated in the satisfaction his body inside hers gave her. Never before had she experienced this wonderful feeling. And each time they made love, it left her longing for more. She smiled to herself, for it also left Emile wanting more of her.

When she woke, she saw a thin chink of daylight coming from a corner of the blackout blind. She looked at the sleeping Emile with his arms still entwining her body, so close that their heartbeats seemed as one. Gently, as not to wake him, she eased from the bed. In the kitchen, she raked at the banked-up fire-grate until a glimmer of flame appeared and pulled a couple of logs from the hearth basket and watched them spark. She filled the small kettle with water from the tap and placed it on the fire. Then she washed in cold water at the stone sink and combed her hair, pulling on her dressing-gown.

Scooping tea into the pot, she set two mugs, milk and sugar, on a tray. She then sliced four rounds of bread to toast. She glanced round the tiny room, feeling a sense of pride. This was her very own domain, and this simple meal her first. The kettle hissed to the boil, and she made the tea, and sat on a low stool to toast the bread, using the long-handle fork. The kitchen utensils and indeed everything in her tiny quarters were second-hand. She didn't mind because now they were hers. The smell of bread toasting evoked memories of when she was a girl at home with her mother, and she smiled to herself. It was then she became aware of Emile standing in the doorway, wearing his trousers and shirt, watching her.

Thinking of their lovemaking last night, she felt her face flush with heat. She hoped he didn't think she was a loose woman who gave herself freely. He continued to gaze at her and she moved to pick up the plateful of toasted bread, but he reached for it before her, their hands touching.

He placed the plate on the table, took her in his arms and kissed her tenderly, and whispered, 'My Cherie. Mon amour.'

Later, after breakfast, she dressed and they donned their outdoor clothes. Finding a pile of old Wellington boots in a cupboard by the outside door, they went for a walk, linking arms.

Charlotte breathed in the freshness of the chilled air, filling her lungs with its cleanness.

Above, the sky was cloudless, a vivid blue expanse stretching further than she could see. Pleasure in each other's company flowed between them as they strolled along the woodland path, their footsteps leaving deep pockets in the virgin snow. A stillness filled the air until a bird, or was it two, landed on a pine branch and showered them with snow. Laughing, they shook themselves and walked on, to circle round towards the pond, now covered in a layer of ice.

The silence was eerie and Charlotte thought of the tragic drowning of the children, and sadness filled her. Emile's voice broke into her thoughts and startled her for a moment.

'Why is there a barrier?' He stretched out his arms to the circumference of the pond.

She told him what had happened that terrible day. 'Two of the children lived in the house and their parents closed it and moved away. The other little girl was Milly, my aunt and uncle's daughter. She would have been my cousin, and I never knew her. So sad,' she whispered.

Emile put a comforting arm about her shoulders and they turned towards the house.

As they approached, they saw the faces of the children looking out of the windows of their recreation room. The younger children had their noses pressed to the glass panes, while the older ones stood behind looking bored with being indoors. Then suddenly a fight broke out between two boys and they wrestled to the floor.

Charlotte and Emile hurried indoors, only stopping to kick off their Wellington boots, to be met by a chaotic scene. A frustrated Mr Grahame was trying to stop the boys from fighting, with no success. The older children egged them on, while two of the little girls were crying. Charlotte gave a quick look round for the volunteer staff, but there were none present. She guessed that because of the weather conditions they hadn't arrived.

Quickly Emile stepped in and separated the sparring boys, while Charlotte comforted the girls. Mr Grahame, exhausted, sank into a chair. Mrs Jolly the cook came from the kitchen and bellowed, 'If you don't stop this racket, there will be no dinner for you lot.' The room went quiet.

The children were still restless, however, and Charlotte quickly introduced Emile to Mr Grahame. 'Do I have your permission for Emile and I to supervise the children to play in the snow until dinner is ready?'

A look of relief washed over his face. 'Most certainly.'

The children made a mad scramble to pull on their boots, coats, hats, gloves and scarves, and within a few minutes, the room was deserted. Mr Grahame lay back in the chair and closed his eyes.

Outside they shrieked and frolicked and Emile was having a snowball fight with the older children. Charlotte asked the younger ones, 'Shall we build a snowman?' In response, they jumped for joy. They began to roll a snowball until it became bigger and bigger. Then they decided to build a semi-circle of little snowmen. Charlotte searched under various bushes and found leaves and bits of twigs and pine cones. These they fashioned into eyes and noses and ears. She looked across the garden to where Emile was referee to see who could throw a snowball the furthest. By the shouts of glee, it was clear the children were enjoying themselves and burning up all their excess energy. As she watched them, she wondered if Emile was thinking of his own daughter, far away in his occupied homeland, an unstable country ruled by Germans. And then there were his parents.

Had he managed to communicate with them yet?

There were calls of joy from the younger children and Charlotte went back to them, her sad thoughts forgotten. 'Shall we hold hands and dance round your snowmen?' she suggested.

Their laughter was infectious as some found it hard to lift their feet out of the snow and fell over. Surveying the scene brought a lump to her throat, witnessing the undiluted bliss on their faces, their eyes shining with pleasure. She looked to Emile, and sensing her gaze, he turned to look at her and she smiled at him.

Emile loved the smile on Charlotte's face. To him she represented one good outcome in this barbaric world. After his wife was slaughtered by the wayside when they were fleeing Paris, he'd thought he could never experience happiness again. It had broken his heart to leave her there, open to the elements, but he had their young daughter, Juliette, to take to the safety of his parents' farm. He had fully intended to go back and bring her to the farm and give her a Christian burial, but circumstances over-rode his desire The Germans were swarming everywhere and he, a serving French officer, would only bring them to the farm and they would all be killed. Later he heard that a farmer, living nearby, had collected the bodies and buried them in a communal grave.

One day, when France was free of its oppressors, he would go and visit the grave and say his goodbyes. But could he tell his daughter of the way her mother had died? His body tensed with fear for Juliette. The lack of correspondence from his parents worried him.

He desperately wanted to go home, to see Juliette, to make sure she was safe. But . . . A snowball skimming across his face, catching his nose, brought him back to the here and now.

* * *

Amid the laughter and noise of the children, a gong sounded. Mr Grahame, not looking so weary now, stood in the doorway to summon them in for dinner.

They all trooped in and soon flung off their outdoor clothes and washed their hands, eager to eat. 'I should be going,' said Emile as he stood on the fringe of the group.

Before Charlotte could invite him to stay, Mr Grahame jumped in. 'You, sir, are our guest of honour.' No sooner had the words left his mouth than the older boys all clamoured to sit next to Emile.

143

After dinner, Charlotte and Emile played board games with the children. She was immersed in a game of tiddly-winks and he in a serious game of draughts.

By three o'clock, the daylight began to fade and glancing up at the sky through the window, Emile jumped to his feet, saying, 'I have to report back to camp, now.' He looked across the room to Charlotte.

She also jumped to her feet, saying, 'I'll walk with you back to the jeep.'

The children were reluctant to see him go, but he promised to visit again.

Outside, they strolled hand in hand, content in each other's company. As they stood by the jeep, Emile drew her close into his embrace, and she felt the roughness of his cheeks as he nuzzled her face. And then the warmth of his lips on hers.

At last, they drew apart.

She held his gaze, fear running through her body, hurting, for she knew he would soon be gone from her life to fight in this senseless war.

He took hold of her hand, kissed it and whispered, 'Au revoir, my Cherie.'

She stood motionless, watching him drive away, tears misting her eyes. She cherished the time spent with Emile, especially last night, when she had given herself to him, with no regrets.

CHAPTER TWENTY-ONE

March 1944

Over the next few weeks, Charlotte and Emile spent precious time together. Every free moment, they were together, talking, walking and making love. The children loved Emile coming to Mornington House, especially the older boys. One Sunday a few weeks later, Emile and Charlotte were busy kite-making with the children in the recreation room.

'What do you think, Charl?' He held up pieces of off-cuts of wood he'd sourced from Jack's workshop.

She knelt on the floor surrounded by a jumble of bits and pieces of material. She looked at him, unsure what the wood was for. He grinned, his eyes saying, wait and see. So she grinned back.

'Come on, lads.' He handed each boy a piece of wood. And soon they were busy sanding to make the wood smooth.

Charlotte was busy trimming the bits of fabric and showing the girls how to sew them together to make diamond shapes. She sneezed as the musty dust itched her nose.

Seeing the concern on Lucie's face, she soothed, 'When we are outside the wind will blow away the dust.'

The three ladies had kindly donated material for the kites. 'Takes us back to our childhood,' they had chorused.

Mr Grahame popped his head round the door. 'My, you are all so quiet and busy. We will miss Emile when he goes,' he said to Charlotte.

Suddenly she felt the happiness surrounding her drain away and evaporate. She'd pushed all thoughts of Emile going from her life to the furthermost recesses of her mind. She glanced at Emile, so engrossed in his work that he didn't hear the remark. She glanced back to Mr Grahame and nodded, not trusting herself to speak. Her hands were trembling as she picked up a piece of fabric and she hoped no one would notice.

Bursts of glee erupted from the boys as they surveyed the wooden supports of four kites now in place. Charlotte stood up. Emile looked happy and light-hearted, as if the atrocities of war had vanished from his mind. At least for a short time. Smiling, she stretched out her hands to him and he took them and she felt his warmth and strength transfer to her. Her heart overflowed with love for him. He pulled her to her feet, and the children gathered round, the joy on their faces infectious.

While Emile held the kite frames, she stretched the material taut and stitched it in place. The younger children finished making the tail pieces, and these were fixed in place while Emile produced the string. And now the children's excitement rose to a crescendo, all of them eager to be outside.

'Come along, children, hats and coats on,' Charlotte called. Outside, the March wind was gusty; ideal weather for kite flying.

Once the children had been given brief instructions, they were soon away, the kites flying high. Emile stood close to Charlotte, both watching the thrilling enthusiasm of the children.

There were shouts of laughter and high spirits and much running about as they attempted to keep the kites in the air. Emile slipped his arm around her shoulder, his fingers touching the nape of her neck, sending electrifying signals through her body. Tonight would be their last night together.

Suddenly there was a burst of shouting. One of the kites had got stuck on a tree branch. 'We'll have to fetch a ladder,' said Charlotte.

'No need,' said Maurice, age nine. He was one of the older boys, whose mother, father and younger siblings were missing. And before they could stop him, Charlotte was amazed to see him climb up the tree extraordinarily quickly. Holding her breath, she watched as he untangled the string and set the kite free.

Everyone cheered as he shinned down to land at her feet, grinning up at her. 'Well done, Maurice.' She watched him run off to join the others, recalling how when he first came to Mornington House, he was thin and gawky and kept himself to himself. Now she saw a lad growing strong and healthy, eating nourishing food and living in a place of safety. He'd lost the haunted look of fear he'd had when he arrived.

And so had the other children, she thought, as she observed them at play. With the war still going on, the future was uncertain, but she would do her utmost to give them hope and happiness to help them forget the nightmarish scenes, which many of them had suffered and witnessed in their young lives. The only thing that frightened the children now was the sound of the siren. Its piercing noise terrified them, especially going into the cellar. Usually, the scares involved the enemy targeting the nearby airfields. But they had been fortunate of late and there had been no recent air raids.

There were a few minor mishaps with the kites, but Emile soon resolved them. She and the younger children ran with the kites. They shrieked with delight as the kites soared high in the sky. Suddenly the wind gusted strongly and Charlotte glanced upwards to see dark clouds scudding across the sky. And then the rain suddenly came, pouring down in torrents. 'Inside,' she called. The younger children ran indoors, but the older ones seemed oblivious. 'Emile,' she called. He rallied the older children round, and they all dashed into the house.

Outdoor clothes were quickly discarded, hair and faces dried and hands washed and it was nearly time for tea. The children were still full of exuberance, and Charlotte didn't have the heart to quell it.

Mr Grahame suddenly made an appearance and a hush fell on them. 'You look a hungry lot. Are you ready for tea?' They went in an orderly line into the dining room. Charlotte and Emile were about to follow, when Mr Grahame said to them, 'Two volunteers are already on duty, Charlotte, so why don't you and Emile take your tea in your quarters. Mrs Jolly has prepared you a tray. We have everything under control and can manage until tomorrow.'

'Thank you,' she replied, surprised at his understanding and generosity.

Once inside Charlotte's domain, Emile set down the tray on the table and took Charlotte into his arms and kissed her passionately. And then, gently, she drew away from him. 'Let's have tea first. And then . . .' She laughed, a merry twinkle in her eyes.

While she poured, Emile poked the fire and when it sparked, put on a log and soon it was ablaze, filling the cosy room with its warmth, adding to the love already there. They sat opposite each other, eating ham sandwiches, sausages and savoury rolls, and delicious warm scones with jam, made from the brambles growing wild in the hedgerows. And then Emile produced a bottle of red wine and a hunk of cheese from his bag hanging on the door hook. When they had eaten and drunk their fill, they sat and talked. They both knew a little of each other's lives before they met, but they felt a need to talk about their family backgrounds in more detail.

He asked about her life before she came to the village. 'I lived with my mother and was an only child. I was never lonely, but a sister would have been nice. I can't remember much about my father, only the faint smell of his tobacco when he smoked a cigarette and blew me smoke rings. He went to work one day and never came home. Mother told me he had gone to heaven. I used to ask, when was Daddy coming home.' She was silent, staring into the fire.

'What happened to him?'

She gulped, then replied, 'Father stopped a runaway horse from going amok in a street where children played. The horse trampled him to death.'

Emile reached across and took hold of her hands and whispered, 'My Cherie, how sad for you.'

'It was a long time ago. When I left school, I worked in the haberdashery shop with mother. Until the enemy bombing raid, which killed her and destroyed our home and livelihood. Then I came to live with my aunt and uncle at the inn.' She didn't tell him that she'd never known of her aunt's existence until then.

'What about you, Emile, where did you grow up?'

'On my parents' farm with my four brothers and two sisters. I was the youngest. My sisters married and moved away. Two brothers joined the navy and the older two have businesses in Paris.' He didn't tell her that they were both involved in the resistance movement. One ran a printing press, and the other ran a bar, which the Germans frequented.

'Tell me about your little girl, Juliette. From your picture of her, she has your eyes and dark hair.'

He ran his hand through his hair, his brow furrowing. 'I worry about her safety, having not heard from my parents nor from my friends on the next farm. It is a long time since I last saw her and I wonder if she will remember me? I have written to both parties and given your address and they also have my army address.' He paused a moment, thinking, then he blurted, 'If anything happens to me, if I am taken prisoner or if . . .' He couldn't finish the sentence. Across the table, he looked directly into Charlotte's eyes. 'Will you take care of Juliette for me?'

She saw the raw fear in his eyes and without hesitation she was by his side, enfolding him into her arms. Her voice clear, she replied, 'I will look after Juliette until you come home.'

149

She felt his body shudder, and she held him until he stilled, and then she whispered, 'Come, we'll have an early night.' She led him into her bedroom.

In the early hours of the morning, Charlotte was still awake, holding Emile in her arms, listening to the rhythm of his breathing and inhaling his male scent. Now and then he would cry out, muttering in his mother tongue, which she didn't understand. His English was better than her French and she wondered what it would be like to live in France. Though she couldn't imagine living under German occupation. She shuddered at the thought, unable to imagine the terror and uncertainty the people must be suffering. Her thoughts drifted to Juliette. She must be three or four years of age. Did she have a carefree childhood? Charlotte doubted it. She knew Emile worried about his daughter, the uncertainty of whether or not she was safe. He was many miles away from her and preparing for battle. He hadn't mentioned it, but there were rumours in the village of a big campaign about to be launched. When and where, no one knew.

Emile stirred in her arms and opened his eyes. 'Are you awake, Charl?' he whispered.

'Yes,' she murmured, pushing back his tousled hair from his face, and kissed him gently on the lips.

This simple loving act aroused him, and they made love slowly, both taking in every touch of the intimate parts of their bodies to imprint on their minds so as not to forget.

'I love you, Charl, with all my heart. When this damned war is over, I will bring Juliette to meet you.' He propped himself up on his elbow to look into her eyes. 'You have made my life so happy.'

She traced her forefinger around his lips and whispered, 'I was lonely until you came into my life. I feel you are now part of me. I couldn't imagine my life without you.'

He buried his face in her breasts, and she felt the wetness of his tears. She held him close, never wanting to let him go, but knowing she must.

CHAPTER TWENTY-TWO

March 1944

Charlotte hurried to Jack's cottage. This was her last chance to see Emile alone. He'd sent word to her that his departure was imminent and that he had one hour to collect his gear from Jack's cottage. As she ran down the garden path, Jip came bounding down to meet her, and Jack poked his head out from his workshop and smiled at her. 'Go right in, Emile's waiting.'

'Bless you, Jack.' She stepped through the open doorway into an empty kitchen. For one wild, panicky moment, she thought he'd already gone.

'Charl.'

He appeared before her. Her heart beat rapidly as he wrapped her in his arms, and she breathed in his heady scent of fresh soap. Their lips touched, so sweet and gentle at first, and then with an overwhelming urgency of passion, the flame between them ignited. She could feel the roughness of his uniform through her thin dress as their bodies melded together in desperation not to be parted. Their kisses deepened. His hands roamed her body, as if he was committing it to memory.

The sound of a vehicle screeching to a halt and the blare of a horn interrupted their passion. They clung together. She didn't want to let go, burying her face in the comfort of his chest, feeling the beat of his heart against hers, ignoring the blast of the horn again. Emile whispered, 'My Cherie, I have to go.' Gently they drew apart, looking deep into each other's eyes.

'Take care, my darling Emile. Part of me will always be with you,' she whispered, tracing a finger across his lips.

'I love you, Cherie.' Their gazes still held. He kissed her once more, a sweet, lingering kiss. Finally, stepping away to pick up his gear on the floor near the door, he turned to her, 'Write to me.'

'I will.' She wanted to fling herself into his arms and never let him go, instead she whispered what she felt. 'I love you.'

She stood on the doorstep until the drone of the engine could no longer be heard. Back inside, she sank into a chair, letting the sobs she'd held back until now consume her. Her tears flowed and flowed, her heart sodden with grief, for she didn't know if she would ever see him again.

She didn't hear Jack come in and put the kettle on to boil. It wasn't until she felt Jip nuzzle against her bare legs that she became aware of Jack placing a mug of tea on the table before her. 'Sorry,' she sniffed, feeling in the pocket of her dress for a handkerchief, which she couldn't find.

'Here.' Jack pushed one of his big white ones into her hand. 'Now drink your tea, lass,' he said softly.

The tea tasted warm and sweet, with a strong flavour of whisky. She sipped it slowly while trying to regain her composure, staring into the mug and not lifting her eyes, grateful that Jack remained silent. By the time she'd drained the mugful of liquid, her heartbeat had steadied. She looked up and watched Jack light his pipe and wondered what he thought of the war. He had fought in the Great War. The war to end all wars, so it had been said.

He never spoke of it, except once he mentioned he'd been gassed, which affected his eyes, and he had spent time in a hospital at Barry Island, in Wales.

She closed her eyes and rested, trying to free her mind.

Jack stirred in his chair. 'Before I forget, Emile has left you a letter. It's on the dresser.'

Quickly, Charlotte sat upright and glanced in that direction, not having noticed it before, but then she'd been too preoccupied. She rose, crossed to the dresser and picked up the envelope addressed to her. She thought about reading it later in her quarters, but she couldn't wait that long. Sinking back on her chair she carefully, with her little finger, slit it open, drew out the single sheet of paper and read.

Darling Charl, You are the brightest light in my life, making it bearable while I have been stationed in Mornington. It is my greatest wish, God willing, that I return to you after the war. You gave yourself willingly to me and so I carry a part of you wherever I am. Write to me and tell me what you are doing and also tell me about the children you care for. If only my daughter Juliette was safe with you. Before I return to you, I must find my daughter and see how my parents are. I must pray and hope they are somewhere safe.

You have their address and I have sent them yours. I have also written my address and you see my battalion is with the Americans under the command of General Paton. I will be constantly on the move though at some stage your letters will reach me and mine will reach you.

Darling Charl, do not forget me. I send you a thousand kisses.

With all my love, Emile

The words danced and merged as tears threatened. Tenderly, she slipped the letter back in its envelope. As if sensing her sadness, Jip got up from where he was lying at his master's feet, ambled over to her and nuzzled against her leg. She patted and stroked his coat, feeling his comforting warmth.

She stayed with Jack for a while longer, for she knew he would miss Emile's company too.

'Aye, I shall miss our discussions and his companionship. I've learned a lot about tanks, something I'd never owt to do with in the Great War.'

They sat in silence and Charlotte wished she could come more often to see Jack but, working more hours, it was difficult and Jack wasn't up to walking to Mornington House.

Then she had an idea. 'Jack, would you be willing to teach some of the older boys about woodwork in your workshop?'

His face lit up. 'Aye, I could do that, lass. Maybe two at a time.'

'After school or on a weekend perhaps. I'll have a word with Mr Grahame.'

'That'll be summat to look forward to.'

As she walked back to Mornington House, she felt much easier at leaving Jack alone.

His neighbours were kind and shopped for him and one now did his washing, but he was always happiest in his workshop and the lads would be company for him, plus he would teach them a useful skill.

She discussed this venture with Mr Grahame and he agreed to go and see Jack and inspect the workshop. And then they could ask the lads if anyone was interested. She had another idea too, but best to wait and see.

The routine of tea, hobby time and bedtime for the children kept Charlotte busy for the rest of the day. She was in demand to read a bedtime story to the little ones. 'Rupert the Bear,' they chorused.

This was their favourite story, and they never grew tired of listening to what antics Rupert and his friends got up to.

'I didn't know that story was in the book,' queried Laura.

Charlotte put her finger on her lips and whispered to her, 'I make it up, inventing more bears and stories.'

Laura laughed.

Later Charlotte was in her quarters where it was quiet and sat down on her bed to read Emile's letter again. She read it again and again, until she'd absorbed every word he'd written.

Fully clothed, she rested her head on the pillow Emile had used, breathing in his lingering scent, and closed her eyes. Sleeping fitfully until the early hours of the morning, she woke up and reached out for Emile, only for her hand to fall into emptiness. She lay still for a while, thinking of him, reliving their time together in this bed making love until her head whirled. Finally, she drifted into a restless sleep, waking up with a headache. Slowly she rose from the bed and pulled off her crumpled skirt and blouse, and slipped on her dressing gown. In the kitchen, she raked the ashes in the fire-grate and added a small log. Hopefully it would catch alight.

Shivering, she sat in the chair and wrapped her arms round her body, hugging warmth into herself. Eventually, the log sparked and a welcome glow appeared.

She made a hot drink of cocoa and assembled her writing pad, pen and ink. She sat down at the table and began to write to Emile. He'd been gone only a short time and already she missed him.

My darling Emile, I miss you. I miss your smile, your lips and your hand in mine. Suddenly I feel empty. You've left a void in my life that no one but you can fill.
Take care, my darling, and be safe wherever you are. Come home to me.

Sobs choked her and tears splashed onto the paper. She couldn't write any more.

Daylight showed through a chink in the blackout curtains. A new day dawned. Quickly she washed and dressed and donned her outdoor clothes. A walk through the grounds in the fresh morning air would help clear her head.

She meandered through the woods, hearing the dawn chorus of birdsong and noticing the fresh new leaves on the trees, a sign of spring in the air. Everything that had lain dormant over the past few months was now beginning to wake up with renewed energy. And yet, the war raged on, oblivious to the seasons, hell-bent only on destruction. And what for; the supremacy of power of one stupid man. She kicked a broken tree branch into the undergrowth, and some poor creature scuttled away. Oh, dear, she admonished herself, behave and think of the children. The care and welfare of the children must be her main concern.

Reaching the end of the wood near the pond, she shaded her eyes from the morning sun.

Then she stopped in her tracks, surprised to see one of the boys sitting by the pond, his head bent low, staring into the water.

She wondered why he was here so early and all alone. This part of the pond wasn't fenced off. Silently, not wanting to startle him, she moved nearer, and then she noticed the glistening of tears on his cheeks. She stood perfectly still, not wanting to intrude and yet she was concerned about him being upset. Was it something which had happened here at Mornington House? Or was it to do with the traumas suffered in his past life? Sometimes the children had the odd nightmare and woke up screaming, but never Philippe to the best of her knowledge. Perhaps he kept what had happened to him sewn-up inside himself.

Tentatively, she took a step forward and her Wellington boot caught a pebble hidden in the grass, which trotted down the slight slope into the pond with a splash. Immediately, the boy's head swung round. Seeing Charlotte, he made to scramble up, but she was too quick for him. She slid down next to him, saying, 'Good morning, Philippe, may I join you?' She didn't expect an answer, so instead she stared into the pond. The clear water reflected her face, and also Philippe's face, so that she could see his eyes. Large, sad, haunted eyes. She recalled that, like the other children now in their care, Philippe had survived by living in bombed-out ruins, scavenging for food. All these children's parents had been killed or simply disappeared. A woman they called Auntie had rescued them and brought them on a perilous journey via Switzerland and then by boat to England and arranged for them to come to Mornington House. Auntie had also organised and paid for the care of the children and the upkeep of the house and staff. This she'd learned from

Mrs Carlton-Jones. Charlotte wondered who this woman called Auntie was.

A plop in the water broke the quietness of the still morning air. 'Was that a fish?' she asked Philippe, not expecting a response.

'A water hen,' he replied, pointing to the right of her.

She followed his direction. Seeing a clump of tall grasses and reeds, she focused her eyes and spied a brood of water hens. 'Ah, sorry,' she said, 'did I disturb them?'

'I suppose,' he mumbled.

They sat in silence, both staring down at the gentle sway of the water. Its therapeutic nuances had a calming effect, and she felt the tension and sadness of being parted from Emile relax a little.

Then into the peaceful atmosphere came the rumbling sound of Philippe's empty stomach. A look of horror filled his thin face. Charlotte laughed. 'That is just how I feel. Hungry! Let's have an early breakfast.' Carefully, so as not to slither down into the pond, she got to her feet, while Philippe just scampered up.

In the kitchen, Mrs Jolly was already putting on a big pan of porridge oats. 'You're early birds,' she announced.

'Yes, we've been nature-studying.' Charlotte didn't mention the pond, which was out of bounds for the children. 'And now we are starving.'

'Breakfast isn't ready yet, but you can toast some bread on yon stove. I've got a pot of tea made.'

'Come on, Philippe, I'll show you how,' Charlotte said. She cut four thick slices of bread from the loaf and sat Philippe in front of the stove with the bread speared on the long-handle fork. His thin, pale face soon became rosy from the fire, and he smiled, his eyes lighting up at his accomplishment. She watched him tucking into the toast and enjoying it, and wondered if he would like to learn woodwork with Jack. Maybe it would help to lessen the anxiety he was obviously suffering from after what had taken place in his home country. She sighed inwardly at the pointlessness of war.

CHAPTER TWENTY-THREE

April 1944

Almost all the boys expressed an interest in going to Jack's shed for woodwork lessons.

Mr Grahame looked thoughtful as he and Charlotte discussed which boys would best benefit.

They sat in the empty dining room; the children were at school, Mrs Jolly and Mrs Grahame were in the kitchen and the volunteers were upstairs tidying bedrooms.

'Jack's elderly, so we need lads who'll behave, so not the two rascals who are always fighting. I think they would be better joining the local lads' football sessions, and use up some of their energy. I'll have a word with the coach.' Mr Grahame scratched his thick thatch of dark hair. 'What about Gilbert and Philippe, they're sensible lads?' He looked at Charlotte for approval, valuing her opinion.

'Yes, good choice. And the other lads are happy helping Tom with the gardening. I hear they have their own plots to grow vegetables.' Charlotte rose to her feet, saying, 'I'm going to have a word with the three ladies, to see if some of the girls can visit their home, for a taste of village life outside Mornington House.'

Twenty minutes later, Charlotte sat drinking tea and eating cake in Dot's parlour with May and Edna. 'Saturday afternoon is best for us,' said May. 'It will save me legs going up to the big house. Besides, I think the girls will like a change.'

'We'll get to know them better,' mused Edna.

They started chatting about what the girls might like. 'Knitting, crocheting and embroidery for starters, then they might have their own ideas.'

'You are so kind,' Charlotte said. 'The girls will love coming.' They chatted some more about the children and crafts.

Then Edna asked, 'Have you been to the inn and seen your aunt and uncle?'

Feeling guilty, Charlotte replied, 'No.' She'd been far too busy even to think about them.'

She glanced at her watch, saying, 'I can pop in and see them now.' Bidding farewell to the ladies, she dashed to the inn.

Pushing open the door, she stepped inside. George looked across from the bar. 'Hey, Hilda, look what the wind has blown in.'

Wiping her hands on her apron, Hilda appeared from the kitchen, and Charlotte was surprised to see her face light up. 'Nice to see you, lass.'

Coming to the bar, Charlotte perched on a stool. 'I was nearby so thought I'd come and see how you are doing.'

'Busy as ever,' George said.

She could see the glint in his eyes, which registered the pound, shilling and pence signs.

Then he surprised her by pouring her a small tot of sherry. She told them about the children, and the hobbies they were organising. 'Just something different from school lessons and to integrate them into village life and make them feel welcome.' Then the conversation lapsed, and she left.

There was just time to go and see Jack. Calling at the bakery, she bought a large rabbit and potato pie for him.

He was sitting in his chair, reading the newspaper. 'I like to keep an eye open to see where Emile's lot is. I think something is brewing and it aint tea.'

'He's not in danger, is he?' she said, a shudder running through her body.

'Nay, lass. I didn't mean to upset you. No. I was just interested in how his battalion is getting on. By that smells good,' he said as she produced the pie.

Later that evening, after the children's bedtime routine, and the story telling, Charlotte retired to her rooms for a few hours as it was her turn to do the midnight shift. There were four volunteers who helped, plus her and the Grahames. Some of the children still had the occasional nightmare, and someone needed to be on hand when they woke up, frightened and confused, to comfort and reassure them that they were safe.

She didn't bother to light a fire, and draped a shawl round her shoulders. Collecting pen, ink and paper, she sat at the table and wrote.

My darling Emile,
I hope and pray you are safe and well. Today I visited Jack, and he has so kindly agreed to teach two of the boys woodwork. This is helpful for his morale because he feels his cottage is lonely without you for company.

She told him about the children, ending with . . .

I miss you so much, wherever you are, think of me as I am thinking of you and somewhere in the great night sky full of stars, our love will meet and light up.

My love and my heart are forever yours.
Charl xxxx

As she read what she'd written, a single tear splashed down onto the paper and as she gazed at it, her teardrop formed into the shape of a star on the word light.

The night was relatively trouble free and only one of the small girls, Maria, woke up crying for her mother. Charlotte enfolded her close, whispering soothing words of comfort.

'Shush, my sweet one, you are safe with me.' She rocked Maria in her arms until her breathing became regular and sleep settled on her. Gently, she tucked the sleeping girl back into her bed, leaving her sucking her thumb.

Checking the other children were not disturbed, she returned to the small staff room.

Furnished with a daybed, small table and chair, it was adequate for its needs. Sitting down at the table, she picked up the pieces of material she was fashioning into a portrait of Emile. As she worked, she thought of every feature of his face, his lively brown eyes, sometimes too sad, his full sensual lips, the craggy lines on his face. As she thought of him, a tingle of excitement ran through her body and she closed her eyes, reliving his touch on her skin as he caressed her.

'Quite a likeness,' came the soft voice of Mrs Grahame, who had quietly entered into the room.

For a moment, Charlotte was startled. 'Is it that time already?'

Mrs Grahame checked the log book. 'Just wee Maria?'

'Yes, she soon settled.'

'It makes me wonder how many more children there are in war-torn Europe who have no one to care for them,' Mrs Grahame mused.

Then Charlotte voiced Emile's fears. 'Emile hasn't heard from his parents in a long time and he's anxious to hear news of his daughter, Juliette. He's concerned for their safety so he's given me their address and sent mine to them in case his letters are held up.'

'As a friend of Emile's, why don't you write to them yourself?'

Charlotte couldn't disagree with Mrs Grahame. Back in her quarters after a quick breakfast and before she caught up on her sleep, she settled down to write to Emile's parents.

Miss Charlotte Kirby Mornington House, Mornington,
East Yorkshire, England.

21 April, 1944.

Delmas Ferme Oradour-sur-Glane France

Dear Madame and Monsieur Delmas,
I am a friend of your son, Emile, who has been stationed
in my village. I know he is concerned for your safety and his
daughter Juliette's safety as well, having not heard from you
for a long time. Have you received Emile's letters?

If you wish to write to me, I can find out the whereabouts of
Emile's battalion and pass your letter on to him.

I do hope you are all well.

With sincere wishes,
Charlotte Kirby.

She sat and pondered, wondering if her words were
adequate. She didn't want to infringe on any laws or add
to Emile's worries, though she knew the letter or parts of it
could be censored. She addressed the envelope and before she
could change her mind, she slipped on her coat and hurried
to the post office. On the way home, it occurred to her that
Emile's parents might not understand English, but hopefully
someone in the village would read the letter to them.

The children enjoyed having activities away from the
house, it gave them, apart from school lessons, a chance to
mix with the villagers on a more informal basis. Charlotte
noted in the children's journal that they seemed more relaxed
and happier. Philippe and Gilbert were busy creating small
wooden boxes, which could be stored under their beds,
to keep some of their private bits and pieces in. And she
could tell by Jack's beaming face that he relished the boys'

company. Six girls went to the three ladies, who made them welcome with baking treats and their knowledge of handicrafts. Mr Grahame enrolled the older boys to play football on a Saturday afternoon. Tom, the gardener, and his small band of helpers were happy with their own tiny plot to cultivate. The girls liked flowers, and Tom had explained to them that the runner bean produced red flowers so they appeared satisfied. Sometimes on a Sunday afternoon, a couple of the ARP wardens came and organised a game of rounders. Charlotte felt her heart burst with delight to see the children so happy and gaining their own independent identities. The girls were confident enough now to walk to the ladies on their own. This enabled Charlotte to help Mrs Grahame with the preparation of the tea, as Saturday afternoon was Mrs Jolly's time off. Tea today consisted of sandwiches, lettuce and radish, which were grown by Tom under his coldframes, and savoury dripping, a favourite of the children. It was made from the cooked meat juices cooled and set in a paste and easily spread on chunks of homemade bread. Mrs Jolly had baked a huge pile of jam tarts, enough for the children's supper.

Hands washed, the children eagerly sat at the dining room table. 'There's two boys missing, not returned from football,' said Mr Grahame. He went outside to see if they were loitering. He walked down the drive to scan the roadway, but it was deserted. Thinking they might be in the woodland area, he called their names. 'Maurice, Jacques.' The only answer was wood pigeons, cooing and then taking fright in case it was a farmer and his gun. Puzzled, he went into the house to ask the other boys if they knew of their whereabouts. Eyes cast down, they shook their heads.

Mr Grahame contacted the football coach, who had no knowledge of the two boys attending the game. 'I must call the police.' Deep lines furrowed his brow, as he turned to Charlotte.

Twenty minutes later, Constable Ganton, the village bobby who was long past retirement-age, rode up on his bike, puffing and panting. Soon settled on a chair with a mug of tea and his notebook and pencil at the ready, he barked, 'Description of lads.'

'Both about 4ft 9inches, one dark haired the other brown, wearing short grey trousers and navy jerseys,' said Mr Grahame.

'Carrying anything?'

Charlotte rushed into the room. She'd just checked on the boys' belongings.

'They've taken a rucksack and their pocket money allowance, and I suspect they raided the pantry for food.'

'So, a planned adventure,' the constable wrote in his notebook. He rose to his feet. 'I will alert all stations and the wardens. They won't get far.'

By nightfall there were still no sightings of the boys. Mr Grahame and Charlotte took it in turns to patrol the grounds, hoping they might be hiding and waiting to sneak into the house. Long past midnight, Mr Grahame told Charlotte to get some sleep for a few hours.

In her quarters, she slipped into bed, not sure if she would sleep, but she did. Four hours later, she was woken up by the bell on the alarm clock ringing. Hastily she washed and dressed and went to find Mr Grahame. He was in the dining room, walking around the table and smoking. His face was ashen.

'Any news?' Charlotte asked.

'Nothing! And I'm shattered.'

'You go and get some rest.'

Alone, she stood at the dining-room window, watching the new day dawning and wondering what Sunday would bring. She made a cup of tea and went outside.

Standing on the drive, the stillness of silence surrounded her, and her thoughts wandered.

Thankfully, the night had been dry, so if the boys had spent the night outside, they probably wouldn't have caught a chill. If they'd gone towards Driffield, there were a few barns and doorways to shelter in. Then her heart missed a beat. What if they had sneaked onto the train and gone to Hull? A city of bombed ruins and pitfalls and the danger of an air raid. They shouldn't have to witness such atrocities again, not in their young lives. The other direction they could have gone was the coast. But that would be heavily guarded and fortified against enemy attack.

Different scenarios whizzed round in her head, making it ache. She gave a deep sigh and closed her eyes. She heard the distant sound of a cockerel crowing, then she heard the engine of a vehicle, or was it her mind playing hopscotch. She listened as the engine sound drew nearer. She opened her eyes to see an army jeep turn into the drive.

It halted and next to the driver sat a boy huddled in a blanket. She hurried forward to look into the tear-stained face of Maurice. The soldier jumped down and lifted the boy out, carrying him in his arms, and followed Charlotte inside.

'Where is Jacques?' she asked.

'Hospital, miss. Broken leg, I fear,' the soldier answered, as he lowered Maurice gently onto a chair.

'Where were they found?'

'On the cliffs at Hornsea. They were trying to scramble down to the beach when Jacques slipped and fell onto a concrete sea defence.'

By now, both Mr and Mrs Grahame had come into the kitchen and more questioning followed. After refreshments, and grateful thanks, the soldier went. Maurice had breakfast, bathed and was now tucked up in bed. Mr Grahame went to the Cottage Hospital in Driffield to see Jacques. It seems they had been seeking adventure, but it could have been so much worse, Charlotte thought. She'd write a light-hearted letter to Emile, of the lads' escapade, and cheerful happenings in the village.

CHAPTER TWENTY-FOUR

Free French 2nd Armoured Battalion, June 1944

Emile concentrated on the task ahead, though at first, the engaging smile of Charlotte and her adoring eyes played on his mind. Now, after many months of training and equipped with the American M4 Sherman tank, under the command of General Leclerc and the American General Patton, Emile, along with his comrades, was ready to take part in the action. Everything was executed with precision and the coordination of the Army, Navy and Air Force. They spent four days at a southern port in England, attending briefings and checking equipment until finally, they were ready to move. The weather was foul on 4 June and the crossing of the English Channel was delayed.

Finally, they were able to make the crossing. They landed on a Normandy beach on 6 June for the D-Day landing, Operation Overlord, combining sea, air and land troops of the Allied forces on French soil. Their objective — to liberate France from the Nazis, had begun. They landed in heavy gunfire from emplacements overlooking the beaches, which were mined and covered with obstacles and barbed wire, making the work of the clearing team dangerous.

Finally, the 2nd Armoured Battalion touched down on home soil. Emile felt a weird sense of exhilaration flood his mind and body. His training, and hopes and dreams of returning to Free France was now being put to the test. He jumped down from the tank to feel the soft earth beneath his boots. On his knees, he dug his fingers into the soil, lifting up handfuls, letting it run through his fingers, smelling its earthy scent, and tears of joy pricked his tired eyes. Looking up to the bright blue sky, he thought of his comrades who were killed in battle and wanted their lives not to have been lost in vain. With that thought in mind, the tiredness swept away from him and he felt a new surge of energy sweep through his mind and body. He climbed back on the tank and moved forward to concentrate on the ongoing campaign of defeating the hated enemy, the Germans and to drive them from his country.

Over the following days they rumbled through towns and villages, passing through Sainte-Mère-Eglise where they received a joyous welcome from its inhabitants, who had flocked from their bombed homes and cellars, so pleased to see their home troops driving away the enemy. Though sometimes the German divisions sneaked back in and were still fighting and trying to regain control of areas, the enemy regime was fast losing control of the war, and was in full retreat. The Free French continued on through their homeland, their main objective to rid France of the Nazi occupiers.

* * *

The village of Oradour-sur-Glane was where Emile grew up and his parents still lived on their farm there. Although it was in the occupied zone of France, the villagers went about their daily lives seemingly indifferent to the German occupation. Secretly, the villagers would hide anyone with Resistance connections, but they never spoke about it. A careless word and someone, however innocently, might tell the Nazis. The Resistance was successfully active in the region and the Nazis ruthlessly sought to crush them by whatever means possible. Everyone knew how, in retaliation for an attack on them, the Nazis had hanged nearly a hundred men from the village of Tulle.

On a quiet day, 10 June 1944, the people of Oradour-sur-Glane went about their daily business, chatting in the street. An ill man was made comfortable in his bed by his carer.

About midday, without warning, the German motorised infantry, 4th SS-Panzergrenadier, advanced on the village and rounded up the villagers, even the ill man, in the market square.

Wondering what was happening, they stood in the village square, whispering in hushed tones. Then, brutally, the SS began separating them.

The men were herded into barns and locked in. Callously, the SS set fire to the barns, burning them to death, showing no mercy. Then the SS drove the women and children into the church, locking them in. Then they committed a most barbaric assault by throwing grenades through the church windows, torching them to death, and shooting those who tried to escape the flames. All were killed, including seven Jewish refugees. Only a handful of villagers survived with terrible injuries. And one child.

The child shivered, squeezing shut her eyes, frightened of the darkness and being squashed into this tightly earth-packed hole. She sucked on her thumb, trying to stop herself from crying. Grand'Mère would be cross with her. She had told her to be good and quiet until she came back for her. But Grand'Mère had been gone a long time. The angry bad men's voices, the shouting, guns firing, and the screams of terror had now stopped. The smell of burning filled her nostrils, hurting her throat, and she stopped sucking her thumb to clamp her mouth shut, not daring to cough. Her tiny body convulsed. She wanted Grand'Mère to come and take her from this horrible hole. Her empty stomach rumbled with hunger. Where was Grand'Mère? After a while, exhausted and frightened, she drifted into an uneasy sleep.

She awoke at the sound of a woman's voice. 'Grand'Mère,' she sobbed as a pair of strong arms pulled her free of the hole and held her close. But it wasn't Grand'Mère.

'What's your name?' the woman asked softly.

She tried to speak, but no words would come. And then she remembered her grand'mère hastily pinning the letter inside her coat pocket, and she pointed to it. The kind woman carefully extracted the flimsy envelope and glanced swiftly at the letter. She gasped out loud on reading the address. The child looked up, seeing the lady had tears in her eyes.

The feel of the protective arm was still around her as the woman carried her towards a waiting horse and cart, whispering soothing words 'You are safe now, Juliette.'

A man with white whiskers sat holding the reins. The woman hoisted her into the smelly cart and climbed in herself. Frightened that the bad men would come again, she closed her eyes, wanting her beloved grand'mère.

They arrived at the next village and she was taken into a small house and bathed and dressed in clean clothes: undergarments, dress, pinafore and woollen socks and boots. Then she sat on a stool at the table and was given a dish of porridge and tumbler of milk. Across the table sat three solemn-faced children, wide eyed, staring at her. She concentrated on drinking her milk.

'What your name?' asked the oldest child, a boy of about eight.

She hung her head, eyes brimming with tears as she stared into the half drunken tumbler of milk.

'She can't speak,' chanted the boy.

'Behave, she's in shock,' scolded his mother.

'Is she an orphan?' He had an inquisitive mind.

'No, her father is fighting in the war.'

'Can I go and fight?'

'Stop asking silly questions and go and do your chores.'

He slid off his stool, muttering to himself, 'When I'm older I'm going to run away.'

After spending two days with the family, Juliette Delmas was collected by the lady who had rescued her from the hole in the ground. As the woman took hold of her hand, Juliette struggled, and a strange guttural sound erupted from her mouth, 'Gaarr . . .' Wildly she looked round for Grand'Mère, trying to break free, but the woman held her close and Juliette sobbed, her heart breaking.

The same man with the horse and cart came to collect them. Once they were settled in, the cart moved off. Gently, the woman eased Juliette away from her so she could look into her face and said softly, 'Your grand'mère has gone to heaven to be with your mère.'

Hiccupping and rubbing away her tears, she asked, 'Will they come back to me?'

The woman, knowing the sorrow of losing loved ones, had no answer for the grief-stricken child. What she did know was that, whatever it took, she would take Juliette to the safety of England, and to Miss Charlotte Kirby of Mornington House.

'I am looking after you now. I am Auntie.' Trustingly, Juliette gazed into the woman's eyes.

Auntie had secured the necessary documents to travel, if they were stopped by the Germans.

Hopefully, not. The plan was to rendezvous on a field doubling as an airstrip, where they would be airlifted to England. The Germans were losing the war, and with the unpredictability of their erratic movements and their indiscriminate massacre of the villagers of Oradour-sur-Glane, they could appear at any time. If the flight escape was blocked, it meant they would have to take the greater risk of travelling overland until they reached a safe port and a boat to England. Auntie smiled briefly.

They said she was mad, perhaps, but her heart ruled not her head. And she was determined not to fail. Her life didn't matter anymore, but the life of Juliette Delmas did.

Their lift was as far as the next village. 'We must walk, now, little one,' Auntie told her, as they scrambled from the cart, thanking the man. Taking hold of Juliette's hand, she said, 'Shall we see how many flowers and birds we can see?' This distraction worked. Then they heard the drone of a vehicle coming in their direction. Quickly, Auntie pulled

Juliette into the roadside ditch. 'Be quiet,' she muttered. They both lay very still, holding their breaths. They stayed for minutes longer until the sound was gone. Auntie peeped along the road, checking for signs of any other vehicles.

'Come, we can go now.' She brushed down the wet, clogged leaves and other detritus from their clothes and they set off, making for a farmhouse where they hoped to spend the night. But when they were in sight of the farmhouse, Auntie could see a Nazi vehicle parked outside. She took a route bypassing the farmhouse and when Juliette could walk no more, their only option was to sleep under a hedge. They ate the bread and cheese Auntie had brought with them and sipped water.

A field mouse came to nibble at the crumbs, and Juliette giggled when Auntie shooed him away. Auntie waited until Juliette slept, then closed her eyes, only half sleeping, aware of their vulnerability. At first light, she woke up Juliette. 'Time to move on,' she whispered, handing the water bottle to her.

The next night they were more fortunate. They stayed in a quiet village in a house next to the church. They had hot soup and bread for supper, a clean bed to sleep in, and the luxury of soap and water for a wash. Juliette cuddled up to Auntie, wrapping her arms around her neck.

They were a comfort for each other. While Juliette slept, Auntie thought of her lost ones.

At dawn, the next day, they moved on, keeping to the lesser used roads, though at one time a motorcycle came speeding along and they hid behind bushes until it passed from sight.

They had short stops to eat and drink, and at one point, Auntie gave Juliette a piggy-back, mindful of the rendezvous time.

In the darkness, Auntie and Juliette waited on the edge of a coppice. Two men from the local resistance were in attendance. All listening for the drone of the pickup plane, and alert for Germans, who wouldn't hesitate to kill them.

They strained their ears, picking up the faint muffled sound low in the sky. The resistance men lit the flares, mapping the landing area. Within seconds of landing, Auntie and Juliette were scrambled up into the aircraft. Juliette was surprised to see a man and a woman run from the shelter of trees and climb aboard too. No one spoke. They were airborne. The whole operation had taken only a few minutes.

Juliette clung to Auntie, frightened of the big sky bird. She shut her eyes tight, not liking this strange sensation in her tummy and feeling sick with panic. Auntie give her a sip of water, and she felt a little better.

A sudden bump, bump, woke Juliette up, startling her. 'We've landed,' soothed Auntie, and gave her another sip of water.

Juliette was told to jump, and she landed in the big safe arms of a man. She asked, 'Are you my daddy?' because Grand'Mère had told her she had a daddy, but she couldn't remember what he looked like. The man said something to her in a strange language, which she didn't understand, but it sounded nice, so she snuggled into him.

They had landed at an RAF station in the south of England and were whisked away by a transport truck to London. Here they were met by a member of the Women's Voluntary Services, recognisable in her smart uniform of dark green tweed jacket displaying her badge, skirt and felt hat. She supplied them with refreshments of sandwiches, tea and milk, and the use of a bed and facilities in a hostel.

Later, the next morning, Auntie washed Juliette and combed her hair, and found her a nice blue ribbon to lift her curls off her face. Holding up a face mirror, she said, 'You look bonny, Juliette. Today and tonight, we will stay here until your papers are in order, and then . . .' her voice faltered. She swallowed hard and continued, 'We go to Mornington House.' She felt lightheaded and sat down heavily on the bed, her head in her hands. She wasn't sure she could do this.

Just then, she felt a light movement and Juliette was by her side, holding the metal water container. Gratefully, she sipped, tears springing into her eyes at the simple thoughtfulness of a child so young. She leaned forward, hugging the child, feeling her warm little body bring comfort to her. Oh, hell, she thought, I'm going to miss this lovely little girl. Then suddenly her professionalism kicked in and she regained her composure. But her pain remained.

CHAPTER TWENTY-FIVE

June 1944

Charlotte and Joyce set off on their bikes to the Majestic Cinema in Driffield. They were going to see a Fred Astaire film, *You Were Never Lovelier*, staring the glamourous star with a mane of red hair, Rita Hayworth.

'If only I looked like her,' Joyce sighed in a dreamy voice. 'Then I could have any airman I fancied.'

There was usually a B film showing first, and they weren't too fussed about seeing it.

Charlotte's stomach was rumbling and as she hadn't eaten since breakfast, she suggested, 'Shall we have a pot of tea and a bun first?' She loved her job, caring for the children, but she needed a few hours' respite once a week to top up her energy levels.

She thought of the children, and how well they were behaving, almost like normal children, mischievous at times, but enjoying playing. Though for some of the children, the terror they had witnessed would always be hidden deep within them. The Mornington House children seemed to have integrated and settled in well with the village children, except for a few skirmishes at school, the odd fight breaking out between the boys. 'It's normal for lads to have a scrap,' Mr Grahame assured her.

'Come on, dreamboat, or we won't get a table!' Joyce and Charlotte parked their bikes at the back of the café. They were in luck; a couple were just vacating their table.

Charlotte rubbed the back of her leg muscles, saying, 'That head wind was strong. Do yours hurt?'

Joyce laughed. 'Nope, I'm used to hard graft, and pedalling a bike is no hardship. You're a softy.'

Charlotte laughed too and soon they were tucking into slices of Victoria Sandwich cake and drinking hot tea. Feeling better for the refreshments, they went to the cinema.

They were squashed in the middle of a row, squeezing past men smoking cigarettes, and well-padded women, munching on dripping sandwiches. Giggling, they fell into their seats amid hushing noises. Charlotte bit on her lip to quell her laughter.

They settled down to watch the divine dancing of Fred Astaire and Rita Hayworth and the spectacular trappings of the glamour of Hollywood, both of them sighing with envy when it ended. 'I could watch it all again,' a wistful Joyce sighed.

'I could as well. It gave me a real feel-good factor, something I've missed since Emile went.'

'Come to the next dance with me and I'll introduce you to a dashing young airman.'

'No, I couldn't.'

'It's only fun. A kiss or two. It isn't as though you're training to be a nun.'

'Shush,' a woman poked them from behind as the Pathé News began. It was the account of the D-Day Landings in Normandy, involving all the allied forces, sea, air and land.

Charlotte froze in horror as she watched the fierce air fighting and the firing of naval guns, protecting the forces and the magnified sound of warfare seem to burn her ears.

She watched the troops coming ashore to stop the Nazis raining more terror on the French women, men and children.

She shifted to the edge of her seat, watching the tanks rumbling on to dry land. Her heart fluttered and her whole body tensed, knowing Emile was there. She strained her eyes just to see if she could catch a glimpse of him as he landed on his homeland. She saw him. She was sure of it, his eyes, the turn of his head. As the tanks rumbled away, she almost slipped off the edge of her seat in her attempt to follow him, but the camera moved to another view.

Hoping to catch another sight of Emile, she watched mesmerised as the tanks and troops advanced through towns and villages, cheered by people coming out of cellars where they had been hiding from Nazi attacks. Now, the enemy was retreating, and as they did so, killing indiscriminately anyone they crossed, however innocent, and shelling homes, setting them on fire, Charlotte could empathise with the people of France, for hadn't she seen Hull, the city of her birth, bombed to ruins by the Luftwaffe, killing her beloved mother. She felt hot tears trickle down her cheeks and her heart ached for all those innocent people caught up in one man's mad bid to conquer nations, only succeeding in causing death and destruction. 'That hateful man will never win. Never!'

Watching the Pathé News had upset Charlotte more than she let on to Joyce. So, as they pedalled down the lane towards Mornington, she kept the conversation focused on the glamorous Hollywood film. They separated at the crossroads, Joyce to Huggate's Farm and Charlotte to Mornington House. All was quiet, and she only saw an ARP warden on his nightly patrol checking on anything dodgy. With British Double Summer-time, it was light until eleven o'clock at night. She recalled the only dodgy thing that had happened in the village recently was a group of young lads pretending to be German soldiers and the warden had called out the Home Guard. It was the highlight of village gossip for days, until tragedy occurred. Pilots from a nearby RAF Station, on their way home from a sortie, hit a bank of fog and two planes collided in mid-air, killing all but one of the crew.

Later, as she snuggled down in bed, Charlotte thought of Emile and prayed for his safety and of all those taking part in the Normandy Landings. War to her was senseless. So many people killed and undoubtedly, more would be. Then her thoughts drifted to the children upstairs, whose parents were missing, presumed dead. Orphans of war. So, what did the future hold for them? Hopefully, having a good education would be helpful for them to gain future employment, but children also need a loving home. Perhaps in time, they would be fostered with families. But, she mused, the children of Mornington House belonged to one big family, and she loved them all.

Restless, she couldn't sleep, so wrapping herself in the big woollen dressing-gown given to her by Dot, she quietly tip-toed down the passage and up the stairs to the children's rooms.

She knocked on the staff room door which was opened immediately by Laura.

'Charlotte, what's wrong?' Surprise registered on her face.

'I couldn't sleep,' she replied as Laura opened the door wider and beckoned her inside, putting her knitting of a pixie-hood to one side.

Laura was a sensible girl, Charlotte thought, as she told her about the Pathé News and how upsetting it was. 'I was thinking about the children in our care and their future. Wondering if they have any family to go back to or whether they are totally on their own.' She looked at Laura, and noticed her troubled face. 'Sorry to sound downhearted and burden you with my thoughts.'

Laura gave Charlotte a quick hug, and brushing her brown hair off her face, she said shyly, 'I know what you mean because I also think about what will happen to the children. I love being with them, but Mother said now I am older, I've got to get a proper job and bring home some money.' Tears pooled in her hazel-coloured eyes and she hastily dashed them away. 'I don't want to leave here and the children.'

Charlotte stared at the girl, no longer a girl, but a young woman and a willing worker.

'Laura, you are a great asset to the care of the children. They love you, especially the older ones who you have a special bond with. Would you like me to have a word with Mr and Mrs Grahame?'

Laura's face lit up. 'Would you, Charlotte?'

'Yes, tomorrow.' She glanced at the wall clock. 'I mean today.' She yawned. 'I'd better go back to bed and try to sleep.'

Laura's mind was now on the children. 'I must check on the younger ones. Ruth was restless earlier.'

Charlotte slept deeply for five hours and then she was up and in the main kitchen having a cup of tea with Mrs Grahame before they started preparing breakfast for everyone. She decided to mention Laura's request. Casually she said, 'Last night I couldn't sleep,' and explained about the Pathé News, 'So I went to see Laura and we discussed the children and I learned that her mother is insisting she should now find paid employment. Is it possible that Laura could become a permanent member of staff?' Before Mrs Grahame could reply, Charlotte smelled a strong odour of tobacco smoke and turned swiftly to see Mr Grahame standing in the doorway. 'Good morning,' she wondered to herself how long he'd been standing there.

'Cup of tea, love?' Mrs Grahame lifted up the big brown teapot.

He sat at the table with them and Charlotte asked, 'Did you overhear the conversation?'

He took a long gulp of his mug of tea before he answered. 'It's a good idea, she's a caring girl and good with the children. I would hate to lose her. I'll have to check our budget and seek Mrs Carlton-Jones' approval and then she needs to have a word with whoever controls the purse strings.'

'Would you like me to write Laura a character reference to strengthen her case?'

'Good idea.'

Before Laura went off duty, Charlotte told her what had happened. 'Best not to mention it to your mother until we know the outcome. Though if she asks, tell her you are making enquiries about jobs.'

From the sitting-room window, Charlotte watched Laura walk down the drive with a spring in her step.

Mornington House was funded privately, but who their benefactor was Charlotte had no idea.

Sunday, a day of leisure and, to a certain degree, the children were allowed to follow their own pursuits within the guidelines. Maurice and Jacques made a bogie from old bits of wood and wheels from an old doll's pram, and were happily larking around the grounds on it. Surprisingly, a mixed group of boys and girls were interested in growing vegetables and fruit, so spent their time with Tom the gardener. Some had made friends in the village, and if their whereabouts were approved, they went to visit them. Mostly the younger children went with Charlotte on a ramble through the woods, spotting various flowers and birds. It amazed Charlotte that the children had easily mastered the English language, far more so than she had grasped French.

When she'd asked the headmistress, Miss Holderness, about it, she'd replied, 'Children can learn a language quite quickly if it is spoken daily.' So the language barrier soon came down when speaking to the local people, but often they lapsed into their own language, especially when they were tired or became frustrated.

'Miss Charl, look,' two girls called, running towards the grassland area at the edge of the wood. 'They are pretty.' As Charlotte drew nearer, she could see the grass was covered by late blooming daisies. The girls bent down to touch the delicate flower heads. 'Can we pick them, Miss Charl?' one of the girls asked shyly.

'Yes, and I will show you how to make daisy chains.' So they all settled down on the grass and picked daisies. 'This is what you do,' They watched, fascinated, as she showed them how to make a tiny slit at the end of the stalk. 'Thread a daisy through and repeat.' Charlotte witnessed the wonderment on their faces when the circle was complete, and felt their joy.

She held up the daisy chain and slipped it on her head like a crown. 'Or you can make it longer for a necklace or shorter for a bracelet.'

There was lots of excited laughter as they enthusiastically began and then quiet concentration reigned. Charlotte heard whoops of joy from where the boys were having a rough and tumble with a ball on the grass. She smiled. A perfect idyllic scene, with no hint of the war raging in Europe.

CHAPTER TWENTY-SIX

July to November 1944

After the Normandy assault on the enemy, the tanks of the 2nd Armoured Division quickly moved inland. It warmed Emile's heart to be welcomed by the citizens of France, who cheered their liberators, thronging from their cellars and every conceivable hiding place where they had sheltered from the Germans. As they rolled through the countryside, towns and villages, Emile felt an immense relief at being back on his native French soil. It shocked him to see the horror of the destruction of the villages and towns of his homeland. Although the British had suffered bombing by the Luftwaffe, the devastation hadn't touched them as much as his own country. He had heard stories of people starving and living in ruins. He thought of Charlotte and her work, caring for the refugee orphans. They were the fortunate ones.

As the tanks rumbled on, stopping in darkness to allow them to eat and to catch an odd hour of sleep, Emile heard the tragic news of the massacre of the villagers of Oradour-sur-Glane. Only a handful of people had survived. His beloved daughter Juliette and his beloved parents were not named as survivors. He didn't sleep that night, but sat on the hard ground submerged in his shock and grief. Morning came unnoticed by him. Hatred of the enemy consumed him and he vowed he would fight to the end to kill the murdering Wehrmacht Army. After all, what else did he have to live for?

Then a few days later, a letter from Charlotte caught up with him. The picture of her beautiful face flashed before him, as he read her words of normality, of everyday things in the village and the children in her care. And then she ended the letter with words of love and hope. He closed his eyes, her words helping him to regain his sanity. If only he could feel the warmth of her body in his arms, touching her, remembering her sweet, adoring innocence as she gave herself to him, completely.

As the tanks advanced deeper into France, news came that General de Gaulle was on French soil in the town of Bayeux, where he was greeted with fervour. Also, Emile was surprised to hear that King George of Great Britain was also on French soil, visiting his troops. And it was at the gates of Argentan that they were ordered to advance towards Paris to conduct reconnaissance missions. Paris faced many skirmishes with the enemy, and after the Parisian uprising, this helped to hasten the departure of the Germans. Finally, General Leclerc received the surrender of the German General Dietrich von Choltitz, and on 25 August 1944, the 2nd Armoured Tank Division, under the command of General Leclerc, had the honour of accompanying General de Gaulle as he arrived in Paris to great tumult as he came to liberate Paris from the oppressor, the Nazis. The atmosphere of the crowds of Parisians and their liberators was triumphant. With great pride, Emile realised he was a witness to a great historic event and tears of freedom stung his eyes.

People had climbed up on statues, waving flags, singing and cheering. Down the Champs-Élysées, people were crushed shoulder to shoulder, celebrating and walking with General de Gaulle, some of them carrying banners. Emile spied two with the Cross of Lorraine on it, and one made of white flowers. Aircraft flew overhead, bands played and everyone cheered, the crowds multiplying as they moved towards the Arc de Triomphe.

Later, the Division celebrated, and amid the electric atmosphere, Emile found he was searching the faces of the pretty girls who wanted to kiss them all, for the lovely face of Charlotte. His mood swung from joy to one of melancholy. He turned away and an old man thrust a glass of wine into his hand, uttering his grateful thanks. Emile found a corner by a statue near the Seine and sat down, lit a cigarette and swallowed the wine. Closing his ears to the noise going on around him, he let his thoughts drift, reliving those precious moments he'd spent with Charl. The first time he saw her across a crowded room at the inn. Their walks together along the leafy woodlands, and the dancing, when he held her so close, feeling the movement of her body in time with his as they danced as one. Inhaling, the scent of her skin, the sweetness of her lips as they kissed. He had seen her blossom into a beautiful young woman dedicated to the children in her care at the home. They had made him very welcome, and he had enjoyed playing games with them both inside and outside. He closed his eyes as he pictured Charl, her big brown eyes that often teased him playfully and that moment when she had welcomed him into her own private sanctuary, her bed. Their nights of intimacy when they snuggled up together and made love until dawn. He whispered her name, 'Charl', and wondered where she was now and what she was doing. 'Charl, will I ever see you again?' He held her picture close to his heart. A strong determination filled him. When the war was over, for surely it could not last much longer — he'd heard talk of it being over by Christmas — he decided that very moment he would return to England and Charl.

Then unexpectedly, from nowhere, a deep guttural sound escaped his lips, as a picture of his beloved daughter, Juliette came into his mind. A sudden fever of desolation raged through him. He swung away from the safety of the statue and lurched forward. He needed to drink himself into oblivion. He wanted to forget the horror of what had happened in Oradour-sur-Glane.

* * *

The next morning, he awoke with a start. Was he in Charl's bed? Back in England? Had those dreadful events been a nightmare? Stirring, he winced as his head raged hot with fire. He sniffed the air. The smell of the room didn't seem right. Jerking up on one elbow, he realised he was in a strange bed. And glancing around the room, he saw his clothes were scattered about. Then he spied a gilded chair upon which were strewn women's undergarments. He groaned and sank back, pulling the blanket over his naked body. He lay there, his head spinning like a wooden top and closed his eyes, drifting back to sleep.

He felt the soft kiss on his lips. 'Charl,' he whispered, stretching out an arm to her. Relieved it had been a terrible nightmare, and he was safe in Charl's bed.

'No, Cherie, it is I, Monica, your saviour.'

Emile squinted up to see a woman of about forty with bright red hair and a seductive smile, wearing only a revealing, clinging dressing gown. He elbowed himself up, saying, 'Where am I?'

The woman snaked herself closer to Emile. Running a finger down his naked chest, she said, 'Shall we repeat what happened last night?'

Horror-struck, he mumbled, 'I have to return to my division at once.'

'Oh, Cherie, no need to hurry.' Her fingers moved lower down his body.

'I must go,' he yelled.

'Of course, I will bring you coffee.' She moved away from him and disappeared behind a screen.

He jumped from the bed, and wished he hadn't as his head and body swayed different ways.

He steadied himself and as fast as he could, he pulled on his clothes; just as she came back in with a pot of strong coffee.

The coffee helped to revive his senses, but his head still swam as he hurried away from the unknown woman, murmuring his apologies. Hurrying through busy streets, he noticed that some people were still partying. By the time he reached his division, the fresh, clear morning air had helped to restore some kind of normality back to him. If normal could describe what he was feeling right now. Although Paris was liberated, the war was still in evidence, and they would be moving on. But first their division was staying on at the request of de Gaulle until his government established itself.

Functioning on reserve adrenalin, Emile stared ahead, blinking the dust from his eyes as the tanks moved off, leaving behind the liberation of Sarrebourg and La Petite-Pierre.

Gathering speed, the tanks roared on towards Strasbourg, but first they had to negotiate the mountain pass of Saverne through the Vosges Mountains. He breathed in the clear mountain air, thinking back to when he was a young boy here on a school excursion. He pulled himself up sharply; he needed to concentrate on the task ahead.

Along the rain-lashed road the tanks travelled, and finally reached Strasbourg on the border of France and Germany, still held by the Germans. After a fierce battle, the Germans surrendered. Thousands were made prisoners of war. And with General Leclerc in command, they liberated Strasbourg on 23 November 1944, to a multitude of loud applause from the jubilant population. As Emile watched the French flag being raised to fly above the damaged cathedral, he felt a burst of pride, so pleased and proud to be French that he almost managed to forget, for a few moments, the deaths of his loved ones. He looked towards his commanding officer, General Leclerc, for whom he had the greatest respect, and felt honoured to serve under him.

In the early hours of the morning, after a couple of hours' sleep, he was on duty watch with others of his division. He yawned and stretched, ground down the butt of his cigarette with the heel of his boot into the damp earth, and took up his position. For a while, he listened to the banter of his comrades, mostly about the Germans on the run, and joined in occasionally, and then their voices became quiet. Emile stared into the darkness, waiting for the morning sky to appear, wondering what it would bring.

Suddenly, the image of Charl's smiling face appeared before him. He tried to erase her, but she seemed insistent. Guilt washed over him. Guilt because he hadn't written or replied to her letters. Now her letters had stopped. So, had she forgotten about him? He couldn't blame her, for what could he offer her? He was a soldier, a man of war, fighting for his country for however long it took.

And then he felt the reoccurring sadness creep over him, the terrible loss of his daughter and his parents. He couldn't even keep them safe in his own country so how could he keep Charl safe in her country. No, it was best if he let her think he was dead. A woman as lovely as her would soon meet a nice man to care for her. Burning tears ran down his cheeks, startling him, and with a swipe of his hand, he dashed them away.

In February 1945 General de Gaulle came to Strasbourg Cathedral and by then, the 2nd Armoured Tank Division was on its way to Germany and Austria, battling against the harsh winter conditions. By spring they were the first to enter Hitler's Eagle's Nest, though there was much debate and confusion with the American forces on this subject.

Later in May 1945, they moved on back to Paris. Emile thought about writing to Charlotte. But how could he write and tell her of the terrible massacre of his family in Oradour-sur-Glane, and of the villagers? He could find no words to express his deep sorrow, and his heart felt so heavy with despair. He needed to feel Charl in his arms, and to kiss her sweet lips, and to walk hand-in-hand with her in freedom. He needed her to heal his heart. But he had nothing to offer her in return.

Emile was thinking of Charl as he crossed a busy road when he became involved in an accident with a motorcycle and his world turned black.

CHAPTER TWENTY-SEVEN

Autumn 1944

Through summer and into autumn, Charlotte checked every day for letters from Emile, but none arrived. She stood at the sitting-room window watching as the postmistress, a young married woman with children, whom her mother looked after, dismounted her bike. Today, Charlotte didn't rush into the hall to collect the post, because she didn't want another disappointment. She'd written to Emile's parents, but they hadn't replied either.

When she'd stopped by the inn, Hilda had remarked, 'Out of sight, out of mind.' And then she'd added, 'You want to court a nice local lad, not one of them foreigners.' At the time she'd laughed at her aunt's remarks, but perhaps she was right. The only eligible young men about were at the nearby RAF station. She sometimes made up a foursome with Joyce, going dancing and to the cinema, having fun. But none of the young men made her heart soar the way she'd felt with Emile. She had given herself to him with no regrets. She consoled herself that the war in Europe was dangerous and he had no opportunity to write letters. Then again maybe, as Hilda said, he had forgotten about her.

'Charlotte,' one of staff called. 'It's time to walk the little ones to school.' They all took turns in accompanying the younger children to school and home again. This morning, she had free time to visit Jack.

Breathing in the fresh morning air, she said hello to two women as she popped into the bakery, loving the smell of newly baked bread and the savoury aroma of meat and potato pies.

'Not seen Jack for a few days,' Mrs Mackay wrapped the warm pie in a piece of muslin. 'And have you heard, war is gonna be over by Christmas.'

'Christmas is a long time away.' Charlotte replied as she left the shop.

'Now, what's upset her chocolate box?' Mrs Mackay remarked to the other customers waiting to be served.

Walking along, Charlotte wondered if the war would really be over by Christmas. If so, and when, how would it change people's lives? she thought miserably.

'Good morning. What a lovely day,' called Mrs Carlton-Jones from her pony and trap as she trotted by.

This made Charlotte pull herself up sharply from her dark mood. She should think of her relationship with Emile as a happy interlude in her life, and cherish the precious time they'd spent together. Those treasured memories would never be erased from her heart. Her steps became lighter as she walked down Jack's path, and she felt happier now she'd made that decision.

As she drew nearer the cottage door, she could hear Jip whining inside. She knocked on the door and Jip whined louder. Turning the handle, she called out, 'Jack, it's only me, Charlotte.' She could see Jack sitting in his chair with Jip at his feet. But Jack didn't move or answer. Moving swiftly to his side, she was shocked to see his pale face and vacant eyes.

He tried to speak, but only gasps came from his blue-tinged lips. 'Jack, you need a doctor. I won't be long.' Her feet grew wings as she flew down the path to the nearest cottage. But no one was at home. She ran further and saw the postmistress coming up the lane on her bike.

'Quick,' she urged. 'Get the doctor for Jack. He's very poorly.' With that, the postmistress swung her bike round and pedalled fast in the direction of the doctor's.

Back indoors, Charlotte held Jack's hand, not wanting to leave him. Jip looked mournfully up at her, his eyes big pools of sadness.

For what seemed an eternity, Charlotte waited. At last, the door burst open and Doctor Metcalf entered. A big burly man of sixty plus years.

Gently, he examined Jack and said to Charlotte, 'Ambulance is on its way.' She looked questioningly at him. 'It's his heart I've being treating him for,' he replied to her unspoken question.

Worried, Charlotte accompanied Jack in the ambulance. She didn't want him to be on his own. The postmistress promised to take a message to the Grahames to let them know what had happened.

At the hospital in Driffield, the nurses took Jack straight to a medical room. Charlotte waited, sitting on the edge of a wooden bench in a draughty ante-room. The hours ticked by.

Stiffly she rose to her feet and peeped into the corridor. But it was deserted. She walked around the room to ease her aching muscles. As she did so, she noticed a framed history of the hospital hanging on the wall. As a distraction, she began to read it, learning that the hospital had been built on land which once had been the kitchen gardens of the workhouse. She shuddered at the idea of being forced to spend your life in such an institution.

Ah, voices in the corridor. Hopefully the doctor coming to tell her about Jack. As the sound of the voices drew nearer, she realised they were foreign. She listened, German!

Quickly she opened the door and saw the retreating figures of two men in orderly uniforms.

Just then a porter came by. He'd come out of retirement to do his bit for king and country, and saw the puzzled look on her face.

'We got four wards of them wounded Jerries, and they,' he pointed down the corridor to the orderlies, 'look after them.'

She nodded. 'Can you help? I came in with Mr Jack Mansfield. It's his heart. Do you know what's happening? I was told to wait here, but it's been hours.'

'Ah, well. There's been a bad crash up at yon airfield, an emergency, so they are busy.'

Then he took in Charlotte's worried face. 'I'll see what's up.'

Another twenty minutes went by and Charlotte was about to search for someone, when a doctor, his face grey with fatigue, entered. 'So sorry, Miss, to keep you waiting.' She just nodded.

'Mr Mansfield has had a severe heart attack. He is responding to treatment, but he will be staying in hospital for some time. I understand you found him and your quick action saved his life. Otherwise . . .' He didn't have to finish the sentence.

'Thank you, doctor. Can I see him now, please?'

'Yes, I will send a nurse to fetch you.'

Charlotte leaned against the wall, her body trembling, and tears welled in her eyes.

A few minutes later, she was sitting by Jack's bedside. There was a screen round him and he was wired up to a machine and his eyes were closed. Panic tightened her throat and words refused to come.

But the nurse understood and smiled reassuringly. 'He is comfortable and sleeping, so just stay for a few minutes.'

Exhausted, but pleased Jack was out of danger, Charlotte was lucky to catch a lift on a farm wagon back to Mornington.

Later, Charlotte was reading a bedtime story to the younger girls. Mrs Grahame had told her to take the evening off, but she politely declined as, alone in her quarters, she knew she would worry about Jack, even though she knew he was being well cared for at the hospital.

'I want to be a fairy,' one of the girls said sleepily as Charlotte finished the story of the fairy with a magic wand.

Charlotte tucked them in their beds and kissed them gently on the cheek, 'Night, night.'

She turned off the overhead light and switched on the night light, which gave a soft, warm glow. It was comforting for the children if they woke up during the night, often having a nightmare, reliving when they were in their homeland trapped by war. She stood for a few moments in the doorway, listening to their steady, rhythmic breathing. As she walked down the corridor, her heart filled with love for the children. They had witnessed atrocities that no child should but, hopefully, the care and love they received at Mornington House had helped to lessen any lasting mental damage they might have suffered. She felt privileged to care for them, and hoped she was making a difference to their young lives by helping to restore some normality to their childhood.

Two of the volunteer ladies were on duty tonight, and they were supervising the older children's bedtime. After a quick word with them, Charlotte made her way down to the kitchen.

Mrs Grahame was making a pot of tea. 'Thought I heard you coming down. You look done in, lass.' She brought the tea tray to the table.

Charlotte sank into a chair and gave a big sigh. Then immediately jumped to her feet, crying, 'I forgot about Jip.'

'Sit down,' Mrs Grahame commanded. 'Neighbours are looking after him.'

Relieved, Charlotte sat back down, and Mrs Grahame passed her a cup of hot tea, sweetened with their precious sugar ration. Neither spoke for a while, then Charlotte said, 'Jack looked terrible. I'm not sure he's going to make it. I feel guilty for not visiting him as often as I should have.' With that, she broke into floods of tears.

Swiftly Mrs Grahame rose to her feet and Charlotte felt the comfort of warm arms holding her close until her body, so racked with guilt, became calmer.

'Sup this, lass,' Mrs Grahame placed a small glass of brandy into Charlotte's hands.

Shakily, Charlotte drank, gulping as the fiery liquid ran down her throat, its heat reaching every vital part of her body. She closed her eyes, feeling the sensation soothing her.

Hearing the faint movement of Mrs Grahame, as she tidied the kitchen, she opened her eyes and gave a huge sigh and pulled herself to her feet. 'Sorry,' she mumbled, 'I think I'll go to bed.'

Mrs Grahame said, 'Have a good night's sleep. Take the day off and see Jack. But first, ring the hospital.'

'What for?'

'They might need you to take some of his personal belongings.' She didn't add the real reason why she said ring first — in case he had passed away.

Jack survived and after two weeks in hospital, he came home. A health visitor called regularly to see him, and so did Charlotte, and when she couldn't because of her care of the children, she organised ladies of the village on a rota system. They shopped, cooked, washed, and ironed his clothes. ARP wardens on night patrol would often call in for a chat. And Gilbert and Philippe tidied up Jack's woodshed and swept the path when they called in to report to Jack.

Today, Charlotte sat with Jack, reading the headlines of the daily newspaper to him. 'Mr Churchill says the war is going on until 1945. Everyone was hoping for it to end by Christmas,' Charlotte said, gloomily. 'Rationing is even tighter, and the farmers say the land can't produce enough food.' Even living in a country village, meat was scarce, the rabbits, which made a good staple meal, had gone to ground and at Mornington House, the apple store was almost diminished.

She glanced at Jack. His eyes were closed and he dozed. At the hospital, she had glanced at his notes, surprised to learn he was seventy-eight. She never thought of him as old, because he had a lively mind. But this heart attack had taken its toll on him, and he seemed quite content to sit quietly with Jip by his side.

'Heard from Emile?'

Jack's voice jolted her. *Oh, Emile, I miss you so much*, she cried inwardly. Turning to look at Jack, she answered, 'No, not a word.' A look of fear flickered across Jack's face. Quickly, trying to make her voice light and jolly, she said, 'I expect he's always on the move. And I will probably receive all his letters together.'

A light tap sounded on the door, and a cheery voice called, 'It's only me.' A villager entered, carrying a tray of delicious-smelling hot food.

Charlotte rose from the chair and exchanged pleasantries with her, kissed Jack, and promised to see him again soon.

Walking back to the house, she thought of Emile and hoped there might be a chance that there would be a letter from him waiting for her. But who was she fooling? Then a terrible thing shot through her mind. Was he still alive?

That night, she tossed and turned, unable to erase that thought from her mind.

CHAPTER TWENTY-EIGHT

December 1944

When Juliette arrived with her escort, Auntie, in London, she was ill with a fever and spent some time in hospital recovering. When she was well enough to travel, she kept asking for Auntie and became hysterical when another woman came to escort her to Mornington.

Auntie pondered on the situation. Her heart raced at the thought of seeing Mornington House. But she must consider the welfare of the child before her own personal feelings. So she agreed to accompany Juliette.

Auntie and Juliette arrived in Hull by train on a cold December night. Auntie set the child down on the platform, while she retrieved the case from a helpful soldier. The station echoed with the noise of the crowds of people rushing to the barrier, anxious to be on their way home. She felt Juliette clinging to her legs, her tears running hot on her bare calves. Bending down, she gently eased Juliette away, wiped away her tears and kissed her on the forehead. 'Soon have you in a nice warm bed.' For a brief moment, she wished she had a home to go to. But maybe it was her destiny to live this nomadic life. What else would she do with her life anyway?

Her steps heavy with fatigue and with Juliette's tiny hand in hers, they made their way through the barrier. The journey from France had been long and arduous. Wearily, she wondered if she had the energy to return to Europe and carry out more missions.

'Ah, there you are,' said a woman's pleasant voice and, holding out her hand, 'I'm Mrs Bishop, from the Women's Voluntary Service.'

Auntie smiled, feeling thankful the woman was on time. Often she'd hung around the meeting places for ages, waiting for someone to turn up. She put down the case and extended her hand. 'Auntie.'

'I have a hot meal waiting for you.' Mrs Bishop picked up the suitcase.

Auntie lifted Juliette up into her arms and the child wrapped her arms around her neck.

As they crossed the concourse and out into Ferensway, the devastation of the city pulled her up sharply and she gasped. Juliette lifted her head to look into Auntie's eyes, and Mrs Bishop turned round as Auntie spoke. 'Hammonds, it's gone.'

'Yes, and many other landmarks have also disappeared.' They began walking again and Mrs Bishop asked, 'You know Hull?'

'Yes, but not since the war.'

They carried on in silence, and Auntie felt the weight of the sleeping child in her arms, comforting her. She drew in a long breath; over the years she'd steeled herself to remain isolated from all emotions. It was her way of coping to do the job she did, rescuing children living in the squalor of buildings bombed by the Nazis and bringing them to safety. But somehow, the child in her arms, Juliette, had crept under her skin and pulled at her heart. She was mad, she knew, to agree to escort the child to Mornington.

By now they had reached Albion Street, where only half of the street remained and she gasped. Mrs Bishop looked at her. Auntie felt her insides quiver. 'The Museum, it's gone.'

The beautiful museum she used to visit as a child with her father, those happy memories of yesteryears all vanished. *Nothing remains forever*, she thought bitterly, a sob catching in her throat.

'Bombed 1941, along with many other grand buildings,' Mrs Bishop replied, a note of sadness in her voice.

They reached the house and climbed up the steps. Someone must have been watching for them, because the door opened immediately and they were ushered inside.

Juliette clung like a limpet to Auntie and cried when a woman in a grey dress and white apron reached out to take her.

Mrs Bishop tutted, she'd had a long day too. 'Come through to the kitchen, Cook has a hot meal for you both.'

The warmth of the cosy kitchen was welcoming and a delicious aroma rose from the pan that Cook was stirring. Auntie eased Juliette from her arms. She washed their hands with a damp cloth and seated the child on a chair with a cushion and sat down next to her. Cook placed a bowl of hot vegetable broth with crispy dumplings floating on the top before them.

And then she retreated to her chair by the fire and picked up her knitting of a multicoloured scarf. Mrs Bishop disappeared to another part of the house, saying she would be back later.

By the time they had eaten their fill and Auntie drank a cup of tea, both she and Juliette were yawning. Mrs Bishop reappeared and took them upstairs to a small room with twin beds. Cook brought up a big jug of warm water and placed it by the side of an ewer on a marble-topped table. Mrs Bishop provided a towel, flannel and a thin sliver of soap.

She hovered by the door. 'Is there anything else you require?'

Auntie motioned to the case on a wooden chair. 'We have everything we need. Thank you for being so kind and offering us such hospitality.'

Mrs Bishop smiled, her face lighting up. 'I have a son at war, and I like to think someone would care for him. Goodnight.'

Auntie tucked Juliette into her bed and held her hand until she slept. In her own bed, although tired, sleep eluded her, and she thought of her estranged husband. The last she'd heard of him he was missing, presumed dead. She felt a dreadful pang of guilt. He had suffered as she had, but she had left him and run away, unable to cope. Now he could be dead in an unmarked grave or none at all. The tears of years of misery fell, running hot down her cold cheeks.

She lay listening to Juliette whimpering in her sleep. Restlessly Auntie tossed and turned, finally drifting into a fitful half-sleep. Suddenly, the child screamed. Shaken awake. Auntie slid from her bed and went to comfort the terrified child, holding her close in her arms, feeling her tiny body convulse. Shivering in the cold room, an icy draught blowing down the chimney, she slipped into bed with Juliette, both drawing warmth and comfort from each other.

The next morning, after a breakfast of toast and a small bowl of porridge, it was time for the last leg of their journey. Cook had brushed and sponged down their travel-stained clothes and the scarf she had been knitting was finished and placed around Juliette's neck. Auntie lifted her up so that she could see herself in the hall mirror. And for the first time, Juliette smiled, her eyes bright. It brought a lump to Auntie's throat. 'Thank you,' she said to the beaming cook.

'A pleasure, Miss, to see little one happy.'

They caught the east coast train, which stopped at Mornington. Auntie sat Juliette near to the window so she could gaze out, pleased that she was not so clingy today. She sat resting her back on the bench and listened to the rhythm of the train as it steamed along, not wanting to see the passing countryside from the window.

At the small railway station, they alighted and were soon out into the lane. There a woman standing by a pony and trap waited. Auntie pulled the beret she was wearing down to cover the side of her face.

The woman stepped forward. 'Had a good journey? I'm Mrs Carlton-Jones.'

Auntie took the proffered hand, not introducing herself. 'This is Juliette, I understand that a Miss Charlotte Kirby knows her daddy.'

Mrs Carton-Jones glanced at the child. 'Yes, he was stationed here for a short time.'

Soon they were seated in the trap, with a Scotch plaid blanket covering their legs. The day shone bright, with a blue sky, the air fresh and tangy on her cheeks. Auntie steeled herself to look directly ahead, averting her eyes when anyone called a greeting to Mrs Carlton-Jones.

They passed the school where children played in the playground. Their joyous voices caught at her heart and she felt compelled to watch them skipping round the playground clockwise and then when the teacher clapped, to change, amid great laughter, to anti-clockwise.

As they trotted by, Juliette stretched her small body and craned her head to watch as well.

Mrs Carlton-Jones, catching the look of her passengers, said with genuine pleasure, 'The children we have staying at Mornington House go to the school. Considering the terrible ordeals, they suffered before coming to us, they are remarkably resilient and have adapted well.' She could have added that some still suffered from nightmares, but she refrained.

As they drew nearer to Mornington House, Auntie felt her body tense and her heart beating too fast. She reached for Juliette's tiny hand, and the child looked up trustingly into her face.

She felt ashamed, for hadn't Juliette and all the other children she had led to safety during this evil war, suffered more than she had. Gently, she squeezed Juliette's hand and whispered, '*Maintenant vous seras en securite.*' Now you will be safe.

As they entered the driveway, she noticed that the lovely ornate iron gates had disappeared, melted down for the war effort, she supposed. Mrs Carlton-Jones slowed down the pony so he wouldn't kick up the gravel and spray it about, and the drive up to the house went into slow-motion and

Auntie felt in free-fall. A weird sensation filled her, reminding her of her first parachute jump. Then the door opened.

A smiling young woman stood on the threshold. She stepped forward, her arms outstretched in welcome. Mechanically Auntie returned the smile, sensing this was the young woman who knew Juliette's daddy. She lifted the child up and passed her into Charlotte Kirby's arms. She then alighted from the trap, and so did Mrs Carlton-Jones. She watched as Tom came to take care of the pony, smoothing its mane and whispering to it. He unharnessed the pony from the trap and led it away to be fed and watered. With nothing else to distract her, it was only then that she followed the others into the house.

She avoided looking round, focusing her eyes on Juliette who was now holding Charlotte's hand, and she suddenly felt bereft and then chided herself. Her mission was complete. Juliette was in safe hands. She felt emotionally drained and weary, and thankful to be returning to London tomorrow. No doubt Mrs Carlton-Jones would offer her a bed for the night.

In the kitchen she met Mr and Mrs Grahame, who seemed a nice presentable couple, and she understood they ran the home for the children. Tea and sandwiches and delicious-smelling freshly baked scones were being put on the table by Mrs Jolly. 'Come and sit down. You look done in.'

Auntie glanced towards Juliette, who sat on Charlotte's knee, and knew she would be well cared for. She hadn't heard any news of Emile Delmas, though the Free French were still active in Europe and communication could be haphazard. At the table, she kept her eyes focused on the group and listened to their chatter, not letting her eyes stray around the kitchen, enjoying the wholesome refreshments because once back in Europe, food was a scarce commodity and she never knew when she would next eat. Realising she was contemplating returning to Europe, her inner voice saying, *for as long as I am needed.*

Suddenly she became aware the chatter had stopped and everyone was looking at her and Mrs Carlton-Jones was saying something to her. 'I'm sorry, what did you say?'

The good lady rose from her chair and spoke. 'Mrs Grahame is kindly going to give you a bed for as long as you wish to stay. I unfortunately have a house full of people. So . . .' here she paused, then said, 'I know your code name is Auntie, but while staying here, it would be nice to know your real name.'

Auntie felt the colour drain from her face. It had been a long time since she had used her real name. She saw their faces, suspended in a moment in time. Her voice trembling, she uttered, 'Margaret Ross.' Her name sounded alien to her own ears.

'We had a family call Ross who once lived here,' blurted Mrs Carlton-Jones. Then her face went a vivid red, and she stared at Margaret Ross. Her voice a whisper. 'Are you the Margaret Ross who lived here?' She looked unrecognisable, so thin and drawn, and shabbily dressed, not like the smiling, smart lady who used to hold the annual summer fayre. And then it hit her, the tragedy of the three children drowning in the garden pond. Something the villagers never talked about.

Auntie, aka Margaret Ross, took a deep breath. 'Yes, I lived here.'

CHAPTER TWENTY-NINE

December 1944

Mrs Carlton-Jones was the first to recover her manners. 'Mrs Ross, I quite understand if you're reluctant to stay here. I shall ask in the village for you to be accommodated elsewhere.' She was on her feet and shrugging on her coat.

'There is no need,' Margaret's voice was quiet but firm. She gestured to Mr and Mrs Grahame sitting opposite her, 'These kind people have offered me a bed.' Her resolve was about to plummet, when suddenly Juliette jumped down from Charlotte's knee and came to climb upon her knee and put her small arms around her neck.

'Auntie,' the child whispered, 'I'm frightened.'

Margaret kissed the top of Juliette's head and whispered, 'You are safe and I will stay with you.' Looking directly at the faces of the people round the table, she continued, 'I will stay until Juliette settles.'

With relief, Mrs Carlton-Jones departed. Mrs Jolly went back to her cooking and Mr Grahame returned to fixing the lock on the outside shed. Mrs Grahame, anxious to return to her household duties, asked Charlotte to show Margaret to her room.

The only room available was the night staff room.

Charlotte led the way up to the room she had prepared earlier. Holding the door open for them to enter, she glanced at Margaret. 'I hope you don't mind, until Juliette settles, for her to share a room with you.'

Margaret looked at Charlotte, seeing her warm brown eyes and the smile which lit up her face. She felt an instant liking for this young woman and knew Juliette would be safe and well cared for. 'Thank you, it is very thoughtful of you.'

The small room held two sofa beds, a chest of drawers, with an ewer on top, a basket chair, a clipped rug, and a blackout blind at the sash window. On one of the beds, propped on the pillow, was a soft rag doll, with bright blue buttons for eyes. On seeing the doll, Juliette looked shyly at Charlotte, who said, 'The dolly is for you.'

The two women watched the child reach out tentatively to touch the doll, not moving.

Suddenly she snatched up the doll and hugged her, letting silent tears slip unheeded down her cheeks.

'She's suffered too much trauma in her young life. It will take time,' Margaret said quietly. On her bed she spied a small bar of scented soap. 'That's a luxury.'

Charlotte smiled. 'Courtesy of my friend Joyce via a GI. Before the children come home from school, would you like a bath?'

'That would be heavenly, even though it's regulation five inches.'

'You will find clean clothes in the chest of drawers for you and Juliette.' Margaret opened the top drawer and peeped inside. 'Sorry, they are donated.' Blushing, Charlotte said, 'I'll show you to the bathroom.'

Margaret's steady gaze met hers. 'I know where the bathroom is.'

Charlotte stood aside and lowered her eyes. 'I'll stay with Juliette.' When she closed the door and turned to Emile's daughter, Juliette was fast asleep on the bed, clutching the dolly to her. Gently, Charlotte removed her boots and drew up the bedspread to cover the tiny child to keep her warm. Then she sat on the edge of the bed, gazing down at the pale face with a halo of dark curls touching her shoulders. Charlotte felt her heart filled with tenderness and hope. Hope that Emile was still alive, but no matter what, she would care for and love his daughter.

* * *

In the bathroom, Margaret stood in the doorway and closed her eyes, trying to shut out the image of her children at bath times. Their shouts of glee, the splashing of water and then the crying when soap bubbles popped in their eyes. She heard a movement down the corridor and, not wanting to see anyone, she pushed the door shut. Leaning on it for a few moments, she forced her feet forward and turned on the tap.

Relaxing in the bath, she let the exotic scented soap of jasmine take over her senses and her mind. She imagined she lounged in a French boudoir of a Parisian Madame. The wild dreams of her thoughts had often kept her sane when in a tight and dangerous situation, though usually without the help of soap.

She stayed in the bath until the water cooled and then, not wanting to linger, she quickly dried her body and hair, and dressed in the clean, serviceable clothes provided.

Checking with Charlotte first, who agreed to stay with the sleeping child, Margaret went for a walk. At first, she stood on the gravel path, unsure which direction to take, if any. She had always known that someday she would have to confront her fears, her guilt. Mothers, she told herself, are supposed to keep their children safe. And she had failed to do that. The horror of the tragedy haunted her. The loss of her children had been an accident, unforeseen, not a deliberate act, she told herself.

As the years passed, and as she scourged war-torn countries for abandoned children to take to safety, she had seen and witnessed such great atrocities, deliberately inflicted.

The unbelievable act of men killing innocent children. She closed her eyes, smelling the terrible lingering smell of death, hearing the screams of terror of those frightened, helpless children.

She gave a huge sigh and turned right towards the woodland path, her booted feet crunching on the gravel until it gave way to a quieter path and she felt the winter earth and the occasional snap of a twig from a fallen branch. She felt the peace and the tranquillity, knowing she had been right to open the house for children in need. Orphans of war.

She was glad she had made the sacrifice.

Suddenly, without warning, a scene came into her mind of her husband, Anthony, when he had first brought her here to the family home and they'd walked hand-in-hand along this very path. Their happiness knew no bounds, and it united even more with the births of their son and daughter. And then one hot summer's day, everything changed. He blamed her for the deaths of their children. Their bitterness towards each other warped their hearts so much that they couldn't comfort each other. The black hole became too deep and communication between them dried up. Filled with guilty, unbearable grief, she had left him to find refuge with an aunt in London, until the war came.

At her aunt's encouragement, she became a volunteer to escort children in London to the safety of the countryside. And quite by chance, she was asked to take part in an operation to help in Europe, bringing orphaned and abandoned children to safety in Britain. This work kept her from thinking of her own children, and she worked tirelessly. Was she paying back a debt, an atonement for the loss of her son and daughter? She wasn't sure. What she did know was that she would continue helping to save children, if needed. Her overnight stay at Mornington House was only a short respite. She must keep on the move. It helped to alleviate her guilt at losing her children.

The overnight stay stretched to two weeks. Juliette did not settle. She seemed to regress into herself and refused to talk. One night, the children were tucked up in bed and Laura watched over Juliette. Charlotte invited Margaret into her small but comfortable quarters. She sensed the older woman's discomfort at being in her old home, where she'd lived with her husband and her children before the tragic accident. None of the staff mentioned this, and neither did Charlotte. That night they sat by the fire enjoying a glass of wine, courtesy of when the Free French were in the village. 'It's the language difficulty, mostly,' Margaret explained to Charlotte. 'Though the children here are French, they have adapted well to the English language.'

Charlotte laughed. 'At first, they were reluctant to talk until they realised if they asked in English, they could have a second helping of puddings. Though sometimes they do relax into their mother tongue.'

The log fire hissed and crackled and Charlotte topped up their glasses. Whether it was the wine loosening her tongue, she wasn't sure, but the need to talk about Emile was uppermost in her thoughts. 'I've only heard once from Emile since he left for France, but I write often to him with the hope my letters will catch up with him.'

Margaret looked at Charlotte's sad face and responded, 'It was rather chaotic when I was over in France.' Which was an understatement. War meant killing and total disregard for human life.

But she didn't mention this. 'You've written to tell him that Juliette is safe and living with you.'

'Yes, I wrote immediately. I didn't want him to believe she was dead after the massacre of the villagers and his parents.'

Margaret looked at Charlotte, knowing that as she said those terrible words, the true connotations didn't register fully with her. Which was a blessing.

Today was the day. Margaret woke early and lay listening to Juliette's steady breathing.

Tomorrow she was returning to London. *So today is the day.* The words reverberated in her head. It was Sunday and the children would be home so Juliette wouldn't feel so lonely. And she knew that Charlotte would take good care of Juliette. All the staff seemed wholly dedicated to the care of the children.

And for this, Margaret felt eternally indebted.

While she was staying here, in her old home, she'd gone up to the attic rooms, opened the old trunk and removed the photo album of her children. She'd sat on the floor for a long time before she opened it. And when she did, she covered her hands over her mouth to stop the screams, and let the silent tears run down her face. And then, her hands moved on their own accord to open the pages of the album, and through her haze of tears, the faces of her beloved children looked at her, bringing more tears.

Gradually, her tears ceased, and she saw the faces of her children so clearly. And as she looked lovingly at them, the sense of guilt she'd carried in her heart for all those years flew away. It was as if her children were talking to her, she heard their voices in her head, telling her they were happy.

And a serene sense of peace filled her.

After breakfast that morning, and seeing that Juliette was happily playing with two little girls, she told Charlotte she was going out. Dressed in her old coat and a headscarf covering her hair, head down, not wanting to speak to anyone, she walked slowly towards the crossroads.

As she approached the church, she could hear the singing of a hymn. The morning service was in progress. Walking down the side path of the church to the graveyard at the rear, where it faced open countryside with the rise of the Wolds in the distance, she stood for a moment, eyes closed, feeling the serenity, hearing the gentle rustle of the yew tree. Opening her eyes, she moved forward and stopped, surprised. The grave of her children was well tended. She glanced about, but she was alone. And then she saw Milly's grave nearby, also well tended.

Hilda Bilton. Tears welled up in her eyes. How could she have neglected her own children's grave? She gave a deep sigh, knelt down on the cold grass and kissed the earth of her children's grave, letting her tears mingle with the soil.

She didn't hear the quiet footsteps approaching, and it wasn't until she pulled herself up on to her feet that she was aware of someone standing close by. She turned and saw Hilda, tears running down her face.

Margaret did something she should have done years ago. She held out her arms to the other mother, who had also lost her child. The two women embraced. Gently, they were aware of a stirring of grasses, a rustling of leaves, and the voices of young children singing.

CHAPTER THIRTY

Christmas 1944 to New Year 1945

Christmas was a week away, and Charlotte felt sorry to see Margaret go. She had grown quite fond of the older woman, but sensed a deep sadness within her. How could you ever get over losing your children in such tragic circumstances? And Christmas, a time to rejoice with family, must hit her hard. And then she thought of Hilda and George. They must still grieve for the loss of their daughter. Since she no longer lived with them, she had grown to understand their offhand behaviour, believing it was their way of coping.

Charlotte and Margaret discussed many topics during their evenings spent together in her quarters, sitting by the fire and drinking wine. The main topic being what would happen to the children when the war was over. Surely, if the news bulletins on the wireless saying that the allied forces were winning the war were to be believed, Charlotte hoped that some of the children might be reunited with their families. But, she feared, it was a very thin line of hope. When Margaret left, Juliette cried for a whole day and withdrew more into herself.

Wanting only Auntie and Grand'Mère.

'Poor little mite,' exclaimed Mrs Grahame to Charlotte. 'How can the Germans bring so much suffering to children? It's not natural.' She banged down a pan she was drying.

Surprised by Mrs Grahame's outburst, because she was not a woman given to displaying her emotions, Charlotte guessed she was concerned for her husband. He was recovering slowly from a bout of pneumonia he'd caught when out fixing part of the fence round the pond, which had blown down in a storm, during which he'd got soaked in a heavy downpour.

'I'll finish off here and prepare the children's tea,' and Mrs Grahame thankfully went to her quarters to see how her husband was faring.

She glanced through the serving hatch to where Juliette was standing with her face pressed to the large dining-room window overlooking the drive, waiting for Lucie to come home from school. Charlotte studied the tea list on the pantry door, beans and scrambled eggs on toast. No fresh eggs, so it would be reconstituted dried egg. The growing children now sported healthy appetites, especially the boys, and would need extra food. She looked through the provisions on the shelves and decided on making carrot buns, first checking the meals on the daily list, not to use any ingredients Cook would require.

Before she began her baking, she went into the dining room to crouch down by Juliette's side, not speaking, but she smiled at the little girl's glance at her. After a few minutes, Charlotte said, 'Soon Lucie will be home for her tea.' At the mention of Lucie's name, a faint smile crossed Juliette's face. Charlotte reached out her hand, saying, 'You help me?' She gave an inward sigh of relief as the child slowly took hold of the proffered hand.

In the kitchen, after they'd both washed their hands, Charlotte tied a small apron around Juliette before sitting her on a cushioned stool. She placed a small enamel basin in front of her and measured out a tiny quantity of the ingredients into the basin. All the time, Juliette watched captivated, and Charlotte wondered if she used to watch her grand-mother baking. Then adding her own ingredients into her large basin: self-raising flour, margarine, sugar, grated raw carrot and the reconstituted egg. There were only a few sultanas, and she decided that Juliette could use them to decorate her buns. She gave the child a small wooden spoon and was about to show her what to do when Juliette began to stir the ingredients.

'Clever girl. Did Grand'Mère show you?' Understanding the words, Juliette nodded, a smile playing on her lips.

Time whizzed by and soon they could hear the joyful noise of children as they entered the house, accompanied by Laura who, after her few hours off duty, had gone to meet the younger children from school and walked home with them.

Juliette eagerly ran to catch hold of Lucie's hand and draw her into the kitchen to show her the buns she'd made.

Laura smiled at the girls and remarked to Charlotte, 'Juliette seems to be slowly settling down.'

'I was worried when Margaret left, but Lucie is brilliant with her, so natural.' Charlotte replied as she went to the pantry and brought out a big jug of fresh milk from the farm.

'Come along, children,' Laura called to those lingering. 'Hats and coats off and hands washed, ready for tea.' The mention of food and they needed no second bidding.

Afterwards was playtime or recreation time, which is what Mrs Carlton-Jones called it, and she was here with a basket full of offcuts of plain and coloured paper and a jam jar full of paste. They were in the dining room because they needed the big table. The children crowded round her, watching, enchanted. 'You are going to make paper chains for Christmas decorations to hang up. Mr Tom will be bringing in the Christmas tree and you can make fairies to decorate the tree.'

'Not me, it's girls' stuff,' Maurice dismissed the idea, and another boy also grumbled his objection out loud.

Without taking her eyes off unloading her basket, Mrs Carlton-Jones said, 'I will need two strapping lads like you to climb the ladder and fix the chains on the walls.'

Watching the show of relief on the lads' faces, Charlotte held back a laugh. 'Both of you go to Mr Tom's shed to collect the bundle of greenery.' They made a quick exit.

Charlotte smiled; Mr Tom would be glad of their company.

Later, when the house was quiet and the children all in bed, Charlotte and Laura were tidying up the room. 'They really enjoyed themselves, making things for Christmas,' Laura put right a chair. 'And I was surprised Mrs Carlton-Jones stayed so long.'

'Yes, I was too. I think she gets lonely at times, especially if her husband is on night duty and she's no committee to chair. And her sons are away in the forces,' Charlotte said as she tidied up. 'Now for a cup of tea before I go off duty.'

In companionable silence they sat in the kitchen drinking their tea, Charlotte deep in thought. Then she said to Laura, 'I think Juliette is now ready to sleep in the same bedroom as Lucie. What do you think?'

'We could give her a try. But my reason is a bit selfish.'

Charlotte looked questioningly at her friend. 'I would love my room back.' Laura had given up her room for Juliette and Margaret.

'Being stuck in the linen cupboard must be so claustrophobic for you.'

'I'm not complaining really, but if you think Juliette would benefit by sleeping in the girls' bedroom, we'll see how she fares.'

'Tomorrow night then.' They both agreed.

* * *

'The transformation in Juliette is remarkable, putting her in the same bedroom as Lucie worked wonders,' Charlotte told Mrs Grahame a couple of days later. It was after tea and they were in the games room, observing Juliette as she sat with Lucie at a low table.

'This bit goes there,' said Lucie to Juliette, as she placed a piece of jigsaw in the picture of Snow White and the Seven Dwarfs. The two girls were now inseparable.

'What happens when Lucie goes back to school?' Mrs Grahame asked.

'I can't predict that, but we'll take one day at a time. It's like the jigsaw puzzle, fitting in the piece until the picture is complete.' Then an idea occurred to her. 'What if we ask Miss Holderness if Juliette could start school after the Christmas break? What do you think?'

Mrs Grahame glanced at the two girls, then answered. 'It would be the best thing, otherwise she would fret.'

* * *

Charlotte watched as Juliette and Lucie walked hand-in-hand in front of her down the lane towards Jack's cottage. She felt rather guilty not having had time to visit him before Christmas and already the days had slipped unnoticed into 1945. Though when Dot, Edna and May visited the House with gifts for the children, they assured her that Jack was being taken care of by his neighbours. Even so, she missed her friend and Jip.

'This is a lovely surprise,' Jack said as they entered the cottage. 'And who are these bonny girls?' They held back, shyly. But Jip bounced up to nuzzle at the girls' feet, checking if they were friend or foe. Satisfied, he then sniffed at the basket of treats that Charlotte carried. She fondled his ears.

'How are you keeping, Jack?' Charlotte asked.

'Fair to middling,' he answered with a twinkle in his eyes.

Putting the basket down on the table, Charlotte ushered the two girls forward, saying, 'This is Lucie, who you've seen before. And this little girl is Juliette; you know her daddy, Emile.' As she said his name, her throat tightened and a wave of sadness washed over her and the smile on her face wobbled. Thankfully, Jack appeared not to notice her distress.

'Juliette, that's a pretty name. Your daddy billeted with me while training.' The little girl didn't say anything, but stared solemnly at him. He glanced up at Charlotte.

'She's beginning to learn English and soon she'll be talking like the other children. Now, girls, shall we show Uncle Jack what we have in the basket. A picnic.'

And both girls repeated together, 'Picnic.' And the atmosphere relaxed as they helped Charlotte to unload the basket, prepared by Mrs Jolly. Plates were fetched from the dresser and they were filled with tasty sausage and sage rolls, various sandwiches, mince pies. 'Look, Uncle Jack,' an excited Lucie showed him a shortbread biscuit in the shape of a Christmas tree. 'We helped to make them.'

'You are clever,' he enthused, looking at the different shapes the girls had created. The kettle came to the boil and Charlotte made a pot of tea and poured milk into tumblers for the girls.

After they'd all eaten and drunk their fill, Lucie sang the carol 'Away in a Manger', which she'd learned at school. Her sweet voice filled the kitchen as her captive audience listened and clapped their appreciation.

'It reminds me of when I was a lad and sang in church choir,' Jack reminisced.

Lucie looked puzzled, asking, 'Where is lad now?'

Jack laughed, 'Hiding.' And before they could ask any more questions, he produced the button bag for the girls to play with.

For a while, Charlotte watched the two girls, lying on their tummies on the fireside rug, making patterns with the buttons, indulging in their make-believe world of playful innocence. It was heart-warming to see Juliette now behaving and playing like any other four-year-old.

Hopefully, living at the House with the other children would help to eradicate the horrors she had suffered and witnessed in her short life.

Jack interrupted her thoughts. 'You look serious, lass.'

She didn't speak, but cast her eyes down to Juliette.

'Aye, it takes time. Heard from Emile?'

Her eyes suddenly brimmed with tears. 'Nothing,' she whispered. 'I don't know if he has received my letters.' A sob caught her unaware and the two little girls looked up at her. Hastily she changed it to a cough, and pulled a handkerchief from her cardigan pocket. She blew her nose, giving time to compose herself. Then she continued speaking in a quiet tone. 'I don't know whether he is wounded and in hospital.' She couldn't voice her darkest thoughts, fearing that he might have been killed in battle. 'According to the news on the wireless and newspapers, there's a great deal of fighting in Europe. I just hope the war will hurry up and end.'

'I'll second that,' said Jack.

They were interrupted by the sound of loud knocking on the door, which opened to reveal a middle-aged bearded man, who Charlotte recognised as one of Jack's neighbours. He was carrying a hot plate of food in one hand and a bottle of stout in the other hand.

'Ah, didn't know yer had company, Jack.' He hovered uncertainly, his big frame filling the room.

Charlotte jumped to her feet, saying, 'It's time we were going.'

The buttons were put in the bag, and the two girls scrambled to their feet. 'Thank you, Uncle Jack,' they chorused as Charlotte helped them into their outdoor clothes.

It was three o'clock, and she wanted to be home before darkness pulled its veil across the sky. She felt the comforting warmth of tiny hands in hers as she guided both Juliette and Lucie along an uneven path. Her thoughts turned to the new year of 1945, wondering if it would bring peace. And if it did, would it bring Emile home to her and Juliette?

CHAPTER THIRTY-ONE

January 1945

A week later, after walking the younger children to school, Charlotte decided to call at the inn to see Hilda. She went round to the yard door and saw George sorting crates for the brewery to collect. 'Morning, did you have a good New Year?' She would have said profitable, but she didn't want to upset him.

He looked at her with suspicion and muttered, 'Aye.'

She found Hilda in the kitchen, busy preparing vegetables for their dinner later on. To Charlotte's surprise, her aunt's face lit up when she saw her.

'I'd never thought I'd ever say this, but it's nice to see you, lass. I'll put the kettle on,' she said, wiping her hand on her apron.

Sitting at the table, Charlotte felt a bit awkward, and her words stilted. 'I expect you were very busy over the festive period.'

'Same as usual, but Maureen, young woman who replaced you, pulls her weight and sometimes her younger sister helps out too.'

'That's good,' Charlotte replied, then sipped her tea, wondering what else to say.

'I hear you had a visitor. Never thought she'd set foot in House, not after what happened. Did she have much to say?' Hilda asked bluntly Charlotte looked across at her aunt and saw the raw grief in her eyes. She wanted to rush to her, hug her, but she didn't think Hilda was the hugging type. She cleared her throat and replied, 'She never mentioned what had happened all those years ago. She came to bring over a little girl from France, whose grandparents were massacred by the SS, along with the rest of their village. The little girl was so traumatised she refused to leave Mrs Ross's side.' She didn't mention that the little girl was Emile's daughter. It hurt too much to say his name out loud.

'France, what was she doing there?' Hilda sniffed.

'Going by the code name, Auntie, she was responsible for bringing all the other French children living at the House. And many more, I guess.'

'She never mentioned it.' Charlotte stared at her aunt, wondering. Hilda busied herself tidying the table, not meeting Charlotte's eyes. 'I thought she'd gone to live a life of luxury down there in London, after she left Mr Ross to fend for himself.' She paused for thought and then added, 'At least, me and George stuck together. At first, it was not easy. Still have me moments,' she whispered and sat down, her mood reflective.

After a few minutes of silence, Charlotte rose to her feet, saying. 'Time I was getting back.'

Walking down the lane towards the House, she thought of Anthony Ross and wondered what had happened to him.

* * *

On a hospital bed, in Leatherhead, Surrey, lay the broken body of a man in a drugged sleep to help relieve his pain. After studying the examination and the case notes from the frontline, the doctors and nurses around the soldier's bed listened to the surgeon's verdict. Left on the battlefield for dead, the German tanks had rumbled over the hole which Major Anthony Ross had been catapulted into. He suffered many superficial wounds, but his main injury was to his spinal cord, causing paralysis. His prognosis for survival was not favourable.

However, the surgeon was renowned for never giving up on a patient. 'The major has a chance, though it's doubtful if he will ever walk again.' He remained thoughtful for a few moments. The other medical staff stood to attention, eyes fixed on the surgeon, ready to follow him to the next patient, when he boomed. 'Prepare the patient for operation.' Then he strode away.

As the staff hurried after him, Anthony opened his eyes. Looking up at the white sterile ceiling, his cracked lips formed the barely audible words, words only he could hear. 'I will walk again.'

* * *

It was past midnight and exhausted, Margaret sank down on the lumpy mattress, hoping to catch a few hours' sleep. The WVS had found her this temporary accommodation near to Blackfriars Bridge. For a few moments she lay awake, her head aching with swirling thoughts, and then she drifted off to a restless sleep and vivid dreams. She could smell the acrid smell of burning, hear high pitched screams, and a loud bang shaking and shuddering the building. She was trapped. Waking up on auto-pilot, she jumped from the bed, ready to flee to safety. Where was she? Which country?

Then she heard the loud English voice of a woman. 'You bloody stupid fool. You've burnt the toast. Can't you do anything right.' Then a string of expletives from another woman.

Margaret groaned and fell back onto the bed and closed her eyes, but sleep eluded her.

Raising herself up on one elbow, she glanced at her watch, which was sitting on a pile of old books; seven-thirty in the morning. She relished the silence of the house when the other occupants departed. Then dragging herself from the bed, she found the bathroom. Washed and dressed, she went downstairs to the kitchen. She surveyed the mess of burnt toast dumped on the table and the half empty cups of horrid-looking brown liquid. Pulling on her coat and hat, she set out to find a WVS mobile kitchen.

Later, sitting on a wooden bench overlooking the Thames, she cradled the mug of hot tea in her hands and contemplated what to do next. She had been told that her services were no longer needed. Suddenly, the reserves of adrenalin, which she'd been running on, evaporated, leaving her feeling mentally and physically drained. She tossed a crumb of her sandwich to a one-legged pigeon, watching its adept movements, and then it flew away. She wished she could fly away too, away from the big black hole which filled her. She stared across the murky water, which held no answer. She struggled to her feet. To survive, she needed a purpose in her life.

Otherwise, it wasn't worth living.

She spent the day wandering aimlessly. No one noticed her. 'I'm the invisible woman,' she voiced out loud. A man walking by gave her a queer look. He probably thinks I'm mad, her inner voice responded. Trudging on, head down, her mind muzzled, she was surprised when she looked up to find herself in St Pancras station. A name dropped into her head from nowhere, Aunt Dolly. She lived in Surrey, in a village, if only she could remember the name. She'd go back to the digs and check in her address book. Aunt Dolly was her godmother, a friend of her late mother's.

Back at the digs, she hurried up the stairs to the room she occupied. Rifling through her bag, she panicked, unable to find the old address book. Then to her utter relief, she tugged it loose from where it was wedged in a corner. Thumbing with trembling fingers through the book, panic gripped her when she couldn't find the telephone number. She closed her eyes and took deep breath to steady her nerves.

She searched through the book again. Slowly, she studied each page. And there it was, Mrs D Morrell.

Hearing the outside door open and voices, she hurtled down the stairs to the pay-phone in the hall, before it could be commandeered by the house's other occupants. In her haste, she bumped into one of the women, just about to use the phone.

'Well, I never!' exclaimed a haughty voice.

'Sorry,' Margaret muttered, reaching for the telephone. She slotted in the coins and dialled the number, hearing the clicking along the line until it engaged and rang. The ringing went on. Almost in despair, she willed Dolly to answer. And then she did.

The warm tone of Dolly's voice brought a lump to her throat and for a few seconds she couldn't reply.

'Dolly, it's me, Margaret.'

'Margaret, my darling girl, how nice to hear from you.'

There was no reproach in Dolly's voice for not keeping in touch over these difficult years.

'Dolly, can I come . . .' Tears welled in her eyes, a sob caught her breath, and she couldn't get her words out properly.

'Margaret, where are you?'

She took a great gulp and then replied, 'London, near Blackfriars Bridge.'

'Come to me. If you leave in the next hour, you can catch the night train from Waterloo Station to Leatherhead. I will arrange for you to be met at the station.'

'Thank you, Dolly.' The coins ran out, and the line clicked dead.

Margaret hastily packed her case and scribbled a letter to the office, informing them of her new address. Not that she expected to be called upon, but as a courtesy.

The train was crowded, but she managed to squeeze on a seat in-between a man smoking a foul-smelling pipe and a woman who constantly fidgeted in her copious handbag. She closed her eyes, listening to the rhythm of the train.

She alighted at the station and the other passengers disappeared, leaving her standing alone on the platform. A feeling of emptiness swept through her taut body. A feeling she'd experienced many times, but could never get used to. Standing alone, she waited.

Then she heard the chugging and engine-spluttering and knocking of a vehicle. As she neared the gate, through the gloom, she saw a van. A middle-aged man wound down the window and shouted to her. 'Hop in missus, before it stops.'

Swiftly, Margaret did his bidding and sat on the passenger seat, her case resting on her knees. 'It's good of you to meet me,' she glanced at the man.

'It's the petrol, you see, it's not pure,' he replied. Then he concentrated on driving down the narrow dark lane to the village of Little Bookham.

They arrived at Dolly's cottage, situated on the edge of the village. Margaret scrambled from the van as it performed its spluttering and knocking. 'Thank you,' she said, not knowing the man's name.

Dolly must have been watching for her. The door opened immediately, and she was ushered inside and the blackout curtain drawn. 'Welcome, Margaret. Leave your case at the bottom of the stairs and come into the kitchen where it is warm.'

Inside the kitchen a wireless played dance music, and a delicious aroma wafted from the pan simmering on the hob. Images flashed before Margaret's eyes as distant memories came back to her. As a young girl, she often visited Dolly. Nothing in here had changed and the war and the killing in the outside world seemed not to exist. A big lump rose up in her throat and tears were in danger of falling. She gulped hard. 'Dolly, it is so lovely to see you.' And without another word, she went into Dolly's open arms for a comforting hug. The warmth of Dolly's ample body released the coiled tension in Margaret's body.

Drawing away, Dolly said, 'I have leek and potato soup and a freshly baked loaf. I expect you are hungry.'

Margaret nodded. Sitting down at the table, she watched Dolly moving about the kitchen. And then noticed the old black cat uncurl itself from a cushion on one of the chairs to stare at her, as if to say, 'I hope you don't want my food.'

'You've still got Snowy, then?' She remembered the day Snowy came. A cold February day, snow drifting deep, when she heard the sound of a pitiful cry on the back doorstep. Opening the door, Margaret saw a little black kitten and gave it a saucer of milk. In fact, she gave him three saucers full. And then she'd gone outside to build a snowman with friends. When she came back indoors, the kitten was sleeping in front of the fire, curled up on the rug. He'd found his home.

Dolly glanced at Snowy. 'He's a good age now and doesn't go far.'

The meal was tasty and wholesome, and Margaret felt quite full. She owed Dolly an explanation of why she'd come, but tiredness overcome her and she yawned. 'Sorry,' she covered her mouth to ward off another one.

Dolly took charge. 'You have a good night's rest, and tomorrow we'll talk.'

Upstairs, in the room, she'd last slept in with Anthony and the children sleeping in the room next door, she bit her lip, not wanting to think of those happy times. Her feet touched the hot water bottle Dolly had placed in the bed, and for a fleeting moment, she felt like the young girl she'd once been. Except she wasn't. Tomorrow, she would unburden herself to Dolly.

But would it bring the inner peace she so much desired? Or was her destiny to remain a troubled, restless soul?

CHAPTER THIRTY-TWO

January 1945

'You're looking peaky,' Mrs Grahame handed Charlotte a morning cup of tea.

'I'm just a bit tired,' Charlotte replied, sinking onto a kitchen chair and wrapping her hands around the hot cup.

Mrs Jolly coming from the pantry carrying a tin of flour, caught the gist of the conversation, and added. 'Young lass like you should make time to have enjoyment.'

'It's Juliette. I don't like to leave her.'

'Fiddlesticks!' Mrs Jolly set the tin down on the table with a thud. 'When I was your age, you couldn't keep me in. Me and my sister used to climb down from the bedroom window onto shed roof and we'd be off with the lads.' She chuckled, a glint in her grey eyes.

'Go to the village dance with your friend, Joyce. Juliette will be fast asleep and won't miss you,' Mrs Grahame poured out a second cup of tea.

'But what if she wakes up? I should be here.'

'Laura will be here and Juliette likes her, so it is not a problem. Ask the postwoman to drop a note off to Joyce,' Mrs Grahame said patiently.

'But . . .' the two women rounded on her.

Joyce was delighted, and cycled over to see Charlotte. They were in her quarters, going through the contents of her wardrobe. 'You've got more clothes than me,' Joyce commented wistfully. 'I've no coupons left. Gave them to Mam for the kids.'

Charlotte brought out the dresses from Jack that had belonged to his wife. 'Try on one of these.' Joyce settled for a green taffeta with a V-neck and cut on slender lines to suit her lithe figure. She twirled around the bed and the hem of the dress flared to reveal her strong legs. Charlotte chose the blue silk dress, because of the frills around the arms and waist, which hid her thin body. She still had the special dress she'd worn for the dance at the Floral Hall with Emile, but she couldn't bring herself to wear it for anyone but Emile. For that was the night he'd stayed over, and they'd first slept together, though they spent more time making love. A magical experience of two bodies and two minds in complete harmony.

That night, as she lay in her in bed, alone, she tried to recapture that enchanted time, but try as she might, only unhappiness filled her mind. 'Emile,' she whispered into the darkness. 'Where are you?' Then she wondered, perhaps he didn't want anything more to do with her? Or was he wounded and in hospital, too ill to write? Or . . . ? She turned over and hid her face in the pillow, not wanting to think of that.

For the Saturday night dance at the village hall Joyce was coming with two airmen from the airfield at Lissett to pick her up. 'I can walk there,' Charlotte had protested.

'What if it rains? You don't want to get your dress wet,' Joyce countered.

There was no rain. It was a fine, clear night. A bomber's moon shone, and she shivered.

She heard the sound of the blast of a horn, and slipped on her coat, wound her scarf protectively around her head and neck, and picked up her handbag. She glanced around the sitting room, wanting to linger longer, but it wasn't fair. These young airmen were fighting a war, they needed some light relief from the thought of not knowing if they might survive the next day. The least she could do was to help them enjoy themselves for one evening.

In the vehicle she said a cheery 'Hello,' and the three greeted her in return. Once inside the village hall, Charlotte glanced at the two RAF pilots and shock filled her. They were so young, about eighteen or nineteen, far too young to be flying planes to defeat the enemy, Charlotte thought.

Introductions were made by Joyce. 'Eddy and Jim.'

Charlotte shook hands with them. Eddy, the taller, had a head of ginger hair and pale blue eyes that looked her up and down with approval. She laughed, liking his cheeky grin. Jim, dark wavy hair and alert brown eyes and a quiet smile, looked the serious one of the two.

Taking off their coats and scarfs in the cloakroom, Joyce asked, 'What do you think of them?'

'They seem very nice, but so young to be pilots and fighting.' Then she noticed a dark cloud passed over Joyce's face. She bit her lip for her insensitive remark as she remembered the pilot who Joyce had fallen for. He never returned. She took Joyce by the arm. 'Come on, let's show them a good time.' And felt relieved to see Joyce's face light up.

There were two visiting bands playing tonight and one of them favoured the American swing style. A couple swept onto the floor and give a fantastic dance routine, like the great Fred Astaire and Ginger Rogers. 'Come on,' Joyce enthused 'Let's show 'em.'

And before Charlotte could utter a word, Jim pulled her onto the dance floor. 'Come on, baby, let's swing,' he said in a mock American accent. And she did. The band tempo quickened and her feet barely touched the floor as Jim swung her around with ease. She felt exhilarated and so full of energy. Then the beat slowed to Glenn Miller's 'In the Mood'. Then the Chattanooga and Charlotte felt good. She smiled at Jim, he was enjoying himself as well. In a slight lull

Joyce waved to them. They went over to the couple, who had secured a table and cool drinks. Charlotte flounced down on the chair. Now she'd stopped dancing, she felt exhausted, but happy. She sipped her refreshing drink, watching the other dancers, as talking was impossible over the music of the band. She glanced round to see other villagers and felt a pang of guilt. Laura would have enjoyed the dance. Instead, she'd insisted on being on duty caring for the children, Juliette in particular. The dance ended and someone announced that the buffet was open. With rationing, the villagers contributed whatever they could spare, so it was always a good mixture. She had brought a dozen cheese scones; which Mrs Jolly had made for her, and a jar of pickled onions. Though she wouldn't be eating them herself as they would leave her with smelly breath.

After the break, and with the food all eaten, the second band assembled on the stage and they began to play a waltz. She and Jim took to the floor. 'I can't do it,' he whispered in her ear.

She laughed. 'We'll shuffle round. Oops,' she cried as he stood on her toes. Once round the floor and they sat down.

He lit two cigarettes and offered her one. 'Thanks,' she murmured. She was only an occasional smoker and tonight it gave her something to do with her hands, while her mind inevitably dwelt on Emile. Wondering where he was. The Pathé News at the pictures sometimes mentioned his unit, and if she saw a tank, she focused her eyes searching for him. Once, she thought she saw a flash of his face. She hung onto that moment for days.

He never acknowledged her letters, so she wasn't sure if he ever received them. Hopefully they would catch up with him, because then he would read that his daughter was safe and in her care.

Startled from her reverie, she realised that Jim was talking to her. 'So you work with kiddies?'

Remembering her manners, she turned to him and smiled. 'Yes, they are refugees from France. Some are orphans and some were separated from their families. It's sad, that so many children's lives are put in danger with the conflict of war.'

He lit another cigarette, offering her one, but she shook her head. He spoke solemnly, staring straight ahead. 'I try not to think of the consequences of war, only that I follow orders to help to end this madness of a conflict' Then he whispered quietly, 'I just want to return to good old Blighty.'

She glanced at his sombre face and just then the band struck up a lively Military Two Step. 'Come on,' she enthused. Taking hold of his hand, she led him onto the dance floor.

After that dance, they had great fun, blowing away all thoughts of war for a short spell in their lives. They laughed and jigged, singing at the top of their voices, 'We've got Hitler on the run.' Finishing with a lot of cheering until their throats were hoarse.

Even on the short drive back to the hall, they continued singing, not quite hitting the right notes, but they didn't care.

Charlotte was just about to jump from the vehicle when Jim caught her arm and pulled her to him, kissing her full on the lips. Startled, she gently eased herself away, saying, 'Thanks for a lovely evening.'

'We'll do it again,' enthused Joyce. And the two airmen echoed her words.

Running indoors to her empty quarters, a sudden spasm of loneliness swept over her, drawing her up sharp. She forced back tears of self-pity and flung off her coat, her shoes and her dance dress, and pulled on her working skirt and blouse, and an old cardigan, and made her way down the passage to the main part of the house.

As she neared the staircase, she could hear the sobbing of a child. She ran up the stairs, two at a time, hurrying along the corridor to the bedroom where the sobbing was coming from. Quietly easing open the door, she saw Laura nursing Lucie in her arms. Tip-toeing in, she noticed Laura's concerned look.

'I think she is sickening for something,' Laura whispered. 'She fell into a puddle of rainwater, wetting her socks and knickers, and instead of coming in to change her clothes, she stayed outside playing.' She gave a big sigh.

Gently, Charlotte placed her hand on Lucie's forehead, and the child looked at her with big, frightened eyes. 'She has a temperature. Bring her down to your room and we can sponge her down with cool water.' She stood aside to let Laura carry Lucie. She turned, casting an eye over the other sleeping girls. She heard Juliette murmur in her sleep and watched as the little girl turned over, mumbled, and then settled down.

In the staffroom, Laura was sitting on a chair still holding Lucie, looking frightened to let go of her. Charlotte filled an enamel bowl with cold water and reached into the cupboard for a clean flannel, towels, and a nightdress. She motioned for Laura to take off Lucie's nightclothes and to lay her on the bed where she had placed a clean towel. Then gently, carefully, she dabbed soothing, tepid water over Lucie's body. Her sobs ceased to a whimper and her eyes lost their look of fear. Soon she was dried and in a clean nightgown.

'Have you a cooling powder?' she asked Laura.

Laura unlocked the cupboard where they kept a small quantity of medicines and brought it to Charlotte to administer. Lucie took it without any fuss and closed her drowsy eyelids.

Tucked up in the spare bed, she soon went to sleep.

'If she's still unwell in the morning, I'll call the doctor,' said Charlotte touching the child's forehead.

'It feels cooler and she is settled. But, if she should become ill again during the night, call me.' Turning to leave, she whispered, 'I will check on the other children before I go.'

That done, as she walked down the corridor to her bedroom, a sudden weariness swept over her. She longed for her bed and, hopefully, sleep.

However, her mind was too active and sleep evaded her until the early hours of the morning. She thought of Jim and all the young pilots who were so full of bravado. Live for today, was their motto. Then inevitably, her thoughts returned to Emile. If only she knew he was safe and well. What if he was a prisoner of war? He's not dead, she told herself, because I feel it here. She pressed her hands to her heart. He is alive! But was she deluding herself? She turned over to weep in her pillow.

The next morning, she was up early to see how Lucie was.

'She seems fine, but best to keep an eye on her today,' said Laura.

Charlotte peeped into the girls' bedroom. Juliette was awake, and she held out her arms to Charlotte. Going over to the bed, Charlotte's heart leapt with joy as she felt the tiny arms encircle her neck. Holding Juliette's warm body close, she kissed the top of her dark curls and a feeling of inner peace filled her.

CHAPTER THIRTY-THREE

Little Bookham, near Leatherhead, Surrey, January 1945

Margaret lay awake, listening to the cheerful chirping of a blackbird. She stretched lazily, relishing the cosy warmth of the bed. Then, glancing at the clock on her bedside table, she sat up with a jerk. It was gone eleven in the morning. She couldn't remember when she'd last slept for so long. Not for years. Giving a reluctant sigh, she threw back the bedclothes and swung out her legs, her toes touching the luxury of a Persian rug. Instantly, it brought back memories of love and stability when, as a child, she'd often stayed with Dolly in the school holidays.

Barefooted, she padded to the bathroom next to her room, another luxury she'd spent the war years without. On missions, the nearest thing she had to a shower was from a hosepipe, held high by a colleague. Now she glanced in the mirror over the sink at her reflection and two dark deep-set eyes stared back at her. 'God! You look terrible,' she said to the staring face.

Shuddering, she turned away to run the five inches regulation amount of water into the bath, adding a sprinkling of Dolly's bath-salts.

Twenty minutes later, feeling much better and more alive, Margaret ventured downstairs.

The house was silent, except for the ticking of the grandfather clock in the hallway. In the kitchen, propped up against the teapot on the table, was a note.

On my visiting rota duties at the hospital. Then I have a committee meeting. Home about three. Help yourself to food. Porridge on the stove. Dolly.

Feeling bereft at being alone, Margaret gave herself a mental shake, and busied herself making a pot of tea and giving the pan of porridge a good stir. After eating her fill, she washed the dishes and went out into the garden. She stood on the crazy paved courtyard, surveying the garden. Gone was the lawn, now dug up for growing vegetables, and the swing she'd played on as a child, and her . . . She closed her mind quickly, counting her steps from the courtyard to the garden path. She walked down towards the rowan trees where the blackbird she'd heard earlier fixed his beady eye on her, as if to say, I don't want trouble from you. Unexpectedly, she laughed. And it seemed as if the burden she carried became a notch lighter. The blackbird cocked his head to one side, then flew off. She walked back down the path, seeing someone had been busy preparing the soil for sowing seedlings.

In the garden shed she fetched a yard brush and shovel and swept up the soil and old leaves off the path and courtyard. In a sheltered spot in the courtyard stood a wooden bench, looking bedraggled. She gave it a good brush and a clean and then found its fitted cushion in the shed. Now all her energy drained, she sat down. The winter sunshine caressed her face.

The blackbird had brought a mate and they were serenading her. She closed her eyes, feeling the peace and tranquillity of the garden. All thoughts of the war receded farther away.

'Margaret.'

She awoke with a start and for a few seconds, disorientation snaked her mind as she looked up to see a woman standing over her. Blinking, she shielded her eyes, the fog of her mind clearing. 'Dolly!' She eased her stiff body up to a sitting position. 'I must have fallen asleep. Though I don't know why because I haven't been up long.'

Dolly sat down on the bench next to her. 'Fatigue, my dear.'

'But I haven't been in battle.'

'Perhaps not, but you have been in battle zones, working non-stop. And no one can do that forever. You must take care of yourself.'

Margaret sighed. 'What for? I've no future to plan for.'

Dolly looked at her, seeing the dark, sunken eyes and the lines etched deep in her face. Once she'd been a beautiful young woman with everything to live for. And now? Keeping her thoughts to herself, she remarked, 'Let's go inside and have a nice cup of tea.'

The weak warmth of the winter sunshine disappeared and Margaret shivered. Indoors, the cosiness of the kitchen, greeted her. She sat down at the table, watching Dolly busy herself, wishing she had her energy. Childless, Dolly had been a widow for as long as she could remember, and yet her life seemed happy and full of interesting activities.

Dolly placed the tea-tray on the table and said to Margaret, 'You pour while I butter the scones.' She went to fetch them from the pantry.

When they had eaten the scones and drank their fill of tea, Dolly turned to her. 'Shall we talk now, Margaret? You can tell me what you have being doing.'

Margaret traced her finger on the plate, chasing the crumbs around, and then she straightened her back and sat up. 'I've been to Mornington House,' she blurted. Dolly looked surprised, but didn't speak. Margaret swallowed hard and then, before she lost her nerve, she continued.

'I had a little girl in my care who was very traumatised and she needed my support to see her there safely.' Fleetingly, she closed her eyes and then focused ahead. 'The house is full of refugee children whom I have brought over from France. I felt like a stranger, looking through a window. It's the first time I've been back since . . .' A sob broke free.

Dolly reached across the table and touched her hand. 'My darling girl, don't torture yourself.'

Margaret's eyes were cloudy with tears. 'I need to.' Composing herself, she began. 'I went down to the pond. So quiet and peaceful. I stood there for a long time, listening, hoping to hear their voices.' She bit on her lip and brushed away the falling tears. 'Then I went to the church, to Stuart and Wendy's grave, expecting it to be overgrown and in a tangle. To my surprise, it is well cared for.'

'Who looks after it?'

'Hilda Bilton. Her daughter, Milly, is buried nearby and her grave is well tended with the same flowers. The children were friends and they . . .' She burst into tears, unable to keep her sorrow at bay.

The scraping of a chair and Dolly's comforting arms encircled her, drawing her close, letting her sob.

From the garden, in the fading afternoon light, the sound of the blackbird's song filled the silence.

Later, freshened up, Margaret found Dolly in her sitting room listening to music on the wireless. Turning it off, she told Margaret, 'You can stay with me as long as you wish. You need to recoup your strength.' She didn't add, *And your mental wellbeing*. For she feared that Margaret was about to have a mental breakdown. Since the tragedy and the advent of war, she had driven herself relentlessly. Now she needed to heal in body and soul. Rising from her chair, she said, 'I'm afraid I've only bubble and squeak and a bit of cheese for supper.'

'Dolly,' Margaret began.

But Dolly cut her off. 'You can stay as long as you want. But I will need your ration book.'

With a twinkle in her eye, she added, 'You can dig the rest of the vegetable garden. Digging plays merry hell with my back.'

Margaret laughed at her godmother. And that tiny molecule of laughter seemed to break a hole in her armour of unhappiness.

The pattern each day for the following weeks was set. Margaret would rise and have breakfast with Dolly, listening each day to Dolly planning her itinerary of the endless good works she was involved in. Today it was the weekly get-together of the retired residents who wanted to do their bit for King and Country. Margaret helped Dolly with a huge container of soup, made from the marrow of a bone and whatever vegetables could be spared, placing it in the basket fixed on the front of her bicycle.

Dolly, full of enthusiasm, relayed to Margaret, 'The oldies love to come along and have soup and fresh bread. Then afterwards we knit or sew. It used to be for the armed forces, but now it's for the kiddies in London who have lost so much. The toys we get donated need a bit of love and care and so the chaps do their bit. Sometimes we have a singsong.'

Margaret marvelled at her energy as she watched Dolly pedal off on her bicycle.

Going back into the kitchen, she washed the pots and tidied up, and slipped on one of Dolly's old wrap-around aprons to keep her clothes clean, and went into the garden to see her friend, the blackbird. Though sometimes, when digging, a friendly robin came to see her too.

Today she was planting potato tubers and thinking ahead to sowing beans and peas and how best to make the support canes with what materials she could source.

Midday, she took a short break and ate some bread and cheese and drank a cup of Camp coffee.

She usually worked until three p.m. when Dolly came home and she would make a pot of tea for them to enjoy together, and sometimes they had a scone or a bun. She liked to keep her mind filled with everyday things. Standing up, she stretched her aching back and looked up skywards to the fleeting clouds, when a picture flashed into her mind. A face she hadn't seen in a long time, not since she'd left him alone in the house of painful memories. Anthony, her husband.

Suddenly feeling very tired, she made her way to the bench seat in the courtyard. She sat down and closed her eyes. After the tragic accident, for months afterwards, she had heard the children's screams every night, and she became suffocated by them. She needed to get away from the house, but Anthony refused to leave. She knew that he blamed her for the accident. He wanted to stay there, to be near his children. So, she left him alone in the house and escaped to London, but she still heard their voices in the night. When war came, she did volunteer work, from scrubbing out hospitals to helping the injured. Then one day, she was asked to escort a party of schoolchildren evacuees on the train to the safety of the countryside. At first she refused, until she saw the sad-looking group of young children at the railway station, then she relented.

She wasn't quite sure how she first came to be escorting a group of frightened, abandoned French children from an occupied zone to the safety of Britain. One such group, with her blessing, were accommodated at Mornington House, only because there was nowhere else for them to be billeted safely. And lastly, the child, Juliette, who had the address of Margaret's old home in her pocket. That had been quite a shock. She hadn't intended to take her all the way, but the child was so traumatised, she couldn't find it in her heart to desert her until she was safe with the young woman at Mornington House. Charlotte Kirby was a wonderful caring young woman, who, Margaret knew, would always put Juliette's interests and welfare first. And, she guessed, with love, too. It was so important for a child to be loved and cared for.

One afternoon, Dolly came home in a pensive mood, sitting quietly while they drank their customary pot of tea together. 'Dolly, are you all right? You're not ill?' Margaret queried, wondering if she'd been overdoing things.

'Sorry, my dear. I was just thinking of those poor boys lying there in hospital, injured, their bodies mutilated. War is so cruel.' She lapsed into silence.

Pouring them both another cup of tea, Margaret said carefully, 'Maybe you shouldn't do your hospital visiting if it upsets you too much.'

'Oh! I couldn't let them down. Those boys rely on my visits to cheer them up. I write letters to their loved ones on their behalf, and I read to the ones who have no one. Often they want to hear from books from their childhood that remind them of happy times. For some, memories are all they have.'

Margaret lowered her eyes, feeling thoroughly ashamed for suggesting such a thing. If she had looked up, she would have seen the twinkle in Dolly's eyes.

The next week, after breakfast, Dolly went outside with a few crumbs to feed the birds, which she often did. Margaret heard a cry. Rushing outside, she found Dolly limping.

'I think I've sprained my ankle,' she said between puffs of breath.

Margaret helped her indoors and sat her on a kitchen chair while she applied a cold compress to the injured ankle. 'There's no swelling at the moment, but you should elevate it and rest.' She went through to the sitting room to fetch a footstool. When she returned, Dolly had her eyes closed. Making her comfortable, Margaret said, 'No hospital visiting for you today.'

'Oh! I must, I must. I can't let those poor boys down.' She let out a plaintive sob.

'Hush Dolly, don't be upset.' And before she could stop them, the words came tumbling from her mouth. 'I'll go.'

'You darling girl. I knew you wouldn't let those poor boys down. Everything you need is in my bag. Just be careful on the bike.'

Margaret wobbled at first, but soon she sailed along. Surprisingly, she enjoyed the wind blowing her hair and whistling by her ears. By the time she reached the hospital, exhilaration filled her. And as she waited at the reception desk for her credentials to be checked, she spied her reflection in a large ornate mirror on the wall. Her cheeks were rosy, and her skin had a healthy glow. The ravages of war, which had plagued her life and body for the past five years, seemed healed.

These last few weeks, she had learned to take one day at a time, which was enough for her to cope with for the time being.

The nurse came back. 'Sorry to hear Dolly isn't well. Give her our best. This way.'

Margaret followed her down the corridor to a ward at the end. A room full of light and whiteness. It took a moment to accustom her eyes to the brightness. She counted eight beds and a table in the centre with a vase of tulips and greenery. A man sitting at the table and another in a wheelchair were doing a jigsaw puzzle between them.

'You're new,' the man in the wheelchair called cheekily.

Smiling, she went over to them. 'I've come in place of Dolly, my friend. She's hurt her ankle, but she'll be here next time. I'll see if anyone would like me to read to them or write a letter.'

The other man said, 'He'll be upset.' He pointed to the bed at the end. 'She was reading to him. See, the book is on his locker top. She was his only visitor.'

She glanced down to the man lying flat in his bed. 'I'll go and read to him.' Quietly, she walked towards the man, a smile fixed on her face. As she stood at the foot of his bed, she thought he was asleep. She decided to see another patient when he spoke.

'Is that you, Dolly?'

Injecting a cheerful note into her voice, she replied, 'No, it's Margaret. I've come to read to you today.' She was about to tell him of Dolly's injured ankle when he raised his voice.

'Margaret! Is that you?'

Tears filled her eyes, and her answer was a sob of his name. 'Anthony.' In a daze, she moved forward to take hold of his thin, outstretched hand.

CHAPTER THIRTY-FOUR

May 1945

The sound of jubilation reverberated around the village of Mornington and the silent church bells rang out in glorious peals to welcome the end of war in Europe. Winston Churchill spoke to the nation on the wireless announcing Germany's surrender.

Charlotte was with a group of young children from the school on a nature ramble along a narrow lane just outside the village, spotting wild flowers growing under the hedgerows. They'd gathered a few to press, and she promised to show them how to make a collage on cardboard with the names of the flowers beneath. She was so engrossed in naming a tiny blue flower to Juliette and Lucie that she was unaware of the distant ringing of the church bells until one of the girls asked, 'Miss Charl, what's that noise?'

Charlotte, who was bent down to the little girls' height, stretched up and listened. 'The church bells. I wonder why they are ringing.' She herded the children together, hand-in-hand in twos and they hurried back to the village.

The first person they saw was Mrs Carlton-Jones as she trotted by in her horse and trap, calling out. 'Splendid news, we've won the war.'

The children, catching the excitement, were eager to reach the centre of the village. Swept along by a tide of mixed emotion, Charlotte shepherded her flock to the hub of the sound of wild jubilation.

Everyone from far and near was congregating at the crossroads. Charlotte was greeted by an unbelievable sight of so many people with happy faces. The vicar stood on the steps of the church surrounded by his congregation and across the road, George the landlord and various drinkers were standing outside the Travellers Rest on the small forecourt, singing, or at least making a rumpus of voices. Charlotte smiled to herself at their obvious high spirits. Then she spied the three ladies, dressed in their Sunday best, faces beaming. She waved to them and would have liked to talk to them, but she needed to keep an eye on her charges. Both Juliette and Lucie clung on to her hands, looking overwhelmed by all the merrymaking.

After ten minutes, she collected the children to report to Miss Holderness at the school.

'Time for tea,' she called in a cheery voice, as she escorted her children back to Mornington House.

'Oh, Miss Charl, can we go and see?' the older girls wanted to know.

'We'll have tea and then we'll see,' she pacified them, knowing tea would be set out ready for them.

After egg sandwiches, jam tarts, and barley water, the older children became restless, eager to take part in the merriment. Laura offered, 'I'll take the older girls down.' And Mr Grahame agreed to take the older boys.

'It's school tomorrow, so not too late back,' Mrs Grahame reminded them. But in the event, school was cancelled for the next day so everyone could stay up late and join in to celebrate the end of the war in Europe.

When the younger children were in bed, Mrs Grahame said to Charlotte, 'You go along and enjoy the fun. I'll be quite happy to sit upstairs with the children. I'll catch up with reading *Rebecca* by Daphne du Maurier.' Off she went, with a satisfied look on her face.

And Charlotte, needing no second bidding, hurried to her quarters to freshen up. She changed her dress for a fresh green cotton one with a pattern of white daisies with yellow faces, then added a touch of bright red lipstick, given to her by Joyce. With any luck, Joyce would be down at the inn with everyone else.

As she entered the Travellers' Rest, someone called her name loudly. 'Charlotte.' Joyce waved, her face bright and sparkling with happiness and a few drinks. One of the RAF crew bought Charlotte a drink, and they stood around the piano for a good sing-song. The favourite being the one sung by Vera Lynn, 'We'll Meet Again'. Tears filled Charlotte's eyes as she thought of Emile. Did he know the war was over? As the evening progressed, Charlotte went to see the ladies in their snug, where they were enjoying the sing-song. The noise was too deafening to have a conversation, so she promised to see them another time.

Automatically, she looked towards the door, expecting Emile to walk in and smile at her. Her heart gave a giant leap and she caught her breath as a man entered the inn. Emile? She pushed her way forward to rush into his arms and feel his body next to hers. The man turned in full profile and she pulled up sharply, colliding with someone behind her. It wasn't Emile. 'Sorry,' she murmured, realising she was sitting on an airman's lap.

'That's all right, darling, anytime.' And before she could move, he kissed her full on the lips.

Startled, she jumped up, looking around — for what, she wasn't sure. Through a gap in the crowd, she saw Hilda at the bar carrying a plate piled high with sandwiches. Hilda beckoned her over and handed her the sandwiches to take round to the customers. Glad of something to do and swinging back into the mode of her days working in the inn, she chatted pleasantly to happy customers celebrating the end of war in Europe. She collected empty glasses on a tray and helped Hilda with the washing up.

Words between them were few, but Charlotte noticed Hilda's dark-rimmed eyes and the deep lines etched at the sides of her mouth. She looked work-weary and in need of a good rest. Charlotte reflected how war pushed so many people to the limits of their endurance, no matter what part they played. She wondered what would happen to the children in her care. Often, when on night duty, she heard them call out names in their sleep, names of loved ones, of family. Hopefully, they would be lucky enough to be reunited with their families, or were they truly orphans of the war? There was so much to think about. As for Juliette, she would care for her until Emile came for her. She must keep her thoughts positive.

Hilda's voice roused her from her reverie. 'Will you join me in a tot of brandy?'

Charlotte nodded in response and followed her aunt into the kitchen and sat down at the table, watching her fill two glasses with a liberal measure and place one in front of her.

'Cheers,' Hilda murmured and raised her glass in a toast. Charlotte reciprocated.

The golden liquid slipped down her throat, giving her a warm, smooth feeling, dulling the ache of an uncertain future.

'I've had enough,' Hilda blurted.

Startled, Charlotte glanced up at her aunt, seeing her flushed face, not sure what she meant.

Hilda continued, 'I'm going to tell him I'm not working myself into a grave, behind this bar. What life do I have, I ask you? I've stayed for Milly, but wherever I am, she will always be in my heart.' Tears wet her lashes and trickled down her cheeks.

Shocked by her aunt's revelation, Charlotte wanted to jump up to hold her in her arms, but Hilda had always been undemonstrative. What the hell! She gently put her arms around Hilda's shaking shoulders and hugged her until her tears were spent. Then she found a clean flannel, damped it in cold water and gave it to Hilda to cool her hot, tear-stained face. Quietly moving around the kitchen, she made a pot of tea and by the time she brought the tray to the table, Hilda had composed herself again.

For a few moments they drank their tea in silence, then Charlotte said, 'Where would you like to go?'

'Scarborough!'

'Why there?' Charlotte couldn't hide her surprise.

'Our parents would take me and Martha there when we were young girls.'

Charlotte was even more surprised. This was the first time Hilda had mentioned her sister by name and without any scathing remarks.

'Cousin Lily lives there, we've kept in touch and I can stay with her until I decide what to do.'

'When will you go?' Charlotte was amazed at her aunt's fortitude.

'I'll write to Lily tomorrow.' A look of fear crossed her face, and she whispered, 'Don't tell him.' She nodded in the direction of the bar.

'Of course not, Aunt.'

'I'll tell him when I've arranged everything.'

Just then, George put his head round the door, and Hilda jumped up and picked up the tray. A look of uncertainty flushed her face.

'I need you out here,' he grunted.

Charlotte glanced at his face, but couldn't see any sign that he had heard his wife's words. She went back to join Joyce and the crowd of merrymakers. As she stood among the packed crowd, a tidal wave of loneliness engulfed her and the singing seemed to recede into the distance.

She slipped outside unnoticed into the freshness after the rain earlier that day. The darkness wrapped around her and she leaned against the inn wall, closing her eyes and willing Emile to come and find her. In the stillness of the night, she heard the flick of a lighter. 'Emile,' she cried out, her eyes open wide. She peered towards the flickering flame. 'Emile,' she said again. Her legs seem to move forward of their own accord. The man didn't move, and when she neared him, through the glare of the flame, she saw the gaunt, sad expression of one of the airmen. She stopped, unsure what she should do next. Mesmerised, she watched him light the cigarette, and he handed it to her. As she took it, she felt the trembling of his hands. She drew deep on the cigarette and the action seemed to calm her. The airman looked too young to have fought in the war. Her voice soft on the night air, she whispered, 'Thank you.' They stood side by side, smoking, neither speaking.

He broke the silence. 'It doesn't seem right.' His voice was strained and sad. 'He should be here.'

She felt the trembling of his body close to hers. 'Who?' she asked.

In a quivering voice, he said, 'My best pal, Jeff.'

She didn't ask where Jeff was, for she knew the answer. Instead, she linked her arm through his and said, 'Shall we have a walk?' She steered him away from the village centre, where the sound of jolly voices drifted on the summer night air, and they walked down the quiet lane, both lost in their own thoughts.

They'd been walking for about ten or fifteen minutes when he stopped to light another cigarette for them both. They sat on a grassy bank near a small copse and smoked in silence.

Carefully putting out the butt of the cigarette, she wondered if they should head back to the inn. Instead she asked him, 'What's your name?'

'Paul,' he mumbled, as if ashamed of saying it out loud.

'I'm Charlotte,' she whispered to the night air. An owl hooted in response.

'We don't hear them birds back home,' Paul said.

'Where's home?'

'Sunderland, me and Jeff have been pals since school.' Then his voice broke. 'I won't ever see him again.' He began to sob.

Charlotte's heart wrenched with sadness for this young man and his lost pal. As if he was one of the children she cared for and they'd woken up from a bad dream, she instinctively put her arms around him and held him close. His head rested on her breasts and she stroked his Brylcreemed hair in a soothing motion, feeling his firm, muscular body against her aching one. Aching for the love of Emile. She pictured the two of them, entwined together in her bed. Their love-making so passionate and fulfilling, taking them both to paradise. She could feel Paul's arms around her, his hands caressing her breasts. She gave a slight moan of pleasure as she pressed closer to him and he eased her down, and slipped on top of her. His hands roamed her body as she pulled him down, revelling in the sensation as he entered her, her hands and legs anchoring him.

Afterwards, they lay side by side on the grassy bank. She looked up to the midnight sky, seeing the bright stars and thinking of Emile.

Paul sat up and lit two cigarettes. He handed her one. Not looking her in the eyes, he mumbled, 'Sorry.'

She put her hand under his chin, looked into his eyes, and whispered, 'No, don't be sorry. It was what we both wanted, to be needed.'

They strolled back to the inn just as the door crashed open and the revellers spilled out, saturated in drink and good humour, singing rowdy tunes. One of the airmen spied Paul and grabbed his arm and pulled him towards the waiting truck to take them back to base. Paul glanced over his shoulder at Charlotte, and she smiled at him.

CHAPTER THIRTY-FIVE

September 1945

Charlotte peered out from the kitchen window, as rain lashed down against the window-panes and battered the laurel bushes. She turned to Mrs Jolly. 'I'm glad I've arranged with the school headmistress for the children to stay and have their packed lunch here.' The lunch she and Mrs Jolly had hastily prepared that morning.

'Aye, no point in getting soaked. I'm making a shepherd's pie to leave in the oven,' Mrs Jolly zig-zagged the fork to make a pattern on the mashed potato topping.

'Charlotte, check the milk. If there's enough, I'll make a rice pudding. Kiddies want something warm and nourishing on a foul day like this.'

It was Laura's day off. Charlotte went to help Mrs Grahame who was tidying the downstairs rooms.

Mr Grahame was outside fixing a loose downpipe. 'I don't know why he couldn't have left it,' grumbled Mrs Grahame. 'He thinks he's still a young whipper-snapper, but he said if he didn't do it, rain would leak into our bedroom.'

'Tea up,' called Mrs Jolly, and they both went into the warm, cosy kitchen.

Charlotte smelled the rich aroma of meat for the pie simmering in a pan. Mrs Jolly certainly had a way of making a few simple ingredients taste so appealing. She placed her cold hands round the cup of hot steaming tea and smiled as Mrs Jolly turned round from the oven with a tray of delicious cheese scones.

'Tuck in, thought they would fill you up till you had dinner with the kiddies later.' Mrs Jolly beamed, her round face flushed with a rosy glow.

After they had their fill, Charlotte went off to iron the children's clothes and Mrs Grahame went upstairs to check through their sock drawers to see if any needed mending.

Sometime later, Mrs Jolly called out, 'Time for me to go.' Mrs Grahame left her darning and came downstairs. 'Pie and pudding in the warming oven, so you've just the peas to cook. Bye.' Putting on her coat and hat, Mrs Jolly picked up her umbrella. 'Dratted rain,' she grumbled.

It was then Mrs Grahame noticed that her husband hadn't been in for his cup of tea and snack. 'Mr Grahame not been in? I called him earlier that his morning cuppa was ready, and he said he wouldn't be long. Men!'

'Not seen him,' Mrs Jolly left the kitchen and Mrs Grahame went off in search of her husband.

Charlotte was putting the ironed garments on to the clothes-airer when she heard a piercing scream coming from outside. Looking through the tiny window of the laundry room, she could only see the rain-sodden garden. Swiftly she pulled her mackintosh off the door peg and draped it over her head and shoulders and went outside. The rain blinded her vision, so she dragged the mac to shelter her face and stared into the bleakness. She gasped.

Mr Grahame lay sprawled on the ground at an odd angle and his wife was bending over him. Charlotte dashed forward. 'What's happened?'

A tearful Mrs Grahame said, 'I can't get him to wake up.'

Charlotte peered closer at the man's grey-tinged, silent face. She whipped off her mac and gently placed it over his body to ward off more rain on his already sodden skin. Touching his wife on the shoulder, she whispered, 'I'll ring for an ambulance and the doctor.'

The doctor arrived within ten minutes, and the ambulance followed ten minutes later.

Charlotte watched as it drove away, its bell clanging. The doctor promised to call at the house of one of the volunteers and ask them to bring the younger children home from school.

Arriving home, the children sensed something was amiss and Charlotte told them, 'Mr Grahame's had an accident. He's in hospital and Mrs Grahame is with him.' They settled down and Charlotte, with the help of Maisie, the volunteer, soon had tea served. When they had eaten their fill, the older children helped to wash up. Maisie stayed until the children were all tucked up in bed. 'I'll come tomorrow, once my kiddies are at school, but I can't stay late. Mam's looking after them, but she's not too good.'

'You've been a great help, Maisie, and I am grateful for whatever time you can spare.' The rain had ceased now and patches of blue sky appeared, enough to make a pair of sailor's trousers, her mother used to say.

That night, sitting alone in the kitchen, in need of comfort, Charlotte longed for her dear mother to talk to. She wasn't sure why she should feel like this, for hadn't Juliette and Lucie hugged her. And there was Mr Grahame's accident and his wife must be so worried. Deep down in her heart, she knew the reason. Emile. The not knowing if he was alive or taken prisoner or wounded in hospital. To take her mind off her dark thoughts, she went upstairs to check on the sleeping children. Only Jacques was awake, reading a book about woodwork by torchlight under his blankets. 'Time to sleep now,' she whispered, waiting until he closed his book, switched off his torch and snuggled down in bed. 'Night, night.'

Her footsteps quiet, she made her way to her quarters to collect her night clothes, wash bag and her writing paper and pen and ink. In the staffroom, she sat at the table and began to pen her words to Emile. She wrote a chatty letter, telling him how Juliette was growing up into a lovely girl and how she talked to her about her daddy, and that she was caring for her and keeping her safe for when he came back. And that she had a nice friend called Lucie and they went to school together and played together. She mentioned Jack, but not that his health was failing. Nor did she mention Mr Grahame's accident. Instead, she told him about Mrs Jolly's delicious cooking and baking, and various happenings in the village. *I long to see you and to hear your voice. When you receive this letter, please write and let me know you are well and safe. Emile, I miss you.* She thought for a moment and then finished with, *Love Charl xxx.* Before she could change her mind, she slipped the paper into the envelope and wrote the address and kissed it. Writing SWALK. Sealed with a loving kiss. She had learned that from Joyce.

The next day Charlotte was in the kitchen with Mrs Jolly and Laura. Having just spoken to Mrs Grahame on the phone, she was giving them an update on Mr Grahame. 'It's not good news, as well as a broken shoulder bone, he has pneumonia, poor man.' All three remained silent as they absorbed the news of Mr Grahame's injuries and what it would mean for the running of the home. 'I told Mrs Grahame not to worry and that we would cope. I've sent notes to the volunteers asking for extra help and I've telephoned Mrs Carlton-Jones.'

'What can she do?' sniffed Mrs Jolly as she jabbed the sausages with a fork with unwarranted ferocity.

'I'm not sure, except she helped to organise Mornington House with the authorities in the first place.'

'Will they send somebody else to help?' questioned Laura.

Before Charlotte could think of an answer, it was Mrs Jolly who spoke. 'Evacuees in the village are starting to go home, so maybe these kiddies will too.' She bent to place the tray of sausages in the oven.

'But have they any homes or families to go to?' Laura looked at Charlotte.

Charlotte, her face serious, answered. 'We mustn't discuss this in front of the children. Understood?' The two women nodded their assurance. 'They may sense a hint of unrest and we must be as positive as possible to calm their fears.'

'I can organise a table tennis competition with the older children,' enthused Laura.

'I can come back one evening and give baking lessons to the girls,' Mrs Jolly offered.

'I can organise craft sessions again. Now the nights are drawing in. Cutting out figures of dolls and favourite characters from books and dressing them and perhaps extra bedtime stories for the younger children.' Charlotte breathed a sigh of relief and then added. 'The children are bound to ask where Mr and Mrs Grahame are? We must tell the truth as near as possible, that he fell off a ladder and is recovering in hospital.'

'What about Mrs Grahame?' Laura asked.

'Hopefully, she may return soon.'

She did, later that afternoon, to collect her clothes. She was tearful, and obviously in shock. Her sister, who lived in Driffield came with her, and while Mrs Grahame went to her room to pack, her sister spoke gravely to Charlotte. 'They can't operate on his injury because the pneumonia has weakened his heart. She's staying with me as it's nearer to the hospital.'

Charlotte stood on the doorstep and watched as the ironmonger's van drove away with Mrs Grahame and her sister. A darkness clouded her mind as she felt the wind of change sweep through her. She pushed these thoughts away as she heard the gleeful voices of children returning from school. She forced a smile and waved to them. Over the top of their heads, she saw Laura's face and knew she must have seen Mrs Grahame being driven away She helped the children take off their outdoor clothes and shoes and led them into the dining room where sandwiches, milk and jam tarts were waiting on the table. They were always ravenous, so they didn't wait for the older children who would be here in about thirty minutes, unless the older boys had football practice.

Two volunteers washed the dishes and tidied the kitchen and dining room. When they went off duty, two more would come to do the night shift. This left Laura and Charlotte free to carry out the daytime care of the children and evening activities.

Later, Charlotte went upstairs to read a bedtime story to Juliette and Lucie and the other girls sharing the room. The older children preferred to read their own books. Tonight, the girls chose a book which had once belonged to the children who used to live in the house. Margaret Ross, when she was here, had given Charlotte permission to use the books and toys stored up in the attic. Tonight, she was reading from *The Child and the Little Lamb*. The girls loved the picture of the little girl and the lamb. 'The sky is blue, and the wind is still, and the young lambs play in sunshine bright on yonder hill . . .' Before she reached the end of the story, both Juliette and Lucie were fast asleep. She gazed upon their cherubic, angelic faces, and her heart burst with love. She smoothed their curls, one dark haired and one blonde, off their faces and gently tucked them in.

From behind she heard a voice whisper, 'Miss Charl, will you tuck me in?' She moved to Ruth's bedside and tucked her in. Kissing her on the forehead, she whispered, 'Night, night.'

For the next week, things ran smoothly. Mrs Carlton-Jones told them she had notified the authorities, but as everything was running as normal, no action was needed, yet.

After school, one of the boys, riding a friend's bike over rough ground, was thrown over the handlebars and hit his head. Charlotte went with him in the ambulance, leaving Laura in charge. At the hospital she waited in the corridor while the doctor examined him. 'He's going to need stitches for the cut just above his hairline.'

Charlotte sat on the hard wooden chair to wait, when she heard the most pitiful cry coming from the end of the corridor. Jumping up, she saw a sobbing Mrs Grahame being comforted by her sister. Hurrying towards them, she wondered what had upset her.

The sister, recognising Charlotte, shook her head and mumbled, 'He's gone.'

CHAPTER THIRTY-SIX

October 1945

Mr Grahame's funeral was held at the village church at 2 p.m. Charlotte, Laura and Mrs Jolly attended from Mornington House as well as many of the villagers. Mr Grahame had been well-liked locally, and was known to enjoy a pint of beer at the inn. Mrs Carlton-Jones and some of the local dignitaries were also present.

Charlotte watched Mrs Grahame, on the arm of her sister, follow the coffin down the church aisle. Her figure was held erect, but Charlotte thought her face looked pale and drawn and her eyes were red rimmed, which was understandable. Mr Grahame had been a man in the prime of life until his accident. The staff at Mornington House were shocked by his untimely death.

The mourners seated, the vicar began talking, the organ played, and they sang, then a florid-face man read the eulogy. As she sat listening, Charlotte couldn't help but think that only a month ago, Mr Grahame had been such an active part of the home. He had been well-liked by the children, and popular with the older boys because to them he represented a father-figure, their own fathers either dead or whereabouts

251

unknown. She had felt touched when the children made a big card, each child adding a decoration, flower, bee, football and much more, and they all signed their name. When the children presented the card to Mrs Grahame, her eyes filled with tears as she read their loving words to her. 'I will always treasure it,' she told them.

After the burial, they were invited for the wake in the village hall. There were the traditional ham sandwiches, cut in triangles, tiny sausage rolls and tray bakes of Victoria sponge with various jam fillings from Mackay's Bakers, an assortment of homemade biscuits baked by the Women's group, and George had sent a keg of ale and a bottle of sherry. The villagers believed in giving a good send off. Mrs Grahame seemed to rally and made an effort to talk to people. Charlotte watched as she made her way towards her, Laura and Mrs Jolly, when Mrs Carlton-Jones and the dignitaries approached her.

Charlotte overheard snatches of the conversation as they offered their condolences, and one of the insensitive men enquired, 'When will you be resuming your duties?' Mrs Grahame's face blanched even paler and she looked to be on the verge of tears.

Jumping up from her seat, Charlotte went over to Mrs Grahame's side and touched her elbow, feeling her trembling. Mrs Grahame turned to her, giving her a pleading look. 'Will you please excuse us,' Charlotte said, in her most gracious voice to the dignitaries and led Mrs Grahame away.

Now seated in between Mrs Jolly and Laura and sipping a sherry, Mrs Grahame's colour slowly returned to her face. They chatted about the children and the food, the lovely service given for Mr Grahame by the vicar until all conversation was exhausted and they lapsed into silence.

'There you are.' Mrs Grahame's sister came up. 'You look tired. Shall I fetch your coat and hat?' Mrs Grahame just nodded and gave a huge sigh.

Later that evening, when the children were in bed, Charlotte and Laura sat in the kitchen having a cup of cocoa, both feeling subdued after the funeral. Laura asked Charlotte, 'Do you think Mrs Grahame will return to work?'

After taking a long sip of cocoa, she answered, 'I honestly don't know.' After a few moments of thought, she added, 'I only hope that the authorities don't close us down. Now the war is over, I suspect efforts will be made to reunite the children with their families.'

'Not all the children will be lucky, so what will happen to them?' Laura's voice was full of emotion.

Charlotte breathed deeply and bit her lip to keep her tears at bay, then spoke. 'They can't make them homeless.'

'Will they be placed in foster homes?' Laura asked.

Charlotte glanced out of the window at the fading light, seeking inspiration.

Suddenly, her voice as angry as her thoughts, she burst out, 'I hope not! This is the children's home, where they are safe and happy.' Through the night, Charlotte tossed and turned, her mind in turmoil, thinking of the uncertainty of the future of the home and the children.

The next day, with half an hour to spare before collecting the children from school, Charlotte was sitting in Jack's cosy sitting room, drinking tea and eating one of the scones Mrs Jolly had baked for him. She was telling him about the man's insensitive remark to Mrs Grahame at the funeral, and he didn't sound surprised.

He explained to her, 'There's been rumours — you know how folks need to take their minds off rationing and such like and enjoy a bit of gossip, nothing malicious, but some folks add bits on and embroider the facts. They're saying that Mrs Grahame won't be back and the house might close down.' He reached for his pipe and began filling it with a rich-smelling tobacco. He glanced at her worried face and remarked, 'It will blow over in a couple of days.'

She sat on the edge of her seat and replied. 'My main concern is if the children hear about it. They are bound to worry and be frightened.'

'Sorry, lass, but it's best you know what's being said so you can deal with it.'

'I'll ring Mrs Carlton-Jones to see what she has to say.'

She met the younger children from school and they were their usual talkative selves. 'Miss Charl, we've learned a new song,' they called out and they began to sing, their childish voices so happy and innocent. She watched Juliette and Lucie skipping ahead while she held the hand of a boy who had hurt his knee in the playground and now sported a bandage.

Arriving back at the house, Laura informed her that Mrs Carlton-Jones had telephoned to say she would be coming to see them at ten in the morning.

'Did she say what about?'

'No, I did ask, but she wouldn't say.'

When the children were in bed, Charlotte told Laura what Jack told her. They were sitting in the kitchen having a cup of cocoa before bed. This was becoming a ritual for them. Both were tired, only managing to snatch the odd hour off duty.

'My mam mentioned it yesterday when I slipped out to see her. It's unsettling.'

Discussing the future of the home and the children had also become a ritual for them.

'Whatever the authorities decide, it can't be done overnight. Juliette is in my care until her father comes for her.' Charlotte thought of Emile, and the uncertainty of not knowing what had happened to him pulled at her heart strings.

'I don't want to leave. I like it here,' Laura put down her empty cup. 'I know it sounds selfish of me, but I can't face going to live back home.'

As she tossed about in her bed, sleep evading her, Charlotte realised that she too thought of Mornington House as her home, just like the children and Laura. She didn't want to live anywhere else. Then she admonished herself for having such selfish thoughts when it was the children's lives that mattered. Far from their homeland, they were now safe and settled, thinking of Mornington House as home. Her last thought as she drifted into a restless sleep was that she would do whatever was possible to keep the home running for the children's benefit.

At six the next morning, sleep impossible, she was up and dressed. She made herself a cup of tea, slipped on her coat and went to stand outside in the tiny courtyard. Here she breathed in the still air, looking upwards, seeing the night sky, dawn waiting in the wings. The quietness was broken by birdsong coming from the nearby wood. She closed her eyes, savouring the beauty of mother nature. Suddenly, she visualised Emile's face, looking so serious that she wanted to reach out and comfort him, draw him close. How she longed to feel the warmth of his body next to hers, giving her strength. 'Oh, Emile,' she whispered, 'I need to be strong for the children's sake, and to keep Juliette safe until you return.' She opened her eyes, dazzled at the brightness of the new day dawning, wondering what it would bring.

Hopefully, Mrs Carlton-Jones would bring good news to quell the uneasiness of uncertainty of the future of the home and children.

CHAPTER THIRTY-SEVEN

October 1945

Mrs Carlton-Jones arrived at ten sharp and walked briskly into the sitting room, wearing her authority hat. Charlotte, Laura, Mrs Jolly and the two volunteers waited for her to sit down before they followed her into the room, all watching her, as she withdrew from her briefcase, a letter.

Charlotte found herself holding her breath as she recognised the handwriting on the envelope, and catching Laura's eye, she saw that Laura knew as well. One of the volunteers fiddled with her box of matches and cigarette packet, quickly putting them back in her apron pocket when Mrs Carlton-Jones gave her a stern look.

The good lady coughed, clearing her throat, and began. 'First, I must thank you all for your sterling work after the sad demise of Mr Grahame and the absence of Mrs Grahame.'

She glanced around the room at them, then continued. 'Sadly, Mrs Grahame is unable to carry on without her husband. This letter,' she held it up in her hand, 'is from her, and you may read it later.'

There followed a shuffling of chairs and the murmuring of voices. Charlotte voiced what was on everyone's minds. 'What will happen to the children's home now?'

Withdrawing a document from her briefcase, Mrs Carlton-Jones replied, 'I am coming to that. We are fortunate. The authorities have engaged a couple, Mr and Mrs Sharpe, who will commence next Saturday. They will be responsible for the running of the home. Any questions?'

Charlotte rose to her feet. 'Yes, while I thank the authorities for replacing Mr and Mrs Grahame, what is the future of the home and the children given that the war has ended?'

There were murmurs of assent from the other staff members.

Mrs Carlton-Jones didn't answer immediately. Then she stood up. 'Truthfully, I cannot answer your question, but what I can say, is that every consideration will be given to the children's welfare, which is our paramount concern. There are organisations involved who specialise in reuniting refugees with their families. It's no easy task, and it may take some time.

'When I have news, you will be informed. Until then, you will continue as normal. It remains for me to say, please give Mr and Mrs Sharpe your full support.'

She then left in a flurry, not staying for a cup of tea and one of Mrs Jolly's freshly baked scones.

'I'm putting kettle on for a cuppa,' said Mrs Jolly. And they all followed her into the kitchen.

'Are Mr and Mrs Sharpe local?' Charlotte asked.

'Not heard of them,' replied Mrs Jolly as she put hot scones on the table. 'Jam, but no butter to spare.'

After chatting for a while and wondering about the replacement couple, Charlotte said, 'If they are like the Grahames, we'll be fine.' She hoped she sounded more positive than she felt.

The two volunteers went back to their duties, and Charlotte and Laura checked the living quarters for the arrival of the new couple. Charlotte opened the windows to let in fresh air and they stripped the bed, ready for fresh bedding, swept the floors and shook the rug, polished the wardrobe and dressing table and tallboy. 'I guess they will bring their own personal bits and pieces.' Charlotte surveyed the room.

'What about the sitting room?' asked Laura, glancing at her watch. 'I've got to collect the little ones from school.'

'You get off and I'll take the bedding to the laundry, then help Mrs Jolly to dish up and we'll clean the sitting room this afternoon.'

With their menfolk returning home to their families, the volunteers were finding it difficult to work as many hours. Mrs Carlton-Jones engaged a woman to launder the children's clothes and bedding, which was a great help. Charlotte and Laura shared the night duties.

In order that they would be able to devote all their time to helping the new couple settle in when they arrived, Charlotte and Laura decided to take some time off beforehand. Last night Laura was off duty. Tonight was Charlotte's turn and she had made arrangements with Joyce to go to the cinema. This could be the last chance to spend time together before Joyce returned home to Hull.

Charlotte puffed and panted as they rode their bikes along the lane against the head wind.

'I'm out of condition,' she laughed as they hid their bikes behind the café.

Exhausted, she fell asleep halfway through the main film, and Joyce nudged her awake for the Pathé News. Charlotte sat up straight, concentrating, hoping to see news about France or anywhere where Emile might be. But nothing. The war was over, and the news focused on people rebuilding their lives and homes. She gave a big sigh.

'Still not heard from him?' asked Joyce. Charlotte shook her head. 'Can't you write to somebody in the unit and find out?'

'I've no idea who his commanding officer is. I just have his French regiment's address.'

Wanting to change the subject, she asked Joyce, 'What about you and the young RAF man you were seeing?'

Joyce gave a big grin, 'He's gone home, but he's coming back to meet me mam and dad.'

Charlotte gave her friend a hug. 'Sounds serious.'

'We get on well together and he's a smashing kisser,' Joyce's eyes were shining. They both laughed, the mood lightening.

Collecting their bicycles, Charlotte was glad the wind had dropped.

In bed that night, Charlotte thought of Emile and the kisses they'd shared and longed to feel his lips touching hers. She tried to hold on to the loving feeling, frightened it would become only a distant memory. And there was Juliette to consider. Surely, he must know she was alive and safe here with her?

Today Mr and Mrs Sharpe were arriving. Charlotte felt on edge, wanting everything to be perfect. She organised the children to practise saying 'Welcome Mr and Mrs Sharpe.'

Maurice and Jacques fell about laughing. 'For goodness' sake, can't you behave,' she snapped at them.

Old Tom stepped in. 'I could do with a few pairs of strong hands.' With relief, the older boys went with him. The older girls amused the younger ones, while Laura checked that everything was clean and tidy. And Charlotte stopped panicking and helped Mrs Jolly in the kitchen.

They were due to arrive in time for afternoon tea. Mrs Jolly made a Victoria sandwich cake and gingerbread men for the children, and volunteered to serve the tea. By now everyone was feeling the strain. Charlotte glanced at the children. By their serious faces, they didn't welcome changes in their lives. To cheer them up, she'd organised for a Mr Caley from Driffield to entertain them with his Magic Lantern Show.

At last, they heard a vehicle coming up the drive. Charlotte and Laura went to greet them, followed by two older boys to help with luggage. The car was a black saloon complete with a chauffeur in a smart dark grey uniform, who jumped down to open the door for Mrs Carlton-Jones and Mrs Sharpe. Mr Sharpe remained seated until the chauffeur opened his door.

Charlotte watched as a fat man waddled from the car, his face red with the effort. His wife, in contrast, was tall and angular with a tight-lipped face. She swept past Charlotte and Laura without a word. Mrs Carlton-Jones nodded, as if to say, I will introduce you inside.

The two boys sprang to help the chauffeur with the luggage while Mr Sharpe stood and watched.

The children, quiet and obedient, sat at the dining table, waiting patiently to devour the gingerbread men and drink the milk.

Their outdoor clothes off, Mrs Carlton-Jones made the introductions, and they sat down to tea served by Mrs Jolly, who glanced at Charlotte as if to say, doesn't she speak? Mrs Sharpe sat upright, drinking her tea and eating her cake and listening to Mrs Carlton-Jones, who was explaining the running of the home. Mr Sharpe was on his third piece of cake and took no notice of the conversation.

Finally, they all rose and Mrs Carlton-Jones said to Charlotte, 'Come and show Mr and Mrs Sharpe their quarters.'

The children went with Laura to the games room for the Magic Lantern Show, and Charlotte wished she was going with them. She hadn't warmed to the Sharpes, but she mustn't be hasty in her judgement. They might be tired after travelling from London.

Mr Sharpe sat down in the easy chair by the glowing fire, which Charlotte had lit for them, while Mrs Sharpe looked around, sniffing. Mrs Carlton-Jones's attempt at a cheerful voice broke the silence, 'You can make your quarters quite homely with your own personal touches.'

'It'll do,' was Mrs Sharpe's curt remark.

Looking at her watch, Mrs Carlton-Jones said, 'I must be off now. I will be here on Monday morning. In the meantime, Charlotte will answer any of your questions.'

Charlotte smiled pleasantly at the couple as Mrs Carlton-Jones hurried off.

Charlotte made her excuses and slipped into the games room, her heartwarming at the sound of the children's laughter, as they enjoyed the magic lantern show. The children were in bed late, excited and wanting to talk about the magic show, but tomorrow being Sunday, they could have a lie-in.

At breakfast, she expected the Sharpes to make an appearance, but they didn't. 'I expect they are having breakfast in their quarters,' she said to Laura. They had the facilities for making tea and toast.

The late autumn sun shone and so the children were outside. The older ones with friends in the village and the younger ones in the garden with Laura, playing games. Charlotte took the rest on a woodland walk, nature spotting. 'Miss, Miss, I saw a squirrel up the tree,' cried an excited little boy. Though by the time everyone looked, the squirrel had scampered away to hide.

Later, hands washed and seated at the dining table for Sunday dinner, the children talked eagerly. Charlotte went into the kitchen to give Mrs Jolly a hand, and was met with a stream of words from the upset woman. 'Who does she think she is? Demand, demanding, not asking.' She shook her head furiously. 'If she thinks I'm gonna wait on her, well she got another thing coming.'

'Mrs Jolly, what's wrong?' She had never seen her so upset.

Mrs Jolly banged down a saucepan. 'That new bit of stuff. She wants me to take their meals on a tray to them. No please or thank you.'

'I'll do it. Let them settle in and then they will take their meals with us.'

But they didn't. They expected to be waited upon.

On Monday, Mrs Carlton-Jones was delayed and telephoned to ask Charlotte to show the Sharpes around the home and explain their duties. Halfway round, Mr Sharpe disappeared, though she guessed he wouldn't be interested in the linen cupboard. 'Your last post, was it with children?' Charlotte asked.

'Children! Can't stand the brats. We're here under sufferance.'

Shocked by the woman's reply, she asked. 'So why did you come to care for the children?'

'Needed a home. He's bloody useless at working. I need a fag.'

Charlotte stared at the retreating figure of the woman, her heart sinking.

CHAPTER THIRTY-EIGHT

November 1945

Mrs Carlton-Jones came to the home on Tuesday morning. Charlotte had to dash off to collect one of the children from school for a doctor's appointment, and Laura was busy helping Mrs Jolly in the kitchen.

Coming into the kitchen, Mrs Carlton-Jones looked around and asked, 'Is Mrs Sharpe upstairs?'

'Not seen hide nor hair of her,' Mrs Jolly banged down a pan lid with such force that it made Mrs Carlton-Jones jump.

She turned to Laura, who shook her head and crossed to the pantry to fetch a bag of flour.

Mrs Carlton-Jones went upstairs where the volunteers were making beds and sweeping the floor. Getting her breath back, she said pleasantly, 'Good morning, is Mrs Sharpe about?'

They both looked dumbfounded. 'Who is she?' One of them asked.

She looked at them with surprise, saying, 'Mr and Mrs Sharpe are the new residential couple who have taken over from Mr and Mrs Grahame. Surely you have been introduced to them?' They both shrugged and carried on working.

She searched the other rooms with no luck. She glanced out of the window toward the vegetable garden where Old Tom was working, but there was no sign of them. Her patient mood disappeared as she marched to their quarters, knocking on the door. She didn't wait to be asked in, but opened the door wide.

And there they were. Both sprawled in chairs in front of the fire, smoking, a bitter smell of strong beer filling the room. Taking a step back, she coughed. They looked at her, neither getting to their feet nor speaking.

Her hackles rising, Mrs Carlton-Jones said, 'Why are you not on duty?'

'There's nowt to do,' Mrs Sharpe stretched out her carpet-slippered feet towards the fire.

'I was expecting you to familiarise yourselves with the running of the grounds, and the children. This is a big house and we maintain high standards and our paramount concern is for the children. Have you met them yet?'

'Heard the blighters, that's enough,' complained Mrs Sharpe.

Mrs Carlton-Jones turned to the man, who hadn't uttered a word. 'You have been and checked round the grounds?'

'Not yet, missus, might do later when it warms up,' he said, taking a swig of beer from the glass in his hand.

'I'll get one of the committee men to show you round and to instruct you on all your duties.' She turned to Mrs Sharpe, saying, 'Come with me.' The woman groaned as she struggled to her feet. 'And put on some sensible footwear.'

'I need the lavvy,' she said.

'Five minutes, then come to the dining room,' barked Mrs Carlton-Jones, leaving the door open as she left.

In the dining room, Laura brought her a strong cup of tea and while she waited, she produced a notebook from her large handbag and began to write.

It was fifteen minutes before Mrs Sharpe made an appearance. 'I've written down daily instructions for the running of the household. On Friday I will check that you understand all that is required of you. Until then, you can leave the care of the children to Charlotte, a very capable young woman.'

How she wished that Charlotte was married and able to take sole charge of the running of the home!

Mrs Carlton-Jones departed, and Mrs Sharpe went upstairs to make an inventory of the linen store and to undertake any repairs needed. Charlotte came back and Laura told her what she had overheard Mrs Carlton-Jones saying to Mrs Sharpe.

'It sounds as though they haven't any experience of running a children's home.'

'No experience of any kind of work, if you ask me,' chimed in Mrs Jolly.

'We'll make sure the children are well cared for,' Charlotte promised. She set the table for dinner while Laura went to collect the younger children from school.

Things went smoothly until Thursday. The Sharpes had continued to take all their meals in their quarters, but Mrs Jolly insisted they came and collected the trays set out for them. Laura was seeing to a boy who had fallen and grazed his knee. Charlotte was in the kitchen filling a water jug, when she heard an almighty crash and a scream.

Leaving the jug, Charlotte rushed out towards the noise coming from the Sharpes' quarters. Here, a scene of chaos met her. Under instructions from Mrs Sharpe, one of the older girls had been carrying the heavy tray with their dinners to them when her wrist gave way and the tray hit the floor, spilling food everywhere. The poor girl was sobbing and Mrs Sharpe was shouting expletives that no child should hear.

Gently Charlotte held the sobbing girl close, leading her to the safety of the kitchen where Mrs Jolly would look after her. Laura was with the children in the dining room so Charlotte went back to the Sharpes.

'I hope you've given that stupid girl a clip around the ears. If not, I will,' said Mrs Sharpe, puffing on a cigarette.

Charlotte shut the door and faced the woman. Her voice was strong and firm. 'Never, ever treat a child in such a despicable manner. They are here in our care, having suffered so much in their young lives. In the future, if you want meals, you either come to the dining room or you collect them yourself. No one is here to wait on you.' She turned to go, knowing if she didn't she may say something she might regret.

'What about the mess?' the woman whined.

Charlotte flung over her shoulder, 'Your mess, you clean it up.'

Going back to the dining room, Charlotte felt her body shaking with anger. Laura escorted the children back to school and Charlotte sat in the kitchen with Mrs Jolly drinking a strong cup of tea.

'I can't see them lasting,' said Mrs Jolly. 'They're a lazy pair of slobs.'

'Mrs Carlton-Jones is coming tomorrow so we'll see what she thinks.'

The couple didn't put in an appearance at teatime, but when Charlotte and Laura finished putting the children to bed and reading to them, they came down to the kitchen for a cup of cocoa. There were traces of food on the table.

The next day, Mrs Carlton-Jones came with a committee man, and he proceeded to show Mr Sharpe the maintenance duties expected of him, while she went round the house with Mrs Sharpe.

Later on that morning, Mrs Carlton-Jones entered the kitchen for a cup of tea, and said to Mrs Jolly, 'Mrs Sharpe will help you in the kitchen.'

Mrs Jolly banged the teapot on the table, making the cups bounce in their saucers. Her voice loud, she insisted, 'I'm not having that woman in my kitchen. I'd rather manage on my own.' Then she added as an afterthought, 'Begging your pardon, Missus.'

Mrs Carlton-Jones quickly recovered her composure. 'If you are sure, I'll say no more.' And she proceeded to drink her tea.

Charlotte and Laura just looked at each other, not saying a word, but both thinking, it wouldn't be wise to upset Mrs Jolly, because if she went . . .

For the next two weeks, the Sharpes seemed to tackle the household and grounds jobs expected of them, but with no interaction with the children. Charlotte and Laura worked long hours, taking only short breaks for sleep. Until one day, Laura caught a nasty cold, which laid her low and confined her to her bed. Charlotte slept in the staff bedroom to be on hand when needed, and her bolt-hole of her tiny apartment became a distant memory. She didn't mind, because her first thought was for the children and their welfare. It was a Saturday morning. The older boys were playing football and four of the older girls were at Dot and Edna's homes for sewing classes. Juliette and Lucie were in the kitchen with Mrs Jolly making jam tarts, and the other children were playing out in the garden or helping Old Tom. Charlotte was outside and, seeing that everyone seemed to be occupied, was about to go inside when the postwoman arrived on her bike.

'Got one for you. It's a foreign one,' she called, handing an envelope to Charlotte.

Indoors, she went to sit in the quiet dining room, the precious envelope clutched tightly in her hand. Her insides jittered and her heart beat faster, her hands shaking as she slit open the letter and unfolded the single sheet of flimsy paper. Her eyes refused to concentrate, crossing over in a peculiar manner until the rhythm of her heart became normal and she could focus. She read . . . It was from Emile, but it didn't make sense until she noticed the letter was dated in April months ago.

My darling Charl,
I miss you. Your beautiful smile is with me every day, and how I long to hold you close and feel your tender lips touching mine. I think of your tiny apartment and you know what else I think of. Now my country is free, the people are welcoming and very generous, feeding us soldiers, and sharing

their wine. There is much rebuilding of homes and other buildings to do, much like your country. The most terrible suffering is the loss of lives in concentration camps. Here, Charlotte noticed a blob of ink, as if Emile had paused to reflect the horror.

How is Jack keeping? I always enjoyed his company and he is a good man for sharing his home with me.

I hope that I will soon be with you my darling Cherie. Keep a light in your heart for me, your true love.

Forever and always yours, Emile xxx

Tears ran down her cheeks. Of joy at his loving words and sadness at the suffering of his people. The war was over, so where is he now? Maybe his unit was helping to restore order in France after the Nazis had been defeated. One of the volunteers' husbands was still in Germany sorting out the mess. Or he could be injured in a hospital anywhere. She banished other terrible thoughts, wanting only positive ones. For him to be alive was her main concern. She had his daughter in her safekeeping. By now, hopefully, her previous letters had reached him and he knew that Juliette was safe. She put the letter in her apron pocket and went to look at Emile's daughter, Juliette.

She was a happy and adjusted little girl, though not so little now. She'd grown taller, and her body was sturdy and well-nourished. Sensing Charlotte's presence, she looked up and smiled, her face dusted with flour. 'Look.' She held up a freshly baked jam tart.

Moving further into the kitchen, Charlotte said, 'They look delicious.' Her heart gave a flutter; Juliette's eyes were so much like Emile's.

After dinner, and free time for the children, the older boys went adventuring, the girls to their sewing with Dot and Edna. And Charlotte took the rest of the children on a nature ramble in the woods. They looked for the squirrel, but he was nowhere to be seen. 'I expect he's still hibernating. Squirrels collect and store food, enough to last the winter, and then they snuggle into their hiding place, and sleep and eat when they want to,' she explained.

'Miss Charl, can we do that?'

She looked at the serious-faced boy and replied. 'No, because you don't want to miss Christmas.' Satisfied, she watched him run along the path to tell the other children what he'd just learned.

Charlotte was back in time for Mrs Jolly to leave and noticed the Sharpes' dinner tray still there with their clean cutlery set out.

'Their dinner's in the warming oven,' Mrs Jolly told her. And Charlotte surmised they must have gone out.

Half an hour later, when the Sharpes didn't put in an appearance to collect their Sunday dinner, Charlotte offered, 'I'll go and see if they are all right.'

Knocking lightly on the door, she waited, but there was no answer. She knocked louder, still no answer. Fearing something must have happened to them, she opened the door and peeped inside. The room was empty, no fire in the grate, and the pantry was bare. The bedroom was also empty, the wardrobe doors stood open, revealing the emptiness inside.

Their two suitcases were gone and the outside door was unlocked. She called Laura, who was now feeling much better, to check, but it didn't make any difference. The Sharpes had gone.

'Good riddance,' was Mrs Jolly's opinion. 'They weren't suitable to look after kiddies.'

That evening, when the children were all asleep, Mrs Jolly came back. She, Laura and Charlotte sat down to discuss a plan to put forward to Mrs Carlton-Jones. They didn't want another unsuitable couple.

It was Mrs Jolly who came up with the best plan. 'There are men in the village home from the war with no jobs. They would jump at the chance of maintaining the house and grounds. And if their wife was employed to do household duties, that should work a treat.'

'But what about the children?' asked Charlotte.

Mrs Jolly was short and to the point. 'Why, you, of course. You know then kiddies inside out and you have Laura to help.'

So it was agreed to put the plan forward to Mrs Carlton-Jones.

Charlotte was surprised when she readily agreed, though she said she needed to interview the couple first.

Betty and Ernie Dodsworth were the choice and agreed to start the following week.

Laura, who had a young man these days, was happy to have Charlotte's old quarters, while Charlotte had the larger quarters. She gave them a good scrub, and Ernie said he would distemper the walls and paint the woodwork. She polished the furniture until it shone, loving the smell of apple blossom. Dot made her curtains from an old bedspread for the bedroom and sitting room and bright cushions made from odd pieces of material. Best of all was the patchwork quilt from May. 'It's a bit creased from being packed away for years,' May told her in a wistful voice, adding, 'It was on mine and my late hubby's double bed, so I've no use for it now.'

Charlotte flung her arms around May's neck and hugged her, whispering, 'I'll take good care of it.'

News soon buzzed round the village that the Sharpes had gone back south to manage a public house. 'Good riddance,' muttered Mrs Jolly.

CHAPTER THIRTY-NINE

Beginning of December 1945

The atmosphere at Mornington House settled into a happy routine, with the staff working in harmony, much to Charlotte's relief. Once a week, she arranged a staff meeting, usually on a Monday morning, over a cup of tea. This was to ensure everyone was in complete agreement with the week's events, and any ideas they wanted to put forward were discussed. Everyone agreed that the children should be involved in all the preparations during December, leading up to Christmas.

And Mrs Jolly allowed the children to stir the Christmas pudding.

Ernie said he would organise a real Christmas tree and collect it in time for the children to decorate it. After the uncertainty of November, which Charlotte knew the children had picked up on, and by their abnormal quietness she was sure they thought they were somehow to blame, December was proving to be a healing month for everyone. So, on an evening, those children who wanted to, made paper chains out of old newspapers, coloured with crayons, paper lanterns to hang on the tree, angels made from wooden pegs, with pipe cleaners for wings, and coloured tissue paper given by a lady who worked in a dress shop. In fact, any bits of packing paper or scraps of material sourced from whoever was willing to give, was made good use of. Glue was made from flour and water, and needle and thread used to connect things together. Some of the boys had a knack of finding twigs and other treasure outside on their adventures, like bits of string and thin pieces of metal. Gilbert and Philippe were busy in Jack's workshop making toy animals and little trucks for the younger boys. They were methodical in cleaning up the workshop after use and always calling to see Jack before and after each visit.

One evening, Charlotte stood in the doorway of the games room just watching the children absorbed in their activities. One of the boys was painting a banner, using pre-war pots of paint given by Old Tom, on an old metal sign long faded and now cleaned up. She moved closer to the boy, Jacques, to watch him at work, though not too close to disturb him.

He was talented, and she pondered on what his chances were of a higher education, and making a settled life in his adopted country. Or indeed any of the children. She knew of organisations trying to reunite children with their families, though no one had been in touch here. The children here had mainly been found living in bombed ruins and foraging for food, living a life no child should have to live. She thanked God that Auntie had brought them here to safety. To her knowledge, none of the children had ever mentioned members of a family. They didn't talk about their past lives, only in their nightmares did they sometimes scream out for their loved ones. Thankfully, their nightmares had ceased now. They appeared happy living at Mornington House, but as they grew older, they no doubt would want to know more of their origins and past life, which would seem a natural progression. For now, she would concentrate on keeping them happy and secure.

About a week later, one of the girls at Dot's sewing class gave Charlotte a note in an envelope. Reading the short message, it was from Hilda, asking if she could visit her. What with everything happening at the home, Charlotte hadn't seen her aunt for some time. On Monday, she arranged to have a couple of hours free and walked to the inn, knowing it would be their quiet time.

When she arrived, George was nowhere to be seen and Hilda was sitting in the kitchen, staring into space. 'Hello, Aunt,' she said.

Hilda looked up. 'I've told him.'

Charlotte sat down opposite her, knowing what her words meant. 'What did he say?'

'Blew his bloody top off.'

'I told him, I've made up my mind and I'm going. Silly man thought I was going off with another fellow. As if I'd want another ball and chain round my neck. No fear.'

Charlotte half smiled at her aunt's words. 'Shall I make a cup of tea?' she offered, and Hilda nodded, relapsing back into her thoughts.

Tea made, they drank in silence, and Charlotte thought of her stay here at the inn. She hadn't been happy, sensing the undercurrent of unhappiness, which she had put down to their losing a child. Perhaps it was down to that, and they had never recovered, but from what she'd seen, George appeared pleased with his life, whereas Hilda always seemed to have bitterness weighed down on her shoulders.

Instinctively, she reached across the table and touched Hilda's hands. They were trembling. 'Where will you go, Aunt?' Charlotte wondered if her aunt was going to live in Hull.

Hilda didn't answer at first, but sat with her head lowered, and when she raised her head, to look into Charlotte's face, she was smiling. 'I am going to live with Cousin Lily in Scarborough.'

Charlotte blurted, 'Will you be happy with your cousin in Scarborough?'

Hilda's face lightened. 'Yes, I'm just going to enjoy not being at George's beck and call.

Then we're going to buy a place together and run it as a guest house. I will enjoy doing that on my own terms. He thinks I can't do it. Said I haven't got the gumption, But I'm not bothered what he thinks anymore.' She lapsed back into silence.

Thinking the conversation had ended, and she had plenty to do at the house, Charlotte rose. Then Hilda spoke. 'Will you look after Milly's grave and the Ross children's for me, please?'

'Of course, I will, Aunt.'

'Right, I'll show you where they are.'

The last time she'd walked by Hilda's side was during the early months of the war, when she came to collect her. Charlotte would never forget that surreal time of grief and bewilderment, the tragic loss of her mother in an enemy bombing raid and the destruction of their home and shop. The days afterwards she'd lived in a dazed fog of unreality, plagued by dreams of going home to her mother, but when she reached the street where they lived and ran towards her home, it kept receding further and further away. She still felt keenly the loss of her dear mother, the feeling of the unjustness of that bombing raid on their home city of Hull.

Within that one night, the person she loved most was taken from her. And her aunt was then a stranger.

Now, she and Hilda strolled side by side towards the church where her daughter Milly was laid to rest, negotiating the old church path to the cemetery where ancient, weather-worn headstones stood at odd angles. The newer graves located farther back looked out to the fields beyond and the distant rise of the Wolds. Birds fluttering about in the yew trees suddenly became quiet.

Beside her daughter's grave, Hilda dropped to her knees, laid down the golden chrysanthemums and greenery she carried, and began to take out the dead flowers from the metal urn. Charlotte stood a few paces back, watching, and when the fresh flowers were placed, Hilda began talking to her daughter about her plans to move on.

Charlotte wandered down the path until she came to the Ross children's grave. Tears slid down her cheeks as she thought of the children whose lives had been cruelly taken away and glanced back to Milly's grave. She understood Margaret Ross's feeling of deep pain and guilt, and her need to flee away. What of Anthony Ross? She'd heard he'd stayed alone in the house, not able to leave until he was called up for war. What surprised her was that the pond had not been filled in. She wondered if the Rosses would ever return to Mornington House.

Then a thought struck her. What if they sold it? She shook her head. For now, she couldn't entertain the idea. Mornington House was the home of children in her care. She glanced back to see Hilda struggle to her feet, and went to give her a helping hand.

Walking back home, Charlotte felt in her pocket, her fingers touching the piece of paper with Hilda's address written on it. She had offered to accompany her, but Hilda said no. Mrs Carlton-Jones was giving her a lift in the morning to the railway station. And on seeing Charlotte's look of disbelief, Hilda gave a rare smile. 'Me and Madge go back to school days.' That stunned Charlotte, because she'd never seen the two women speak or acknowledge one another before.

CHAPTER FORTY

December 1945

Charlotte was having an afternoon off duty to see Jack. Mrs Jolly and Betty had had a marathon baking session that morning and generously given a few pastries for Jack. She wrapped up warmly in her winter coat of dark green with a matching beret and a thick wool scarf of multi colours and a pair of mittens, and her stout shoes and lisle stockings. Her pair of nylon stockings from Joyce, who'd been given them by a GI she had befriended, were for special occasions. It had been ages since she'd been to a dance or the pictures, though she didn't mind because she was happiest looking after the children. Did that make her dull, she wondered, but she didn't care.

As she approached Jack's cottage door, she could hear Jip barking inside. Hurrying, she knocked on the door and entered to see Jack lying on the floor. 'Jack,' she cried. 'What is it?'

Fearing the worst, she dropped to her knees. He was puffing and panting, but still had his faculties and gradually she managed to get him into a sitting position, resting his back against his chair. She waited for him to get his breath back before she asked him what had happened.

'I only leaned forward to get a spill for me pipe, when my knee gave way and I went down.'

'You stay still while I go for your neighbour to help me.' The neighbour's husband, a brawny man, came, and with ease, he lifted Jack back onto his chair. Then he went off on his bike to fetch the doctor.

'Don't want all this fuss. It's only me knee,' Jack gasped.

While they waited for the doctor, she made a cup of tea and sat with her old friend. The doctor came and strapped up Jack's knee and gave him tablets to help relieve the pain. He said he would make arrangements for the district nurse to call tomorrow. Jack's neighbours both came in once the doctor went.

'We'll take care of him, love, don't you worry,' said Mrs Jameson. 'Stan will help get him into bed and up in the mornings. You get back to them kiddies.'

Reluctant to leave him, but knowing Jack was in capable, caring hands, she went.

Mrs Jolly was still in the kitchen when she arrived back at Mornington House, and Charlotte voiced her concerns about Jack's vulnerability. 'You try to take on too much. You've enough with the kiddies and the running of the home. If you overdo it, what will happen? Just you think on that,' replied Mrs Jolly. 'Now sit down and I'll make you a strong cup of tea.'

Charlotte sat down. She didn't want another cup of tea, but Mrs Jolly had the best of intentions.

* * *

The next morning, after she had taken the younger children to school, she did a detour to see how Jack was faring. As she entered the cottage, she was delighted to see his beaming face as he chatted to one of his old mates. Then Mrs Jameson popped in to explain that she and her husband, Stan, had organised a band of willing helpers to visit Jack on a regular basis, for company and anything he needed. 'So you have nowt to worry about, lass.'

As Charlotte walked home, her steps felt lighter and so did her heart, now that Jack had plenty of help and company. But she was still determined to see her dear friend, as often as possible.

Later that week, Joyce called to see her and Charlotte showed her around her new quarters 'A bit posh after your other tiny place,' Joyce commented, admiring the sitting room, kitchen and bathroom. 'And you've got a double bed.'

Charlotte didn't reply, but ushered her friend back into the sitting room. Here they sat drinking cocoa and toasting muffins on the open fire, like when they were young girls, long before the war changed everything.

'I'll be going home next week for good,' Joyce was staring into the fire.

Charlotte felt bereft at her friend's news. 'I'm going to miss you. Won't you miss the life, the freedom of working on the land?'

Joyce laughed, 'You're joking. I certainly won't miss old misery-guts, though his wife is a good cook. Nothing happening now the airmen are being demobbed or moving on to other stations. No more dancing and no fun. At least, Hull's got dance halls, that's if they haven't all been blown to smithereens by Jerry.'

'Have you got a job?'

'No. I'll need a bit of a rest, and then I'll look at what's on offer. I've got a bit of money put by to pay Mam for my board and lodging.' With a mischievous glint in her eyes, she laughed, 'Maybe I'll go to college and train to be a film star.'

They talked about clothes and whether ration coupons would end, both agreeing they were fed up with make do and mend. Charlotte told Joyce about Hilda leaving George. 'I've heard, it's all round the village, and it's rumoured he's got his eye on the new barmaid, a bit of a glamour puss.' They both laughed. 'He could meet his comeuppance, the old sod,' said Joyce.

Charlotte threw another log on the fire, and they both watched it catch and flare up, crackling and sparking. There was something comforting about a log fire, and her thoughts turned to Emile, wondering where he was. As if Joyce had read her thoughts, she asked.

'Heard anything from Emile?'

'Only an out-of-date letter, but nothing current. I just hope he received my letter letting him know that his daughter, Juliette, is safe and with me. It's strange, Juliette never asks or speaks about her daddy, though I suppose she was very young when she last saw him.'

Her voice serious, Joyce said, 'I don't know how you do it, looking after lots of children. Will any of them be going home?'

Charlotte shrugged. 'Nothing is certain, but I live in hope that some of the children will be reunited with their families. Long term, I have no idea. Maybe eventually some will go to foster-parents. But while they are in my care, I will do whatever's in my power to make them happy and safe.'

Joyce's voice was still serious, 'Rather you than me.'

'I have a favour to ask of you. Will you go to Mam's grave for me and tidy it up?'

Joyce stared at her and put her hand over her face then released it, saying. 'I forgot to tell you, Mam and the other neighbours take it in turns to see to her grave and also the ones who have no one left to care.'

Charlotte felt her eyes swim with tears at this loving act of kindness, and she flung her arms around her friend and hugged her tight, whispering, 'Thank your mam and the other neighbours for me, please.'

When Joyce had gone, Charlotte sat alone in front of the dying embers of the fire and thought of her dear mother, so cruelly taken from her. Not wanting sadness to overcome her memories, she focused on the good things they had shared, letting her mind drift back. She recalled from a very young age, helping her mother in her shop. Fascinated, she loved tidying ribbons and putting buttons in rows, and when she grew up, she loved working in the haberdashery shop. Her most treasured memory was the precious bond of mother and daughter they shared. That love would always be hers to keep safe in her heart.

Standing up, she stretched and felt as though a ton of bricks had been air-lifted from her body, leaving her much lighter in spirit and clearer and more positive in mind. She hummed a carol, 'Silent Night', which she sang with the children. They were all going, staff as well, to sing to Jack and his neighbours the next evening. The three ladies, Dot, Edna and May, were invited for afternoon tea and the children would sing for them too. Christmas would soon be here. Already the children were filled with excitement and anticipation. Charlotte loved Christmas with the children, sharing their magic time.

Charlotte slipped a shawl around her shoulders and went into the courtyard. The night sky shone clear and bright, and she gazed upwards, seeing the twinkling stars. 'Emile,' she whispered. 'Where are you?'

CHAPTER FORTY-ONE

Christmas 1945

Coming in from the vegetable garden, Charlotte shivered and stamped her booted feet. The December day was raw. She put down the heavy basket while she shrugged off her coat and changed into indoor shoes. From the kitchen drifted a tantalising aroma of baking, and her nose twitched as she breathed in the smell of sweet spices. Mrs Jolly was having a mammoth Christmas baking session with her helper Betty, and both were working extra hours. Charlotte had agreed, in an irrational moment, to cook the dinner tomorrow, Saturday, so that the two women could have extra time off duty to spend with their families. Both were working on Wednesday, Christmas Day. She decided to enlist the help of the older children and asked for volunteers. Surprisingly, Maurice and Jacques were keen to help by washing the muddy potato skins. On the menu were bangers and mash with tinned beans. 'What about pudding?' she asked the girls.

After much perusing of Mrs Jolly's cookbook, they couldn't make up their minds and began squabbling over two recipes. 'Why not make both?' Charlotte offered.

'Can we, Miss Charl?'

'Yes, providing Mrs Jolly has currents to spare for the countess pudding. We have the ingredients for treacle tart.'

'I wanted to make jelly, Miss Charl.' pouted the smaller of the girls.

Charlotte smiled, enjoying the playful interaction with the girls.

'Let's check the store cupboard.'

Later, after a hectic morning of cooking, Charlotte was busy plating up the meals, and heard Laura's commanding voice from the dining room, 'Sit down everyone and be quiet.'

Charlotte smiled to herself. She and Laura worked well as a team.

Her face was flushed with heat. Cooking the meal had taken longer than she anticipated as the old oven proved temperamental. 'Ready,' she instructed her willing helpers, and they began taking out the meals to the hungry, impatient children. But when she sat down to eat her own meal, her appetite seemed to have deserted her.

'Don't you want those sausages, Miss Charl?'

She looked up to see Maurice looking hopefully at her plate. She pushed the plate across the table to him.

Only later, when the washing up was finished, and the kitchen tidied, and a pile of spam and egg sandwiches had been prepared, keeping fresh under a damp tea towel, ready for tea-time, did Charlotte relax. While Laura supervised the children in the games room, Charlotte went to her quarters, a short respite to relax with a strong cup of tea and her feet up. How Mrs Jolly managed to cook, day after day, amazed her.

After tea, she and some of the children made two cards, in appreciation of all the wonderful meals cooked by Mrs Jolly and Betty, from pieces of card and coloured bits of trimmings left over from the Christmas decorations. Charlotte knew that since Mrs Jolly had been cooking at Mornington House, she made the most of the limited ingredients available, especially with rationing, though being a children's home, they did receive a few extra rations.

On Sunday evening, the children dressed up warmly in coats and boots, the boys wearing woollen Balaclavas and the girls pixie-hoods, knitted by the three ladies, and scarfs knitted by the older girls, in an assortment of colours including red, orange and green. Miss Holderness had come a couple of times to play the piano in the sitting room so the children were familiar with the tunes, but this evening, they were singing a cappella, and Charlotte had a tin whistle, to give them the right note. They set off, the older boys carrying lanterns made from old tin cans with a candle inside. They went first to Jack's cottage where he and his neighbours were waiting to hear them sing 'Away in a Manager' and 'Silent Night, Holy Night'.

Suddenly, the night air became filled with the most beautiful sound of the children's pure voices singing the timeless carols celebrating the Saviour's birth. Tears sprang into Charlotte's eyes and she saw the audience, which had grown, had shining eyes too. A surreal, magical moment. And when the last word echoed away, the gathered audience were silent for a few moments and then an outburst of rapturous applause filled the stillness.

Afterwards, there were hot mince pies and blackcurrant juice and much chattering among the children with the villagers. This gave Charlotte a chance to talk to Jack. He sat on a stool outside his door, dressed in a warm jacket, cap and muffler, a big smile beaming on his weather-beaten face.

'This reminds me of when I was a lad. Me and my pals would go singing around the village. Thank you, Charlotte.'

She kissed his cheek and whispered, 'My pleasure. I'll come and see you after Christmas.'

It warmed her heart that this evening had evoked such happy memories for Jack. And also she was pleased that he would be having his Christmas dinner with his neighbours.

She and Laura rounded up the excited children and walked through the village to sing for the ladies and their neighbours. When they arrived, someone cheered and this added to the magical atmosphere.

To settle the children down, Charlotte said, 'We will do breathing exercises.' Then when they were ready, she gave the note on the penny whistle and their voices soft and clear, they began singing. Tears welled in Charlotte's eyes again, her heart bursting with pride and love for the children. The gathered audience were mesmerised by the singing and called for an encore, naming carols they wished to hear. The children looked startled, unsure. Then Charlotte stepped forward and suggested, 'If you all would like to start singing, the children will join in.'

A man stepped forward, and with his mouth organ played the first notes of 'Once in Royal David's City'. By the time they began singing 'The Twelve Days of Christmas', Charlotte could see the children tiring and nodded to the ladies, who promptly brought out refreshments. They soon devoured the treats of shortbread biscuits shaped like Christmas trees and a cup of warm juice. Some of the audience decamped to the inn to carry on with the merry-making.

Once back home, the children had a quick hands and face wash, teeth cleaned and into bed.

Charlotte had only read a few lines of a Christmas story to the girls when Juliette and Lucie were already fast asleep. She watched their steady breathing, and gulped as her throat tightened with pure love for these two precious children. She vowed they would never be parted.

Leaving the nightlight on, she tip-toed from the room.

Downstairs, in the kitchen, she joined Laura, who sat at the table. In front of her was a tray with two glasses and a bottle. Charlotte's eyes widened.

Laura laughed, 'Homemade wine from Edna.' She began to pour. 'I need this.'

The outside door opened, and they heard a voice say, 'It's only me.' One of the new women Mrs Carlton-Jones had engaged as permanent night staff came into the kitchen. The volunteer staff had dwindled and both Charlotte and Laura were relieved at the extra help because they realised they couldn't work day and night without a break.

'All the children are sound asleep,' reported Charlotte.

'Right, I'll go up. Enjoy your drink, from what I've heard, you've earned it.'

Alone, Charlotte said, 'We can now adjourn to my quarters where it's more comfortable.'

Laura looked round appreciatively at the cosy sitting room, the two upholstered fireside chairs and the couch, covered with a chintz cover and matching cushions, nestling under the window, the polished wooden shelves fitting in the nook next to the stone fireplace. Sitting on one of the chairs, Laura stretched out her legs on the clipped rug and watched as Charlotte lit the kindle and added two logs, and soon the fire was ablaze.

Charlotte placed the tray on the small round table between the chairs and Laura poured the wine. 'I have a tin of savouries, which Mrs Jolly made or a tin of biscuits from Mrs Mackay?' They settled on both.

The wine slipped down Charlotte's throat, warm and relaxing. 'This is delicious,' she murmured. They chatted about the children and the evening of singing and Christmas Day.

When the bottle of wine was empty, Laura yawned. 'Sorry I'm so tired. I'd best have an early night.'

Alone with her thoughts, Charlotte sat staring into the dancing flames and thinking of Emile. She pictured his face the first time she saw him, across the crowded bar. She was busy, and yet their eyes met in unison. His beautiful brown eyes. She saw his eyes every day in his daughter's and wished she had a picture of her daddy to show Juliette, for the child never mentioned him. When she first came she asked for Grand'Mère. Now she didn't mention her at all. From what she'd been told, Juliette's grandparents had both been killed. She glanced at her watch, gone ten, time for bed. There was much to do before Christmas Day.

* * *

At last Christmas Day dawned. The night before, Charlotte and Laura had filled the stockings, made by the ladies, for each child. In each stocking was a new penny, an orange, a small packet of goodies, and cards with riddles to solve. Their main presents were under the tree in the sitting room, all wrapped up in mostly brown paper for the boys and with fancy bits and pieces stuck on for the girls. This year, Ernie was dressing up as Father Christmas.

The younger children gasped in wonderment at this jovial man in a red suit trimmed with white cotton and a slightly askew beard, but the older boys sniggered, the give-away being Ernie's scuffed boots which he wore every day. Charlotte silenced them with a finger on her lips.

They all congregated under the tree, after a delicious meal of goose and all the trimmings, with vegetables, carrots, sprouts and plenty of roast potatoes and rich onion gravy, and for afters, Christmas pudding and custard for the children, and with brandy sauce for the adults.

Afterwards, the children played with their gifts. Two of the older boys went into the games room, where they now had table tennis set up, and the younger ones, for now, seemed contented.

Charlotte gave gifts to all the staff, which were from Mrs Carlton-Jones' women's group and were handmade. Socks for Ernie, aprons for Betty and Mrs Jolly, and handkerchiefs for her, Laura and the other staff. After a small glass of sherry to toast the day, the others departed for home.

The next day, Boxing Day, was Laura's day off to visit her family, and Betty and Ernie were also off duty. Mrs Jolly came in and made stew and dumplings and they had the rest of the Christmas pudding.

For tea, there was plenty of food, sandwiches, sausage rolls, buns and jellies, which the older girls were keen to serve.

The children had played outside in the morning so now they were happy indoors. The older boys gravitated to the games room and Charlotte stayed in the sitting room with the younger children. Outside, the sky darkened and snow began to fall. She was reading a story to four of the girls about a snowman when Lucie piped up, 'Miss Charl, there's a snowman outside.'

They all looked. Outside a man, covered in snow, was slowly walking down the drive. The children dashed to the window, waving at the snowman.

Charlotte rose to her feet and followed the children to look, wondering who it was calling.

The jangling of the bell sounded, and the children began jumping up and down, excitedly calling, 'Miss Charl, the snowman wants to come in and play with us.'

Slowly, she went to answer the persistent ringing of the bell. With caution, she released the bolt and opened the door slightly to peer out. A man leaned against the door jamb, his body bent and covered in snow. For a dreadful moment, she thought he was going to fall over. And then he spoke.

'Charl.'

She gasped, hand over her mouth, peering closer, unable to believe who she saw, then recovering her senses, she opened the door wide. And then, in a dazed voice, she spoke his name. 'Emile.'

CHAPTER FORTY-TWO

December 1945 to January 1946

Emile stumbled and Charlotte caught hold of his arm to steady him. Then firmly, she put her arm around his waist; the snow covering him was cold and icy, making her shiver. His body felt so fragile, as if it would break in two. Slowly, she manoeuvred him into the hall, taking care to keep him upright, not wanting him to fall. There was an upright chair in the hall and she eased him onto it while she took the bag off his shoulder, and then began to peel off his outdoor clothes. She gasped when she felt the thinness of his body through the woollen pullover he wore. When she turned round, it was to see the children watching in total silence, which was unusual, their eyes wide with amazement as they gazed at the real live snowman.

She smiled, saying, 'Children, go back into the room and read, while I help the snowman to thaw out, for he is very cold.'

They began whispering together as they went back to the playroom. One of the children was Juliette, and she and Lucie giggled together. A strange feeling rushed through Charlotte's body. Juliette hadn't recognised her daddy. But when he was thawed out and had something warm inside, she would surely know him.

With her arm securely round his body, she led Emile into the kitchen and seated him on a chair near to the stove. She watched him for a few seconds, in case he toppled over. She busied herself making a pot of tea, though she knew he would prefer coffee, but not the Camp coffee, which was all they had. Searching in the cupboard, she found a measure of brandy in the bottle left over from the brandy sauce, and added it to his mug of tea. She knelt before him and held the mug while he slowly sipped the hot liquid. She studied him, taking in his gaunt features and the way his hair flopped over his forehead. His dark eyes held oceans of fatigue, and the stubble on his chin was unkempt and felt rough. Exhaustion plagued his body and no doubt his mind as well. He needed sleep, and she guessed, by the state of him, he must have been travelling for days.

When he'd finished, he looked at her with dark, gaunt eyes and whispered, 'Charl.'

She bit on her lip to stop from crying out. Gently she wrapped her arms around his trembling shoulders as she held him close, feeling his body rack with sobs. When he calmed, she said, 'You need sleep.' He nodded.

She left him dozing on the chair and went to quickly check that the children were happy and behaving. Coming back to him, she whispered, 'I've a nice warm bed for you.' Supporting him, she led him to her quarters, where she removed his boots and helped him take off his outer clothes, leaving his under garments on. She guided him into her bed and tucked the covers round him, like she did for the children, and kissed his forehead. It was then he caught her hand and whispered, '*Merci, Cherie.*'

She wanted to cry, but instead, she sat on the edge of the bed, holding his hand until he slept, and listened to his uneven, rasping breathing. She decided to see how he was when he woke up, before sending for the doctor.

When the night staff came on duty, she went to check on Emile. He was still sleeping. She would have loved to slip into the bed and wrap her arms around him and feel him close to her body. Instead, she made up a bed on her settee, though she didn't sleep much. She lay awake, listening to Emile's irregular breathing and hearing him call out in French. She got up a few times during the night to give him a sip of water and cool his hot forehead with a cold, damp flannel.

Next morning at breakfast, the children were excited, chorusing, 'Miss Charl, where is the snowman?'

'He's fast asleep, because he has been working so hard and now he's a man again.'

'Ah,' was the disappointed response.

Laura, Mrs Jolly, Betty and Ernie were on duty and the house resumed its normal routine.

In the kitchen, Charlotte told them about the unexpected visitor. 'Emile is Juliette's daddy, and he's in such a bad state that she didn't recognise him.'

'When did she last see him?' asked Betty.

Charlotte shrugged. 'I not sure, maybe three or four years ago.'

'Poor little mite. I expect she was too young to remember him,' said Betty.

Emile woke up late afternoon. Charlotte soothed his hot brow with a cool flannel. He was muttering incoherently and tossing about and his eyes were unfocused. The telephone was out of order. She hurried to find Ernie. 'Emile's worse. Can you go for the doctor, please?'

'Of course, I can, love. I'll nip on me bike.'

The doctor came before evening surgery and examined Emile, while Charlotte waited in the sitting room. She paced up and down, praying it wasn't anything serious.

At last the doctor emerged from the bedroom. 'Pneumonia, a result of a combination of terrible conditions and internal wounds, which have left him weak. I have given him medication and left the bottle with instructions on the dosage to administer. Sleep and care is what he requires for now and he needs an extra pillow. I'll call again in the morning, but if his condition worsens, send for me immediately.'

'Yes, doctor.'

After seeing the doctor out, she returned to Emile and added the extra pillow. She stood watching him. His breathing had steadied, but his body kept twitching, so she stayed with him until his body rested. Then she collected his clothes to take to the laundry room. She monitored his condition every half hour. Each time he was sleeping, though often the blankets were rumpled, so she tidied them, glad to be able to do something. The children hadn't mentioned anything more about the snowman, for they were being well entertained by Laura and Betty, and Ernie organised a table tennis tournament for the older boys and girls. As Charlotte watched the table tennis ball pinging back and forth, she felt as if her emotions mirrored the game, bouncing from here to there like the ball. She was eternally grateful to the staff for rallying round by taking the responsibility of the home off her shoulders. She bit on her lip, praying that Emile would soon recover.

Later, the children were all in bed, Charlotte had checked on Emile, and now sat in the kitchen with Laura having a welcome cup of cocoa and a shortbread biscuit. Laura was talking about the children, and how natural Betty and Ernie were with them.

'Yes,' Charlotte roused herself. 'We are fortunate to have them and the night staff. But I'll tell you what's on my mind: Juliette. Has she mentioned her daddy at all?'

Laura frowned in concentration. 'No, not a peep.'

'We'll have to wait until Emile's health improves and introduce them to each other gradually. What do you think, Laura?'

She hesitated then offered, 'Juliette and Lucie are inseparable playmates, perhaps the two girls together . . .' her voice trailed off.

Charlotte's face brightened. 'That's a good idea.' And she jumped up and hugged Laura.

Through the night, she slept intermittently, getting up regularly to check on Emile. Before taking to the makeshift bed on the couch, she'd given him his medication and cooled his brow and sat with him. He began muttering in French, as though he was giving an order, and his body thrashed about. She laid a protective arm across his body until his movements subsided and he became quiet. Shivering, she waited by his bedside until satisfied he was asleep and what troubled him no longer did.

The night passed without any more disturbance. She awoke about seven and hastily washed and dressed in a clean skirt, blouse and cardigan, glad of her thick lisle stockings.

She poked at the banked-up fire and threw on two logs, watching as they sparked into life, soon warming the room. The kettle sang on the hob and she made a pot of tea. Then quietly she opened the bedroom door and peeped in.

Emile stirred, and opened his eyes. A ray of light from the sitting room beamed across his face and he turned towards her, his expression puzzled. Then recognition dawned, and he rasped, 'My Cherie.'

Slowly she crossed to his bedside and took hold of his hand. Feeling its bony thinness, she gently squeezed it. 'How are you feeling?'

He tried to lift his head from the pillow, but couldn't. He groaned, his muttering words mixed up, but she caught the sense.

She gave him his medication dose, then sat on the edge of the bed saying softly, 'You will soon be well again. You are exhausted and need to rebuild your strength, so rest is your best cure. The doctor will visit again this morning to check on you.' She watched as his eyelids fluttered and he dropped back into a restless sleep. Placing her hand on his forehead, she felt the burning heat. Rising, she went to rinse the flannel with cold water and to dab it on his brow, to try to bring down his temperature. She wasn't a nurse, but she knew he was quite ill. She hoped the doctor would come before morning surgery because she didn't want to leave him, but she had the care of the children to consider.

An hour passed when a tap sounded on the door. It was Laura with a message. 'Doctor's wife telephoned. Doctor will be coming after morning surgery, unless there is a crisis.' She glanced at Charlotte's concerned face. 'We can manage this morning. You stay with Emile.'

Charlotte hugged her, saying, 'Thank you and the rest of the staff.'

It was midday when the doctor came to examine Emile again. After what seemed an eternity, the doctor emerged from the bedroom. Charlotte who had been standing staring unseeingly out of the window, turned round.

He came straight to the point. 'He's no worse and at this stage, he would benefit by not being moved to hospital. I will arrange for the district nurse to call each day to monitor him, and see to his needs, and give him the medication as prescribed.'

When the doctor departed, she sat by Emile's bedside, watching his laboured breathing. A thousand things rushed through her mind, but she couldn't articulate any one of them. A light tap on the door broke her reverie and stiffly, she rose to answer.

It was Mrs Jolly carrying a tray with a cloth covering what was beneath. 'I've brought your dinner. What about your young man?' She nodded towards the bedroom.

'He's not well enough to eat just yet. Thank you, Mrs Jolly, I'd forgotten about food.'

'You must keep up your strength, love.'

Charlotte sat at the table and removed the cloth from the tray, breathing in the lovely aroma of shepherd's pie. One of her favourite meals. Afterwards, after checking Emile was sleeping, she sat down by the warm fire and dozed, only to be woken up an hour later by the district nurse. She was a bustling, capable middle-aged woman, who said to Charlotte, 'I can cope here, you may leave us. I will let you know when I am leaving.'

Although she was concerned about Emile, she couldn't help but smile to herself at her dismissal.

As the week went by, Emile, much to Charlotte's delight, slowly began to recover and gain his strength. Mrs Jolly made him nourishing broths to tempt his appetite. The only thorn was Mrs Carlton-Jones, who requested to see Charlotte in the sitting room.

'Most irregular, Miss Kirby, you an unmarried woman sharing your quarters with a man.'

Charlotte faced Mrs Carlton-Jones, her voice quiet but firm. 'Yes, a wounded man who fought for his country and he is Juliette Delmas' daddy. I would not turn such a man away, would you?' She turned, her head held high as she left the room.

Not another word on the subject was heard from Mrs Carlton-Jones.

At the end of the second week, Emile was able to get out of bed, and for a few hours a day, rest in a chair in front of the sitting room fire. Charlotte sat with him, listening to him talking about what happened, though only in short bursts, because he soon tired. His voice, still weak, he began. 'It's still hazy, but the explosion of the tank still rings in my ears. I was the only survivor.' He stopped talking, his eyes dulling over.

Charlotte reached for his hand, feeling the trembling. After ten minutes, she was about to ask him if he wanted to go to bed and rest when he spoke.

'I was in hospital a long time, my internal injuries needing operations. My head wound gave me headaches until it healed. In my mind, I wasn't in a good place. I thought my daughter was dead and what did I have to offer you? Until your letters caught up with me.'

He stopped talking, his breathing rasping.

The district nurse had told Charlotte about the head wound, noticing the scar when she'd washed his hair. Rising to her feet, Charlotte helped him to his feet and guided him. 'Time for bed and rest.' He offered no resistance.

One evening, on the third week, Emile was feeling much stronger. He sat with Charlotte in the sitting room. She listened while he told his story of making his way through Europe and crossing the English Channel by boat with American soldiers and hitching lifts until he ended up in Driffield. 'And then I walked the rest of the way to you and Mornington House.'

'A horrendous journey, but you made it here, my darling.'

'I wanted to see you again.'

She rose from her chair and went to his side and hugged him, feeling his body, still too thin, but not bony. She kissed him lightly on the lips. He smiled at her, reminding her of his old self, and a bubble of desire filled her. He looked deep into her eyes. 'My Cherie, what is bothering you?'

'I need to ask something important.' This had weighed heavily on her mind since Emile's return. 'Emile, did you receive my letter telling you that your daughter, Juliette, is safe and well and living here?'

His gaunt eyes stared at her, as if he'd not understood. Then slowly he shook his head, and whispered, 'I thought she was dead, along with my parents in the massacre of the villagers.'

CHAPTER FORTY-THREE

February 1946

Charlotte watched Emile's health improve daily, becoming stronger in mind and body. He regularly joined the children at mealtimes, so they were used to him being around and referred to him as the snowman. Today, Charlotte observed Juliette and Lucie giggling together and looking at him. She loved Emile's happy reaction at seeing his daughter, but then his sadness, knowing she didn't recognise him, was heartbreaking to watch. And this worried Charlotte. Her dearest wish was for father and daughter to be reunited, but her instinct cautioned her not to rush. She knew she should wait for the right moment, when the child was used to Emile being in her daily life and not a total stranger.

Serendipity presented itself one Sunday. The children were in the grounds, playing before tea, when Juliette slipped on an icy patch. Leaving Laura in charge, Charlotte took hold of the sobbing little girl's hand and led her indoors to the quiet sitting room. Sitting Juliette on a low chair, she examined the injured knee and fetched the first-aid box to clean the wound and apply a sticking plaster. 'There, all done. Would you like me to tell you a story?' Juliette nodded her head, her dark curls bouncing, and shyly she climbed up to sit on Charlotte's lap.

They didn't see the man quietly enter the room and sit in the farthest corner from them.

'A long time ago a little girl lived in a country far away with her mammy and daddy and they were all very happy together. Then one day the bad men came, so Daddy was taking . . .'

She stopped and put her finger under the girl's chin. 'Can I call the little girl Juliette?' Her big brown eyes gazed into Charlotte's trustingly, and she nodded. Charlotte kissed her warm cheek and the little girl snuggled closer. She continued. 'Daddy was taking Mammy and Juliette to safety, to a farm in a village to live with his parents, Juliette's grandparents.

But on the way . . .' Here Charlotte's voice faltered, and she forced back a sob. 'The nasty men came from the sky with guns. Daddy, was carrying Juliette and they hid in a ditch with Mammy. But the nasty men hurt Mammy and she went to heaven to live with the angels.

Juliette went to stay with her grandparents on their farm, while Daddy went to fight the nasty men. Then one day, the nasty men came to the village to hurt people. Grand'Mère hid Juliette under a bush with the soil around to protect her.'

Suddenly Juliette sat up, saying, 'Grand'Mère hid me under a bush, but she didn't come back for me.' She began sobbing, her body shaking against Charlotte's, who held her, gently soothing back her hair.

This was the first time that Juliette had talked about her terrible ordeal. The noise of a chair scraping on the polished wooden floor made Charlotte turn sharply to see Emile. She put a finger to her lips, and he sank back, perching on the edge of the chair.

When Juliette stopped sobbing and Charlotte had dabbed her wet eyes with a clean handkerchief, she asked, 'Would you like to see your daddy?' The child blinked, flicking away her tears.

Juliette sat up and looked earnestly into Charlotte's face. 'My daddy?'

'Yes, your daddy.' She smiled at the child's puzzled look and explained, 'You remember the day the snowman came, and he became ill.' Juliette nodded in response.

'Sometimes he sits at the dining table to have his meals.'

'Ah,' she whispered, her face lighting up. 'Is he better now?'

'Yes, and do you know why he came?' The puzzled look appeared on her face again as she shook her head. Charlotte swallowed hard as the lump constricted her throat. 'He came to see his daughter. His daughter called Juliette. He is your daddy.'

'I have a daddy?' She slipped off Charlotte's lap, turning to see Emile, who was now standing, looking at his beloved daughter. Slowly, she walked towards Emile and when she reached him, she took hold of his outstretched hand. 'I can look after you, Daddy.'

Charlotte couldn't see their faces, for her eyes flooded with tears of happiness and joy.

She left father and daughter together, pausing before she opened the door, to see him showing her a photograph of when Juliette was a baby with him and her mother.

In the kitchen, Mrs Jolly looked at her, saying, 'You've been crying. Whatever is the matter?' Charlotte explained. 'Well, I'll be blowed, that's a turn-up for the books. Now you sit down and I'll make you a strong cup of tea and one of my fairy buns.'

Afterwards, she sat quietly, while Mrs Jolly busied herself preparing tea. Gradually Charlotte felt in control of her emotions. Suddenly the house rang with the welcoming sound of children's voices coming in from their play. And then the excited sound of Juliette's voice as she proclaimed to everyone. 'The snowman is my daddy!'

And then Lucie's voice. 'Is he my daddy as well?'

Emile smiled at Lucie. 'Yes, I can be your daddy.'

The children crowded round Emile, asking if he could become a snowman again. Charlotte clapped her hands, saying. 'Children take off your outdoor clothes and wash your hands for tea.' There were grumbles, but food wasn't to be missed.

At the tea table, Emile sat with Juliette and Lucie on either side of him and in-between eating egg sandwiches and jelly and custard, and fairy buns, and drinking milk, the children hung on to Emile's every word as he told them about his journey through Europe and England to Mornington in East Yorkshire. Of course, he left out the gory bits, the hunger and the dangers. And the children loved how he became a snowman and then melted into a real man. 'Magic!' they exclaimed.

That evening, it took longer than usual for the children to settle at bedtime, especially Juliette and Lucie. Charlotte stood in the doorway of their bedroom and watched the sleeping girls. The thought most uppermost in her mind: would Emile now take Juliette back to their homeland of France? Lucie would miss Juliette, and she would too, and Emile. Her heart sank at the thought.

So that Mrs Carlton-Jones couldn't raise any objections to Emile staying, Charlotte now slept up in the staff bedroom. She wasn't sure how long this arrangement would last.

Charlotte watched from a sheltered corner of the garden as Emile kicked a ball about with some of the boys, while Juliette and Lucie seemed content to play a skipping game with the girls. He looked quite fit now, just like the Emile she once knew. Surprisingly, he fitted quite naturally into life at Mornington House, bonding with the children, and they with him. She racked her brain to think if he'd ever mentioned to her what work he did before the war, but nothing came to mind.

The following Sunday afternoon, Charlotte had a couple of hours free. She was in her sitting room. Feeling at that moment her life hung in limbo, she gave a deep sigh.

'Ah, my Cherie, you are sad?'

She spun round at the sound of Emile's voice. She gazed at him, noticing the return of the sparkle to his brown eyes. Then she lowered her eyes, feeling self-conscious, as if he could see into her very soul. The next moment, she felt the strength of his arms around her, drawing her close into an embrace. So close. The beating rhythm of his heart seemed in tune with hers.

She felt the soft exhale of his breath gently on her hair, and then his fingers under her chin, lifting her face up. His lips brushed hers, gently at first and then crushingly.

When he released her, he looked deep into her eyes, saying in a husky voice, 'I've longed to kiss you. The thought of you over those terrible months was what kept me alive. And now I am fit again, my Cherie. I need you more. I need to talk to you.'

Charlotte glanced through the window. The February day shone bright and the sky was blue. She turned to him, saying, 'If we wrap up warm, we can walk and talk at the same time.'

They headed towards the wood, walking hand-in-hand. She waited for him to say the first word. She knew without doubt that she loved him and wanted to spend the rest of her life with him, and if that meant going back to France with him and Juliette, so be it. So, when he spoke, his words surprised her.

'There is nothing left for me in France, I want to settle here in Mornington with you.'

She stopped in her tracks. The rustle of a breeze lifted the heads of the snowdrops, as they seemed to wait for her to speak. Still holding his hand, she looked into his face, seeing in his eyes the depth of his love for her. She wanted to cry. 'You mean it?' she whispered. 'You'll live here?'

'Yes, I do. I want to marry you, Charl, for you to be my wife.' And with a mischievous twinkle in his eyes, he said, 'And for us to have lots of children.'

His lips touched her burning ones. Eager for his kiss and the promise of more to come, she felt his arms encircle her, drawing her to him. A wonderful sensation cruised through her body, one she wanted to hold on to forever.

Coming up for air, he gave her a roguish smile and, holding hands, they walked on until they came to a gap in the hedgerow of an adjoining field. 'If we cut through here, we can go and see Jack. He's been asking after you.'

'Yes, I wish to see my old friend. I have a request to ask of him.' She glanced at him, but he didn't enlighten her further.

As they strolled down the garden path, they heard Jip bark at their approach. She gave a light tap on the door and called as they entered, 'It's only me, Jack, and look who I brought to see you.'

Jack beamed on seeing Emile, saying, 'Good to see you, my friend.' Emile shook his proffered hand.

While the two men caught up, Charlotte made a pot of tea, and placed the tray, and a plate of shortbread biscuits on the small occasional table. She poured and they chatted.

Emile gave her a quick glance and turned to Jack. 'I have a favour to ask you, Jack.'

He put his teacup down. 'Fire away then, lad.'

'Could I lodge with you for a short time? While I have been ill, Charlotte kindly gave up her bed for me, though I understand that Mrs Carlton-Jones did not think it appropriate. I am intending to stay in Mornington, and this beautiful lady,' He reached out to take hold of Charlotte's hand, 'has agreed to marry me.' Both men looked at her and she felt the heat flush her face.

'By heck, that's the best news ever. And of course you can come and stay with me, lad.

Where will you live when you are wed?'

Emile looked at Charlotte and she smiled at him saying, 'At Mornington House, as long as there are children to care for.'

'Though sometime in the future, we will have our own home, for my daughter Juliette is here and maybe her friend, Lucie, and then our own children.' He smiled at Charlotte.

'Sounds to me as though you will need a big house,' Jack mused. They all laughed.

CHAPTER FORTY-FOUR

May 1946

They set the date of their wedding for Saturday 4 May 1946. 'Fancy,' said Mrs Jolly, as she peeled vegetables in readiness for dinner, 'The first wedding since war ended.'

Everyone seemed pleased and excited, and planning for the wedding was just what folk needed to lighten the mood and create happiness. Although the war was won, austerity and restrictions were still in place, so a wedding was a lovely diversion.

Charlotte knew, despite food still being on rations, that folk would rally round and produce what was needed. It seemed that most people in the village wanted some part in the wedding preparations. Joyce and Laura agreed to be her bridesmaids and Juliette and Lucie her flower girls. The children, under Laura's supervision, were making her cards. She pretended to be unaware of it, because one of the girls told her it was a secret.

Mrs Carlton-Jones arranged for the wedding reception to be held in the village hall and Charlotte was banned from entering until the day, because there was a group of happy women busy decorating it. And a crew of village men, now demobbed, were eager to reform their pre-war band and were busy practising. The ladies, Dot, May and Edna, were busy with their needles and thread embroidering her veil and wedding dress. Both Emile and Jack were engrossed in perfecting their speeches. So Charlotte escaped on a train to Hull.

On seeing the once magnificent historic buildings, now piles of ruins, she felt angry that the enemy had destroyed such treasured landmarks of her childhood, and hurried by, not wanting to linger. On the bus to the cemetery, she saw more destruction of family homes, offices and the docks, as well as the prison, which she'd heard had been bombed.

After all the devastation she'd seen, here in the cemetery she felt an oasis of calm and peace as she walked along the gravel path, listening to the chirpy sound of sparrows and the blackbirds warbling their song. On reaching her mother's tidy grave, she laid the posy of delicate, blue forget-me-nots on it. Gazing down, a sadness crept into her and loneliness swamped her, she missed her mother so much and especially now when she was to wed. Every girl wants her mother at this special time. Tears began trickling down her cheeks, as she remembered the years before the war when her mother was alive and they'd shared so much happiness together. Dropping to her knees, the soil felt soft and comforting, and she let her tears flow freely. She stretched out her hand to touch the earth, running her fingers through it, feeling the strong presence of her mother by her side, embracing her with love.

When she was ready to leave, Charlotte felt her heart lighter in spirit, knowing she had her mother's blessing.

That evening, she felt content as she put the children to bed and read a story to Juliette and Lucie. They were enjoying *The Fairy Dell*, where the tiny fairies went on adventures.

In the kitchen, Laura made a cup of cocoa and they sat at the table. 'Only one week to go before your wedding. Are you nervous?' Laura asked, looking over the rim of her cup at her friend.

Charlotte answered honestly, 'No, I'm not. Though on the day I might be.' Both of them were silent, lost in thought, then Charlotte said, 'I'll tell you what is on my mind. The children's future.'

'It's been on my mind, too,' replied Laura.

'The war ended almost a year ago, and the evacuees who were staying in the village, all except two, have gone home. Mrs Carlton-Jones mentioned some time ago about an organisation who were trying to find refugee children's families.' She paused, sipping her cocoa, then continued. 'The children are happy and feel safe here, but it is their right to know if they have family members alive. It's their future that important. Though I do worry about Lucie. She and Juliette are so close, almost like sisters. She was very young when she came here. I can't recall her mentioning any family.'

* * *

A week later, Charlotte lay in bed and felt her nerves tingling through her body. She glanced at the clock, only six o'clock. Flipping back the bedcovers, she swung her legs over, pushed her feet into her slippers, and opened the curtains to look out on the day. Her wedding day. As often in May, there was a slight ground frost, and she marvelled at its magical sparkle as the early morning sun rays caught it. Shivering, she pulled on her dressing gown and went to make a cup of tea. Mentally, as she sat by the log fire, she ticked off things in her mind. Today she would become Mrs Emile Delmas or Madame Emile Delmas, whatever, it didn't matter, most important was that she and Emile were marrying. Last night, Juliette, her face solemn, had asked her, 'Will you be my mammy?' And she answered, 'Yes my darling.' And then Lucie asked the same question. Charlotte was saved from answering by one of the night staff reporting for duty. Now she wondered about Lucie. If no relatives came forward to claim her, she would ask Emile what he thought about adopting her as their daughter. They had already agreed that she would formally adopt Juliette as her daughter.

As she sat dreaming, she heard the sound of a light tap on the door. Charlotte opened the door to a beaming Mrs

Jolly and Betty who carried a laden tray with a cloth covering it. She ushered both women in and Mrs Jolly said, 'We brought your breakfast and, so you don't feel lonely, we are joining you.' They both bustled about, setting the tray on a white damask tablecloth on the table. Charlotte brought her bedroom chair, and they all sat down. She suddenly felt tongue-tied, but looking at the two women's expectant faces, she began to pull out words, like a magician, pulling rabbits out of a hat. 'A splendid spread. You've both been very busy.' Then a sudden thought occurred to her. 'The children, I meant to sort out entertainment for them.'

Mrs Jolly patted her hand. 'All taken care of, my dear. It's your special day, so make the most of it and tuck in.'

Charlotte glanced down at the plate of toast and scrambled eggs and wasn't sure she could eat it, as her stomach suddenly felt queasy.

'It's nerves,' Betty told her, as if she'd read Charlotte's mind. She lifted up the big pot and began pouring out the coffee.

Charlotte looked up, savouring the delicious aroma. 'It's real coffee. Where from?' Betty tapped the side of her nose with a finger, and they all laughed.

Afterwards, alone, she actually felt much better for having eaten.

Stepping into the bathtub, she luxuriated in the lovely warm water, scented with lavender bath salts. Lying back, she closed her eyes, and truly relaxed. She must have relaxed too much, as the voices of Joyce and Laura woke her with a start. They were helping her with hair and make-up.

She stood looking in the full-length mirror, unable to believe it was her in this beautiful wedding gown of ivory silk, overlaid with delicate lace, with a sweetheart neckline and long sleeves, its skirt full, swirling around her slim figure. Her headdress was a simple band of artificial white flowers and a two-tier lace veil. On her feet she wore delicate white satin shoes.

'It's hard to believe that your dress is made from parts of three different dresses.' Laura smoothed it out, and teased the veil to perfection. 'Ready?'

Leaving her quarters, she walked on air to where the children waited in the sitting room.

On seeing her, they stood looking on in awe, even the boys. Someone opened the outside door and a gentle breeze drifted in, lifting her veil outwards and upwards. 'Are you an angel, Miss Charl?' one of the girls asked.

Just then, Betty came in to say, 'Time to go to church, children.'

Watching them go, Charlotte felt a lump rising in her throat and tears threaten her eyes. She thought of them as her own children.

'Don't you dare,' said Joyce. 'You'll spoil your make-up.'

At last, she arrived at the church in a Daimler, driven by the owner, Major Carlton-Jones.

He sprang from the car and first helped out Jack and then Charlotte. Proudly, she linked her arm through Jack's, who looked so debonair in his dark navy suit, crisp white shirt and holding an ebony cane with a silver top. Walking down the aisle to the traditional Mendelssohn Wedding March, she floated, seeing only a sea of faces until she reached the altar and Emile turned to her. She felt her heart melt as she looked into his deep brown eyes, seeing his love in them. He reached for her hand and she felt his strength as they stood side by side ready to take their vows of marriage, of love for eternity.

Now the ceremony was over and they walked down the aisle out of the church to a rapturous cheering of well-wishers. And blissfully looking into her husband's adoring eyes, they kissed. 'Later,' he whispered to her.

The wedding reception was attended by most of the villagers, who loved the enchanted, light-hearted atmosphere. Charlotte, in a short interlude, sat observing the children scoffing the remains of the buffet, the band in full swing, and the dancers twirling round. Emile stood talking to men who, like him, had fought in the war. She felt a sense of pride that her husband had also fought to help make the country safe for everyone. She looked to the children again. They were the future. Dreamily, she wondered how many children she and

Emile would have together. Juliette and Lucie both looked over and waved, looking so lovely in their pretty pink dresses. They were happy and carefree, so very different from when they first came to the home.

'May I have this dance, Madame Delmas?'

She smiled, and replied, 'With pleasure, Monsieur Delmas.'

Later, leaving for their short honeymoon in a cottage snuggled high in a Wolds village, she threw her bouquet of spring flowers into the cheering wedding guests and saw Joyce catch it.

Her young man was by her side and she waved to them both.

'Goodbye,' waved Major Carlton-Jones, as he drove off in the Daimler.

'Emile.' Charlotte giggled like a girl as he carried her over the threshold, bypassing the sitting room and taking her straight up to the bedroom under the eaves.

'Happy?' he asked as they lay entwined after their love was spent.

Her heart spilling over with love for him, she said, 'I'm overjoyed with happiness,' and to seal her love, she kissed him gently on the lips. And except for a brief walk over the hill in the morning, 'To blow away the cobwebs,' she told him, they didn't venture out. Instead, they spent all their time in bed, indulging and satisfying their love for one other.

CHAPTER FORTY-FIVE

May to October 1946

All too soon, the honeymooners arrived home, happy to see everyone. The children crowded around them, saying, 'You're not going to leave us again?' Charlotte noticed that both Juliette and Lucie's bottom lips quivered. She held out her arms and drew them close, saying, 'I will always be here for you both.'

That night, sitting by their fireside, talking, Emile said to Charlotte, 'I will need to find employment.'

She looked at him, surprised, and replied, 'Aren't you are content here?'

'Yes, but I need to work.'

'Male pride,' Jack told her later when she mentioned the subject to him.

'Before the war when he was a young man, Emile worked on his parents' farm, and later as a teacher in Paris.' She shrugged. 'So I'm not sure what he will do. Though I do know he enjoys being with the children, he seems so natural with them.'

Jack finished filling his pipe and lit it, then puffed on it thoughtfully.

'What about young un?'

Charlotte looked up. 'Juliette? She calls Emile Daddy and so does Lucie. I don't think she fully understands who he really is.' She sighed heavily, then added, 'I hear from Mrs Carlton-Jones that plans are in motion to find any surviving families of the children. Lucie doesn't remember anything of her time in her homeland, or if she does, she has it locked away deeply within her. If anyone comes forward to claim her, it will break her heart to be parted from Juliette. They are close, like sisters.'

Jack puffed on his pipe once more, then commented, 'War is brutal. Truthfully, there are no winners. All those people killed and maimed and separated from their loved ones, their homes and work places destroyed. They said the Great War was a war to end all wars, and that only brought misery and hardship. Afterwards, many men were out of work, not able to provide for their families. At least this new government consider the working class and are bringing in welfare reforms.'

Leaving Jack in a pensive mood, Charlotte went to meet the younger children from school, and while she waited, she mulled over what she and Jack had been discussing.

'Miss Charl, look what I've made.' One of the girls came racing up to her, waving in her hand a small knitted hat. 'It's a pixie-hood,' the girl chanted.

Charlotte smiled at her enthusiasm. For the past two years, May, Dot and Edna had been going into the school twice a week to help the girls with handicrafts.

On Friday of that week, when the children were preparing for bed, Charlotte was sitting at one of the dining tables, doing the monthly accounts for Mrs Carlton-Jones. They were well over budget that month due to the expenditure of the wedding, the money mostly being spent on new clothes for the children. She put down her pen and rubbed her brow, feeling the tension of a headache, when she heard someone cough. Looking up, she was surprised to see Betty and Ernie standing in front of the table, both with solemn faces. She gave a deep inward sigh, sensing something was wrong.

Betty spoke. 'Charlotte, can we have a word?'

'Yes, please sit down.' Was she going to like what they had to say?

Betty was the spokesperson. 'Ernie's been offered a job, with better money, which we desperately need to rebuild our home again,' she blurted out.

The stunned silence hung in the air. Then Charlotte found her voice, trying to sound upbeat. 'That's good news for you, Ernie.' He glanced at her and nodded, shuffling his feet.

Then Betty, looking sheepish, said, 'Can I still keep my job?'

'I'm not sure, but I'll discuss it with Mrs Carlton-Jones.'

Later, when the house was quiet and Charlotte and Emile were in their quarters, she told him of the conversation with Ernie and Betty. He lit a cigarette and went to stand by the open door, looking out at the courtyard. She busied herself pouring two glasses of wine, from one of a few bottles which had been left over from their wedding reception. She brought the glass to him. 'Shall we sit outside and enjoy the peace?'

They sat on a wooden scrubbed bench, watching the dappled sunlight through the trees, listening to the gentle rustle of the leaves and the evening song of a blackbird, sipping their wine.

Emile broke the silence. 'Charl, would you be in agreement if I took over Ernie's duties and then Betty could keep her job?' He turned to her.

She gazed into his serious brown eyes. She removed his empty glass and placed it alongside her own under the bench and then took hold of his hands, feeling their strength in hers. 'Is that what you want to do, my darling?'

'Yes, I enjoy being with the children and I think they like me.' He paused, then added, 'Being here, with you, Juliette and the children, for me, it is healing after the brutality of war.

'My Cherie, do you think we can work together?' He released a hand to put a finger under her chin, looking into her eyes to see the truth in them.

The next morning, Charlotte telephoned Mrs Carlton-Jones. She wasn't pleased about Ernie leaving. 'Just when everything was settled. My greatest worry now is that the authorities might decide to close us down.'

Charlotte's heart dropped at the thought of the children being forced to leave the only home they had known for years. 'Mrs Carlton-Jones, I have a request to put to you.' She outlined the plan for Emile to take over Ernie's duties, and for Betty to continue with her work with the children. She listened to the silence that followed and crossed her fingers.

Finally, Mrs Carlton-Jones spoke. 'It is a good plan. I will put it to the committee.' The line went dead.

Charlotte went into the kitchen and Betty looked up from preparing vegetables. 'I did my best. Now it's a waiting game.' Abruptly she turned and went outside into the garden. In the distance she saw Emile working alongside Tom. She walked the other way, towards the wood to the far side of the pond. She eased round the fence and sat down on a lump of grass and weeds. She smoothed down her skirt and drew up her knees, clasping her arms around them.

As she watched a dragonfly, zig-zagging rushes and skimming the water, her thoughts drifted to the fate of the three young children who had drowned here. So sad to die so young. As she'd promised Aunt Hilda, she kept their graves tidy. She wondered about Margaret and Anthony Ross. Would they ever return to the house they still owned? According to Mrs Carlton-Jones, Anthony had been seriously wounded in the war and now his wife was caring for him, and they were living down south. So the future of the house could be in jeopardy if they decided to sell. She quickly pushed that thought from her mind.

She wasn't certain how long she'd been sitting there, but she couldn't linger any longer. She had work to do. Sighing deeply, she rose to her feet, brushing bits of dried grass from her skirt, and made her way back to the house.

As she neared the house, Laura came out and waved, calling to her, 'Telephone.'

Quickening her pace, she went to answer it. It was Mrs Carlton-Jones, her voice sounding even more booming than usual. Charlotte listened. 'Thank you,' she said, when the woman finished talking and replaced the receiver on its cradle. Then she promptly sat on the hall chair.

'Everything okay?' asked a worried-looking Laura, who was standing by.

Charlotte looked up. 'Yes, the authorities have agreed for Emile to replace Ernie, and for Betty to stay on.'

'That's great news. You must be relieved.'

'Yes, so relieved. I am pleased for Emile, and also for Betty. But mostly that the authorities are not considering closing us down and the children still have their home. You must not mention this to any child or staff member.'

'I understand.'

Later that afternoon, when they were in their quarters, Charlotte told Emile the good news.

She saw his eyes light up, and he startled her as he swung her in his arms and then kissed her passionately. She felt her heart contract with joy and happiness for him as she felt the uncertainty lift from his shoulders.

That evening, Charlotte was reading a bedtime story to Juliette and Lucie, and Emile came up to listen as well. The two girls giggled when they saw him and waved.

As was her custom, she always kissed the girls goodnight. A few nights later, the girls asked, 'Daddy, will you kiss us goodnight?'

Charlotte watched with tears in her eyes. Such a simple question, yet the look on Emile's face captured the preciousness of that special moment. One of their favourite nursery rhymes which they loved Emile to sing to them was 'Wee Willy Winkie'. His voice hit just the right note, and the other younger children begged him to sing to them as well.

Looking back, that summer was idyllic, and Charlotte had never felt such happiness. Married to the man she loved, both of them caring for the children they adored. Usually after tea, Emile organised games outside, rounders, cricket, football. He built swings for the younger children, and somehow, although she wasn't quite sure how he'd managed it, a sandpit.

Come October when the nights were drawing in, he organised different kinds of activities for the boys, stamp collecting, a thriving table tennis team, a pool table, and making an aircraft from balsa wood.

Charlotte and Laura kept the girls busy with their own activities, though a couple of the older girls played table tennis as well. Everyone, children and staff, with thoughts of the war receding from their minds, felt their spirits rising, and embraced their new-found freedom.

One night, as Charlotte lay blissfully in Emile's arms, she whispered to him, 'I wish we could stay in this time-bubble forever, don't you?'

'Yes,' he murmured, sleepily.

A sudden darkness clouded her mind, and sleep eluded her.

CHAPTER FORTY-SIX

November 1946

The bubble burst in November. Philippe's mother had been found. She had been a prisoner in a work camp. Arrangements were being made to reunite mother and son. Normally a quiet boy, he kicked up a tantrum and broke a chair in the bedroom. When Emile tried to calm him, Philippe broke into sobs, shouting, 'I don't want to go.' Emile stayed the night in the boys' bedroom and comforted Philippe when he awoke during the night from a nightmare, reliving past terrors. He discussed with Charlotte the next day how to help Philippe. 'I think he's remembering how it was for him during the war.'

'It's understandable. But how best to help him?'

An idea came to her when she overheard one of the staff talking about what was showing at the cinema that week. That evening when she and Emile were sitting by the fire in their quarters, she put her idea to him. 'The cinema is showing two films and the Pathé News. From what I've heard, the Pathé News is showing France as it is now. We could take the older children to see it. What do you think?'

And so it was arranged for them to attend the early viewing on Saturday afternoon of the film, *The Road to Utopia*, a light-hearted comedy starring Bing Crosby and Bob Hope. Philippe and Gilbert, and two of the older girls accompanied Charlotte and Emile. This was the children's first visit to a cinema and they were excited. They caught a coach that now operated between the local villages and Driffield.

Charlotte noticed that Philippe's troubled expression was slightly relaxed, and she prayed that seeing his homeland no longer at war would calm his fears of returning.

The party settled in their cinema seats, the four children in the centre and Charlotte and Emile at either end. For the interval, each child had a paper cone bag of Mrs Jolly's homemade toffee, and a shiny red apple each. A gift from the Canadian government, having shipped over a supply for all schoolchildren.

Hoots of laughter sounded from the children as they marvelled, wide-eyed, at the antics of the two vaudeville characters on their journey to find gold. At the interval, Charlotte passed the treats to the children, and looking over their heads, she caught Emile's gaze. He blew her a kiss, and she felt a warm glow light up her whole body.

In good spirits and their appetites satisfied, the children were in a relaxed mood when the Pathé News was shown. Mostly it showed various victory parades taking place in Britain, and then America and Europe, and a fleeting glimpse of an event in Paris. Would that help to alleviate Philippe's fears? Indeed, would it help any of the children, destined to return to their families and homeland? It was a question Charlotte couldn't answer, though she suspected there could be problems later.

After the news, the B film was a slapstick one, full of daft things, which made the children laugh.

Leaving the cinema, the children were in a happy mood, and for that, Charlotte was thankful. She linked her arm through Emile's, feeling the warm reassurance of his presence.

That evening, as had become their custom. Charlotte and Emile discussed the day's happenings. 'It will come,' he told her. 'Some of the children will be reunited with their loved ones.'

She had to agree with him.

The next day, the house was a hive of activity. The four children who had seen *The Road to Utopia*, with Emile's help, were busy drawing maps and hiding the treasure, leaving clues for the others to find and discover the chest of gold. It was at times like this that Charlotte wished she had a camera. She watched them awhile, feeling their enthusiasm.

Smiling, she went into the kitchen to prepare vegetables for dinner. It was Mrs Jolly's day off, and she'd made a meat and potato pie, ready to pop in the oven to bake. As Charlotte stood at the sink, listening to the laughter ringing through the house, an idea occurred to her.

They should take a photograph of all the children, but she didn't know anyone with a camera. She stopped chopping cabbage — of course she did. The man who had taken her and Emile's wedding photograph. First thing in the morning, she would telephone him.

The photographer came the following Sunday morning, and thankfully, the children were still reasonably tidy. Two photographs were taken in front of the house. One of the children and the other of the children and the staff, and Charlotte arranged for them to be framed.

Also, she ordered a postcard-size photograph for each child, signed on the back by all the children. A memento for them to have of their time living at Mornington House.

Philippe was leaving next week, and soon more children would be going too. Mrs Carlton-Jones had informed her that plans were in motion for those children who had no one to be placed with foster carers. Ideally, Charlotte would have loved to care for all the children here at Mornington House, which they considered to be their home. But foster care was deemed in the best interests of the children, though Charlotte could not whole-heartedly agree.

Charlotte and Emile had already seen a solicitor for her legally to adopt Juliette as her daughter. And they had discussed with Mrs Carlton-Jones, spokeswoman for the authorities, their desire to adopt Lucie as well.

After the photographs were taken, Emile was talking to the photographer, and Charlotte watched the high-spirited children tumbling on the lawn. She called to Laura, 'Come and help me bring out refreshments.' In the kitchen, Mrs Jolly was setting out plates of homemade biscuits, and Charlotte, surprised, noticed she had tears in her eyes.

As the children prepared for school the next morning, Charlotte called out, 'Settle down.' She raised her voice higher. 'Stop messing, you two.' The boys, who were flicking crumbs across the table, lowered their heads, and the other children giggled, all but one.

Philippe sat staring into space, trapped in his world of uncertainty. She wanted to hug him.

Tell him everything was fine, and he could stay. But then, how would she feel if she was a mother and war had torn her and her son apart, and he didn't want to be reunited with her? It would break her heart. She watched him go off to school and was thankful that his friend Gilbert accompanied him.

Home from school for their tea, the children still chatted about the photographer.

Emile caught Charlotte's eye and she smiled. Afterwards, it rained and activities were confined to indoors. Emile was coaching the table-tennis players, and she and Laura were playing board games with the other children. Soon it was bedtime for the younger children and story reading, and the night staff came on duty, seeing to the older children. Laura was having an evening off, going to the pictures with her boyfriend. Charlotte yawned. She and Emile enjoyed relaxing in their quarters, once the children were all safely tucked up in bed.

Charlotte woke with a start, switched on the bedside light, and glanced at the clock, twenty minutes past midnight, wondering what had woken her. Then she heard the sound of heavy knocking on the door. Jumping from her bed, she flung on her dressing gown and hurried to open the door. One of the night staff stood there looking stressed as she gabbled, 'We've looked everywhere, but they've gone.'

'Who's gone?'

'Philippe and Gilbert.'

By now, Emile fully dressed was by Charlotte's side, asking, 'When did you last check on them?'

'Eleven, we check every hour.'

Hastily Charlotte dressed, and she and Emile went up to the boys' room. A quick search revealed that their school satchels, minus their school things, outdoor clothes and other belongings, plus food from the pantry, were missing.

'Have you been outside to look?' asked Emile. The women shook their heads. Moonlight flittered across the night sky. He turned to Charlotte. 'I will fetch torches and we'll search the grounds.' Charlotte hurried in the direction of the wood and Emile, to the kitchen garden and the sheds.

Charlotte called out, 'Philippe, Gilbert.' Her voice sounded eerie. She flashed the torch around the undergrowth, and upwards, expecting to see the boys perched high on a branch as a dare. She heard a scuffle, her heart beating faster as she headed towards the noise, only to see the eyes of a fox glaring at her. She hurried on, calling their names until her voice was hoarse. Reaching the pond, she stopped to regain her breath, seeing beams of moonlight filtering through the far trees and sending weird patterns across the pond. She heard the hoot of an owl and the sound of a creature she couldn't identify. She focused her eyes on the far bank of the pond, seeing only rushes, bending slightly, but hiding no one.

She met up with Emile, who gave a big sigh as he shrugged his shoulders. 'A fruitless search.'

Back at the house, she telephoned the police constable. 'I'll ring Mrs Carlton-Jones later.'

At first light, they trawled the village, but no one reported seeing the boys. The constable alerted the police station at Driffield and the railway staff to look out for the runaway boys. Even Farmer Huggate took part in the search, looking in his barns and outbuildings.

Every inch of the village and surrounding area was combed, the village hall unlocked and searched. Even grumpy George at the inn looked down his cellar.

Nightfall again. No moon shone, and Charlotte stared out into the darkness. 'I'm not giving up,' she stated. 'I blame myself for not keeping a proper eye on Philippe.' She sighed heavily.

Emile came up behind her and wrapped her in his safe arms, saying softly. 'We will go and search the woods and grounds again.'

Both equipped with torches, and sticks to beat at the undergrowth, together they raked through the grounds and woods in the hope they had somehow missed somewhere, calling the boys' names.

The police had been in touch to update them on the situation. No sighting of the boys had been reported on trains or hitching a lift with vehicles. The beaches had been combed, and the coastguards alerted, but there was no trace of the boys.

'It's as if they have vanished off the earth.' Charlotte was tearful now.

'You must rest,' Emile told her. 'You cannot stay up all night.'

Reluctantly she agreed to go to bed, and the night staff promised they would call her immediately if they heard news. But they didn't call.

The next day she and Emile rose at first light and set off to tramp the fields around the village, looking under hedgerows and beating with their sticks at any tangle of undergrowth, but to no avail. Towards the Wolds they tramped, climbing the hill, where on higher ground they had a wide view of the surrounding area. Emile lifted the binoculars which one of the village men had loaned him, and scanned the countryside, focusing on every building, tree, blade of grass, bush, and anything that moved. On a distant road he saw a police patrol car drive slowly, pulling into a farmyard to check it out. As they began their downward descent, they met a man on the road, travelling to Driffield. Hopefully they asked whether he'd seen the boys, but he hadn't.

Sitting to rest awhile on a fallen tree trunk, Charlotte said to Emile, 'I think the boys might have hidden on a train and they could be anywhere in the country by now.'

Back at the house, the railway police report was negative.

On the third night Charlotte was up again at first light and dressed quickly, leaving Emile sleeping. She went to the boys' room, hopeful they might have come home, but no. She sat on Philippe's bed, her heart aching with despair, and covered her face with her hands, trying not to cry.

After some time, feeling more in control, she opened her eyes. The first thing she saw was the wooden animal figure which Philippe had carved when he and Gilbert first went to woodwork classes.

Within seconds, she was hurtling down the stairs and out of the house. Running at speed, willing herself on faster, she didn't stop until she reached Jack's cottage. Down the path, past the front door until she reached the shed. Yanking open the door, she startled the two sleeping boys.

CHAPTER FORTY-SEVEN

January to June 1947

Charlotte felt bereft seeing Philippe trundle off. His head down, hiding the tears in his eyes.

He had an official escort, a middle-aged man, taking him to London on the first leg of his journey to be reunited with his mother. A week later, Ruth, one of the older girls, left to be reunited with a married sister. And so now, the exodus was almost complete. The mood of the children left behind was subdued, and also of the staff too. Everyone, it seemed, could sense the ending of an era. Plans to foster the remaining six children, who had no living relatives, were underway. Two applications had been made from families in the village, and they hoped to place the others as near to Mornington as possible so they could keep in touch with their friends.

Charlotte stood at the dining-room window, watching the flakes of snow fluttering down, like blossom from a cherry tree. Soon the children would be home from school, hungry for their tea, and delighted to see snow. It would help them to take their minds off the uncertain future they now faced. Yesterday, the authorities had confirmed that by summer, Mornington House would close, Mrs Carlton-Jones had informed all staff. Apparently, Mr and Mrs Ross were putting the house up for sale, as they intended to settle down south. Charlotte and Emile hadn't yet discussed what to do when the house closed; they had only just got used to married life, and Emile loved working with the children. Their future also hung in the balance, like a dice spinning on a rotary wheel, wondering where it would stop.

Her mood lightened, and she smiled as the children came running down the drive, thrilled to see the snow falling, which now was settling like pure white fluffy fur. She watched as a boy threw a snowball at one of the girls, and then a full-scale snowball fight ensued.

Normally, she would insist they change out of their school clothes before playing out in the grounds, but today was a Friday, so she would make an exception. Laura waved to Charlotte, indicating she would stay with the children, to ensure no one got hurt.

Mrs Jolly and Betty came out of the kitchen to watch. 'I shall miss the kiddies,' sniffed Mrs Jolly, brushing away a tear. 'It's a sad day.'

Charlotte turned away, because tears threatened her eyes too.

It snowed all night and continued next day. Emile and some of the children were down in the garden shed, making sledges out of old pieces of wood, thick fallen tree branches, any bits of metal or tin that they could find, and lengths of skipping ropes.

Charlotte busied herself checking the contents of the store cupboard, for she had heard on the weather forecast on Mrs Jolly's crackling wireless set that the snow would be here for some time.

Bread, milk, eggs and meat came from local shops and farms, and they grew their own vegetables, having a good store of potatoes, cabbage, onions, carrots and turnips. They also had a weekly supply of dried goods and cleaning and washing materials from the village grocery shop.

That job finished, Charlotte donned her coat and thick woollen scarf, with matching gloves and socks in rainbow colours, her feet snug in Wellington boots.

As she walked down the garden path, she heard shrieks of joy coming from the shed. As she appeared in the doorway, Emile said, his voice full of humour, 'Cherie, you will never get lost in the snow, you are so brightly coloured.' The children, absorbed in making a sledge, just gave her a cursory glance.

She caught the twinkle in his eyes and her heart filled with love for this wonderful man.

'I'm going to see how Jack is faring, and how Juliette and Lucie are with Laura.'

Observing the snow-laden sky, Emile said, 'Be careful underfoot.' He leaned forward and kissed her cheek.

She hurried on, eager to spend time with Jack, recalling when she last visited. He had looked frail, though always cheerful. Passing Mrs Jameson's cottage, she knocked on the window and beckoned her to the door.

Opening it, Mrs Jameson told her, 'Jack's not been well. It's his chest and breathing so doctor called and prescribed tablets and medicine. My Stan, or one of his mates, sits with him at night and helps him into bed. Then I call in the mornings to get him up. And I make sure he has plenty to eat. He'll be pleased to see you.'

Charlotte stepped forward and hugged Mrs Jameson, saying, 'Jack's so fortunate to have you and Stan to care for him. I only wish I could get out here more often.'

'Now, don't you fret, lass. You have enough to cope with looking after kiddies.'

Giving a gentle knock on Jack's door, Charlotte opened it and went into the cosy room.

Jack was dozing by the bright fireside, and Jip looked up and wagged his tail, then closed his eyes.

'Jack, it's only me, Charlotte,' she spoke softly.

He opened his eyes, and smiled at her. 'Hello, lass, nice to see you. Still snowing, I see.'

He indicated her appearance.

She laughed, shrugging off her outdoor clothes and putting them to dry on the back of a chair. 'Looks like the snow's here for a few days.'

Jack glanced toward the window, 'Weeks or months, it's here to stay for a while.'

She extracted the small bottle of brandy from her coat pocket and placed it on the small table by Jack's chair. 'Fancy a drop now?'

'Aye, put kettle on.'

She stayed the afternoon, chatting about the children and how Emile loved working with them. She described their activities, especially building sledges for fun in the snow. She didn't mention the unsettling future of the remaining children, except the two children being fostered by families in the village.

Before leaving, she banked up the fire, putting the fireguard in place. With Jack being unsteady on his feet, he could easily fall, so this was a necessary precaution. She tucked a plaid blanket around Jack's knees and legs, and he was soon dozing. She kissed his forehead and fondled Jip's ears. Before she opened the door, she glanced back at Jack, and saw he had a contented smile on his face.

Back home, she looked in on Emile's and the children's progress. The sledges they were making would be invaluable, becoming a mode of transport: for ferrying the children around the village, to collecting bread from Mrs Mackay's bakery and other shops in the village. Also, Emile and the children shopped for the three ladies, as they had become housebound. School was abandoned, mainly because the boiler had broken down, and the snow made it impossible for the teachers to travel. It snowed relentlessly, all through January, February and March. The railway lines became blocked with drifting banks of snow.

Charlotte, Emile, Laura and Mrs Jolly, who was now sleeping at Mornington House, listened to the wireless in the kitchen, the warmest room in the house. The sombre voice of the announcer said, 'Coal is frozen and unable to be mined or moved to any destination.'

'Well, I never,' exclaimed Mrs Jolly. 'Coal frozen!'

Just then, all the lights went out. Quickly, Emile fetched the candles from the store in the pantry and placed them in holders and lit one for each person. They were now sleeping upstairs in the empty children's rooms, to be on hand if the remaining children should need them. Not wanting to frighten the children, it became a game. Charlotte told stories of magical people living in an enchanted ice castle.

In the village, a few people had fallen, slipping on icy patches hidden beneath the snow. The postmistress, wearing snow boots, bless her, came to Mornington House twice a week, delivering her post by sledge. And on one visit she brought tragic news. 'It's Farmer Huggate, he's missing. Missus said he went out to tend to lambs and never came home.'

His body was recovered a week later. He had collapsed into a snow drift and became buried. One of his sons, who had returned from the war and was working in Driffield, came to help his mother, but stressed he didn't want to run the farm. 'I don't know what will happen to the farm,' the postmistress told her.

Charlotte felt saddened. 'He was quite a grouchy character, when I worked in the inn, but he often turned up trumps.'

Days later, Charlotte woke up feeling anxious about Jack and wanted to see him, but the snow was even deeper and getting around the village was becoming impossible. She and Emile were in their quarters having a quiet respite before the children's bedtime. Charlotte pulled aside the curtain to peer through the window at the surreal white landscape. 'I'll never get to see Jack if it doesn't stop snowing,' she lamented.

Emile came and slipped his arms around her waist, hugging her to him. 'I will take you tomorrow morning on the sledge.'

She half turned to gaze into his loving, warm brown eyes. 'Oh, Emile, thank you. It means so much to me.'

'And me, I remember Jack's kindness to me.'

Next morning, Emile was up early, and in the shed reinforcing the best sledge with firmer seating. After a quick breakfast, they were ready to go. Mrs Jolly and Laura were taking care of the children and they all stood at the dining-room window to wave them off.

They encountered a few hitches along the way, when the sledge slipped sidewards on a camber and Emile couldn't correct it. Charlotte sat feeling helpless and was about to tumble off the sledge, when two men appeared and helped Emile pull the sledge and Charlotte until they were on a level path of snow in Main Street, where a farm tractor had scooped a path down the centre of the road. Off the beaten track, it was hard going, because the snow was so deep and at one point, a party of schoolboys playing in the snow came to relieve Emile, while he got his breath back.

Eventually, they came to the lane leading to Jack's cottage. Mrs Jameson, ever vigilant, opened her cottage window and shouted, 'Jack was fine earlier. He's sleeping a lot, though.'

Charlotte heaved herself off the sledge with the help of Emile. She kissed him lightly on the lips. 'Thank you. I will reward you later.'

'That's a promise?' She laughed softly in response.

'Hello Jack,' she called softly, as they both entered the cosy warm cottage.

He was sitting as usual by the fireside, but on hearing Charlotte's voice, he turned round and smiled at her saying, 'I knew you were coming.'

Shrugging off her coat and boots, she went over to him and kissed him on the cheek, and replied, 'How did you know?'

'My Doris said you were coming.'

Charlotte glanced towards Emile, and a cold shiver ran through her body. She repeated, 'Doris?'

Jack looked around. 'She was here a moment ago.'

Emile came forward into Jack's line of vision. 'Good to see you, my dear friend.' The two men began reminiscing about the time Emile spent lodging with Jack.

Charlotte made a pot of tea and plated the tin of Mrs Jolly's shortbread biscuits. They settled with their drinks. Jack said, 'Have yer poured a cup for Doris?'

Feeling the cold chill run through her body again, Charlotte geared herself to speak in a natural voice. 'I'll pour her one in a moment, don't want it to get cold.'

They drink their tea and Jack didn't mention Doris again. Emile went to check on the store of logs for Jack's fire. Charlotte sat with Jack as he dozed. She reached out to hold his hand, and he smiled to himself, giving a sigh of contentment. They sat in companionable silence, save for the tick of a clock and the soft flickering flames of the fire. It was then that she realised that Jip wasn't here. She was just about to ask Jack about him when . . . he let go of her hand and startled her by sitting upright in his chair, his eyes wide open, but not focused. 'Doris, are we ready to go?' Then he turned to Charlotte, his eyes now focused on her. 'I'll be all right, lass. Doris has come for me. I always knew she wouldn't leave me alone, now that Jip's gone.' He reached out for Charlotte's hand and held it firm.

Charlotte's heartbeat thumped loud in her chest, her eyes filling with tears. 'Jack, my dear friend,' she whispered. He squeezed her hand, and she heard him gasp.

When Emile came back indoors with logs to replenish the basket, he saw tears running down Charlotte's cheeks as she held Jack's limp hand.

EPILOGUE

Jack was laid to rest by the side of his wife, Doris, in the church graveyard. Jack had left instructions that the passing of his life was to be celebrated rather than mourned. After the burial, the wake was held in the Travellers Rest Inn, which surprised Charlotte. Most of the villagers braved the snow. The main paths to the church had been cleared by a volunteer posse of men. Someone had provided a brazier outside the inn, for hardy men who defied the cold day, and with tankards of ale they circled the fire, breaking into song, Emile joining in. Sitting inside with Dot, May and Edna, Charlotte listened to the rousing songs of the Great War, which no doubt Jack had sung too in his day.

By June, the snow was almost gone, and Charlotte stood in the silent, empty Mornington House. She closed her eyes and felt the presence of the children, hearing their joyful voices in her head. Her tears flowed freely, as slowly she walked to the door, knowing that once she closed the door behind her, that life would be gone forever.

Outside, waiting for her, Emile sat in the driving seat of a truck, on loan to him. Behind him, stacked neatly, were their belongings. She climbed up beside him, he leaned towards her, and brushing away her tears, he kissed her gently on the lips.

He drove slowly through the village, and people going about their business stopped and waved. Charlotte forced herself to smile and wave back to them.

They left the village and were now travelling on the open road, passing green pastures and cows grazing, and wheat shimmering and swaying in a light breeze. Then ahead, coming into view, was a farmhouse and barns. Into the yard, Emile drove. And the door of the farmhouse opened to reveal Mrs Jolly and Laura, and the tantalising aroma of food assailed their nostrils. Emile helped Charlotte down and they stood side-by-side. Then both turned, looking towards the barn where the noise of a dog barking and children laughing sounded. Mrs Jolly banged on a saucepan with a metal stirring spoon. The barn door burst open and out rushed Juliette, Lucie, Maurice and Jacques, the two mischievous boys who no one wanted, but who Charlotte and Emile had welcomed into their family.

Later that evening, after the delicious meal of meat and potato pie had been consumed, the children tucked up in bed, and Mrs Jolly and Laura had gone home, Emile poured out two glasses of wine, giving the smaller one to Charlotte. They raised their glasses, saying, 'To our dear friend, Jack Mansfield, for his legacy, enabling us to purchase Farmer Huggate's farm and land. And for the new life to come.' Charlotte's hand encircled the swell of her belly. Emile reached out to her and drew her close. And melting into his embrace, she lifted her face to feel his lips warm and tender on hers. A loving kiss of happiness and of hope for the future.

THE END

ACKNOWLEDGEMENTS

The village of Mornington is loosely based on an East Yorkshire village where some of the Free French were billeted. My friend, Joyce Calvert, provided me with lots of written material provided by villagers and the Free French Association. A colleague, Ted Hoar's mother, went out with and corresponded with a Free French soldier and he kindly lent me the letters, and give me many details of the Free French. Ian Sumners, a local writer, pointed me in the right direction to various online sites of information. Katie Wells, a writing friend, found me a book written by villagers and one mentioned the Free French.

Thank you for reading this book.

If you enjoyed it please leave feedback on Amazon or Goodreads, and if there is anything we missed or you have a question about, then please get in touch. We appreciate you choosing our book.

Founded in 2014 in Shoreditch, London, we at Joffe Books pride ourselves on our history of innovative publishing. We were thrilled to be shortlisted for Independent Publisher of the Year at the British Book Awards.

www.joffebooks.com

We're very grateful to eagle-eyed readers who take the time to contact us. Please send any errors you find to corrections@joffebooks.com. We'll get them fixed ASAP.